The Elucidations of Drake

Bill Koch

The Elucidations of Drake

Bill Koch

ISBN (hardcover): 9781915952516
ISBN (perfect): 9781915952523
ISBN (epub):9781915952530

First printed September, 2025
by Sphinx
(an imprint of Sul Books, LTD)
Lewes, UK / Rodenbourg, LUX

Cover and Interior Design: Sul Books

Find our books at SULBOOKS.COM

I dedicate this book to Hope, my niece, who might one day write books of her own and to Joseph, my husband, whose support makes all things possible and who has patiently lived with Drake almost as long as I have.

I would also like to express my deepest gratitude to my editors Mirna Wabi-Sabi and Rhyd Wildermuth whose careful and loving work vastly improved this text.

The book you hold is based on several previous versions, one of which was diligently edited by my friend Jeremiah Kleckner who also helped Drake come alive.

Within

Suffer the Small Children

Wearing a silk Victorian dressing gown, he sat in lotus position in a room lit dimly by candles. The walls were paneled in dark stained oak; there were no windows.

The floor was marble inlaid with a circle of silver of eight-foot diameter, ringed about with writing in an ancient tongue. All was silent as the light of the candles set on the circle, in the four cardinal directions, glinted off the silver, but only moments before, the room had resounded with a deep, mellifluous chanting.

The man sat in the middle of the circle, and before him, on a velvet cushion, rested a mirror with a black obsidian face that cast no reflection. It was a scrying mirror, a tool of witches and magicians used for visions. To his right, a brazier filled with hot coals filled the air with the thick, heady smoke of myrrh, mistletoe, and Oil of Abramelin. His eyes were immobile as glass, gazing down upon the surface of the black mirror, and his face was expressionless and smooth like polished marble.

It was impossible to put an age on him. His features looked young, perhaps no older than thirty-five, but even still as a statue he bore himself with an air of age and wisdom. His black hair had hints of white at the temples. Drake, the famed or infamous mystic and magician, gazed into the mirror.

The night air outside shivered with a barely present breeze. All around the old country home, the hills of northern England rose empty and desolate. One cherry tree was just putting forth buds. Drake had been here, on retreat from the world, for six months and had been considering making that retreat a permanent retirement. He had thought that his time with the world might be over.

But upon staring into the mirror, another story was told. Images rose from the dark. At first, they were unclear and appeared too swiftly to make sense: a boat, a knife, a ring, the sea, a painting, a dried bouquet of flowers. But then the images coalesced and resolved into one solid figure. It was the shape of a person cloaked in shadows. There was little visual information, but the form radiated a sense of danger, and a force of hate aimed at Drake; an enemy was coming such as he had never faced before, and it was someone he hadn't yet met. That ruled out a good number of known opponents.

The next vision was of Drake standing alone on the Northumbrian heath. The meaning was apparent: he was not ready and could not face what was to come alone.

He grunted and muttered an invocation to Alethea, Goddess of Truth. Suddenly, the mirror filled with golden clouds which, clearing away, revealed to him the aid he required. Five human figures stood side by side. To Drake's other-worldly ears, a ringing voice granting them titles accompanied each image: the Socialite, the Artist, the Priestess, the Student, the Friend.

"All is sewn," spoke the voice, "but you must husband the harvest."

Then the mirror was dark, and there was silence. The brazier was cold — the candles had burnt out. Drake stood and offered aloud a chant of thanks. Then, his movements swift and sure with purpose, he left the room to pack. It was a long trip to London. From there, he would go to America, because each of the five figures in the vision had been standing on the Boston Common. He was returning home.

Lady Victoria Chetwynd, Grand Mistress of the Order of the Golden Lamp and Ruby Flame, was sitting alone in her private library at the Order's London headquarters when the door inexplicably opened. The opening of the door was inexplicable because there were standing orders not to disturb her — any emergency would have brought a soft knock and not such a boorish intrusion.

The sharp retort that rose to her lips was silenced by shock when Drake marched into the library. She had known he had been at his country estates in Northumberland for months; but, aside from a visit over half a year ago, no one had seen or heard from him. It must be confessed that she was not pleased to see him, though not because of his abrupt intrusion — normal rules of behavior never applied to Drake. Rather, she was distressed to see him because Drake was an uncontrollable variable, a swerve of chance or hand of fate muddling any plan, and she had many plans.

"I will need the assistance of the Order," Drake stated abruptly before she could speak. He was one of the most high-ranking members of the Order (higher-ranking, she feared, than even she knew), so he had a right to the Order's assistance. But requests for assistance were usually, well, worded as requests and not demands.

"Is that so?" Her voice was cold, but proper.

"I am returning to America and will likely need the cooperation of the Chapter Houses there."

"Cooperation with what?"

"I don't know."

Lady Victoria groaned silently and turned away in disgust to walk to the window.

"I see," she said. "We can use your assistance also, my absentee brother." She had to counter with something. Drake always got what he wanted in the end, but you couldn't just give it to him or you would find yourself enmeshed in one of his webs with little say of your own. "Andrew Weir and his lodge have been extending their international sway. War may be coming."

Drake chuckled and sat, uninvited, in a plush leather chair by the unlit fireplace, "War has already begun, Victoria dear. But Andrew is an amateur as is his brothel of Satanists.

Something bigger is afoot." He twirled his black silver-tipped cane between his fingers as she waited for more. Rather than explaining, he stared at her quizzically.

"Well," she burst out in exasperation, "we could use your help with the dangers we do know about."

"As I said," Drake responded, "I am going to America." With that, he stood and moved towards the door. "If you won't help me, I will go it alone."

"Good gods, of course we will help," she responded in exasperation. "But you do realize that Andrew is coming for you, right? His grudge won't end until one of you is in the grave, and maybe not even then."

"Well, then he will have to find me in Boston," Drake responded over his shoulder, unconcerned.

"Boston?" Victoria frowned, having just read an odd request from the chapterhouse in Boston. "I have a job for you in Boston."

"I do not take jobs."

"You said you will need our help," Victoria countered.

"No, you will need mine." Drake sighed, "But I suppose that help starts now, what do you need?"

"We have a case of possession. The son of one of our top members in Boston."

❧

It was spring in Boston, and the weather shifted wildly back and forth between winter and summer. Hot, humid winds ripped apart frigid rainclouds, and cold nights kissed temperate morns. By day, the esplanade along the Charles River filled with half-dressed sunbathers basking in the end of the brutal Massachusetts winter. The Commons were displaying the first blush of summer green, and the dogwood in the Public Gardens were flushing pink and white. However, it was raining in Cambridge as, sheltered under a large black umbrella and wearing a fitted black silk suit and silver tie, Drake ascended the steps of a weathered townhouse.

He paused for a moment before ringing the bell, marveling at the sense of foreboding emanating from the house. The Order of the Golden Lamp and Ruby Flame was, on its surface, an international secret society comprised of intellectuals participating in yoga, meditation, ceremonial magic, kabbalah, divination, and the basic disciplines of the Western Hermetic Mystery Traditions. In other words, it was a group of mainly rich mystics and magicians. There was, however, much beneath the surface. People whispered of its obscure social and political goals and of an inner circle of hidden leaders pursuing ambitious world-historical purposes. This house was the abode Gerald Wood, one of the Order's wealthiest Boston members, and an uncanny tragedy had struck his family. At the request of Lady Victoria Chetwynd, Drake was to assist the family in addressing the unusual crisis.

Gerald Wood met Drake at the door. "Mr. Drake," he exhaled with relief, "I can't tell you how relieved I am to see you." The man spoke effusively as he led Drake out of the rain into the luxurious trappings of the family home. "We have never met, though I have seen you in the past at Order events. I have, of course, heard all about your skill and wisdom. We are so grateful you have come."

"My name is Drake, sir. Just Drake." Wood had been holding Drake's elbow as he led him into the house, and the mystic's cold gaze and even chillier voice made his indiscretion apparent. He dropped his hand and stepped back.

"Of … of course. I am so sorry, sir. I trust you can help."

"There is precious little in this world we can trust," Drake said as he walked ahead of Wood into the parlor room where a small fire was burning next to a table holding bottles of brandy and cognac. "I would reserve your supply if I were you." Drake looked around, then asked, "Where are your wife and son?"

"My wife is at church, praying. It is where she spends most of her time these days. And my son — well, my son is upstairs, safely locked in his room." Drake raised an eyebrow. "Yes, well, he gets violent sometimes, and there is no telling what he might do next."

Drake frowned for a moment and then sat in one of the chairs arrayed around the fire. "Make a drink, sir," Drake said, "and tell me everything." He then lit a cigarette smelling lightly of foreign spices and sat back in his chair, waiting.

Moments later, Mr. Wood sat opposite Drake with a glass of brandy in his hands. "I don't know where to begin."

"How old is your son?"

"He is nine. No, ten? Yes, ten."

Drake nodded. "And his name?"

"Thomas, for my grandfather."

"Go on."

"It began less than a year ago. The doctors call it a psychotic break, or early onset of schizophrenia, or the late onset of autism. They haven't got a clue. My wife thinks the, um, occult work of our Order opened him up to demonic possession."

Drake raised an eyebrow again at this, "And what do you think?"

"I think he is the victim of an occult attack upon me and my household by the enemies of the Order." Drake made a deep sound in his throat and gestured with his cigarette for the man to go on. "It started fast. First, he would have nightmares at night and wake up screaming. Each time it happened, it would take several moments of us calming him before he realized he wasn't asleep anymore. Then he started to become absent-minded during the day. At school, at home, he would be found gazing blankly into space. The things he would say became odd. He would burst out with things sometimes. Predictions about the future, comments about the past as if old events had only just happened, strange observations about what people were thinking or feeling."

"Did you take him to a doctor then?" Drake asked.

"No, we consulted friends from the Order and took him out of school to rest. He was in a private school in the country where he often stayed during the week. We thought it best for him to be home, perhaps the stress was getting to him."

"Was he often stressed?"

"No. He was — is — brilliant. He found none of the schoolwork difficult. In fact, his intelligence measured off the charts on his I.Q. tests."

"Intelligence can be measured no more than physical beauty," Drake said absently, his eyes distant in thought. "How was his social life?"

"Social life? I don't really know."

"What are his friends like?" Drake pressed.

"Friends? Well, I don't think he has any here in the city. No, not even at school, I don't think. Though I could be wrong. He was always busy with projects of his own. Reading, writing, inventing things. He really is a genius."

"I see."

"But he got on great with people. They loved him at the Order Chapter House. He is its youngest member ever. He used to debate the ins and outs of metaphysics and theology with the other members for hours. Can you believe it? At nine years old!"

"Ten," Drake corrected. "How is he now?"

"Not himself," Wood stated bluntly. "He doesn't talk directly to anyone. He won't respond to you at all, and when he talks, it is as if to himself. Babbling, sometimes ranting, often in foreign languages."

"You mentioned he is violent? What has he done?"

"Well, perhaps I misspoke a bit. He hasn't been violent, but the things he says, sometimes, are very violent and passionate. He gets very worked up."

"But he hasn't harmed, or tried to harm, himself or others?"

"No. But wait till you see him. He could do anything, the way he talks."

Drake nodded. "So, your wife prays, your son rants alone locked in a room or else stares silently into space. And what do you do?"

"Everything," Wood responded. "I have researched every protection ritual, purification, and exorcism I can find. I have performed them all over him, along with the help of Order members. But I know, I just know, that you with your magical prowess will be able to turn aside this attack!"

"Magic, sir? I assure you, I have no magic to offer," Drake retorted sharply.

"But, I thought —"

"I neither know nor care what you thought. I have a reputation, sir, for solving problems. I solve them, always, in my own way. But I don't engage in magical rituals to fix other people's messes as if the world should bow to our whims just so long as they are stated in the proper antediluvian tongue. I have no patience for superstition whether it comes bearing a cross or a wand. Now," Drake stood, walked to the window and noted that the storm had passed and the sun was once more out, "I would like to meet Tom. Bring him down and we will go for a walk about your back gardens."

"Down? Outside? I really don't think that is wise, sir —"

"Drake, call me Drake," the mystic interrupted in a voice far softer than any he had used so far. "If you truly love your son, and I think you just might, you need to trust me. Bring him outside, I will await you there."

Outside the house was as nice a garden as a wealthy home in the city could allow. It stretched forty feet or so back from the house, and a wrought iron fence enclosed it. Small paths wandered around little garden plots in which roses and herbs grew. A few benches were placed amidst the growth.

Drake found one, nestled between a trellis of freshly planted jasmine and a large rosemary bush. As he sat and thought, he ran his hand along the pine-like rosemary branches and leaves, releasing their fresh smell into the air. Rosemary was good for memory and cleansing spiritual infection, he reflected.

The boy's case was the task Victoria had set him in exchange for the Order's assistance in his future work, whatever that as yet mysterious work might be. It was a challenge, of sorts, but not the challenge those around him thought. Victoria was as convinced as Gerald Wood and his wife that occult forces were at work, and likely ones coming from Andrew Weir's lodge of black magicians. Whatever Andrew was up to made little difference, however. Every problem was multifaceted: seen from one angle, you have demons, and from another, you have a sad child in a failed family. The same went for mental illness: from one perspective you had a disease, and from another, a seemingly superhuman talent. Many a genius and artist had been destroyed in the flip of that coin.

As these thoughts passed through Drake's mind a sudden wind arose in the clearing sky and a fierce swirl of leaves kicked up at Drake's feet. On the wind was the memory of the past winter as if an edge of January had hidden huddled beneath the bench and was now roused by Drake's reflections on the boy's case. A few houses away a murder of crows, disturbed by the sudden wind, set to flight with their deep harsh calls filling the air. They circled above the garden in terrible warning for a moment and then winged their way towards the Charles River. A small smile chased,across Drake's face as he stonily ignored premonition and omen alike.

The back door opened, and Gerald led his son, blinking and shuffling, out of the house. Drake jumped to his feet amidst the dripping bushes and walked forward, taking Tom's elbow as Gerald had previously taken his own. The boy was thin, dressed in pajamas with disordered blond hair and glasses slightly askew. His cheeks were dotted liberally with freckles. Drake stooped down so that the boy's eyes and his own were level. The boy stared through him, still blinking slightly.

"Hello, Tom," Drake said softly, "my name is Drake and I have been wanting to meet you. It is very nice to make your acquaintance." The boy's eyes might have flickered, briefly, but then went glassy again. Drake stood tall once more. "Thank you, Mr. Wood," he stated. "You can go back inside, we will walk around out here for a bit." Wood made to object, but Drake cut him off, "I said, thank you." Wood frowned, then turned and went inside.

Leading the boy slowly by his elbow Drake walked him to the back of the garden and then around a loop back to the house. They continued in this way, the sun glinting from time to time from the boy's glasses.

"They tell me you are sick," Drake stated casually. "Well, I don't know anything about that. I'm not a doctor of any sort. But I do know that nothing makes one feel better quite like a stroll in the sun and fresh spring air. Don't you think?"

Once more the surprisingly chill breeze kicked up as if to contradict the mystic's words. Drake looked to the boy who still stared into space. They stopped for a moment in a patch of direct sunlight, and Drake placed himself firmly between the sunlit boy and the cold wind at his back. "Just feel that warmth, eh? Rather an improvement from the winter, or some dusty bedroom."

Drake put his arm around the boy's shoulder and crouched down next to him conspiratorially, both of them staring into space, and continued talking in a casual manner, "You wouldn't imagine what they think about your sickness. Such silly rubbish about magic and demons! No. I say where there is a cough there is a cold and not Beelzebub."

"Tom's not sick — not sick — not sick," The boy said suddenly in a sing-song voice, staring into space.

"No?" Drake asked, but the boy acted as if he hadn't heard him.

"Not sick — not sick. Tom's all gone. Poor Tom, dead Tom. Dead as dust and ducks for dinner. Dead-ding dong dilly-oh."

"Really?" Drake asked. "What an amazing thing. And yet here he is strolling the garden with me."

"Tom toms gone!" The boy said vehemently and then launched into a loud string of foreign speech.

Drake laughed. "That is Ancient Greek, my boy, Attic Greek from the time of Plato actually, but with some hints of Aristotle as well. You can mark the Aristotle because it is more cosmopolitan. Hard stuff, but hardly magic. How is your Homeric Greek? That, I imagine, is rather harder for a boy your age — even a genius." Drake then switched to speaking in impeccable Homeric Greek.

The boy did not respond. Rather, he turned, stared Drake in the face, and launched into a diatribe in modern French that translated, roughly, to: "My mother is the whore of God and my father is Satan's banker."

"Yes, I am quite sure," Drake responded in French. "Come, let's sit down."

He led the boy to the bench next to the rosemary and sat them both. The boy continued ranting, though his body remained still aside from the horrifying animation of a face grown bestial.

"You know," Drake spoke over the boy's rants just loud enough to be heard, "you would be amazed at the things I know. The secrets I could teach you. All that stuff you learned from the Order, all your reading, pales in comparison to what I could tell you. The things I've seen, the mysteries uncoded."

Drake continued to speak, but slowly lowered his voice until it was hard to hear over the ranting of the boy. In response, the boy's ranting became softer as well, as Drake held a comforting hand on his shoulder.

"I'll tell you a secret. I knew a boy once who climbed to the top of a mountain and found an ancient, ruined temple there amidst the snows." Drake's voice was a whisper, and the boy went still, staring straight ahead.

"The marble was cracked, but most of it still stood. The white of marble reflecting the white of stone. White on white, all clean and crisp in the fresh high mountain air. The wind rustled the snow about his feet, all white and clean, white and clean. The sky was clear and empty." Drake's voice was soft but insistent, carrying an odd note of command.

"See the white marble stone and the white clean snow, the empty sky all around, empty and free, empty and silent. Feel the wind die down so there is only silence. Up the stairs and into the temple we go, into a wide room with no roof — open to the clear blue sky above. White all around, white stone, white snow." Drake paused, feeling out the extent of the boy's rapt attention.

"Feel how clean and calm the open temple is. Feel the light of the sky shining down onto the white of the floor, and there we are, you and I, surrounded by white light with the open space above. High above the world. All is calm and still. Feel how the mountain air cleans out your lungs, washes clean your skin and hair, silences your thoughts, and clears your mind. There is nothing to worry about here, above the world amidst the sky." The boy was lost in the images Drake wove.

"Now close your eyes to see the temple better, see every detail, feel the white and the air. Feel the space and the silence. Close your eyes and rest." The boy's breathing was deep and even, his face relaxed, and his eyes softly closed. "Until I say so, you will hear nothing but the mountain silence. Think nothing but the white around you and sky above you."

At that moment, the back door of the house flew open, and Tom's mother, Magnolia Wood, flew into the yard. "I don't know what devilry you are working here, but it stops now!" She fumed. Drake shot her a look that froze her in her tracks as she looked at her sleeping son. She opened her mouth to speak, but Drake shook his head softly and patted a space on the bench next to her son. She came and sat, and Drake nodded.

"Tom, focus on the white of the snow and the openness of the sky. Can you hear me?" The boy nodded to Drake's question. "Can you speak?"

"Yes," the boy said, his voice sounding weary. Fearing trouble, the boy's father had come out into the garden as well. Drake motioned for him to be silent, and he came and stood behind the bench — one hand on his wife's shoulder and the other on Tom's — as Drake drew his own arm away from the boy.

"Tom, we are all here now. All people who love you. Can you feel our love?" Drake asked.

"No. No one loves me," the boy responded.

"That is not true, Tom," Drake responded. "You can feel the love radiating off the marble of the temple and the white of the snow. The sky above you is the openness of love. Breathe deeply now, Tom, and look around. The temple is no longer ruined. It stands in a complete, perfect circle around you. The marble, pure and smooth, forms an uncracked ring about the open sky above. The temple is full of the love of your mother, Magnolia, and your father, Gerald."

"And you?" the boy asked.

Drake smiled. "Yes, and I, your friend. You can speak freely now, here with the crisp air and white light of the temple protecting us. What is bothering you?"

"I'm so lonely," Tom said. "Lonely and scared."

"Why are you scared?" Drake asked as he saw both mother and father squeeze the boy's shoulders.

"There is so much to know, so much I want to know and think." The boy sighed wistfully. "But my mind doesn't stop, even when I am tired or afraid." His voice reflected a growing frustration and strain as he spoke, his shoulders growing tense. "There is no one to help me understand it all or help me sleep." He took a shuddering breath and then continued, "Everyone leaves me. I am alone. And grasping, always grasping."

Drake nodded. "Forget the books and your thoughts for a moment. Forget wanting to understand. Your thoughts don't bother you up here, amidst the clear air of the white temple."

"No," the boy agreed.

"How do you feel?" Drake pressed.

"I feel ... free."

"You are free. Here you can rest whenever you want. Not for long, just for moments of peace and quiet when your thoughts are too much. I want you to breathe deeply, close your eyes, and come to the pure temple and free sky every night before bed to help you sleep. Can you do that?"

"Yes, I think so."

"Good. And any time your thoughts are too much for you, do the same for a moment. I have a secret I want to tell you, Tom. Do you want to hear it?"

"Yes."

"The world can't be known. You can never know it all because it isn't just about thinking. The world is also beautiful, and beauty can only be felt and loved like now in the peaceful silence of the beautiful temple. Do you understand?"

"I think so."

"Good. From now on, I want you to look for beauty as much as you look for understanding. And when you find beauty, it will bring you peace and comfort, just like now. Will you do that?"

"Yes."

"Now I have a question for you, Tom. Your mother and father are here, and they want to make you happy." Drake looked at them firmly for a moment. "Forgetting books and study, what above everything else would you like to do with your parents?"

"I want to go boating on the river like before." Tom's mother stifled a sudden sob and Drake looked to the parents.

"Gerald, what does Tom mean by 'like before?'" Drake asked.

Gerald Wood cleared his throat, "When he was a young boy, we used to go rowing on the Charles River on the weekends. Then we would picnic along the banks, all three of us. We have been too busy to go for years. Tom had school and —"

Drake cut him off, "That is enough." Then he looked back at Tom, his expression growing softer, "Now, Tom, I want you to remember everything I have told you about the temple and beauty. When I say so, you will wake up, hug your parents, and tell them you love them. Then you will spend this week resting up and spending time with your parents. There will be no more trances, or voices, or outbursts in foreign languages. If you get agitated, just take a moment, close your eyes, and breathe back in your temple. Then return to the world and tell your parents what is bothering you. If you can do that, the three of you will go boating this weekend, and every weekend thereafter as long as the weather is nice." With this last comment, Drake cast a stern look at the boy's parents. "Can you do that, Tom?"

"Yes," Tom said. "Can we really go boating again?" His voice had a hint of excited schoolchild to it now. Drake cast a quizzical look at the parents, who both stumbled over each other.

"Of course!" cried his mother. "Yes, son," agreed his father. "Very well, Tom, wake up."

The boy opened his eyes and turned to look at his mother. Crying, he hugged her, the tears of the parents blended with those of the boy as they told each other how much they loved one another. Drake turned and walked back into the house and, grabbing his umbrella, left without another word to any of them.

❧

That night, Drake sat in his flat, sipping a cup of tea and writing with a neat, tight script in a leather-bound book, when the phone rang. It was Lady Victoria Chetwynd calling from London. Gerald Wood had told the Order in Boston what Drake had done, and they, in turn, had contacted Victoria to thank her.

"I won't say I am surprised," she noted, "You have yet to fail at a task you set yourself. But I do need details. Was this some demonic attack from Andrew's group or not?"

"I haven't the foggiest idea, dear Vicky," Drake drawled, noting with a smile her exasperated grunt. "But it doesn't much matter since the crisis is averted."

"Yes, but did you need occult means to cure the boy?" she pressed.

"All means are occult to those who don't understand," Drake commented clinically. "A home, a family, is like a temple," he continued, "no evil can enter except what we bring with us or invite in. That family's temple was in ruins. That alone would cause trouble, especially with a talented and brilliant child playing amidst the wreckage. If there was outside influence, that was why it could get in, and if not, the solution was the same. Rebuild the structure."

"So, what are you planning to do there in Boston?" she asked after a moment's silence.

"I do not have a clue, my dear." Drake sighed in frustration. "Apparently," he said, "the universe thinks I need to make some new friends and reconnect with old ones."

Victoria burst out laughing in response, "Good luck with that. It might just prove the one challenge you aren't fit to meet."

"Let's hope not," Drake said darkly, "I suspect far more hangs on my success than any of us know."

As Drake hung up, the spring night wind picked up outside, shaking the dogwood in the Gardens and casting waves upon the banks of the Charles River. The city, long awaiting the mystic's return, was preparing unknown challenges for him. Out there somewhere, the socialite, artist, priestess, student, and friend required his help.

When Dreamers Weep

The townhouse was a fine brownstone in Brookline, just a step outside of Boston. The stones of the building were meticulously clean and glowed like polished bronze. Several evergreens sat precisely positioned and trimmed in the front, amongst which sat three rose bushes in full bloom. The white of the roses caught and reflected the light of the quarter moon as the guests arrived.

The cocktail party was a classy and common occurrence at 235 Harvard Avenue. At least once a month, the owner of the immaculate townhouse would invite his several friends and fellow artists over for a "quaint gathering," which was neither quaint, considering his taste for the dramatic, nor ever only a gathering. John Crisman, owner of the much-used townhouse, had an expansive definition of art, and it was one of his several affectations that he never associated with anyone whom he did not consider an artist of some kind. When the time came for his "gatherings," he always felt the need to invite every artist in Boston.

Crisman's idea of art included political art, social art, the arts of the theater, the arts of business, the arts of human deception (usually practiced by criminals and popular religious leaders), the classic arts, liturgical arts, and (most objectionable of all) the occult arts. For this reason, his parties were never small and often filled with friction and conflict, not to mention more than a little eccentricity.

This party, however, was different. It was subdued, almost lifeless. The energy of the entire occasion was ruined by the reclusive mood of David Bore, the pampered darling child of Boston's inner circle of Bohemian writers and poets. The poor lad, no older than twenty-three, had become convinced that he had reached his artistic peak two years before upon his completion of a book of poems he called *The Sirius Cycle*.

The cycle dealt with the sexual relations practiced between the old pagan gods of Gaul. It was widely acknowledged to be a masterpiece of creative plot weaving, Neo-Pagan thought, and classical history. Now, however, he had fallen from his lofty peak of poetic genius and had failed to write a word worth printing since. He had become convinced that the old gods, in response to his revealing work, had cursed him and revoked his muse.

He and his confidantes were so worked up over this sad situation that they did not mingle, they did not flirt or flutter, and they hardly even spoke. The brightest of Boston's poets sat in the corner smoking clove cigarettes with a dire air and seeking relief from the torments of the dark master we call life. David was all but curled up in a ball of misery amongst his grim guardians, drowning his sorrows in glass after glass of O'Doul's. He despised beer, and his distraught state was revealed through his descent into the world of debauchery and vice inherent in strong drink.

All this was driving the glowing host of the party to distraction. Nothing could calm him. Even the presence of the illustrious and aloof mystic Drake failed to console Crisman. Drake's appearance at the party was a complete surprise, as he had spent the last several months in Europe on some unknown business of his own. He now sat calmly in the corner, sipping a glass of red wine and smoking a cigarette while watching the entire flow of the gathering.

His too-wise eyes wandered time and again to the clutch of puffed-up poets as they drowned in their self-pity. No one spoke to the solitary mystic, though many wished his advice or even the slightest sign of his attention. Every magician and guru in the civilized world envied his knowledge on all subjects, mystic and occult, and his wisdom concerning all else was legendary. Few would have dared to interrupt his vigil or thoughts for personal matters that were certain to appear petty and unimportant to so distinguished a character.

Were John Crisman not driven to complete distraction by the possible failure of his party, he would never have considered asking Drake for help on so earthly a problem. But surely, he reasoned to himself, the curse of the gods and the failure of a great poet were sure to interest the mystic. So, in complete desperation, John turned to Drake to supplicate him to aid the poor poet David Bore.

"My darling host," murmured the distant mystic, "far be it from me to allow one of our finest and brightest poets to fall into the pit of strong drink to the exclusion of his responsibility to his gift and calling." Drake smiled then chuckled to himself, his voice honest but smelling of sarcasm, "It would be my pleasure to rescue, if not this party, then perhaps any you may have in the future. Fear not, I am humbly on the case." With that, he leaned back in his large, comfortable seat and sipped his wine as his eyes slowly closed in complete lack of concern.

John was reassured. If the esteemed Drake were on the case, then all would be well. He returned to mixing with his guests and flirting outrageously with any victim to come his way.

The party wound on into the evening until David, feeling overwhelmed by his indulgence in the devil's brew, wandered out onto the balcony for air and to stare at the city in melancholic desperation. Sighing, he gave voice to his pain: "Life is meaningless without art." He did not expect a reply, but he received one.

"But art is meaningless without life, my dear boy. What is well planted cannot be uprooted. What is well embraced cannot slip away." The mystic, who had joined David on the balcony unobserved, smiled and nodded, but the boy only looked confused.

"Sir, I am losing my mind. The gods have cursed me. My life is over, ended along with my art. I have been robbed of my muse. I am cursed." Tears of pain glimmered in the young poet's deep eyes.

The mystic chuckled in response. "Man is always slave to the gods he creates himself," he muttered. Keenly, he watched the boy who showed no sign of understanding. The mystic smiled in resignation and moved on to small talk. "I was in Europe recently and heard the most interesting legend. Would you care to hear it? Perhaps it might inspire a new muse within you."

The poet shrugged in a noncommittal manner.

"Well," started Drake, "In the time of Elizabeth in England lived a man named Dr. Dee. He was a famous astrologer and scholar. He and another man claimed to speak with angels, and a complex system of magic grew out of these conversations. A system which came to be called Enochian magic, for the Biblical patriarch Enoch spoke with angels himself. Now, one of the first actions of the angels was to give Dr. Dee a stone, a crystal ball if you will, which he was to use to see and speak with them. This stone is claimed to have materialized out of nowhere, appearing in Dr. Dee's study one day during a conversation with the angels."

Drake told the story in a manner devoid of interest as if he were passing time. He languidly lit a cigarette and stared up at the moon, ignoring the poet as he continued. "The story now moves to the late 1800s in England. A much more modern-day magician by the name of Mathers was studying the works of Dr. Dee and Enochian Magic for use in a secret order of which he was the leader."

Drake gestured idly with his cigarette and continued staring out into the night as he spoke, "While studying the Enochian manuscripts within the British Museum, Mathers stumbled upon the story of the crystal ball of Dr. Dee, which was also housed in the British Museum. Using the pull he had within the museum, he gained access to the stone one night and began to study it."

Drake glanced out of the corner of his eye and saw David

Bore enrapt in the story, "Mathers formed the opinion that the stone actually materialized from a world between worlds, a netherworld of sorts. This was a world made of mental impressions, dreams of the spirit, and pure energy. Mathers found that the stone, coming from a world not our own, had a tendency to return to its place of origin. Putting it simply, the stone wanted to go home and had a tie to that other plane of existence."

Drake took a long, slow draw on his cigarette and released a cloud of smoke with deep satisfaction before continuing. "It was this tie with a world between worlds that allowed Dee to see the angels through the stone."

The wind picked up as the moon slipped behind a bank of clouds. "Mathers could not perform any drawn-out studies of the stone in the middle of the museum, but was not about to be thwarted in his quest for unearthly knowledge. One night, in the dark museum amongst the musty display cases, Mathers chipped away part of the stone and part of the special metal holder that Dee had made for it. He then had the stone samples melted down into a single stone and mixed the metal with silver. From the metal, he formed a band into which he had the stone placed. He made a ring of it and performed many unknown ceremonies and occult experiments upon it, using the whole body of his magical order to study and refine its power." Drake turned slightly from his study of the moon and was pleased to see the young poet's eyes gazing into the distance with a fire kindled by what the mage and mystic was saying.

"What was done with the ring, and what powers it was found to have, is cloaked in mystery to this day. We do know that it was thought to be tied somehow to the world of dreams and visions and to have a connection to inspiration. Mathers wore it for a long time as a symbol of power. However, as his mind declined into madness, he stopped wearing it."

Drake finished his cigarette and turned to leave. "Well, I hope the story helped cheer you," he yawned in boredom. "The night is old and I have matters of no small importance to attend to." With that, the mystic walked into the now nearly empty party and moved to leave.

The poet, however, ran after him. "Mr. Drake! Mr. Drake, wait!" he begged. "Where is the ring now? What happened to it? I must know, Mr. Drake!" He tugged at Drake's long black overcoat and received a cold stare of disdain in response. David realized his sin and dropped the fold of the coat he had been holding, stammering an apology.

"The name is Drake, just Drake." Slowly, he turned to leave again, then seemed to remember the questions the boy had badgered him with. "The ring? Where is it? How should I know?"

The mage paused in thought. "It was lost after Mathers' order broke into revolt; however, it eventually came into the hands of one of the order members. Arthur Macken, the famous English poet. It was said to have granted him visions of some of his greatest works. He disdained to use it after a time, though, claiming it had driven Mathers mad. So, upon continual requests from a friend in America, he sent it across the sea. I suppose it is still in the possession of the family of the man who gained it from Macken." Drake yawned again and turned to leave once more.

"Please, Sir!" begged the poor poet David, "Who in America got the ring? Where did he live? What was his name? Please, this is my salvation!"

Drake frowned in irritation. "Why, it went to H. P. Lovecraft, my boy, the famous master of the macabre. He was a good friend of Macken's and begged him for it. Rumor has it he used the ring to inspire his Cthulhu Mythos stories and many of his other great works. He lived right here in New England."

The mage yawned one final time, nodded to himself, and swept from the party into the dark Boston night.

David was ablaze with hope; his soul smoldered and flared with the thought of tapping into the source of the great Lovecraft's fount of inspiration. The subtly contrived net of an apathetic angler named Drake had ensnared the poet. He must have the ring, and it was somewhere right in New England. It was so close it seemed providential.

David left the party with neither a nod for the host nor a smile for his forgotten friends. He wandered the dim city streets for hours, his mind feverish with hope and desire. Upon arrival at his loft, he immediately went to his desk where he penned a poem about the tantalizing hope now kindled in his soul. The lyrical masterpiece expressed the pinnacle of pain, desperation, and need he had reached. Throughout the work ran the electric dream of a possible reunion of the broken poet with his inspiration. It ended with the pleading and crazed whisper of a chance that some-day he might again be able to write. One day, perhaps, his muse would return.

The next several weeks were lost in a whirlwind search of New England. The powerless poet made every effort to run to ground the mythical key to Lovecraft's genius. But the ring turned out to be as elusive as the inspiration that had left the poet in such a fickle manner.

David grew feverish and slept little; his eyes were blood-shot and smoldered with an unearthly lust and terrible long-ing. His friends never heard from him, and his days and nights were spent in contact with the oddest characters. He developed a squint from the dim lighting of pawnshops and antique dealers, and he developed allergies to the dust of the old warehouses and collectors' lairs that had become his haunts.

He repeatedly contacted the family of the late H. P. Love-craft to implore desperately as to the whereabouts of the ring, but none of the family had ever even been aware of its existence. His hopes were dashed against the jagged rocks of futility again and again, and, had there not been hope that the ring would be found, the poor poet's body would have decorated more material rocks at the bottom of the Charles River. But the possibility of hope drove him on, his need was insatiable, and his spirit became an ever-burning flame of desperation.

It was in this state of impaired sanity that David Bore stumbled into another one of John Crisman's cocktail parties. It had been several months since David had last attended such a gathering, and his disheveled and distracted entrance caused quite a stir.

David did not grace the party with the questionable pleasure of his presence for just any reason; rather, he had given up all hope of finding the ring on his own. His sleep-deprived and desperation-warped mind had thus realized that the only man who might be in any way able to help was the man who had started the entire affair. He came in search of the mysterious Drake who had become like a god in the corridors of the crazed poet's head.

Unfortunately for David, and fortunately for the guests of the party, Drake was not in attendance. The poet soon removed the fine evening of his maddened and excited presence. Before his merciful withdrawal, however, David accosted the long-suffering host John Crisman in hopes of some information on Drake's movements.

John had been worried about the young poet who had rarely before missed any of his gatherings, and he was surprised to see David after so many months looking so much like a common madman. No longer was he the fine, pampered poodle of the upper-class poetry circles. Now he appeared to be more of a common lunatic or homeless alcoholic. The delicate artist of lyric and verse now appeared truly ruined to John's eyes. It was a sad sight, and even sadder since John could in no way help him. Drake's movements and whereabouts were as mysterious as his ambitions and motives. Drake was a riddle, and nowhere to be found. David left without hope and, in utter despair, drove his expensive sports car towards the river where he planned to end his agony.

The night was chill as the hand of death, and a constant bombardment of ice and water filled the airy voids above the city of Boston. The clouds tore and thrust at one another in a sick parody of Satan's archfiends battling for the souls of the damned. The wind wove amongst the chaos with the rushing might and sly speed of the lord of Hell himself. From above, the savage forces of Mother Nature watched on in freezing disdain as David parked his car at the foot of the Harvard Bridge and stumbled into the wild night air.

The wind doubled in intensity as if to keep David from his dire purpose. Shivering and sliding in the freezing muck along the road, the broken poet fought his way to the center of the bridge's span to stare in utter horror at the raging waters below. The roar and whistle of the wind filled the night and seemed to whisper to David and then scream his name in either supplication or summons. The rushing air beneath tore at the tips of the reaching waves below, whipping them into a heavy spray that covered the entire bridge with freezing river water.

David was soon soaked and horrified to find even his motivation in this last and most awful endeavor failing. He turned from his dire contemplation of the dark river to scan the bridge. For a moment, he thought he caught the outline of a tall man in a long coat on the end of the bridge.

The stranger was watching with intensely cold eyes.

A moment later, he was gone. David shivered harder as he convinced himself he had just seen the Great Tempter himself come to take his soul after this most fatal act.

David turned back to the waves below and clutched the

cold railing in his trembling hands. Tears leaked from his eyes as he contemplated the awful outcome his life had reached. All the moments when he had dreamed of the glory his amazing talent would bring him paraded before his mind's eye, mocking him. Nothing — and his mind itself choked on the thought — nothing had come of his once great promise. He had come to nothing, was nothing, and would never be anything. He had sinned against the gods, and so his muse had been stolen.

The grim outline of the last several months came into focus in his diseased perspective. All paths had led to this moment, he could now see. It was fated that he should die: the universe had cursed his wretched soul. His eyes flashed, and he suddenly stood straight. His finger pointed in second-rate dramatics at the sky as he hurled curses to all the gods who had taunted him so with seemingly inevitable fame. David's fury passed and ended in his dejected collapse onto the barrier before him.

"Good Lord, David, my boy, you look positively like a drowned cat. What in the name of all the gods are you doing out here?" asked a cheerful voice behind the crumpled form of the suicidal poet. David yelped in terror and surprise as he spun about to face the intruder. There before him, in a long black overcoat and dark hat, leaning on a silver cane while cheerfully smiling in a friendly if obscure manner, was Drake.

David could do nothing but stare in amazement at the man he had been desperately seeking. In an incoherent rush, David babbled the entire story of his search both for the ring and for Drake. Drake, behaving as a true gentleman, refused to notice the subhuman and maddened state of his current companion and so merely nodded, smiled, and ignored everything the mad poet said.

"Yes, yes, my boy," he murmured distantly. "Now come, my car is waiting. I was just returning from the airport — important trip to Europe, don't you know — and who should I see but the greatest poet in Boston hanging about in this ac-cursed weather. Lord knows, this isn't a fit night for man or beast. Come and warm yourself in the car."

He turned to head back towards the end of the bridge when suddenly he turned as a thought struck him, "Oh, and perhaps I might have something to cheer you. It's only a trin-ket, mind you, but a friend passed it on to me a couple of weeks ago, thinking I was still in the habit of collecting point-less antiquities. I passed that hobby on to less serious men years ago, but some people can simply not manage to keep with the changing times. So, anyway, here I am with a piece of the past which is without value for me, but perhaps it might help warm your shivering form a bit, eh?" He chat-tered on kindly as he led David back towards his waiting Rolls-Royce.

The car was perfection itself, seeming never to have re-ceived the slightest scratch or smallest blemish upon its smooth black surface from either weather or dirt. Drake's chauffeur opened the doors for them and wrapped a warm blanket about David's shoulder. The interior of the lovely car was deliciously warm, and the soaking poet was grateful to be out of the sleet and winds. Drake sat next to him and cast him a lazy, indulgent smile, reminiscent of a kind uncle hu-moring a silly young nephew.

"I say," murmured Drake, "I just don't know about the younger generation these days, wandering about in the heart of such a storm. One would think that Boston's most renowned poet would have more sense." Drake seemed to be thinking out loud, and though his tone was that of a very old man, he did not in any way appear old. Nor, however, did he appear young.

David noticed with a small start that he could not seem to put an age to Drake at all. He had the energy of a very young man and yet the manner of a much older gentleman. His eyes seemed ancient, though alive with a youthful fire.

So engulfed was David in these observations that it took him a moment to realize what Drake was saying.

Once the term, "Boston's most renowned poet," sunk in, David shuddered as if physically struck. It took all his willpower not to break into sobs on the spot. Drake, however, was oblivious, or at least seemed to be. Little did David know at the time that neither the seriousness of the situation nor the terrible condition of the poet had in any way escaped the wise man's observation.

Drake continued to ramble calmingly as he rummaged about in a leather traveling bag that rested at his feet. In a moment, his conversation with himself stopped, and he turned to face David with a wry half smile on his face. In his hand was a smooth, heavily lacquered wooden box.

"Well, now, here we are. Nothing ever seems to be quite where I left it these days. But here it is nonetheless. I'm not sure if you remember, I'm sure your mind is full of more important things of a poetic nature, so I shan't blame you for forgetfulness, but quite a while ago we held a conversation at that chap Crisman's house during one of his impeccable cocktail parties. I won't bore you with a recapitulation of the entire conversation as I'm sure you were bored enough at the time."

Drake spoke on in a singsong way as if he had neither a care in the world nor a thought in his head. His voice was free of the least tone of irony, which demonstrated the supreme control with which he ruled every aspect of his life.

"The point is, however, that the conversation revolved around the subject of a ring made by MacGregor Mathers and once owned by both Arthur Macken and Howard Phillips Lovecraft.

"Well, quite by chance, I happened to stumble upon it. In fact, it was a gift from a friend, as I have already mentioned. Now, besides some small eccentric value due to its history, it has little value for me. You, however, seemed to have been interested in my poor story in some small way, and so here is the ring. In truth, I'll be grateful to be rid of it, lord knows it serves no purpose in my hands."

With that, it was done. David, having never said a word, was handed the goal of his mad quest. He took it with shaking hands. He was too dazed to speak, yet somehow found his way back to his car. He supposed Drake had had his driver drop him off, though he couldn't remember. He drove back to his loft in an utter daze. David's life seemed to have become a dream, awash in surreal fog and violence.

Later that evening, Drake sat in one of John Crisman's finely arrayed sitting rooms, smoking an expensive cigar brought back from London and sipping a marvelous glass of champagne. John was just ending a long-winded speech about the fears he harbored for the once great poet David Bore.

"He is not at all well, my friend," he complained to Drake, who responded with a bland smile. "I hear he no longer writes, and when he appeared this evening, he looked like a destroyed man who had suffered many years from some terrible disease. I even suspect," he whispered in a conspiratorial tone, "that he has taken to drinking in excess." John was clearly troubled, or as troubled as he could bring himself to be. David had been, after all, a gem in the social life of the famous Crisman gatherings.

"My dear sir," Drake said gravely in response, "did you not ask me to help the poor boy? Have I ever before agreed to do something without fulfilling all I promised and more? I am not a man to go back on my word nor fail on a course to which I am set. My methods simply take more time than those of less successful fools."

Drake stopped speaking abruptly as if that put the topic to rest. John, though he knew enough of Drake to realize that once he agreed to do something, one could do nothing but be certain all would be well, was still very much afeared for the safety of David Bore.

"But the poor boy is ruined!" John blurted out.

"I once had a friend," Drake broke in, "who was struggling with a troubling addiction to nicotine. After having tried everything, he came to me in complete desperation seeking help. I promised to cure him of the disease."

Drake took several satisfied puffs from his cigar before he continued talking, "I first made him swear by the most binding of oaths never again to smoke without first gaining my consent. Having accomplished that, I took him to one of my cabins in the Appalachian Mountains, where there would be no chance of his gaining the drug behind my back. I also took one pack of extra-strong cigarettes and left him to wait."

"Several days went by during which I allowed him none of what he most craved. In the isolated mountain retreat, there was nothing for him to do all day but obsess over his craving. It grew within him more and more each passing day until he was near insane with his need."

"Finally, his sanity seemed almost at an end. He raved, he screamed, he begged, he degraded himself in the depths of his craving. I watched and waited until his withdrawal was at the peak of its intensity. At that point, I smiled and agreed to grant him what he most desired, with one condition."

"If he had one cigarette, he would have to smoke them all. The entire box, one after another, until all were gone. He was too desperate to refuse, and so we sat, and I gave him the box."

A chill smile crossed Drake's face. "The reason he had desired to quit was the toll the habit had taken on his health. After smoking half the pack, he was forced to stumble from the cabin to vomit. He returned feeling awful and sought my pity. I smiled and sympathized with him, then lit him a cigarette and forced him to finish the rest of the pack. He was sick several other times in the process and was in bed for the next two days."

"He never smoked again, nor could he so much as stand

the smell of smoke from that day on. He was cured by simply keeping him from the thing he most desired until the flame of craving had burned his mind clean to the point of madness and then quenching the fire with a total dose of the object of desire. In this process, one's mind is left cleansed of the obsession and the madness, life is seen in a new way, and the soul's lens has been cleared of the addiction."

Drake took a calm sip of his champagne and smiled.

"So all will be well, fear not." With that, the conversation ended with John more confused than ever, yet certain that Drake was right. The conversation meant nothing to John, but Drake's tone and complete certainty left no room for doubting him.

At the same time, David Bore sat in his humble artist's loft and lovingly ran his hands along the finely crafted box in which his redemption resided. He attempted to appreciate the fine craftsmanship of the box, but he could postpone the moment no longer. With the determined air of a soldier, the shivering and broken man opened the lid of the dark wooden box. There was a small click, and then he looked upon the object of his obsession.

It rested on midnight blue velvet and, to David's unbalanced mind, seemed to have a faint glow. The band of the ring was smooth, with neither a scratch nor a sharp edge. It was sleek and made entirely of curves. The lack of sharp edges, so associated with common jewelry, made the ring seem otherworldly. The metal of the band had a silver sheen and was cold to the touch, but it was different from mundane silver. It had an almost green gleam to it.

Knowing the story behind the ring, David realized that the metal was made of silver mixed with some of the metal from Dr. Dee's original stand for his crystal ball. Who could say what mysterious substances Dee may have used?

All this flashed through David's mind in an instant, but it was the stone that most caught his attention. The stone was oval and smooth. It seemed to be one with its frame, bulging out of the metal seamlessly. At first glance, it appeared dark blue, but upon closer inspection, David saw that it was made up of spirals and concentric circles of different hues, from dark blues to light greens. The colors got consistently, though subtly, darker as one looked towards the center of the stone, drawing the vision towards and into darkness. David felt the stone pull at his mind, trying to draw his thoughts into itself.

With expectation and a touch of dread, David slipped the holy object onto the ring finger of his right hand. It fit snugly and made his skin tingle for a moment, though that could have been due to his overexcited state.

Besides that, nothing happened. He took a deep breath and tried to concentrate. Nothing happened. In frustration, David realized he was not a magician and had no experience with such things. He had no idea how to make the damned ring work. He tried to clear his mind and closed his eyes.

Perhaps it was only his need to notice something, but the darkness that had always awaited him behind his closed eyelids seemed darker and somehow more alive. He waited in expectation — and nothing happened. His frustration got the better of him, and he sighed heavily like a spoiled child. *Damn it*, he thought. There had to be something to the ring if both Macken and Lovecraft had used it.

It was late, and David had experienced a very long day — a very long month, for that matter. Indeed, it seemed he had aged many years in the short time since he had first heard of the ring.

Overexhausted, the young man could no longer avoid slumber, and having gained at least part of his quest, some of the strain was lifted from his mind. Sitting in his loft and still wearing both his damp clothing and Mathers' ring, David fell asleep.

Suddenly, he awoke, if he was indeed awake, to the experience of floating in a silent void. Emptiness stretched in every direction, with nothing in sight to ease the terrible blankness of the ultimately extended abyss. Unaware of his body, it seemed that he had no form. He was mind alone, floating in darkness. He was a disembodied eye, transparent and dimensionless.

Yet, now that he became more aware of his surroundings, or lack thereof, he realized the void was not as empty as it seemed. True, he could see, hear, smell, and feel nothing. However, some deeper sense beyond his physical form insisted that there was more to his surroundings than was immediately obvious. The void in which David was so oddly suspended seemed to be made of a complex layering of realities.

The poet was ignorant of how he knew this; he seemed to sense it with some yet undeveloped part of his puny mammalian brain, or perhaps some part of his not so puny immortal soul. The metaphysics of the situation resisted description, but one must attempt such an impossibility for the sake of a careful record.

The supposed "emptiness" seemed, in reality, to consist of everything. The dark void was an infinite number of interwoven universes, each of which was the absolute opposite of another. Hence, the sum of the infinite multiverse was the nothingness David found himself contained within. More than this, however, soon became apparent. Within each universe, every single form, function, and reality, indeed every particle itself, had a complete opposite that in turn canceled the entire universe to nothingness. The void about David was pregnant with the completion of an eternal string of possibilities, and that completion was emptiness. It was the fullest emptiness anyone could ever know. His mind reeled from the pressure of too many paradoxes and shuddered back from their implications.

Slowly, David became aware that the void was not empty; he sensed first and then faced a strange sight. It was a point of light, almost like a star in an empty night sky. The light was a pure white color and grew brighter and larger as David slid closer to its beckoning. Like driftwood on a calm sea, he and the light grew near until it floated only a short distance in front of him.

It was not a ball of pure light as David had expected; rather, it seemed to be a crease in the fabric of the void. The edges of the crease gave off the light, which had seemed brilliant from a distance, but which now was soft and calm. David found what his new "sense" told him of this phenomenon even harder to grasp than the nature of the void itself.

It seemed to him that the crease was a small fold in the multi-dimensional material surrounding him. Trying to picture three-dimensional space alone, "folding" made his mind scream in agony, but seeing what he somehow knew to be an infinite number of dimensions folded was inconceivable. The fold seemed to contain a bit of misplaced "space." It was similar to how one can pinch a piece of cloth, leaving a pocket. To his utmost alarm, the poet began to slide through the crease, into the fold beyond.

The moment David entered the fold, some of the common laws of the universe returned. He could tell this because he began to fall. The fold itself did not seem to have any limits, as it naturally should have. Instead, blackness once again stretched to infinity, with only the swiftly receding light of the crease to tell direction by. David could even feel air fly by as he plummeted through infinity, which brought to his attention that he could once more see his own body, moving and sensing as he should have been able to do before.

He also noticed that the ring was still planted on his finger. It glowed faintly and pulsed with a similar light to that which the crease had given off. The void through which David now fell was both different and similar to the one he had only just left. Not truly void, it too was a complex fabric of overlapping realities. These realities, however, had a different flavor to his strange new sense. It felt as if these realities were of the mind and imagination. They too cancelled each other out but seemed of a lighter, less physical nature than the ones that made up the great void David had left.

Perhaps it consisted of alternate dream realities. One thing was certain, however, it was just as "real" as the other void and what made it up.

David had, by this time, been falling for quite a while. His original panic slipped away as he realized no bottom seemed to exist in the vastness through which he was plummeting. No ground reached forth to crush his bones and rend his body as he had first feared. He wondered if there was, in fact, any earth, land, or substance anywhere in this new void. The moment the poet thought this, he felt the entire fabric of reality about him shiver, and he lost consciousness.

At first, there was only light — pure, white, blinding, without pain. Then the cascading and crystal. He stood, suddenly aware of his body, on a translucent stretch of shimmering stone. Everywhere rose crystal, natural and shining. Sharp impossible angles cut into pillars, maybe mountains, of ice-like surfaces. All of it reflected and refracted light. The light danced like a presence more real than the stone. Amidst the pillars and crevasses poured streams of water that caused the air to sing and ring with the sound of a million wine glasses humming in different tones. But the air was warm and not at all wet, at that temperature where skin and breeze meld without friction or contrast. There was no sun or sky, just endless drops sheathed in diamond and spiraling chimneys of glass.

But then, through the natural hum, he heard what could only be a human sound. Far away, tantalizing from out of the megalithic forest of light, came music with a set meter and voices raised in accompaniment. He could almost pinpoint, amidst echo and hush, where the sound originated. As if in response to his thought, the ring on his hand warmed and pulsed softly. Then the air around him blurred, and he felt as if he were bent, tilted sideways to reality, and he found he had moved to a new vista.

The monstrous crystal pillars and peaks still rose all around, but now he stood on a small ledge looking down on a plateau stretching flat amidst the endless crystal. Here he could see there was a sky, a stretch of pink shot through with opalescent auroras free of cloud or sun as if light lived in the stone itself and danced forth into the air. But music and voices filled the air here, for the plateau held human habitations.

Seamless walls with arching windows rising in terraced pyramids covered the plane of glass. The buildings seemed molded or blown like glass. He could see people, both spread along the balconies and terraces as well as through the windows and transparent walls themselves.

The music he had heard before was clearer here, sounding almost like a waltz, and he saw figures dancing and playing instruments. He shouldn't have been able to see much at all, but it was as if the atmosphere magnified his vision as he looked down upon what could only be a complex of pyramid palaces engaged in a vast celebration. He wanted to see more, to look close, and with that thought, the ring gave another warming throb, and he blurred and folded once more.

Then he was there, amidst the palaces and music, standing at the corner of a terrace. He was relieved that he was alone on the terrace, but he could see the dancing through the transparent walls and on the terraces below him.

The inhabitants weren't human, though he had taken them to be at first. They were far taller and thinner than any human, their skin an impossible powdery milk white. Their eyes were ovals stretching long up into their foreheads, and they were hairless. They danced with a slow swaying grace that would unexpectedly break into swift spins and leaps. They were mostly naked, though devoid of distinguishing sexual characteristics. Their only clothing seemed to be scarves and sashes wrapped at random about their forms.

Behind the dancers, musicians played instruments the likes of which he had never seen. They were crystal rods or pipes used as both percussion and wind instruments. Several singers accompanied them with voices that reminded him of nothing so much as whale calls.

Oddly, amidst the dancers on a terrace below him, he saw several figures fencing with long silver swords and spears in movements appropriate for both dance and competition. The entire sight was so beautiful, such a combination of grace and terrifying foreignness, that he found he was weeping silently as he gazed.

This world amazed and confused him. Everything seemed alive while, at the same time, lifeless. He gazed off the balcony into the distance, over the environment of cascading crystal, and wondered if there were plants or trees anywhere in this strange land.

In response to his wandering thought, once more the air about David shivered and the ring pulsed. Space folded and, after a moment of disorientation, he stood in the depths of a forest. New trees in odd shades of lavender and orange resembling ancient oaks and mighty pines towered about him. The ground was not grass or dried leaves, but rather a carpet of soft mosses of green and browns. The heavy, healthy fragrance of summer filled the air, and birds sang in the higher branches of the trees. David strolled about the wood when he saw a clearing in the distance. Towards this, he aimed his slow strides.

The clearing was a perfect circle, defined by seven towering violet oaks and seven mighty crimson pines, each evenly positioned in relation to the others. Reverently, David entered the hushed circle of trees. Breeze and bird song alike had ceased, but the sky was still pulsing opalescence above him. There he stood in breathless wonder at the sense of peace, and then he heard music, or perhaps several different forms of music, shimmering in the air once more.

Small multicolored points of light began twinkling in between the trees and amongst the mosses and branches. These lights seemed to wink and dance to the music, and David suspected the points of light were either the music or were producing it. More lights appeared, and the music grew louder.

At first, it was simple, but each strain of the unknown melody was soon overlaid by another that was then greeted by another. The sound was of thousands of faint pipes, or multiply-pitched bird songs in consistent rhythms and melodies.

It was marvelous, yet troubling.

The songs, if songs they were, had no words and did not match in their complex melodies or rhythms. Each was original in its wild freedom. Soon, there were thousands of songs and millions of points of light, all whirling and spinning about the clearing until the trees themselves disappeared amidst the glow, and all David could see was a dancing rainbow swirling about him in every direction. The melodies were fantastic, and complete chaos. The light became brighter, the music sweeter. His mind whirled with the lights and soared with the millions of songs. It was anarchy, no order hid in the dance of the lights or their song.

Perfect anarchy, the true essence of beauty and the vitality of life. He could lose himself forever in this splendor, this wild release and ultimate freedom. Looking for order or reason in this glory seemed to be a quest to bind all that is free. The chaos of the scene was the fulfillment of every possible perfection in one. Sighing, David wondered if there were any imperfections in this world, with all this pleasure and beauty. He hardly noticed when the ring pulsed once more and was taken by surprise when the air shivered and space folded around him.

He stood amid madness.

Waves of flames crashed amongst rivers of smoke at his feet. The sky was a raging expanse of whirling shards of wicked ice and sheets of lightning that melted into thunder. Mountains of fire erupted from nothing to spiral into the frightful sky.

The sky was a maelstrom above. The air was sweltering and freezing, flashing from one extreme to the next.

David stood upon nothing; he floated in the horror, then the liquid destruction of both sea and sky sucked him in. There was no up, no down, only the rush and roar and crash of the fury. Caught in a streaming inferno that tore at his clothing and scorched his skin, he could not breathe or see.

The sounds, the speed of his flight, the color and glare of the light, the smell of the smoke, all grew worse by the moment. Every particle of the chaos escalated to insane levels as if seeking an impossible crescendo.

The poet's body throbbed in agony as the wind sought to rend his limbs to pieces. All was pain and force and fury. David screamed and knew that it went unheeded. There was nothing here to witness his suffering. Had not a strange shield of light projecting from the ring and protecting his body surrounded him, he was sure he would have been dead before he even knew where he was.

With a shock, he was born upwards through the clouds of hurling ice and flashing lightning. He was torn away into the blackest depths of the rushing skies above. Looking down desperately, he saw the seas of smoke and fire.

A giant snake made all of flame, larger than any building he had ever seen, burst from the seas and rushed toward David. At the final moment, it stopped its ascent and crushed in upon itself, driven by its own momentum. Its form flowed into that of a giant screaming face, and then the howling winds tore it to shreds.

Every cloud became a form with some resemblance to meaning. He rushed past laughing children made of smoke and flame, screaming women with hair of lightning and red lips of blood colored ice, and things even harder to explain that appeared half human and half animal. Explosions filled the air at random, without cause or reason. The realization dawned on David that he was caught in a vortex, swirling and rushing inward towards some awful center and climax.

New sounds invaded the poet's brutalized ears. Some were commonplace, but escalated to the point of unimaginable volumes. It felt as if David's eardrums must soon burst from the pressure under which his mind was already crumbling.

The sounds of summer evening crickets and children laughing boomed amongst the howling blare of car horns and ear-rending songs of birds in terror-twisted trees of nuclear holocaust. Simple conversations tore through the air at impossible pitches. In the distance, pipes played with no order or rhythm. They called forth the fury of the entire cacophony.

David's eyes lost focus, and his mind followed; he knew only that he was nearing the horrible center of the vortex.

He could no longer discern smoke from flame from ice from lightning. All colors blended and flashed, becoming undefined. Everything lost distinctness as one sound bowled into the next.

David felt his mind torn to shreds and become but another part of the meaningless hurricane of insanity about him. He began to lose his own sense of self, his own definition, as his maddened screams blended with the howling orchestra of hell about him. He knew that the moment he truly forgot who he was and became but a part of this nihilistic anarchy, he would cease to exist. With that realization came the despair that would inevitably push him over the edge.

Then he saw it: the horror of horrors, the king of blasphemies, the crown of dementia. All was lost, and his mind slipped into the dark abyss as he stared upon that awful nucleus of all chaos, surrounded by its insane pipers of meaningless cruelty and eternal frenzy. He felt his mind leave his body along with the scream that sought to tear his own throat to shreds. He felt his soul burst into flame and rend the air about him, flowing with the unending howl he did not recognize as his own. There was only horror as he screamed the scream he knew would never end, the scream that transformed man to animal, and animal to demon, and demon to the flame that burns in the heart of lunatic nightmare.

The sun streamed through the open windows of David's loft to warm the room and dry his still-damp clothing. Slowly, fearing what he would see, the poet opened his eyes. A smile of wonder dawned upon his face as the pleasure of being back in his own safe home filled him. He could not believe he was alive.

His mind reeled from the shards of memories that remained of his experiences the night before. The ring had certainly inspired the works of the great H.P. Lovecraft, for David had a gnawing feeling he had seen the crown of all Lovecraft's horror: Azathoth himself, lord of chaos. The aching beauty and transcendent horror of all he had seen could have inspired a thousand works of genius or insanity.

David Bore tore the ring from his finger and flung it into the air to soar across the room and land sullenly in the dark corner. Shivering, he ripped the damp clothing from his body and ran to the shower. In a matter of moments, he was cleaned, dressed, and practically jogging through the streets of downtown Boston to his favorite coffee house.

He sat in the dark corner of the establishment for a short time, running over everything that had befallen him both the night before and over the past several months. He felt as if he had awakened from a horrible nightmare, but it did not consist of last night's adventures alone. The nightmare was years of self-involvement and shallow histrionics. He saw himself for the pretentious fraud he had become. The shadows in his corner of the room slithered and stared at David. He couldn't deal with it any longer and hastily left the cramped room to wander the bright streets of Boston.

The storm of the night before had passed after David returned to his loft, and the sun now dried and warmed the streets. It was a pleasant day, and the poet was grateful for it, yet he still felt uneasy. He could almost feel the ring pulsing in his loft, calling him back. It called him to return to the all too lovely paradises he had wandered and called him to once more be torn by the insanity at the universe's heart.

Though the sun was warm, he shivered violently, convinced he would never forget what he had seen and certain it was all either too marvelous or malevolent to be put to paper. His experience transcended his poetic skill. In addition, part of him was afraid of what might happen if he attempted to record any of it. The experience had a life of its own, a seductive and cancerous life. Azathoth's mighty force was reaching out, awful and claw-like, to take his soul and mind back to the nucleus of madness.

Most horrifying of all, part of David longed to be taken.

He found himself standing before a church, seeking redemption. But the cold statues and dogmatic phrases that surrounded the "holy sanctuary" mocked the beauty of last night's wonder. It was utterly puny beside the force of that ultimate anarchy. There was no salvation there.

He seated himself on a bench at the edge of the Boston Commons as cheerful and busy people wandered by. In his mind, the first conversation he had ever had with the enigmatic Drake was replaying itself. "Life is meaningless without Art," the poet had whined. David grimaced as he remembered the self-pity dripping from his words at the time.

He halted his recollection, struck by a scene that unfolded before him. Across the Commons was a middle-aged woman carrying a young child tenderly in her arms. Her face was lit with a secret smile of joy, that of a mother. The words of a new sonnet began in David's mind, for he had never quite seen an image as lovely as that of the mother with her child.

Here was something so simple. Yet, in its structure, it entangled all of history. The legends of powerful Goddesses and virgins bearing the children of Gods blurred and unfolded to the simple truth that to every mother, her child is born divine. To every child, mother is the name of God. Love transfigures all the flaws and failures of the comic tragedy. It became a perfection made greater by each potential flaw.

The pulse of poetic creation flooded David's mind, and he got up and rushed home where his writing books awaited him, too long unused. This would be his greatest work yet. "Ode to Human Divinity." As he ran for his studio, all the horrors and adventures of the last several days forgotten, a few sentences from his first conversation with Drake whispered in his soul, "But Art is meaningless without Life, my dear boy. What is well planted cannot be uprooted. What is well embraced cannot slip away."

The townhouse was a fine brownstone in Brookline, just a step outside of Boston. The stones of the building were meticulously clean and glowed like polished bronze. Several evergreens sat precisely positioned and trimmed in the front, amongst which sat three rose bushes in full bloom. The white of the roses caught and reflected the light of the full moon as the guests arrived.

Inside, the latest cocktail party of John Crisman was well underway. The crowd was cheerful and laughed often as David Bore amused them with stories of the misadventures of Boston's inner circle of writers and poets. His days of seclusion and depression had passed like a momentary cloud over the moon. He was now, however, a much-changed person from the pampered darling of Boston's high society he had once been. No longer did he amuse and annoy his spectators with the melodramatics of his spoiled life and the pompous, if finely written, poetry of a self-centered prodigy. Now people commented on the tone of humble appreciation in his works and in his personality. No longer did he write of impossible Gods or Elizabethan romance; rather, his works were the creations of a lover of humanity and a realist. He had torn down the flashy mansions of puffed-up phraseology he had once used and rebuilt his edifice upon the sturdy foundations of human love and folly.

The party had seemed to reach its peak when the aloof mystic Drake strolled into the gathering. John Chrisman beamed. Things were going wonderfully, and this was going to be his greatest social event to date. David noticed Drake as well and solemnly walked to the throne-like chair in the corner that the mystic occupied. Neither said anything for a moment; Drake waited with a wry and expectant half smile on his face. "I see you are back into the swing of artistic creation, my fine young man," he said at last. David only nodded and then drew from the confines of his pocket the smooth lacquered wooden box that contained a ring once owned by both H.P. Lovecraft and Arthur Machen.

"I believe this belongs with you, sir," the poet said. "Lord knows," he imitated the tone Drake had once used himself, "I have no use for it."

The mystic nodded solemnly and took the box, slipping it into his coat pocket. "I must compliment you on your latest work," Drake said. "I especially liked the last line, 'Man is always slave to the Gods he makes himself, save only when he makes himself a God.'"

The lights came up, following the final bow of Mozart's *Idomeneo*. Drake stood, chuckling to himself over the inherent humor of the master's music and the foolishness of characters seeking to escape Poseidon's wrath by fleeing over the sea. It was labeled a tragedy, but truly, the work was a comedy.

In the opera house's lobby, the mystic was met by John Crisman, who deposited a fine glass of champagne in Drake's hand and gushed over how nice it was to see him again. It had been some time since their last meeting at one of Crisman's famous soirées, a reprieve for which Drake was more grateful than Crisman distressed. Nonetheless, once more, the fates had thrown the flighty socialite and the astute magus together.

The conversation wove in strange spirals, wrapping from one topic to a mildly related other, mostly due to the furor of talk Crisman bore while Drake sipped his champagne and cast his martyred glance into space. Following a lengthy monologue on the "rather peevish silliness of those old-time gods," Crisman launched on an entirely different track: "I say Drake, speaking of cranky old gods, what do you think of this entire mess with the ancient deities of Atlantis?"

Drake was taken entirely by surprise. "I beg your pardon, but I am afraid I have positively no idea what you are talking about," Drake responded.

"What, but surely one with your particular interests would have heard?"

"I have been rather busy; I had need to retreat for a time from the mundane."

"Oh, but it's anything but mundane, my boy! An archeologist struck down by a curse from ancient Atlantis, that is, if he wasn't killed by more human means, of course."

"Atlantean curse, you say?" responded Drake. "Heavens help us if a society whose very continent hasn't lasted came up with curses that do! Oh, Crisman, is there no end to your charity? Perpetually filling my life with parlor talk, mystery, and caviar! Now be a good man and, in the spirit of Mozart, get me more champagne and tell me the whole story."

And so things happened in that very order, with Drake and Crisman firmly ensconced in the lounge of the opera a few moments later, sipping merrily as Drake smoked a pipe and Crisman a cigar from Havana.

"You see," Crisman explained, "the man was an archeologist with an obsession for Atlantis, an unpopular interest in academic circles, I might add. He had just recently returned from the Island of Bimini, where he had uncovered a statue off the coast that he believed to be evidence of Atlantis. Well, four days ago, he left his wife in Beacon Hill to go work on his boat in the harbor. He was never seen alive again.

"After three days, his body was found floating in the harbor. There was no sign of assault or physical trauma; he did not hit his head, and his heart was fine. He was a strong swimmer who had spent his life on and in the water. Not a mark on him."

"Yes, well, my dear Watson," Drake mumbled around his pipe stem between puffs, "it's all elementary. The butler did it. But you mentioned a curse and murder, I believe, as of now, it's just a drowning."

"My dear Drake, healthy swimmers don't just drown."

"And dead men are rarely healthy, so we can dismiss the healthy hypothesis. But continue."

"Yes, the curse," Crisman agreed, "the statue he brought here to Boston is the center of a dispute, to say the least. It seems that natives of Bimini, the Lucayan people, consider the area where he found it to be a holy stretch of sea. It is strictly off limits. They are enraged, and he came back to Boston with the artifact to flee legal complications in Bimini.

"The Lucaya not only accuse him of being a thief but have declared him a grave robber who has been cursed by the gods. So, we have grounds for a murder and a curse. As I said, though, there is not a sign of murder beyond motive — unless one considers, as I am sure you will, occult murder."

"It's harder to kill a man through the potency of the spirits than one might think," Drake responded in a droll voice. "It is much easier and more pragmatic just to stick a knife in the fellow or at least turn to poison for the sake of aesthetics."

"Well, how was it done?" demanded Crisman.

"How was what done?" parried Drake.

"How was the man killed?"

"Ah, so we assume he was killed, do we?" Drake enquired as he finished his champagne.

"Good Lord!" exploded Crisman in frustration. "How did he die, then?"

"Ah, my poor Crisman, have you no sense of dramatic effect? If I told you how now, what would we do with the rest of our weekend?" Drake stood up and stretched like a cat. "Come, my boy, to work!" Purposely, he marched outside to Crisman's waiting limousine.

For a few moments, they sat in silence as the limo sped through the night streets. Finally, Crisman spoke, "I say, Drake, where are we going?"

"Well, at 12 on a Friday night in Boston, we are going to the only place we can go. Namely home. Mine first if you please. Meet me tomorrow around noon in the Public Gardens, and the chase will begin in earnest."

Drake went home and read, for a time, from *Fleur du Mal*, and Crisman, returning to his own flat, rejoiced in becoming part of one of Drake's undertakings at last.

⁂

When Crisman strolled into the Public Gardens, he found Drake sitting cross-legged on the grass in his Sunday best, despite it being Saturday.

"My dearest Drake, I had no idea this was a formal occasion," Crisman murmured, unused to being outdone and despising the feeling of being underdressed.

Drake smiled and gracefully uncurled himself into a full standing position, "One must always approach the mystery of death with respect, my friend. Moreover, I have ulterior motives. The chief priest of the Lucayans, or rather the Luku-Cairi, as their original name was pronounced, has arrived in Boston. I intend to pay him a visit later this evening. For now, we must visit the grieving widow."

The two investigators traveled in Crisman's limousine through the streets of Boston and over the Charles River, which stirred restlessly beneath them. Crisman noticed that Drake's eyes lingered on the dark waters as if boring beneath their surface in search of some hidden clue or specter of ancient, angry Atlantean Gods.

"A widow and no children?" Drake asked Crisman suddenly, drawing the man out of his own morbid brooding.

"What? Oh, yes. Um — no children as far as I have heard," responded Chrisman.

"I wonder if his work will die with him, then," murmured Drake.

The home of Nancy Durem, the widow of the archeologist Thomas Durem, was a pleasant New England-style cottage nestled in an affluent sector of Charlestown. Upon arrival, they found it surrounded by a simple yard with an anchor leaning against a lobster trap as the only decoration. The yard was impeccably kept and had no bushes or trees. The house's façade was likewise perfectly maintained, but plain.

Without even pausing at the door, Drake knocked firmly. While they awaited a response, he glanced about the yard and frowned slightly before murmuring, "How very Puritan."

Nancy Durem's face betrayed creases of mourning, half-smoothed in an effort to look presentable. "I'm sorry," she said, "but I am not seeing any visitors."

"Of course," Drake said softly in a comforting voice. "I am so sorry to bother you. It is only that I am assisting in the investigation, and I thought that perhaps I could ask you a few brief questions. My name is Drake, and this is John Crisman."

Her eyes met Drake's, and even as she shook her head, she pushed the door open and stepped aside. Within an instant, Drake had her hand in his and guided her, seemingly by instinct, directly to her own kitchen. All the while, he spoke about making her a cup of tea.

They sat at her kitchen table, her eyes clouding and unclouding with tears, while Crisman rummaged about the kitchen and made tea in as disgruntled a manner as possible.

"I adore peppermint," Drake said as he sipped his minty cup. "It can be so refreshing, don't you agree, Nancy?" She had not given her name, but in moments, she and Drake were speaking together like old friends whispering over the agonies of loss and the terror of fate's sudden turning.

Subtly, Drake turned the conversation to other subjects, commenting on the neighborhood and driving her to discuss the weather. Random topics, unimportant and distant from her grief, were all that they discussed for a long while, as her tears dried and her bearing returned.

"And what a lovely home you keep," Drake said at last. These were no empty words, for out from the well-appointed kitchen opened a tasteful sitting room in High Victorian style and decorated with scattered artifacts from the world over.

Drake stood and led her into the sitting room, and it was clear to Crisman that he was leading her towards the point of this visit as well. On the mantel, at the far end of the room, sat a statue. It seemed to be made of black marble or obsidian and betrayed signs of great antiquity.

With intense interest, having slid into startling silence as his smile faded to a troubled frown, Drake studied the statue. It depicted a forceful god holding a spear in his left hand with his right hand open as if grasping the air. The top half of his body was that of a man, strong-chested and thick-necked. From the waist down, the body split into two tails where legs should have been, covered in detailed scales and curving fish-like.

The face was the most commanding aspect of the artifact. It had a mouth set in grim resolution, and the deep-set eyes glimmered under heavy eyebrows. Crisman thought that there was something sinister about the long, rectangular cut beard and the simple diadem covered in unknown writing that sat on the form's forehead.

"Ahh," Drake spoke at last, awaking as from a trance. "The god Dagon."

Nancy Durem looked at Drake in surprise. "Yes," she responded, "that is what Tom thinks as well."

Drake nodded, ruminating out loud, "But found off the island of Bimini — your husband was quite certain this isn't a hoax?"

"Yes, quite certain." Her voice quavered again as the weight of her tragedy descended once more. "I hate it!" she raged suddenly, "It's an ugly, vile thing! It — it watches me! I know it sounds crazy, but it does! I can feel it smile sometimes..."

Drake nodded and drew a monogrammed handkerchief from his coat pocket. This he placed respectfully over the statue, whispering something that sounded like a psalm in another language as he did so.

"Well, Nancy, perhaps in time we can help you get rid of it." He turned his back on the statue and smiled brightly. "And such a lovely house," he repeated his statement from earlier, as if the conversation had never broken off. "But no pets, my dear?" he asked as they meandered into the dining room, which looked out into the sparse backyard.

"Pets? No. Tom — he — Tom doesn't — I mean didn't – like pets..." Her voice broke again, and Drake gently put his arm around her shoulders.

"Easy, my dear," he soothed her as Crisman watched her pain drain away, leaving her looking simply weary and a little dazed. "Now, tell me about the day Thomas disappeared."

"He said he was going to work on his boat," she began. Nancy's voice was distant now, as if she spoke from out of a dream. "When he didn't come home, I drove to the harbor. He wasn't there, but his car was and the boat was open. Doors and hatches left unlocked. I knew something was wrong. I called the police, and they searched for three days. Then..."

Drake interrupted her, "But the boat was in order? No sign of a robbery or struggle?"

"No, nothing. He had just disappeared."

"They say he was a strong swimmer and in good shape. No heart problems or health conditions?"

"He was in perfect shape," she answered, her eyes following the flight of a wren in the back yard. "He swam like a fish, was even athletic."

Drake nodded. "I assume he was a diver?"

For a moment Nancy's eyes looked startled. "What? No — he said he got claustrophobic down there. He had other people who did the diving for him. He just told them where to dive and what to look for."

"Hm, and were there any strange visitors before this all happened?"

"No, just disturbing phone calls from those people down in the Caribbean, saying he was a thief and cursed."

"And where are his crew, his colleagues?"

"They all stayed down in Bimini. He left in such a hurry, worried about losing that statue, and sailed all the way back here alone."

Drake stood and led her back towards the front door. "That will be all, Nancy," he said, "and thank you. Now, you go to bed and take a long nap. Dream of brighter times."

She nodded solemnly as Drake opened the front door and gave her shoulder one last reassuring squeeze. He turned to leave, then thought better of it.

"One last thing," Drake said, "What is the name of the boat?"

"*Poseidon's Steed*," Nancy replied.

Within moments, Drake and Chrisman were back in the limousine. The day had passed swiftly towards evening as they had spoken with Mrs. Durem. Drake informed the driver to take them to a hotel near the heart of Boston.

"Good lord, Drake," Chrisman said as the car sped off, "the way you handled her seemed almost like hypnotism."

"My dear Chrisman, don't speak nonsense."

"Do — do you really think that creepy statue is from Atlantis?" asked Chrisman.

Drake frowned for a few minutes, "I assume I think pretty much what Thomas Durem thought. The statue is obviously that of the sea god Dagon. The same god who was worshiped by a Middle Eastern people called the Philistines, who appear often in the Bible as the enemies of the Hebrew people. Finding an ancient depiction of a Middle Eastern God in the Caribbean is unusual, to say the least, and certainly very provocative.

"Also, the age of the statue raises certain questions. History, as it is known now, doesn't place any inhabitants on Bimini at the right time period who would have been likely to create a piece of art in such a style. It is highly unusual for the location and time. Finally, Atlantean legend and folklore have always contained rumors about the Philistines being descendants of the Atlantean people. Together, it is all rather suggestive. One can't, however, make a clear jump from that one statue to the existence of an over 2000-year-old legend. But let us return to reality. Did you notice how clean the house was?" Drake asked seemingly out of nowhere, causing Crisman a moment of confusion before he began to nod his head excitedly.

"Of course," Crisman said, "and I follow your thought for

once. She has been cleaning compulsively since he died. A sure sign! She is trying to wash away her guilt for his murder!"

Drake laughed, "Yes, impeccable logic, thus dooming all maids to lives of crime."

Crisman frowned, "So, the maid did it?"

"No," Drake responded, "The butler did it. Call your cook."

"I beg your pardon?" Crisman said, clearly confused.

"Call your cook at the townhouse, have him prepare a rich feast for us and an honored guest. We are going to pick up the religious leader of Bimini Island, the representative of the Lukku Cairi."

"Oh," Crisman said, reaching for the car phone. "Is he expecting us?"

"That depends on how good a shaman he is," Drake responded.

"Um — ok. But, Drake?"

"Yes, my dear boy?"

"I don't think the Durems had a butler."

When they arrived at the hotel, they discovered that they were not the only ones visiting the priest from Bimini. In the lobby, they ran into a ster- looking man with two uniformed police officers.

"Ah, Inspector Fitzgerald, so nice to see you diligently at work," Drake said brightly as he bowed to the scowling man.

"Drake," the inspector acknowledged with distaste. "How are you involved in this whole mess?"

"Mess?" Drake asked. "What mess? I am merely paying a social call. Now, what are you doing here?"

"Just interrogating a suspect."

"Really? I trust he has been informed of his rights and of the fact that he is a suspect."

The inspector's scowl got even darker, an event Crisman had not thought possible. "Possible suspect," Fitzgerald corrected himself.

Drake nodded and winked in a conspiratorial manner. "Oh, of course. I was unaware the police had the time to trouble themselves with cases of accidental drowning."

"To be honest, we don't have the time. But this case is causing such a stir, and there is the issue of an international crisis over an old piece of stone as well. But, you stay out of it! The Feds are even considering getting involved, and we don't need you barging in, confusing things."

Drake smiled beatifically. "But of course, Inspector! It is clear you have things well in hand, and far be it from me to interfere with the honest hand of the law. I shall stringently attempt to keep all barging to an absolute minimum and avoid confusion at all costs. Now," Drake said primly as he glanced at his pocket watch, "I am late for a date with an alleged suspect. A very fine evening to you, gentlemen."

With a bow and a swift turn, Drake and Crisman were away into a closing elevator even as the inspector opened his jowls to yell after them. Whatever he had to say was lost in the closing of the elevator doors and the hearty chuckle of Drake.

When they reached the appropriate door and knocked, they were met by a stout man of middling height with tan skin and long black hair adorned by woven charms of shell, wood, and stone. His eyes, which seemed accustomed to the serenity of sure command, were dark with rage.

"Honored sir," Drake said as he bowed low with respect, "Please, allow us to welcome you to Boston. This is John Crisman, and I am known as Drake."

"I don't care who you are," the man snapped in a heavy Caribbean accent, "I have already been greeted by the authorities of this place, and I don't believe I can stomach any more greeting."

"Sir," Drake insisted, "I beg you, do not judge the people of Boston based upon the foolishness of our misrepresentatives. It is not proper that the spiritual leader of another people should dine alone on his first night in our land. Please, join us as an honored guest. I think you will find we have similar interests to pursue."

The man's eyes narrowed, and his face became more thoughtful as he considered Drake. Still obstinate, he responded firmly, "It is not my custom to share meals with those who suspect me of being a murderer."

Drake nodded, nonplused, "Nor, sir, is it my habit to dine with those I suspect of murder. So, I trust we are both safe on that count."

The man was now puzzled. "Surely you are not some sort of priest here," he said.

Drake smiled. "Surely not indeed. I am but a student with due respect for fellow novices. Please accept my hospitality."

Something Crisman did not understand passed between the two men as they stood staring silently. It seemed a mutual testing occurred in which neither was found wanting.

"Very well, I accept. My name is rather complex for your people, so you can call me Papa Joseph."

The drive to Crisman's townhouse passed mostly in silence. Papa Joseph still seemed out of sorts from his police interrogation and showed an interest in getting a visual feel for the city of Boston. Drake was more than willing to let the silence rest undisturbed. He sat like a Buddha, looking neither thoughtful nor uncomfortable.

Crisman, on the other hand, felt as if he had never passed a minute in silence before in his life. The stretches of empty time made him anxious and restless, but the superhuman silence of the two mystics was impenetrable and suffocated Crisman's innate need to babble.

Two mystics they were indeed, Crisman now realized. Papa Joseph was a creature steeped in spirits and living more in the mysterious otherworld than in this one. The feeling of power passing between the two was palpable and made clear just how out of place Crisman was.

For Crisman, the situation was rather surprising. Here he was, a rich, cultivated, civilized American aristocrat, being made to feel out of place and foolish by some native barbarian witch-doctor from the tropics. This was ridiculous, the man had probably never seen an opera, read Shakespeare or Montaigne. Most likely he made his living sacrificing chickens to bring the rain!

Drake, however, was a social god, lord of all things civilized and refined. Where Drake showed respect, normal men were wise to show great caution. But it was possible that all of this was a ploy of Drake's to lure the suspect into a deceptive sense of comfort.

Crisman looked up from his inner monologue and visibly jumped. Both enigmatic men were looking right at him. Drake frowned in disappointment and Papa Joseph grinned a large toothy smile of amusement. It was for all the world as if the two had heard every word that Crisman had thought silently to himself.

"Ever been to the Caribbean?" Papa Joseph asked in his deep voice.

"Um, yes," Crisman said. "I have taken several cruises in the area, and a few trips by private yacht."

Papa Joseph snorted loudly, "Cruises, yachts! Ha! So, you've seen the sea through silk curtains and walked beaches of imported sand raked to perfection and guarded by hidden soldiers with machine guns. You haven't ever been to the Caribbean. You have never truly spent time upon the wild sea's bosom. You have never passed alone in your canoe, made by your own hands, over the ocean's silent moon-drenched roads. The winds have never whispered for your ears only.

"You have never laughed with the gulls as they raced the surf, wetting their wings in the salty spray. You have never faced the sudden squall, fighting and feeling your body strain at one with the heaving storm. The palms have never hidden your passage to the secret homes of your ancestral gods.

"Each island speaks with a separate voice, but you have never listened. Each stretch of sand tells its own holy history, but you have never heard. Oh, I may not know your ways either. Your cars may deafen me, and your neon may blind me. But, how well do you know your own home? This river by which we pass, what you call the Charles River, had another name once before its original friends and children were driven by your ancestors from their home.

"What was its name when it was addressed as family and neighbor, when it flowed clean and free, unbridled by your bridges and untainted by the black blood of your machines? You do not know its name. Your own home is a stranger to you. You can have your cities with their art museums and poverty, but they were far more civilized when trees grew here to be used for shelter or for sustenance and not for hanging witches or feeding the hungry furnaces of poison factories."

At that moment, the car stopped. They had arrived at Crisman's luxurious townhouse.

Dinner was prepared for them, consisting of New England clam chowder, lobster thermidor, and a chocolate soufflé for dessert. Despite Crisman's anticipations, Papa Joseph did not eat with his hands and displayed perfect etiquette. After the first course, before the arrival of the lobster, Drake stood and raised his glass of wine to Papa Joseph.

"We welcome you, may the spirit of our city welcome you as well." Papa Joseph nodded solemnly, and they all began to eat their lobster. Maddeningly, Drake seemed set on not discussing anything important. He and Papa Joseph bantered back and forth in a cheerful, friendly way about reef diving and whale migration. "The humpback whale," Drake mentioned as he finished his lobster, "gives birth off the coast of the Dominican Republic in the Caribbean, and then migrates with its children north all the way to Maine, the very place from which this lobster came. Our homes, Papa Joseph, are not so very far removed at all."

Papa Joseph nodded, "The children of the sea can course the entire earth in a year. The ocean ties us all together. But when we anger it, there is nowhere to hide."

Crisman nodded to his servant: the port that was served before dessert was to be brought out.

"Well, enough pleasantries, I suppose," Papa Joseph said as he took a large cigar out of an inside pocket of his coat after Crisman had offered him a tray of exotically flavored cigarettes and pipe tobaccos, "I suppose you are wondering why I am in Boston."

Drake shrugged. "Why you are here is your business," he said as he selected a pipe from Chrisman's collection and filled it.

Papa Joseph grunted as a servant lit his cigar. "My business alone? Hardly. Why I am here seems to be a matter of international dispute. But, alas, I am too late, and the curse has already taken its price."

"Too late?" Crisman repeated inquisitively. "Surely, with Thomas Durem dead, there is a greater chance of you getting your statue back."

"Getting my statue back?" Papa Joseph said in a mystified voice. "The statue is certainly not mine, nor do I wish it to be. And getting it back has never been my primary concern. The lords of the sea roads, to whom the statue is dedicated, are not gentle masters. My concern was for the safety of Mr. Durem, and now for the safety of whoever else may gain possession of the statue. I assure you, if I were to receive guardianship of the holy icon, I would return it to the sacred and forbidden undersea byways from whence it came, after performing the appropriate sacrifices of apology and reconciliation."

Drake let loose a large fog of pipe smoke into the still air. "Lords of the sea roads? Undersea byways? You reference, I assume, the Bimini Road?"

Papa Joseph frowned and nodded, puffing for a moment on his cigar. "I refer to what you people call the Bimini Road. We call them, for there are many such roads, the Deep-Ways or Silent-Passing. They are the provinces of the gods alone, and they are very jealously guarded and defended. The fact that Mr. Durem lived long enough to steal from them at all is amazing. Their desecration endangers anyone who possesses the stolen icon, yes, but also endangers the fragile treaty my people have with the Deep-Ones. The guardians of the roads are not of the same clan as our gods, you see. They are a different, older family who only barely tolerate men. Never have we risked angering them, and now they have been robbed and insulted."

"Roads? What are we talking about?" Chrisman asked in desperation.

"Hm — where to begin," Drake mused, swirling his port contemplatively. "At the turn of the last century, there was a man, Edgar Cayce, who became known as the Sleeping Prophet. He would put himself into deep hypnotic trances and then diagnose diseases, heal people, tell strangers about their past lives, and make strange prophecies and predictions. Over the years, he dictated massive amounts of information.

"One of the things he claimed was that the island of Bimini was an ancient mountaintop of Atlantis, and that in 1968, people would discover evidence of Atlantis' existence off the coast of Bimini. That year precisely, pilots flying over Bimini noticed large underwater formations resembling roads. To this day, these roads are highly debated and mysterious. Some claim they are natural rock formations resembling roads, others claim they are actual ancient sunken roads. Scientists don't like to muse about the strange coincidence of Edgar Cayce's prediction and the discovery of the roads. It is near one of these roads that, I assume, Mr. Durem discovered the statue, yes?" Drake looked to Papa Joseph.

"Yes, he dug into the ruins of a temple at a crossing of the roads, the blasphemous bastard," Papa Joseph growled. "I don't know much about when you silly folks think the roads were 'discovered,' but we have known about the Deep-Ways for as long as we have known our own history. More importantly, we know that the Deep-Ways are not for men. Vengeful gods walk the Ways from a time before the time of men.

"That is why I am here. No distance can attenuate the force of the curse, and I knew Mr. Durem was in danger. This is the reason we demanded the artifact back, not because we claim ownership. We are not foolish enough to claim or desire ownership of what belongs to the Deep-Ones."

"Hm," Drake murmured, "Crisman, have your people bring out the dessert. This conversation needs some levity added, and the airy delicacy of your chef's soufflés will serve perfectly. Papa Joseph," Drake then said, turning to stare the priest in the eyes, "if I were to get the statue into your hands, you would accept it?"

"Of course," he said.

"And you would take it immediately back to Bimini and perform all appropriate rituals to end the curse upon both your people and Durem's people?" Drake pressed.

"You have my word, I shall use the full power of my wisdom and years to appease the angered gods and end the danger to all involved," Papa Joseph said in a grim voice.

"Good, good," Drake said, finishing his port. "Good lord, where is that soufflé?" Nothing more was said of the matter over dessert, and then Papa Joseph was driven back to his hotel with a promise from Drake that he would be in touch soon.

Despite his demands for information and explanations, John Crisman was sent to bed that night with no new information and with instructions to meet Drake at the docks where Thomas Durem kept his boat the next day at noon.

Moments before Chrisman fell asleep, he thought wearily that, caught between two mystics, an ordinary man never stands a chance.

❧

Poseidon's Steed tugged restlessly against the lines that bound it to the dock. The sky was overcast, and the clouds raced swiftly across the turbulent skies. The waters of the Charles River were equally disturbed, with chop slapping petulantly against the boat's hull as if to further inflame the vessel's spirit. All in all, it was a forbidding and damp scene that hardly suited John Crisman's spirits.

When he had first arrived at the late Thomas Durem's dock, he had found Drake and Papa Joseph already there, staring thoughtfully out over the roiling waters.

"I never did understand how to distinguish a boat from a ship," Crisman said jauntily as he joined them, seeking to break the weird silence.

"A boat can be put on a ship," was Papa Joseph's laconic answer.

"I have already spoken with Mrs. Durem; she will join us soon," Drake said. "She has given us permission to press on with our investigation, which I believe will reach its completion soon. I have, likewise, invited the charming Inspector Fitzgerald to join us soon. First, let us see what *Poseidon's Steed* has to tell us."

Graceful and spry as a man half his age, though his age was itself always unclear, Drake leapt off the dock onto the rolling deck of the boat. "Well, come along, gentlemen. Mysteries do not solve themselves."

"I will not join you," Papa Joseph said. "It is bad luck to board a boat onto which you have not been invited. Something tells me Mr. Durem would not have been likely to invite me. We had met and spoken when he was in Bimini, and our relations were not cordial."

"Of course. John," Drake said, looking at Crisman, "you

have no excuse. Come along, the final scene of the opera is drawing near when the wrathful lord of the sea rises to drag the hero tragically to the murky deep."

"I'm no hero," Crisman said in consternation as he shakily climbed aboard the boat.

"Of course not," Drake agreed, "and thank god for that, you would make a pitiful lunch for Poseidon."

"I find your humor unnaturally whimsical and distastefully lighthearted," Papa Joseph said sharply to Drake.

Drake simply winked at him roguishly. "Just whistling in the dark, my dear Joseph," was all he said as he led Crisman on a brief tour of the boat in an observant fashion.

"Let's reconstruct the scene," Drake said. "Thomas is here on the boat. He has no intention of actually taking it out to sea; he has come to do some rather regular upkeep on the vessel. We know that, when the boat was searched, the hatch to the engine room was open, as were both the door to the cabin and the bathroom within.

"There was a toolbox Thomas had brought from home, unopened, on the deck. The engine was not on and does not seem to have been run at all while Thomas was here. When the engine room was searched, nothing unusual was found, and no work seemed to have been done."

"I don't know what this babble is supposed to get you, Drake," a voice growled from behind them. Crisman jumped and spun around to find Inspector Fitzgerald and two other officers standing threateningly on the dock, "You are trespassing at a crime scene, and I am going to enjoy arresting you."

"Indeed, Inspector, indeed. I am sure I will enjoy the fine decor of your prison cells. For now, however, since we are both here and I, unlike you, have explicit permission from Mrs. Durem to be here, let us discuss this case a bit. Mrs. Durem is on her way, and I am sure you will want her to be present before you serve her interests by carting away from her property one of her own guests."

"Damn it, Drake, someday you're gonna realize no one finds you funny but yourself," Fitzgerald grumbled as he climbed clumsily onto the boat.

"I find him funny, Inspector," Papa Joseph said, grinning.

"Oh, shut up," the inspector said. "Watch him," he ordered his men, pointing to Papa Joseph.

"Well," Drake said. "Since you are here, why don't you enlighten us as to what has been altered here from how it was on the day of the disappearance."

"Only the very bare minimum has been changed," Fitzgerald said. "Our crime scene specialists have already been here, so a few minor things could be altered. Basically, the deck was cleared, the toolbox was taken away, and such. The doors to the cabin and the hatch to the engine room have both been bolted. Beyond that, the inside of the cabin and engine room have been entirely unchanged."

Drake nodded. "Excellent. Now, please provide us with an analysis of the engine room. What did you learn from it?"

"I don't know why I am humoring you madmen. I should just get on with arresting you all. But fine. We learned nothing. The engine room seemed in a normal engine room state. Nothing had been obviously worked on, disassembled, or changed from how a normal working engine room would look."

"Thank you, you are uninformative as usual. But," Drake held up his hand to silence the sputtering inspector, "let us assume that your complete lack of insight is appropriate. Thomas Durem was here. He was planning on doing work in the engine room, but didn't get to it. Instead, he was doing work in the cabin. The fact that his tools were clean supports this."

"How do you know that?" Fitzgerald demanded.

"Oh, I have read the police report, of course," Drake said with a wave. "I do have some friends in the department. The profession is not entirely devoid of the intelligent and civilized. But let us continue. He is doing work in the cabin when disaster hits. Fitzgerald," Drake said with a flourish, "open the cabin door!"

Complaining all the while, the Inspector complied. Drake led Fitzgerald and Crisman into the dim cabin.

"Now," Drake continued, "we know as well that the bathroom door was open, which it is not at present." Drake led them to a small door at the opposite end of the cabin and opened it. The bathroom was tiny and cramped, with a closet-sized shower, a toilet and a small sink. On the floor was a deck brush, an empty bucket, and an empty bottle of bleach next to a bottle of soap. "Your police report mentioned the cleaning products. Apparently, before doom struck, Thomas was in here cleaning."

"Get to the goddamn point," Fitzgerald demanded.

"The point is an ambiguity in your report that I hope you will explain. The police report mentioned that elements of the bathroom were in disarray as if the victim had left swiftly. What does the report mean by this?"

Fitzgerald frowned and looked around, "I don't know. Nothing looks like it is in disarray here now. I mean, there is a cleaning brush on the floor, but that doesn't seem very unusual if one is cleaning."

Drake nodded, "John, take a look at the bathroom and tell me what you see."

John ducked in as Fitzgerald backed out. "I don't see anything strange," he said.

"Very well. Do you smell anything strange?" Drake pressed.

"It smells clean — and like bleach," John said.

"Good. Where is the bleach smell coming from? From the empty bleach bottle? Where is the clean smell coming from? From an empty bucket?"

"Well," John answered Drake, "the bleach bottle is open."

"I am getting the hell out of this box! Small spaces make

me feel stifled," Fitzgerald complained. Drake and John followed him back up to the deck and found that Mrs. Durem had arrived.

"Nancy," Drake greeted her warmly from the deck of the boat, offering her a hand to help her aboard. "I think, my dear, we shall clear up any mystery connected to this tragedy soon. I just need you to be strong and answer a few last questions as honestly as possible."

Nancy Durem nodded solemnly, and Crisman noted for the first time that she was rather gingerly carrying a large traveling bag. Drake took the bag from her and put it aside in a corner of the deck.

"Now, Nancy," Drake said, "we have already talked about the strangeness of such a strong swimmer as Thomas drowning. He was, as you have attested, in generally good health. He did not, however, like diving because it made him claustrophobic, and he didn't like pets. Am I right?"

"Yes." Nancy sounded hesitant and looked confused.

"Damn it, what the hell do pets have to do with anything?" Fitzgerald burst out.

"I am afraid a lack of pets and an empty bleach bottle, both of which you think are of no importance, explain perfectly how a strong athletic swimmer drowned in a calm river," Drake snapped.

At that moment, a speed boat, being driven by college kids, shot past the docks at a wild speed. The wake set off by the vessel approached *Poseidon's Steed* like shock-waves, causing the boat to pitch to the side and rock violently. Drake, his feet spaced wide on the deck, rode out the wake firmly and caught Nancy Durem when she lost her balance. Fitzgerald and Crisman yelled and both fell against the railing, coming dangerously close to falling overboard.

"I believe that type of behavior is illegal, inspector," Drake said, pointing to the swiftly departing boat.

"Damn right it is," he grunted. "But tell the coast guard

about it. These damn rich kids with their toys are impossible to control."

Drake nodded. "A similar event probably occurred while Thomas was cleaning the bathroom. The rocking caused his bucket of soap and bottle of bleach to fall over, covering him and the bathroom in bleach and soap. It was this mess that the original inspecting officers noted, but which has since evaporated."

"That still doesn't explain how he ended up in the water drowned," the cop grunted.

"You're right," Drake said. "Until you take into account the fact that the bleach fumes would have filled the bathroom and cabin, driving him to the deck."

"So."

"Back on deck, he suffered a severe asthma attack, which is the reason he never kept pets and the reason his yard and house were always kept so clean. It was also the reason that he never actually did his own diving, but rather let others dive for him, despite the fact that he was a very good swimmer. In fact, I bet he didn't even have a diver's license. Isn't this correct, Nancy?" Drake pressed.

"Y-yes. He did have asthma. I never mentioned it because I didn't think it mattered much. I didn't know how it could have led to him drown. And, well, he was always very embarrassed by the fact. Tom thought it made him seem weak. He hated the disease," Nancy said sadly.

"So," Drake continued. "He is standing on the deck, beginning to wheeze. The bleach is on his shirt or pants. The fumes in the cabin set off the attack, but he is still breathing the fumes outside from his clothing. He leans against the railing, gasping for air. Suffocating, he passes out and falls into the water, where he drowns."

Inspector Fitzgerald's eyes bulged, making him look a little like a horrific, mutated frog, while Nancy Durem's eyes became suddenly clear as, at last, she understood. She nodded. It made sense and cleared up the uneasy darkness of supposed curses or murders that had surrounded his unexplained death.

"Now," Drake said crisply, drawing everyone out of their thoughts and surprise as he picked up the bag Nancy Durem had brought with her. "This is the center of the confusion surrounding this case," he said as he hoisted the bag in his hand. "Papa Joseph, Nancy Durem reasonably wants nothing to do with this artifact. She is giving it to you, that you may make right whatever wrongs have been done."

Drake walked to the back of the boat and stepped onto the dock, handing the bag to Papa Joseph, who nodded solemnly and spoke a swift blessing and prayer over the bag in his native tongue.

"I will return it to the deep where it belongs," Papa Joseph said solemnly.

"No, you won't!" Inspector Fitzgerald said as he scrambled off the boat, tripped, and fell face-first on the dock. "You are a murder suspect, and not going anywhere, and ownership of that object is a matter of international dispute," he insisted as he climbed back to his feet and grabbed hold of one of the handles of the bag.

Papa Joseph, who was no small man to begin with, drew himself to his full height as he and Inspector Fitzgerald stared each other down over the bag they both now held. The wind picked up, and the waves lapping at the boat and dock became louder. "My patience with this foolishness has reached its end," Papa Joseph said in a deep, threatening voice.

"I will not be threatened by some savage witch-doctor!" Inspector Fitzgerald retorted. The faces of both men were quickly becoming darker as was the sky that was swiftly filling with more threatening storm clouds. The two officers who had accompanied Fitzgerald stood back in confusion, unsure what to do or unwilling to interfere in the frightening confrontation.

Drake cleared his throat humorously. "As amusing as it might be to see Inspector Fitzgerald turned into a frog," he said, "this is not up to either of you. The statue was a matter of international dispute because Thomas Durem was forcing the matter. Now, whatever claim to ownership Thomas had has transferred to Nancy. The two sides of the dispute are now Nancy Durem and the people of Bimini, as represented by Papa Joseph. If Nancy wishes to give up her claim to ownership, there is no more dispute. So, Inspector, let go of the property of the people of Bimini, or I shall have to summon a police officer." Drake grinned mischievously at Fitzgerald's own officers.

"This man is still a murder suspect," Fitzgerald insisted.

"Yes," Drake said. "Except that there is now no reason to think that any foul play has occurred. We have a reasonable explanation for how the accident might have happened and no reason to suspect murder. The widow herself is no longer suspicious. And, we might note, it was originally her insistence that it could not have been an accident that led to the murder investigation. I dare say, my dear inspector, that should you insist on holding Papa Joseph, there will be an international scandal, or rather another one, but this time with you in the center."

It was clear that the air had been stolen from the inspector's sails. Growling, he let go of the bag and turned on his heel, calling over his shoulder to his men as he marched away.

"Job well done, officers," Drake said cheerfully as they passed.

Papa Joseph bowed deeply to Nancy Durem and expressed his hearty regret over her loss. Following this, Drake had John Crisman lead her back to Drake's waiting limousine, which had driven her here. Before she left, she gave Drake a firm hug and cried softly as she did. Little was said, little had to be said. Then, only Drake, John, and Papa Joseph were left standing on the dock before *Poseidon's Steed* with the Atlantean statue of the Deep God.

"Perhaps you shall someday visit Bimini," Papa Joseph said to Drake, "and I shall be able to return the hospitality you have shown me."

"I would very much like that," Drake said.

Papa Joseph turned and bowed as deeply to *Poseidon's Steed* as he had to Nancy Durem, "This is a noble vessel, and it served its master well. It is sad that its master aroused the anger of the gods." Then Papa Joseph also left the dock, carrying the cursed statue with him.

John, bitterly, noted that no one had bowed to him, "Drake, shouldn't that statue have gone to the scientists? I mean, it seems to be a rather important discovery, especially if it verifies the existence of a lost civilization."

Drake shrugged, rather unperturbed, "The statue had the bad luck of being associated with an unpopular mythology. Even if it did prove conclusively the existence of an ancient civilization of high technology and developed culture around Bimini thousands of years ago, it would never have been accepted by any scientific community. We, all of us, see what we look for. Our prejudices create the world we see. No statue is going to prove Atlantis to a world of 'objective' observers set on not seeing."

"So that's it," John Crisman said, as he and Drake turned to leave, "all that hype and there was no curse after all. It was all just a strange accident." Crisman sounded rather disappointed.

Drake shook his head. "Did I say that? How do you want your curses to work? With lightning from the heavens, perhaps, or demons rising from the deep? Thomas Durem insulted an ancient myth, and he died shortly after. Why use lightning, my friend, when bleach will do just as well?"

A Bitter Draft to Drink

Jonathan exhaled a cloud of smoke from the depths of his lungs and then gulped at the cold night air like a drunkard gulping beer. The night was crisp and quiet, yet the city streets seemed to shiver with electric energy. Jonathan liked the night, liked the enshrouding darkness that cloaked him from the prying eyes of the condemning masses. He took another slow, loving drag off his cigarette as if the poisonous smoke were his life's blood.

Ah, blood — that brought a tingle to his spine. He watched as a couple strolled by in each other's loving embrace. Yes, blood was nature's true perfection, an ambrosia of the gods that was both the essence of life and the harbinger of death. Even the night air had a pulse, a slow, succulent beat that filled the air with a shivering flow of vitality.

Jonathan could taste the blood of the night. It consisted of hidden passions and perverted dreams, a pulse created by all that was human and all that man sought to hide under veils of darkness. Shivering and smiling, Jonathan walked in the direction the couple had gone.

Had the couple turned at that moment, they would have been greeted with a not uncommon scene. The man strolling behind them was perhaps twenty-five years old; he had longish black hair and wore a brown leather coat. Between his fingers dangled a half-smoked cigarette, and his smile and swagger were that of a kid thinking he owned the world.

Only his eyes, hidden in shadows, would have revealed the strange fire that burned beneath the surface. Only the eyes, those portals to the truth within, could have portrayed to the blissful couple the depth of the bitterness that followed them.

Perhaps they would have overlooked the telltale shadow in his strangely shining eyes. That shadow spoke of years of forced loneliness that taught him to always be solitary, even in a crowd, and to be grateful for it. Anger burns like a fire and is gone, but hatred festers to a bitterness that gnaws upon the soul until nothing remains. The streets are full of the soulless gnawing upon their own emptiness, finding nothing to sustain them but illusions.

The couple turned a corner and wandered into a peaceful city park. Jonathan followed closely after.

The day was slow and lazy behind the forbidding doors of the elite private club known as the Hasan Society. It was named after the powerful figure of the Old Man of the Mountain, Sheikh of the Assassins, a secret society which held the Arab World in terror starting in 1090 and was rumored to have never ceased. The modern club, however, was founded much more recently by a collective of anarchists and multi-millionaire adventurers.

Within the club's plush mansion which towered majestically over Beacon Hill in Boston, everything was lacquered hardwood and champagne. The interior was a mix between the Elizabethan decadence of a royal palace and the succulent comfort of a Persian opium den. The members of the club strolled about the building, playing chess in one corner, reading or writing a book in another.

In truth, the entire club consisted of anarchists who took great joy in proving that even they could be elitist aristocrats. It was required that every member be able to prove themselves a heretic in at least three of the orthodox religions of the world and to have performed at least five acts which would nationally be considered treason against capitalism, society, and state.

Surprisingly, most members could just as easily be found in Congress, courts, or corporate offices. Many of them were upstanding judges, lawyers, and business magnates. Most believed that empires only fell from within, which is why they snidely snuggled up to the cold, calculating breast of mother bureaucracy.

This day was much like any other inside the protective walls of the club's palace of elite separation. Lazy and epicurean, the hours rolled by as the members smoked, drank, and talked of everything and nothing.

In the corner, the club's most honored and enigmatic member, known only as Drake, sat smoking a Cuban cigar and sipping a fine white wine. Lounging in a throne-like chair positioned so he could observe the entire gathering, Drake played a game of four-player chess with two other club members. The fourth player was believed to be a spirit whispering its desired moves into the ear of Drake's close friend, Matthew Macgregor.

Matthew conversed with his spirit opponent and with Jacob Harris, who mused aloud about his latest case. He was the city's greatest private detective and had sold his talents in most major cities around the world. Members of the club whispered in hushed tones that he had also worked as a bounty hunter and assassin. He was rumoured to be wanted in Russia in connection with several mysterious deaths and to have fled Paris decades earlier after clashing with the military.

"Surely you have seen the grislier details of the case in the papers," Jacob murmured to Drake while agonizing over his next move. "The entire city is ablaze with conjecture and rumor, and now two of the city's wealthier families have hired me to hunt down the mystery."

"My dear sir," Drake drawled, "I find that anyone who has even the slightest fondness for the truth avoids the papers and other creatures of the news industry. I have no need for my understanding of the universe to be poisoned by fairy tales woven by the fiction writers of the *Globe, Journal,* or *Times.*"

Matthew Macgregor chuckled to himself and waited to see what climax this conversation would reach.

"Allow me to share with you some of the most recent 'fictions' then," Jacob said as he pulled a paper from his traveling case and passed it to Drake.

Vampire Murderer of Boston Strikes Again!

The midnight horror of Boston's streets has added two more victims to its list of kills. Over the period of the last four weeks, the serial killer, now referred to as the Vampire of Boston, is suspected of being responsible for six deaths. Investigators are mystified. The killer, who gains his name from the bloodless state in which he leaves his victims, has added the lives of a couple on honeymoon to his list. A list that includes the names of young and old, rich and poor alike. Investigators say that every murder has been perpetrated in the late hours of the night. Victims are drained of large quantities of blood extracted from large, knife-like wounds to the throat. Residents of Boston are advised to avoid the streets as much as possible in the late hours and to travel in large groups whenever travel at night is necessary.

"Well, Drake?" Jacob Harris pressed, "what do you think of that? And two of the victims are the golden children of two of Boston's wealthiest families! Now, it is my job to find this freak. It's unsolvable, I swear. Six deaths and not a single lead."

Drake smiled indulgently and sipped his wine. Then his eyes grew distant in a distinct way that only occurred when he had a sudden burst of insight, or premonition. Frowning, he graced Jacob with a response.

"My dear sir, despite your long history of success, I assure you that this case shall be different from any other you have ever taken. To begin with, you find the case so difficult because of your lack of understanding, both of the psychology of the human mind and the more important sciences of the human soul. With appropriate knowledge of both, this case would provide you with more than enough leads. Already, your own psychology has tainted your view of the situation to the point where there is more obfuscation than clarity."

Jacob snorted derisively. "Is that so? Perhaps you would like to enlighten me about these obfuscations," he growled.

Drake smiled before responding, "I fear that such education would take more time than even I have the energy and desire for. I can, however, point out key examples. First, you refer to the murderer as 'he' and 'him' and yet you have no evidence for even this most basic of claims. It is possible the murderer is female, and you could have been running all over the state hunting the wrong sex."

Jacob made to respond, but Drake silenced him with a look.

"Second, you most likely have overlooked the simple fact that names have more meaning than one would suspect. This bringer of death is called the 'Vampire of Boston,' and it is very true indeed that a vampire is what we are dealing with."

At this, Jacob could hold his silence no longer. "Oh, please! What trash! And here you are accusing the papers of spinning fantasies. Are you actually suggesting that a preternatural monster is committing these crimes? A horror fiction? And you accuse me of obfuscation? What madness," exclaimed Jacob.

Drake yawned and sipped his wine. "I believe that by the end of this case, you will discover there are many more types of vampires than you would imagine. One feeds because one lacks sustenance in one's body. Likewise, a vampire feeds off others in a certain way because it lacks a certain something in both soul and mind. Your killer is attempting to fill a void with the blood of his or her victims, which I assure you this vampire is ingesting. If you want to find this killer, look for a vampire, and not a man or woman."

Jacob broke into disbelieving laughter.

Matthew Macgregor, however, knew better than to ever doubt Drake's acute observations. He also knew Jacob to be an obsessive gambler. Seeing a chance for an entertaining and perhaps profitable game in this argument, he jumped in. "Gentlemen, if I may suggest a wager. It would appear that you both believe yourselves better equipped than the other to solve this case. I suggest that we begin a race; the first to solve the crime wins. I, myself, put three thousand on Drake."

Jacob's eyes lit up for a moment in interest. Then, the flame died as he remembered his earlier claim that the case was unsolvable. "And what if neither of us prevail?" asked the detective.

"Then, sir, whoever bet that the case was unsolvable wins the pot," replied Matthew.

Drake interrupted, "Matthew, I do not enjoy being brought into one of your vain attempts to turn life into a game. Nor do I approve of this covetous maneuvering of meaningless symbols of debt. One's mind should be on higher matters than the movements of paper."

Drake drew on his cigar and stared into space for a moment in thought. "However," he continued, "I accept the challenge if only to see justice done and to teach our friend here the value of the study of the sciences of the human soul. I swear to see all parties responsible for these murders duly punished." He moved one chess piece and placed all three of his opponents in checkmate at the same time.

So, the deal was done. In a matter of moments, the entire club had cast bets for one party, the other, or neither. It proved to be one of the most popular of Matthew's games yet.

⁊⁊

The following day, Jacob set off into the city with a determined tilt to his prominent chin and a resolute clench to his jaw. He visited each of the crime scenes and interviewed anyone who knew any of the victims, searching for a common factor that might point to a motive. He also bribed an officer at the police department for all information pertaining to the case.

He went home that evening exhausted, having gotten himself nowhere. Frustrated, he mulled over following up on the vampire lead Drake had suggested. Injuring his pride only a little, he decided the next day would be spent investigating the few "vampire clubs" in Boston where gothic role players went to pretend to be the undead. He was determined to beat Drake no matter the cost. As far as anyone knew, no one had ever bested the mysterious mystic. Jacob would be the first.

Drake, meanwhile, spent his day at Harvard Square. The area was filled with bohemian street performers and quiet cafés that suited Drake's mood. He engaged in a few games of chess with the self-aggrandized students of Harvard and found their so-called "competition" neither threatening nor stimulating.

In a cloud of boredom, he wandered back across the river to the Boston Commons, where he spent several hours reading beneath an oak tree and watching the public pass in that self-important haste designed to keep them busy and away from such dangerous activities as thought. The tone of the city had changed, however: for now the words upon everyone's lips pertained to the horrific murders and the stalking vampire whose reputation had grown to supernatural proportions.

More than one seemingly rational man whispered to a friend, as they passed Drake, that the police's inability to catch the killer suggested the crimes were being committed by a real vampire. Soon, rumors of men changing themselves into bats and wolves would fill the streets as well. Boston was aflame with conjecture, fear, and the sickening excitement often displayed at the scenes of accidents where passers-by stare in grim fascination at the blood littering the area. The public preferred anything to the monotony of their self-inflicted pointlessness and boredom, Drake thought.

As the sun sank below the horizon, Drake left the Commons and wandered to one of his favorite coffee houses to meet a friend. Matthew's talk aimed at pulling details of Drake's theories of the crime from his vague silences.

Drake, on the other hand, lazily watched the smoke from his cigarette curl towards the roof and sipped at his mediocre coffee.

Between puzzling statements of esoteric philosophy, he watched the patrons come and go while listening to them discuss the murders. More than one of the eclectic coffee drinkers claimed to know for a fact that several real vampires were on the loose; three members of different coffee clutches even claimed to be vampires and killers themselves. Drake smiled in benign amusement and turned his conversation with Matthew to more mundane areas.

"So, my friend, what do you know of my worthy competitor?" asked Drake between a sip of coffee and a drag off his cigarette. "He must have a very interesting history."

"Not much is known; he is almost as much a mystery as you are." Drake did not respond to Matthew's obvious attempt to pry into his past; instead, he spun his cigarette in a circle for Matthew to go on.

"Jacob Harris has spent his life traveling the world, and most of that time was spent hunting one criminal or another for profit. He is an incessant gambler, as his current situation shows, and he believes himself the modern Sherlock Holmes."

Drake chuckled at that. "Perhaps he should pick up a cocaine addiction to add to the dubious resemblance."

"He was born in New York City," Matthew continued, "and, finding he hated living there, moved to London. How he came by his money is also debated, but there are rumors of possible illegal activities. Despising London as well, he left for Paris, where he became a private detective."

Drake frowned and gazed into the distance in thought, "What was he doing before he became a detective, and what motivated him to become a detective once in Paris?"

Matthew shook his head, "No one knows. There are rumors of everything from working as a hired killer to smuggling drugs. There are also rumors that, since becoming a detective, he has been hired to not only find criminals but also to kill them if possible, which is perhaps a reason for his constant movement. A country's law enforcement agency rarely likes private detectives who exact their own justice."

Drake stared across the room at various groups of college students coming and going, socializing and studying while Matthew spoke. Almost as if he wasn't listening at all, but Matthew knew better than that. Drake, as always, heard and saw everything.

"He spent three years in Paris, where he had several affairs, which is no surprise considering he has robbed any city he visits of its virtue as far as he can. He does have a most confusing affinity for justice. It is said that he performs the jobs for the enjoyment he obtains from catching the criminal, with an almost religious obsession with the concept of justice, and has alluded to viewing himself as the hand of justice. Above the law, as it were."

"Unfortunately, there are laws which no man is above," Drake mused aloud.

"He did leave France in a hurry, some say with the military police on his heels. It is also rumored that, in the current situation, he has been hired not only to find the criminal but also to apprehend or kill him. Having failed in his last two cases, he is driving himself mad over solving this one." At that, Matthew's information drew to a close.

Drake nodded and sipped his drink, "Yes, to a man in a situation like this, with a history like Jacob's, the criminal becomes the devil himself. He does not hunt men; he hunts all he hates about society, and most often about himself," Drake mused aloud. "Justice pursued for the wrong reason turns on its executor."

Drake paused in grim thought before speaking once more. "I wonder if you would do me a favor. I am planning to be busy all evening; however, there is information I need. Could you perhaps contact my dear friend, the Marquis de Nizet in Paris, and request any information he can dig up on Jacob Harris and his actions in Paris?"

Matthew was slightly taken aback. "Of course I will, but don't you think that you should focus on the case? There is a wager at stake here, my friend. Shouldn't you be hunting this supposed vampire and not collecting information about your competitor?"

Drake sighed and shook his head, "My dear friend, will you never learn the subtlety of the real game I play? I am already on the very edge of solving these murders — that shall be little trouble. However, modern Quantum theory has proven that the simple act of investigating a particle changes its properties and behavior. One must study the method of study itself to understand the true properties of the particle and how it behaves. Our friend Jacob is the investigator in this. I do not investigate. I wait and watch. He is the one who is hunting the particle that, at this time, happens to be a killer. We must understand him to understand the killer. In fact, there is always something of a pre-established harmony between a seeker and what they seek."

Matthew shook his head in befuddlement, "Very well, my friend, I trust you. I'll get you your information as long as you win me this bet."

Drake smiled, his eyes running over a group of students upon whom he had been eavesdropping while Matthew spoke. Then he returned his eyes to Matthew decisively, "I am involved in no bet and no wager, Matt. I swore to see those responsible for this crime brought to justice, nothing else. I am afraid I have no interest in who wins the bet." With that, the conversation was over.

Drake put out his cigarette with a clear sense of finality and stood up. Matthew watched in chagrin as he wandered over to a group of college students playing chess and challenged the winner to a game. In a matter of moments, Drake had skillfully turned their topic of conversation away from the murders and focused them on a lively debate about Brahm Stoker's *Dracula* and the motivation of the vampire in the book.

"What do you think the noble count was after, good sir?" Drake finally asked his opponent, a soft-spoken boy who had said little more than a word the entire time.

"I really couldn't say," he replied with a slight European accent. "I have never read the book. Check," he finished decisively.

Drake moved his knight to block the attack of the boy's bishop. "You don't have to have read it. Just what do you think would motivate a vampire? Any vampire?" Drake asked absently as he concentrated on the game.

"Hunger, I would imagine. Don't vampires drink blood because they have to? To survive or something. To sustain their eternal life, I would suppose," muttered the boy as he attempted another line of attack against Drake's king.

"Oh, I wouldn't say that, friend. I would imagine that some vampires at least could give up the hunt for blood and drink wine or orange juice. No one ever made clear the entire issue to my personal liking. And why not break into a blood bank and not have to kill, eh?" Drake moved his king to the side, just sidestepping an attack from the boy's queen. The boy was a very assertive and offensive player for one so soft-spoken.

"I suppose the actual act of the killing has as much to do with the hunger as the blood does," the boy said softly. "Maybe the blood is a symbol of the life the living dead lack.

They have to feed off other people's life force. The killing is where they get to feed, the act of taking life proves they exist, proves they have power, proves they can affect the world and are not simply phantoms." He stopped and sipped his coffee.

Drake smiled.

"Precisely, my boy," Drake responded and moved his own queen out to checkmate his opponent's unprepared king. He looked up from the board and stared the boy right in the eyes. "You seem to understand the mind of the vampire well." Drake smiled and did not break eye contact. The boy shrugged and began clearing the chessboard.

"Good game," he mumbled as he put his pieces away one by one.

Drake continued to watch him and smile. "I would imagine the life of the vampire is lonely. Perhaps that is the hunger he must feed with blood and murder? Man is often defined by other men. Someone who is alone, even in a crowd, can feel very undefined. Like a phantom if you will. It is a sad and powerless life — or so I would imagine."

There was a moment of intense silence while Drake gazed at the boy who did not meet his eye.

"You're right, though," Drake continued. "By killing, the vampire proves he is not just the living dead. He can affect the world. He is real and does exist in the few moments of slaughter." Drake chuckled to himself and grinned. "A rather grim topic, I must admit. I am known as Drake. You play a good game of chess, perhaps I shall have the opportunity to play against you again sometime."

The boy nodded absently and shook Drake's extended hand. "I'm Jonathan, it's nice to meet you," the boy said softly.

Drake nodded and removed a card from his coat pocket. "This is my phone number and my address when I am staying here in Boston. If you ever want to discuss your game and perhaps look for some guidance, call me or stop by. I would, however, suggest that you not stop by after dark. I'm afraid I am rarely available at night and would find any intrusion then quite rude." Drake smiled as he completed his multi-meaningful introduction. He walked over to collect Matthew, and the two left.

"What was that all about, Drake?" Matthew asked. "I've seen you play chess thousands of times and that was by far the worst game you ever played. You let that boy control the game the entire time."

Drake smiled mysteriously and replied, "The best way to win any game is to allow your opponent to think that they have the upper hand and then to reveal their own weaknesses to them — in the end, just before you claim checkmate."

Drake turned to leave Matthew at the door of the coffee house, intending to wander the dark streets by himself. "Oh dear," he joked as he strolled away, "I fear I have forgotten my garlic and stake. Good lord, what kind of vampire hunter am I?" And with that, he disappeared into the chill Bostonian night.

Watching him go, Matthew felt sorry for any would-be killers. Drake was not a man to toy with.

The next day dawned clear and crisp, and the morning papers were abuzz with word of another attack by the Boston Vampire. This time, the victim was a young man returning from a punk rock concert. The city was in a frenzy. Even the inner sanctuary of the Hasan Society was inflamed, mostly because the members were worried about their wagers.

While the city buzzed, and the club wondered, Drake sat in one of the club's private rooms and spoke on a telephone to the Marquis de Nizet in Paris. He received the information he needed, smiled, thanked his friend, and hung up.

Meanwhile, Jacob sat in a separate room of the club, poring over his notes and the information he had gathered from the police and from his own investigations. He still had no leads. Hearing the sound of a cane clicking upon the hardwood floors, Jacob raised his head from his notes to see Drake approaching him in good humor. He swung the black lacquered staff with a fine silver handle absently between his fingers.

"Well, old chap, any luck?" drawled Drake as he smiled.

Jacob snorted in disgust and shrugged. "Nothing much, a lead here, a lead there. I dare say it must be more than you've got. I hear you've spent your time sipping coffee, reading books, and playing chess," Jacob replied.

Drake chuckled. "Ah, not so; my friend. I've been doing quite well for my old self. Granted, I'm not the most distinguished investigator on four continents, but I have been holding my own," Drake responded.

Overhearing the conversation, others drew near, hoping to find out which side of the battle held the lead.

"In point of fact," Drake continued, "I have seen the killer. Last night, I saw him fleeing the scene of the crime. Alas, I was too late to save the poor victim's life. Indeed, it was I who phoned the police, though I neglected to give them my name. I attempted pursuit, after making sure there was nothing I could do for the departed, but the braggart got away. He had a frightful head start, and I am no longer the man of my youth. I did, however, catch a view or two of his retreating form. Rest assured, I am well on the tail of our mysterious vampire."

There were a few sighs of relief and some small cheers from the crowd that had gathered. There was also more than one curse of frustration from those foolish enough to bet against Drake.

"I am sure, however, that you are just as close on his trail. You are the worthiest of opponents." Smiling, Drake finished his sarcastic speech and wandered from the room.

The second he was out of the room, Matthew caught up to him. "Good Lord, Drake, did you really see the man? Are you so close already?" His voice carried wonder and joy at the prospect of winning his bet.

Drake chuckled to himself, "Matthew, my dear boy, you are so obtuse. I knew who the murderer was two days ago. I simply had to confirm the fact so that no doubt could be summoned up. The killer's identity is as clear to me now as the sun is to you."

"Then announce it! Call in the police! Save the day! Win the bet for Christ's sake!"

Drake spun on him with a stare as cold as ice. "Macgregor, there are lives at stake here. This is not a matter of a bet! You would do well to end the entire deal now. I warn you, this is a forbidding situation, and none involved shall depart from this game without losing something dear to them. End the game now while you're ahead." His words were cold as ice and sharp as daggers.

Matthew was in shock. Drake never behaved so bluntly unless he was under great strain. He must truly be troubled by the situation. It was a rare occurrence. Matthew's musings were halted, however, by Drake's final words.

"I am not in this to win some bet, my friend, I tell you this once again. I swore to bring all responsible to justice, and that is what I prepare even now to do. Justice is a cruel goddess who has killed her every lover. Remember that, always, my friend."

Drake then strode grimly from the club into the streets of Boston.

❧

It was 6:30. Jonathan was just preparing to go out for the evening when there was a firm knock on his apartment door. He went to the door to see who was there and found only a simple note on expensive parchment.

> I know who you are and what you are doing. If you val-
> ue your secret, meet me tonight. 12:30. The Public Gardens.
> If you are not there, expect to hear next from the police.

Shivering, he read the note over and over again. It could only be that man Drake! All his talk of vampires and loneliness. Jonathan choked back a sob. Drake knew, yes, he knew about the murders, but more importantly, he knew about Jonathan. He knew why he killed. He knew the hunger, the terrible loneliness. The man had hit the mark seemingly by accident.

But, damn it, Jonathan was not a phantom! He was not the walking dead, as he so often felt. He didn't need the love, the friendship, the family he had always lacked! He had shown the entire city that.

Weeping now, the boy crumpled into a ball on the bed. It was over. Thank God it was over. He had not wanted to kill those people, but he had no choice. They didn't care, they didn't know him, they didn't see him. He was just another shadow as he had always been. Worthless, a nothing.

But they had known him at the end, as he had tried so desperately to drain from them that which made them real.

He begged God to kill him every day, and every day he lived on in the limbo that is a worthless, empty, lonely life. He had grown cold. All the years of his childhood had taught him to be cold, the years of being the unwanted illegitimate child. Left to himself for days on end.

He was too cold to kill himself, so he prayed that someone else would. Every time he stalked someone through the dark, empty streets, he prayed this would be the man to pull a gun on him and kill him. He only existed when he was the vampire, and once he was dead, he would be someone. People cared about him now for the first time in his life.

But it was over now, he knew it. Drake had proven too good a player and had found him out. Unless — he could go to the man's house and hunt him down now. But no, Drake would be prepared for that. The only choice was to go to the meeting tonight and see what the man wanted. Perhaps he wanted to help him; he had seemed to care when he gave Jonathan his card. Yet, now even the caring of another just revealed to Jonathan the horror of what he was.

Drake seemed wise, kind — maybe even merciful. He might gain redemption from Drake, redemption or mercy. If not mercy, then perhaps death. And if those two options did not come about, then he himself would kill Drake. Alone in his dark room, Jonathan wept bitter self-hating tears. As always, there was no one there to notice.

About the same time that day, Jacob Harris received a simple letter in the mail. He noted with suspicion that there was no return address.

> Murder has haunted the streets long enough and justice has come to punish all those responsible. The Vampire of Boston will be in the Public Gardens tonight at 12:30. Be prepared for the extraction of Justice.

There was no signature. Jacob found the entire situation odd, but he could not pass up a possible lead now. Turning to his desk, he took out two handguns and began to load them.

Tonight, he was the hand of justice, and the victory would be his.

❧

The sun set that evening in an explosion of pinks and purples as if the light were trying to make up for the horror its passing allowed to wander the land. That night was silent and peaceful in Boston. The wind that had blown throughout the day settled to a gentle breeze, and a light snowfall blanketed the ground.

The streets were empty, for all feared the mysterious death that had taken over their once safe city. Alone, Jacob Harris stalked into the Public Gardens. All was still as if the world itself held its breath. Tonight, Jacob was hunting the devil himself, and tonight he would win.

The trees parted before him as if revealing a secret they

had harbored for too long. Before him, Jacob saw a figure standing still in the dark. The figure became a boy in his mid-twenties, wearing a long black coat and a dark, concealing hat. His hands were in his pockets. The boy saw Jacob and stiffened as if waiting for him. He walked in Jacob's direction and soon the two were divided only by a small footbridge. There, both stopped as if the bridge was a gate into another world, the world of the dead.

"You're not Drake," said the boy in worried wonder.

Jacob stared for a moment. Here he was at last, the devil who had slaughtered men, women, and children with no regard for propriety or justice. Justice would not be mocked this night. Jacob swore to see to that.

"Drake? What does Drake have to do with any of this? I am not Drake, I am justice! Why did you kill them? Did you think there wouldn't be a price?" Jacob's voice shook with self-righteous fury.

A boy! A simple boy! The world was insane when such evil grew out of children. He hated the world at that moment and realized he always had. He was too good for this world of criminals and idiots. Justice had no place in this sick, stupid, meaningless planet.

That, he realized, was why he had chosen the career he had. In some way, he hoped to bring the entire world to the judgment of justice it deserved. There was no excuse for the evils he saw every day on the street. The evils men perpetrated behind closed doors when no one was looking. Justice was looking, and Jacob was, at that moment, justice.

Men use words like freedom and liberty to justify their inequity. Jacob was not fooled. Justice knew no liberty, believed in no freedom. All were answerable before her mighty throne. No rationalizations or political backtalk could slow her true wrath.

Jacob saw it all so clearly, the inadequacies of his fellow men, men that were little more than beasts. They would all learn to fear the sting of judgment soon enough.

The boy was no longer a boy, he was a vampire. He was a killer, he was the devil himself and the embodiment of every cruelty the world had shown Jacob in not appreciating his true value. Every snide comment, every time he had been forced to flee a country for seeking justice, every man who had doubted his talents and judgment. And Drake, a devil himself. Well, Jacob had won now, this devil must die.

His reverie was broken as the boy pulled a long razor-sharp dagger from his coat pocket and flung himself at Jacob. Jacob did not hesitate; he did not regret what had to be done. Justice had no weak heart. Justice was cold, quick, and sure. He pulled his gun and fired twice. The boy fell, dead, in the center of the bridge. His blood flowed over the path to drip into the small pond beneath. The two gunshots echoed for a moment, then all was silent. Jacob laughed. He had won! Won the bet and beat the devil himself! He was a God.

Drake stepped out of the shadows and onto the bridge, and Jacob's laughter was cut short.

"Well done, my friend," said Drake. "You have won the game and the bet. Congratulations!"

Jacob was amazed.

"Y-you set this whole thing up, didn't you?" He stuttered in surprise and horror. The damn mystic was stealing his triumph!

"Don't worry about that. But let's see what has come to pass this evening, shall we?" Drake smiled a cold, sad smile. "Jacob Harris, meet Jonathan. He is twenty-five years old, born in France to a high-class Parisian lady by the name of Madame Julien. He was born approximately eight months after you were forced to flee the French military police while they were investigating the murder of an officer.

"At the time, you had been living in Madame Julien's home when her husband was away on foreign business. Rumor has it you helped ease her loneliness. Eight months after you left her, this boy, Jonathan, was born. An unwanted bastard child and a social embarrassment. A child you knew you had created." Drake gazed at the still form of Jonathan.

"You left and never contacted her again. She could not keep him and so paid the owner of a brothel to raise him. How he came to Boston is anyone's guess, but he did. His years of abuse in the brothel and being abandoned by his mother at birth warped his innocent mind. Never having, knowing, or seeing a father and being abandoned by mother and father alike wounded him worse than we can ever know. Years of loneliness, neglect, and being unwanted made him cold and hungry. Supernaturally hungry for the humanity that was never shown him. He became a killer because he was sick. He was sick because he was rejected by everyone, especially by those who had caused his inopportune entrance into this world. He is a victim of the worst injustice. Your injustice."

Drake's face was cold as stone, and his eyes were sharp as shards of ice. "Jacob Harris, meet Jonathan Harris, drawn by fate and preternatural instinct to his father. Jacob, meet your son."

There was no pity for Jacob in Drake's face; there was no forgiveness. Justice did not forgive those who acted unjustly in her name. Drake did, however, lean down and tenderly close the eyes of Jonathan. A boy who was never loved received a moment of kindness only after his death. Then, grim as death itself, Drake walked across the bridge and past Jacob. Before he disappeared into the night, he turned one last time to look at the private investigator who stood now staring and unmoving.

"Call the police, Jacob. Call them and tell them of your victory. Tell them how you killed the murderer you had created. Tell them how you killed the son whom you turned into a monster. The only vampire walking the streets these last few nights has been you, my friend." And with that, the mystic departed.

He walked down the dark path that would no longer be haunted by vampires. He left the gardens just as he heard the third and last gunshot of the night. The sound of the shot shivered in the air for a perfect moment like the final crystal note of an opera. Jacob Harris was dead by his own hand.

Nodding, Drake moved on, knowing father and son both lay now upon the cold surface of the bridge. Divided in life, united in death.

⁂

Later that night, Drake sat in his usual corner at the Hasan Society. He spoke to no one, and neither drank nor smoked. He was silent and serene, but his eyes shone with deep sadness. Finally, Matthew went over to find out what was going on. The response he received shocked him to the extreme. Drake dictated to him the entire story. How he had sensed from the start that Jacob was, all unknowing, intimately connected to the killer. How he had heard about the reclusive French immigrant Jonathan while at Harvard Square. The boy was a poet for a time and had gained a reputation amongst the students of the city. Drake knew immediately, from his description and psychological profile, that Jonathan must be the murderer.

He had then discovered his favorite coffee house, which was Drake's as well, and had arranged the meeting with Matthew to be in the right place at the right time. The entire conversation over the chess game had been the final evidence of Jonathan's guilt, and the accent hinted at the connection to Jacob he had sensed earlier. Drake had offered him salvation by offering him his card and friendship. He gave him one day to respond. Had he responded, Drake would have aided him in seeking help and escape from his demons. He did not seek help.

Meanwhile, Drake had looked into Jacob's past and discovered his actions in Paris and the son he fathered and left to fate. The fact that the son was the murderer was a tragic twist of fate, a cruel one that seemed to have taken an interest in father and son alike. The rest was allowing justice to run its course, as it always does of its own accord.

"I swore to see all those responsible for the murders brought to justice, and that I did, Matthew," Drake finished sadly. Matthew was shocked to the bone by the horror of the story and the god-like reserve of the man known as Drake.

Shortly, however, his aristocratic bearing returned, and Matthew regained his air of flippant indifference. "But, you lost the bet. You could have won and saved Jacob the shock which caused him to kill himself," he muttered.

"What came to Jacob was what Jacob himself had sown. He found the justice he so loved to speak about. As for winning, there are no real winners in this game, my friend. There are only those who lose more and those who lose less. The bet was meaningless, and it is perhaps another aspect of Justice's plan in this game that you lost the bet you had created in such cold-blooded humor. You, too, have tasted a touch of the bitter draft of judgment. This has not been an easy game for any of us."

Matthew shook his head in wonder and remorse. "So, everyone lost," Matthew MacGregor said.

Throughout the conversation, Drake's voice had been as deep and somber as his face. Slowly, however, a small melancholy smile drifted onto his countenance.

"Not entirely, my friend. Though I have lost a thousand wagers worth of winnings in sorrow, I do have something to show for all this. I knew this was a game I could not truly win, so when everyone began placing bets, I had a friend place a fair sized wager of my own money. You see, I bet on Jacob, and by losing, I won."

To Kindle a Fire

It was April 30th. The sun was sinking below the horizon like a soldier defeated, giving up its burdensome battle. The sun's surrender was apparent to those ending their day, but not seen, for a blanket of disheartening gray hung heavy upon the city of Boston. The sky was obscured as if by the veil of some forgotten corpse, long since laid to rest, which refused to die and begin proper decomposition. Boston lay in the stupor that comes just before the poor victim passes on, the prelude to death by apathy. The few products of the clouds fell without energy or purpose, as if even the rain had lost all ability to feel. The sounds of drip after drip echoed through the gray canyons of the city's streets.

Jess walked about her expensive apartment, moving for the sake of motion rather than towards some purpose. The space felt like a sealed tomb, a locked prison, and she felt like a dead phantom within it. She knew she had something to do that night, but couldn't seem to connect the present with any possible future. She was hungry, that much she knew, but she couldn't seem to muster the motivation to either make food or go out somewhere. Growling in frustration at herself and mumbling about acting like a child, she threw on her overcoat and made herself ready to walk down the street to the small café on the corner.

Just before leaving the rooms that should have been her home, her mind touched upon the subject she had been avoiding.

"What can I do?" she asked herself. The news was too sudden and yet expected. Sighing, she came to the answer. "Nothing, I can do nothing. We are doomed to live in circumstances we do not choose and cannot control. There is only chance." Diffidently, she walked out into the drooping skies and dripping rains.

The walk to the café was short and familiar to Jess; she had trodden it countless times over the past several years of working in Boston. She knew every sight along the way: the statue in honor of some random patriot across the street, whom no one remembered and whom no one cared to honor anymore; the closed stores sliding by her vision on the right; the broken cement of the sidewalk filled with spreading cracks like some strange creeping disease; the leafless trees planted in hard dust blown about by passing cars in their rush to nowhere.

Finally, the last sight: at the corner before the café sat Reggi. He slumped into a little hump, huddled against a wall, covered by a blanket, and clutching a bottle of whiskey in his thin, pale hands. Sighing, she handed him a five-dollar bill. She knew he would spend it on alcohol, but she figured he deserved whatever meager comfort he could get.

Reggi was once a musician living in a beautiful flat in a nice area of the city. He was promising. He had lived every day as if it were his one and only day, a day to be feasted upon and cherished.

He challenged the monotony of the modern world with the reckless grin of passion, until he found out he was sick. The realization of his approaching death, that would be heralded by tremendous suffering and unknown depths of humiliation, ruined him. The knowledge that he would be broken and degraded broke and degraded him well before the disease had the chance to.

He had lost his flat, his inspiration, his purpose, his meaning, and replaced it with a bottle, a street corner, and an empty wait for pain and death.

Reggi was the incarnation of inevitability to Jess, and she pitied him.

"Let him drink," she thought, "it is the least we can do for him. It is all we can do for him." She entered the familiar café.

Conversation, true conversation, is a joining of minds; a

pure connection of souls struggling to know one another, to see what the other sees. This raises people above themselves and creates all art. In contrast, thought Jess, what passes for communication is a rather pale shadow. We make empty sounds to fill empty moments. And Jess entered the café to the usual mumble of "conversation."

"But you have to vote," claimed the waiter to one of the regulars. "If you don't vote, you have no right to complain when the country goes to hell."

"But what will voting do, John? Eh?" asked a wrinkled businessman sitting in a booth next to the door. "Have you seen the candidates they offer us? There isn't even a lesser of two evils. Voting won't do any good and you know it."

"Sure, I know it, Shawn. Who knows it better, what with my business being driven under the way it is by the economy. But one has to vote, if only to make a token attempt at caring. I mean, what can anyone do besides that?"

"Exactly. Vote or not, it makes no difference, guys. The government will be run the same way anyway. It's not politicians who make decisions but the corporations and rich bastards who fund their parties, and that doesn't change. We get different faces for the same old lies. I won't vote. I prefer not to waste my time pretending to matter. There ain't nothing I can do about it, so I'll stay home in bed."

Jess sighed as she walked in and took a seat in the corner. John noticed her at once and hustled over to her table. "Ah, Jess, how are you? Well, you don't have to answer that. How would anyone in your position be? I'm so sorry about the news. Yes, we have all heard, just this afternoon."

"I heard this morning," replied Jess.

"I'm so sorry, my dear. But what can one do? Move on as always, I would say. What can I get you today? It's on the house." Jess nodded and ordered numbly.

The food slid down her throat without being tasted. The coffee she sipped was just warm water to her clouded mind.

Time ticked away, and the people around her talked, debated, and fought, but it was all a blur of sound to her. She wasn't sure at what point during her listless meal the voices of others started to make sense again. First, it was just a word here or there, then phrases about an art exhibit: opening night, big party, very exclusive. Then it hit her, she was supposed to be there. That was what she knew she had to do, but couldn't muster the energy to remember. Leaping to her feet, she ran from the café, slicing through the haze of empty talk and cigarette smoke. Past Reggi and past the bones of dead trees, she flew with a purpose she had forgotten. Finally, she sprinted into her apartment to throw on the appropriate clothing and hail a foul-smelling taxi to take her downtown to the opening of the exhibit she had promised to attend.

❧

The gloom of the outside world was banished the moment Jess entered the glimmer of Boston's social world, though nothing could dispel the internal gloom that wreathed Jess' spirit like a shroud. Light glimmered off elegant gowns in bright spring colors and danced along the crystal glasses that held expensive champagne like mini stars amongst the flowing galaxies of socializing men and women. Along the walls of the gallery hung the newest works of Boston's brilliant young artists. The entire scene reeked of pseudo-civilization. Sighing, Jess leaped into the waves of socialites and put on her fake smile and plastic voice. She nodded and made small replies to the multiple condolences she received, telling everyone not to worry and that all was well.

No matter the interlocuter, the response was always the same: "What can one do about bad fortune but live with it?"

The hours rolled by at an agonizing pace, yet whenever Jess glanced at her watch, only minutes had passed. Finally, in the corner near a large rendering of Dante's Inferno in sickeningly gray colors and an indistinct modern style, Jess found some solitude. The painting made her sick for some reason. It seemed even the fires of hell had gone out, as if even the Devil had given up with a shrug. It was devoid of passion, replacing fear and pain with monotony and meaninglessness as hell's torments. Yet, as awful as the piece seemed, Jess could not look away. She stood there, trying to appear contemplative so as to avoid anyone talking to her anymore.

"The past is of no importance. The present is of no importance. It is with the future that we have to deal. For the past is what man should not have been. The present is what man ought not to be. The future is what artists are."

Jess turned at the sound of the voice quoting Oscar Wilde solemnly, like a prayer. The sight that met her eyes was a surprising one. The man was tall, his bearing such that it seemed to make him twice as tall as he was. He wore a black three-piece suit with a bright maroon tie and a handkerchief of the same color peeking out of his pocket. He held a fine silver and black cane in his hand. His face was serious, and his eyes were too deep and too intense, as if the entire universe could be hidden there. She knew this man, if by reputation alone. It was Drake, mystic and philosopher, a supposed magus of great power and a man of mystery and influence.

Everyone seemed to fear and respect him, though no one knew why. Jess's first reaction was sharp hostility, as if the man had attacked her by intruding upon her personal space and time.

"If artists are the future," Drake said again, "what are they telling us, eh? Look at that lovely rendering of our dear earth." Drake motioned towards the piece Jess had just been contemplating. The man chuckled, and the sound seemed to have an evil, villainous quality to her ears. She was about to disagree about what the picture portrayed when she chanced to glance down at the plate that held its title. The scene she had taken for a lifeless depiction of Dante's Inferno was titled

Earth 2001 A.D.

"So, Jessica, what do you think of the piece?" Jess shivered. Maybe the stories about Drake being some strange servant of a devil, stories she had never believed, were true.

"How do you know my name?" she demanded.

Drake chuckled once more.

"Come now, my dear, I know many things. You are rather of interest in today's social circles, what with your most recent tragedy and all."

She frowned, and her eyes lost their flare as she prepared to endure another spree of well-wishing and pity.

"No, my dear, don't worry," Drake said softly, almost secretly. "I'm not here to offer condolences. I make it a point to never apologize for the actions of the universe. I let others deal with their own supposed tragedies while I deal with mine. Pity masquerading as sympathy, or worse, a simple show of false pity, does nothing but degrade the recipient. You're as strong as the rest of us and will deal with nature the same as the rest of us. We share the same lot, and so you're no more deserving of sympathy or pity than anyone else." Drake smiled and studied her face.

"Then why are you here?" Jess demanded, still angered by this unseemly intrusion by this would-be sorcerer into her personal time and space.

"Why am I here? Why, to enjoy the art." Drake waved his arm as if to motion to the works on the walls, but the sweep of his gesture seemed more to take in the fluttering crowds of socialites and scurrying forms of servants. "I fear the art is getting cold these days, however. There seems to be a lack of passion and inspiration in it." Smiling, he wandered on towards the next display.

Jess could not say why, but she was drawn to this man despite her initial resistance. She followed him. They wandered together from piece to piece, speaking only of the art before them. It seemed almost as if the strange nature and content of their meeting and the implications found there did not exist.

She found Drake stimulating, as she had found no one else for a long time. Soon, she discovered she was enjoying herself, lost in the flow of genius's creations and the challenge to interpret them.

Finally, they found themselves before a work that seemed different from the others in its use of color and contrast. The piece consisted of small portraits set up in rows. Each row contained fewer faces as one moved up, until arriving at the top row, which contained only one small depiction in sharp contrast to the others. The bottom row showed five portraits done in bright flashing colors that seemed to exude life and energy. The figures were those of Buddha, Jesus Christ, Lao Tzu, Confucius, and Mohammed. The next row contained four figures done in the same flashing, brilliant style. Here were Shakespeare, Galileo, Plato and Hypatia. The next row was similar but with the faces of Kant, Mary Shelley, and Ralph Waldo Emerson. Each row was painted more brightly and energetically than the one before. The second row to the top held only two faces, those of Albert Einstein and Emma Goldman.

Jess's eyes reached the top of the pyramid, which she expected to be the grandest, the crown, of all the others. What she found shocked her.

It showed a contemporary man in a business suit crossing a street in the rain. The entire thing was painted in tones of gray and brown as if the color had died before reaching the top. The man's shoulders hunched in some terrible defeat, and his face was twisted by bitterness and self-hatred. He was on a cell phone, arguing. Behind him, the landscape was that of a city, but it was cloudy and indistinct. Shivering as the cold of the top picture radiated into her bones, Jess looked away to find Drake's too-sharp eyes boring into her.

"What do you think of it, Jess? I ask because a dear friend of mine is its creator. If, as Wilde so passionately believed, artists are the future, what is this one telling us about it?" Drake's voice was cold and solemn as if he were speaking at a funeral.

"I think it's obvious," Jess replied, her voice soft and hopeless. "It portrays a collection of the greatness of the past, and then reveals the emptiness of the present. It observes that what made these people great is lacking in the common modern-day person. The striking color contrast is designed to show the difference between genius and mediocrity, to show that the fire found in the greats is not found in the common."

"Do you think so, my dear? As we both know, the interpretation of art lies in the observer and not the artist, but I happen to know this is not what my friend had in mind when he painted this. Why, look at the title, my dear." Jess looked below the work and found that its title was *Ode to the Common Folk.*

"It must be for the sake of irony. Obviously, the entire thing is not a tribute to the one commonplace man at the top."

Drake laughed. "Of course not. It's a tribute to all the commonplace people in the work. That, my dear, is the point. Each person portrayed in the work was just a person like any other. There are no 'geniuses' in this work, only men and women. Men like Einstein, who failed math as a young boy, or Jesus, who was the son of a humble carpenter and a member of an oppressed nation, or Confucius, who never held a decent job in all his life, or Buddha, who was a sheltered, spoiled prince, or Hypatia, whose murder was celebrated among Christians. They had no inherent spark that others lack, nor flame unique to only a few."

Drake continued. "The color that makes the majority of them so interesting and striking is created through their own work and acceptance of themselves. The color lacking in the top scene is waiting to be painted with pigment drawn from the veins of the living. But, for whatever reason, he refuses to let it out. He is afraid to, perhaps. Or has been trained not to, or has accepted chains that hold it in. But all these figures are the same common, simple, honest, mortal people. There are no gods in this picture and no giants on earth. Just many people who tried and one man who hasn't. The title is literal and not sarcastic."

Drake stared intensely into her eyes for a moment and then smiled, his eyes glancing away and granting her rest from the terrible scrutiny. At first, she had no response to give. She glanced back at the *Ode to the Common Man*. Her eyes scanned the flash of the rainbows of color and fire, then settled on the emptiness at the top. Then, slowly, a glimmer of something of her old fire returned like a desperate ember too long hidden amongst the ashes.

"You yourself assert that art is not limited to the intention of the artist," Jess observed. "And if the value of art is that it shows us what we could be, then it offers a mirror not a di-dactic lecture. I suspect neither you nor your friend exhaust the meanings of this piece."

Although she couldn't say why, Drake's eyes glimmered in pleasure at her response.

❧

At just that moment, a woman rushed into the event. Her eyes were wild, and she seemed to be both weeping and an-gry.

Jess looked at her in surprise as she rushed to the back of the gallery to a single-occupancy bathroom and shut the door behind her.

"My word," Drake said softly.

"I know her," Jess told him, frowning and speaking in a thoughtful tone. "That's Bernadette Cushman. She is a major financial advisor for the city."

"She seems rather distressed; perhaps you should check on her."

Jess squinted at him, a part of her stirring in objection to being ordered about, but eventually nodded and walked to the closed bathroom door. She could hear crying interspersed with soft yelling in anger. Jess knocked, and there was no answer, so she knocked harder.

"Bernadette. It's me, Jess. Are you alright? Let me in."

"I'm fine," Bernadette's muffled voice responded. "I'll be out in a moment. Please, just leave me alone."

Jess hesitated, feeling like she should do something more, but then her general malaise descended once more, and she decided she could let people deal with their own tragedies. She had enough tragedy to deal with as it was. She walked back to Drake.

"Is she quite well?" He asked softly, not wanting to be overheard by several of the guests who were glancing quizzically at the locked bathroom door.

"I don't know. She said she was fine and would be out in a moment, but she was clearly crying and angry." Jess shrugged, "But she can take care of herself."

Drake raised one eyebrow, "If you say so, my dear."

They continued wandering about the gallery, and Drake even induced Jess to enjoy a glass of champagne.

"Did you know," Drake said as he held his glass of champagne up to the light to admire, "that Oscar Wilde supposedly requested a glass of champagne on his deathbed? His dying words are said to have been 'I have lived beyond my means, I might as well die beyond them.'" Drake raised the glass to his lips and sipped slowly, enjoying himself.

"Hardly practical. He no doubt left his family in debt," Jess responded shortly.

"Without a doubt," Drake agreed, "but humanity owes him a great debt as well."

"Not much comfort to his family."

"Perhaps. But ultimately, my dear, we must first be responsible to ourselves before we can be responsible for others," Drake said.

They continued their cycle through the show and came upon a canvas full of colors and motion, tiny brushstrokes suggesting the form of feathers or flowers or flame. Perhaps it was all three, or none of these. She was entranced. Light and life had been captured in canvas and paint.

"Abstract impressionist," Drake said softly.

"Don't you mean abstract expressionist?" Jess provoked him.

"No, a lesser-known movement, perhaps, but a far more vibrant one. Tiny, careful details building to prismatic suggestions of meaning and form."

"It's beautiful," Jess said, losing herself in that beauty.

"It's life," Drake responded. "Blossoming chaos, driving creation, ever transitioning form, and from it all meaning arises."

"Or doesn't," Jess murmured. "Fire kills as much as it shines."

She looked away from the painting and realized the gallery was almost empty. The show was over.

Drake touched her arm gently, "Your friend never came out of the bathroom."

Looking at the back of the gallery, Jess saw it was true. Two gallery employees were knocking on the door but receiving no response. Frowning, Jess drifted to the bathroom door and the employees. Drake followed.

"Excuse me," Jess said, "but what is going on?"

At first, the docent looked as if he would tell them to leave, but then he saw something in Jess' face that changed his mind. "The door is locked from the inside. Someone must be in there, but they aren't responding," he said in a voice expressing impatience and annoyance.

"My friend went in there," Jess responded, "she was upset. Let me see what I can do." The two men stepped aside, and Jess knocked softly on the door a few times. "Bernadette, it's Jess. Are you ok? The gallery is closing, please come out. We can talk, I'll take you home." There was no response, just an aching silence.

"Should we call the police? Break it down?" The docent asked.

"Please, allow me," Drake said, and moved to the door.

He rested one hand against the doorknob and the other next to it along the wood of the door. He stood there, stock still, exerting a slight pressure on the handle, pushing against the interior workings of the locking mechanism, and then offered a swift jiggle to the handle as he exhaled suddenly. With a slight pop, the door swung open.

"I have some unsavory talents, I must confess," Drake said, sounding slightly embarrassed on the surface, though the tone didn't really ring true. He stepped aside and gestured for Jess to go in.

It was a small bathroom, but well-appointed. Designed only for one person at a time, it consisted of two rooms with no windows. One contained a toilet, the other a small marble sink, a mirror, and a nice leather chair in the corner. There were no windows or other doors, and, unless faced with someone with Drakes' skills, the main door locked and unlocked only from the inside.

There was one other presence in the bathroom, in the larger room with the sink, mirror, and chair. It was the body of Bernadette Cushman, wearing her austere business suit with her briefcase flopped on the floor beside it, lying on her back, staring open-eyed at the ceiling.

The first thing that struck Jess was that Bernadette's face didn't look right. It was slack and grey, more than just pale, almost as if there was a touch of green. There was blood around her nose and right ear as if it had recently trickled out.

Jess knew the woman was dead. She just stared, in silence, frozen in place. In that small room, that little bathroom, she faced the death of her friend. But something more, something else, stared her down. She faced Death itself — a sordid, sudden, inexplicable death. Jess felt it, like a swift stab in her guts, the utter and complete pointlessness of the entire human drama. It always ended, one way or another, like this, in a stupid little dirty room with each person utterly alone.

Drake and the two docents looked over Jess's shoulder into the room. "My god," the one docent said, "is she alright?" Drake stepped into the bathroom and slipped past Jess to kneel beside Bernadette. He held his hand before her nose for a moment and then pressed his fingers to her throat.

"Now you'd better call the police," Drake said softly. The two docents stepped shakily away from the door and went to find a phone, in too much shock to realize they probably shouldn't leave the body with two strangers. Drake stood and looked to Jess with a slight question in his gaze. She hadn't moved.

"Well, my dear?" he asked, softly.

Her distant gaze snapped back to the room, and she shook her head. "I'm sorry, what?" she asked in a dead voice.

"What do we do, my dear?" Drake pressed.

"Do? Nothing. What can we do?"

"Ah, yes, what can anyone do, eh?" Drake muttered.

"Let's get out of here and wait for the police," Jess said with a slight tone of disgust in her voice.

"Well, yes, I suppose we could do that," Drake agreed, "but I'm not really one to let others uncover truth for me. I'd rather see what I can figure out myself, first."

"Best of luck," Jess said and turned to leave. "I'm going home."

"Of course. But first, my dear, I wonder if you could offer me the benefit of a little of your knowledge. You did, after all, know the poor woman here."

"Yes," Jess said, "and I failed her."

"You feel that something could have been done, and we missed the chance?"

Jess glared at him, her eyes flashing dangerously, "Yes!"

"Well, surely we can't be certain until we know better what happened," Drake said, spreading his hands before him. "So, would you take the chance to help me find her murderer?"

"Murderer?" That snapped Jess out of the turmoil of her dark reflections and self-punishment.

"I can't rightly know, of course," Drake responded, "but there is a feel of violence, of darkness, to this. Why do you think she is dead? Physiologically, what killed her?"

"Are you asking me to medically examine her body without the presence of the police?" Jess pressed.

"It would appear so," Drake said, nonplussed. "Now, let's see. As we've established, I know something about you and your current situation — as most of Boston's socialites do, though, I shudder to group myself in their class. That includes knowing something of your past and your experience. You have a medical degree and worked for a time as a doctor. Then, for reasons unknown, you gave up medicine and went into business selling medical equipment — or rather, ultimately running businesses that do. One of the most successful female C.E.O.s in America, revolutionizing the field of illness profiteering."

"Profiteering?" Jess growled indignantly.

Drake held up his hands apologetically, "I'm sorry, of course, I am sure you only charge for your equipment prices that allow desperate, sick people to afford their benefits. It was wrong of me to presume otherwise." He smiled slightly at her and raised one eyebrow.

She clenched her jaw, but before she could speak, Drake continued, "But, please, take your medical expertise in hand and help your friend here. What caused her death?"

Jess frowned down at the body, successfully diverted from an angry retort. "Blood from the nose and ear, eyes unevenly dilated, but no visible bruises or damage about the face." She frowned for a moment, "I would look at her skull for a crack or bruise, she likely died of a severe cerebral edema — swelling of the brain because of head trauma."

Drake nodded, "I see. Now, let us presume accidental death. Look around, are there any signs on walls, or corners, and so on of having been struck by her head — for example, as if she fell? It doesn't seem so."

Drake swiftly knelt back down next to the body and pulled Jess down next to him. He delicately ran his hand through Bernadette's hair and along her scalp. He focused first on the back of her head that rested against the floor. "No fracture or bruising on the back of the head, which she might have hit against the floor when she fell. The fall doesn't seem to have been that bad, and didn't seriously injure her."

"I don't think we should be touching the body," Jess said, her voice concerned.

"Indeed, we shouldn't be," Drake agreed, "but alas, it is too late. Aha!" His hand had stopped around her left temple. "No blood or visible contusion, but there is bruising here and, if I am not mistaken, fracturing. We are definitely looking at an epidural hematoma."

He looked at her questioningly for confirmation and, after an extended moment of deliberation, she ran her hand along Bernadette's left temple. After all, Drake had already disturbed the body. With a nod, she agreed with his assessment; it was clear she had suffered a severe injury to her left temple.

Drake stood and offered his hand to Jess to help her up. She refused it and stood on her own without noticing the approving nod Drake gave her in response. "Now, how did she injure her left temple that badly? Enough to kill her? She would have had to hit it rather hard and possibly with something compact like a corner." Drake glanced into the room with the toilet, "Nothing in here she could have hit her head on," he glanced about the room with the body, "nothing in here either. The sink is rounded, and she wouldn't have landed the way she did if she had hit her head on it. She couldn't have struck the side of her head on the floor like that. Her shoulder and arm would have protected her. The chair is soft, fully padded with leather and cushioning."

"Still, something could have happened," Jess offered.

"Yes, something could always have happened. But this was a dramatic injury capable of causing her death. It is commonly a sports injury, or derived from a car accident, or from a violent confrontation and fight."

The two docents returned, "The cops are on their way," they said, beginning to look at Jess and Drake skeptically as if about to object to their presence.

"Very good," Drake said, reassuringly, "you have done an excellent job." He walked to them and put his arms around each of their shoulders, walking them into the middle of the gallery. "The police shall be most thankful for your assistance. Please wait for them out front to show them where they are going." Somehow, amidst their haze of surprise and confusion, the reassuring and authoritative presence of Drake convinced them to put all doubts out of their mind and leave him and Jess with the body.

Drake returned to Jess. "So, she wasn't engaged in sport or driving in here. She had neither the space nor the proper environment to fall hard enough against a sharp surface to cause her injury. So, the injury must have come from someone assaulting her. And," Drake knelt down once more and held up Bernadette's right hand to reveal several broken fingernails and, under one of them, bits of black hair, blood, and skin, "she seems to have gotten a good scratch out of her assailant. Notice the hair is black while hers is a natural raspberry blond. Those hairs are short. Very likely the hair of a man with black hair."

"Good," Jess said, "then the police will have DNA evidence."

"Just so," Drake agreed, "which will be worthless without the right suspect. And, unfortunately, I find it unlikely there will even be a search for one."

"What? Why ever not?"

"Think about it. Look at the setting. She dies in a sealed room. Locked from the inside. None of us saw anyone go in, and even if someone did go in, how did they get the door locked behind them from the inside as they left? No windows, no other doors, no way in or out. This is a murder, my dear, but an impossible one."

"The killer would have had to be able to walk through walls or doors," Jess said softly.

"And, it would seem, to be able to do so undetected. It is too much to ask that the police even entertain the idea. They will see an injury that can occur accidentally weighed against a murder that would require supernatural capabilities and side with an accident, despite any evidence to the contrary. People, after all, naturally dismiss the anomalous to the point of not even seeing it without rather extensive training to the contrary. So, we must do something that no one else can or will. We must solve your friend's murder and then explain and prove it to the authorities. That is, of course, if you care to."

Jess stared into the fixed eyes of Bernadette for a long moment and then gently pulled her eyelids closed. "Very well, what do we do?"

"Means and motive, my dear, we address means and motive." Drake glanced around. "Of course, I don't mean to consider the means of murder but rather the means of access to the victim. But we can put that aside for right now, since we are pressed for time. I would like to get us out of here before the police show up so we can complete our investigation before getting wrapped up in theirs."

"Isn't that illegal?" Jess asked uncertainly.

"What? Leave the scene of an accident we did not cause?

Surely not." Drake smiled in a mischievous manner. "So, on to motive. When she arrived here, she was clearly distraught. It might help if we knew where she had come from."

"Work, I would imagine," Jess said.

Drake nodded and flipped open the briefcase. "Financial papers dealing with the Big Dig construction here in Boston," Drake said.

"Yes, she works for the mayor's office. She is one of the Assistant Comptrollers, in charge of keeping track of the city's budget. She is assigned to keep track of the budget of the Big Dig."

"A rather nightmarish job," Drake said softly.

"Very. The Dig is the largest construction job in the history of the state, and it is far behind deadline and even further over budget. She has been working on an audit of the funds for the project."

"Yes," Drake said, "these papers all involve tracking construction expenses for the project. She has highlighted several sections involving funding for a given portion of the project." Drake put the papers back and closed the case, then glanced at Bernadette's shoes, "Look there."

Jess looked at the shoes and saw that there was yellow dirt and sand caked on them along with bits of gravel.

"Hardly the leavings of standard city streets," Drake murmured. "Alright, let's go." Drake led her out of the bathroom after taking one last moment to look carefully over the door's lock. "Quick," he said at last, "out the back." The lights of several police cars had just appeared near the front of the building. Drake led Jess out through the kitchens and out the back door of the gallery. He led her down an alley and around the block to where his driver, Alexander, stood smoking a cigarette and leaning against the hood of a long black Lincoln Towncar.

Drake opened the door for Jess to climb in and then followed her into the well-appointed, spacious terrain of the car. "Please take us downtown, Alexander, towards the waterfront."

Alexander looked meaningfully at the police lights flashing near the front of the alley, "Trouble, sir?"

"Perhaps. A mysterious death we hope to clarify."

In the rearview mirror, Alexander's raised eyebrow was clear. "How do you get yourself in these situations?" he asked softly, but was only answered by a frown from Drake.

※

They drove for a time in silence, and then Drake said, "And so we find ourselves on a rather unexpected adventure."

Jess considered saying no in that moment and telling Drake to drop her off at home. Part of her wanted to thrust this weird man from her life and return to the solitude and numbness of her apartment. But then, the image of her apartment joined in her mind with that stark little bathroom, each a prison in which to die alone, and she felt a deep sense of horror that made her feel she would rather be anywhere but home.

Another part of her, a deeper part that seemed to remember what it was like to breathe and hope and create, wondered if adventures were still possible and if she could help find justice for her friend.

"Sure. Why not? But where are we going?" she asked.

Drake smiled. "Out into the city night, my dear. The evening is young yet, and it's such a lovely evening, isn't it?"

Jess looked up and noticed that the sky had cleared quite a bit since she had entered the building. There were large tears in the clouds through which stars seemed to spy from infinite distances away. The gloom seemed to have been shredded, ripped away by some powerful wind or oncoming light.

"Yes," Drake said at last, "a lovely evening to hunt a killer and bring one to justice." Drake seemed exceptionally cheerful, a fact that Jess found more than a little disconcerting.

The luxurious car seemed to float through the misty streets of downtown Boston. Churches, which in the night air appeared to be ancient ruins, rolled by in a dream-like haze; impossible towers of glass shot out of the mist to the sky, only to fade once more. The world was a surreal blur as the city slid past Jess, stirring unknown feelings within her.

Was that a grand palace born out of a fantasy? No, only the same church she had passed almost every day for years. Was that a monument to some eternal divinity? No, only the bank to which she often went to deposit checks. The endless gray moments of her life seemed to take on brilliant new colors, only to lose them once more in the miasma of her mind.

Drake's voice called her from her reverie. "Well, let us address this riddle then, and a rather fascinating problem it is too. A murdered body in a sealed room."

"I've never heard of such a thing. It is surely impossible," Jess stated.

"You would be surprised. I know of several cases like this one, and even once heard a learned doctor give a lecture on the various possible solutions to locked-room mysteries. The key is usually to lay out clearly the various possible solutions and eliminate them one by one."

"But there is no possible solution, that is the whole point. It is an impossible problem," Jess insisted.

"No," Drake corrected, "it is a problem with the appearance of impossibility. That is a key aspect of all locked-room cases. They all appear impossible." Drake stared at Jess for a pregnant moment and then glanced out the window, "I suppose life is something of a locked-room crime."

Jess refused to rise to the bait, and so Drake continued. "So we face deception, whether through the ingenuity of the killer or through coincidence, which leads either to the conclusion that the killer was superhuman or that the case is suicide. In fact, locked-room murders are one of the most famous variations on the attempt to achieve the perfect crime.

The situation involves a series of assumptions, and the trick is to figure out which assumption and appearance is the heart of the deception. So, my dear, what assumptions are we making that might be wrong?"

Jess frowned out the window for a moment. "Well, we assumed there wasn't any other way in or out."

"Just so," Drake agreed, "so the first thing to do is to assure oneself that there isn't any hidden passageway. In this case, I am confident there is not. The bathroom was a rather simple space, and there was clearly no hidden mode of entrance or exit. What else?"

"I'm not sure," Jess gave up.

"I'll offer two, and then it is your turn again," Drake responded. His treating this as a game, and his almost childlike enjoyment of the challenge, struck Jess as ghoulish, but she had to admit she was growing just as fascinated as he was. "We assume that the victim died in the bathroom, while she might have died somewhere else, and that she was actually dead when we found her."

"What do you mean? She was certainly dead."

"In this case, yes, she was. But I knew another case in which someone ended up being killed twice, since he was mistakenly assumed to be dead earlier when in fact he wasn't."

"And we saw her enter the bathroom and no one saw her leave it again," Jess stated. "Plus, even if she had left and been killed somewhere else, there still would be the mystery of how her body was locked into the room from the inside after the crime occurred somewhere else."

Drake smiled and nodded, "Yes, very good. So, what else are we assuming?"

Jess was beginning to see the trick of this mode of thought, and something came to her almost immediately, "We are assuming that the killer actually left the room, I suppose he might somehow still have been present."

"Exactly, the killer could have been hiding and then could have either slipped out somehow as we entered or could have waited for us to leave. Here, however, there was nowhere to hide. There was no space behind or under the chair, I checked behind the door, and the ceiling is solid as is the floor. What else?"

"Well, I suppose a clever killer might come up with a way to kill from a distance. Say with poison or something."

"Yes, there are cases of released spiders, poisonous snakes, dart guns, timed devices, people killed while leaning out of windows, even something like a robot, and so on. This is a possibility if we can figure out a way to hit someone in the head — hard — from outside of the room and leave nothing inconspicuous. Anything else?"

"I don't think so. Basically, we can be deceived that a crime occurred, that the killer had left, that there was no exit, that the crime happened in the room, and that nothing could have done this from a distance." Jess summed up the case.

"One final thing. We assumed that the door was locked," Drake added.

"But —" Jess frowned deeply. The docents had been the ones to try the door. If they had been the killers, it would have been possible for them to enter and kill Bernadette and then pretend the door was locked. "Wait, you tried the door yourself and then opened it somehow. How did you do that?"

Drake nodded, "Yes, I can confirm that the door was indeed locked from the inside and that no one could have left and locked it from the outside, even if I could open it from the outside. As for how I did it, well, one must have some secrets. But you seemed willing to doubt the report of the docents just now. Why don't you doubt mine?"

Jess stared at Drake's oddly ageless face and felt a chill shoot through her. "You couldn't have killed her. You were with me," Jess said.

"Indeed," Drake agreed, "but couldn't I have been working with the killer or killers?"

"It's possible, but then we are talking about some extraordinary conspiracy, and you would have had to know that Bernadette would hide in the bathroom, and that the killer would try to make it appear locked, and so on. It would just be too great a coincidence," Jess insisted.

"We are in the realm of deception and extraordinary crime; coincidence is most often just another deception. You'll have to do better than that."

"I trust you," Jess said at last.

Drake nodded. "Thank you. It is most foolish, but we shall put that aside for now. I assure you, I was not involved, but you'll have to decide for yourself whether that assurance is to be trusted. So, our best option seems to be that she was killed in the room, but by someone outside of the room through unknown means. Let us think upon that as we travel to where, I hope, we shall be able to uncover something concerning the motive."

Drake smiled slightly, leaned back against the plush leather of the seat, and closed his eyes. Jess took his lead and joined him in resting her eyes and mind.

She was not sure how long she leaned back upon the soft leather of the car's seat with her eyes shut. Her mind wandered in a way that was neither restful nor productive. Honestly, she didn't think much about the case at all. She thought about her life, and it seemed, in those moments, that the sad image of Bernadette locked alone and dead in that gloomy bathroom became the perfect symbol of Jess' own situation. How afraid she must have been, isolated with whatever terrible, shadowy force bludgeoned away her successful life. If only Jess, or Drake, or anyone, had forced their way in — it might have diverted the mysterious events that led to her demise. Now, on top of all else, Jess felt a failure once again, but rather than just failing herself, she had failed her friend.

A sudden change in the sounds around her made her open her eyes. The car was driving on gravel. She started forward as she saw that they were driving through a pit, surrounded by partially completed construction. Tools lay about haphazardly as if it were a junkyard and not a construction site. Half-formed supports and rusty metal girders rose from the dust and grime like the ruined remains of Atlantis. It was dark and empty; there was nothing but blighted attempts at creation for miles. She shivered and then noticed Drake watching her. She opened her mouth to ask a question, but he spoke first, his mouth forming a knowing smile.

"The Big Dig, which has wallowed in failure and incompetence for years now. Sprawled out like a rotting corpse, the ground torn and rent all about it." His voice was cold and critical.

Jess suddenly felt hurt and ashamed, as if the judgment in his voice was directed at her and not the surrounding ruin.

"You feel guilt right now," Drake said, as if reading her mind, "not despair, and that makes all the difference; guilt over your dead friend, guilt about your own situation. That wasn't how you felt earlier this evening, but surely enough, it is how you feel now."

"Thanks for telling me how I feel. So, what does that get me? Nothing has changed."

"Absolutely right, my dear. Guilt changes nothing, much like despair. But unlike despair, it can motivate. In this case, it motivates us to find your friend's killer, to bring justice to her unnecessary end." The car ground to a halt over the gravel and dust. "Ah, here we are." They parked in front of a trailer in which a light still burned.

As they stepped out of the car into the night, Jess noticed the ground was covered in the same yellow sand they had found in Bernadette's shoes. She saw that Drake noticed, too.

They walked up to the door of the trailer, and Drake knocked in a solemn manner.

"Go away, it's after hours and I am very busy," a gruff male voice yelled from inside.

"This is a rather serious matter, sir. I must insist that you let us in," Drake's voice rang with a note of impatience and authority that would have immediately identified him as some police official to any casual listener, though Jess knew he was no such thing. The voice worked, however, and the door soon opened.

"Yes? What do you want?" Asked a large man with dark hair and the blurry eyes of someone fairly deep in drink.

"Are you Robert McDonald? The chief foreman of this portion of construction?" Drake asked in a staccato tone.

"Uh, yes. Why?" At that moment, Jess noticed a long fresh scratch running down the side of his face.

"We need to speak with you, sir," Drake said in a dismissive fashion and brushed him aside to enter the trailer. Jess followed.

"What is this about?" the man demanded.

Drake seemed to gain in height in order to tower over him. In his long black coat with his silver-tipped cane and piercing eyes, he cut an imposing figure. "Sit down, Mr. McDonald." As if the crack in his voice pushed the man down, Robert McDonald almost collapsed into a tattered couch that dominated one wall of the trailer. "To begin with, this is about your finances," Drake said in an almost off-handed manner.

"What about my finances?"

"That's an awfully nice car you have out there," Drake said casually.

"So? I am a major foreman of a huge government project. I make good money."

"And your home?" Drake pressed. Jess could see he was bluffing, but it was a good bluff.

"A relative left me money, what about it?"

Drake turned and paced the small space in a stern manner, pausing to glance at the battered wooden desk while running his finger along it as if checking for dust. "Is that so? Well, we will be needing the details on which relative, how much, and when. I am sure the tax information will all check out. But that doesn't account for the missing materials here, and the work orders for work undone, and the missing funds to account for all this missing work."

The man sputtered for a moment, his face going through alterations of pale and red. Finally, he settled on a course of action. "Who are you? Show me some identification. Am I under arrest or something?"

"Arrest? Not yet. Perhaps after we discuss the murder," Drake responded.

"M–murder? What murder? I haven't killed anyone!" The man seemed sincerely confused, but Drake did not seem surprised.

Drake nodded. "I see. How about you tell us what happened earlier tonight — between you and Miss Bernadette Cushman."

"So that is what this is about. Did that—" he caught himself and modulated his tone, "She went to the police, huh? Well, it wasn't anything. Just an accident."

Drake stared at him for a long moment and then pulled a chair over in order to sit facing him, "Bernadette Cushman is dead, Mr. McDonald, so you had better tell us everything."

"D-dead? What? How?"

"Just tell us what happened," Drake pressed.

The man sat, stared into space, and breathed heavily for a while. A trickle of sweat rolled down the side of his face. Then he took a deep breath with a look of surrender. "Ok, look, it was nothing. She came here, making all kinds of accusations about money and embezzling from the Dig. She was crazy. I told her so, and she got angry, then I got angry. She came at me, and I fought her off. She tripped and fell—" he stopped speaking.

Drake continued for him. "And hit her head on the side of your desk there, right on her temple."

"She was fine. She got up, told me she would see me rot in jail, and stormed out. I didn't kill her, I swear."

"But you did throw her into your desk, whether or not you intended to," Drake pressed.

"I didn't kill her."

"You didn't try to kill her; they are not exactly the same thing," Drake corrected.

The big man burst into tears, blubbering and repeating the phrase "oh god" over and over again.

"It's over. Your finances will be exposed, and her death will be traced to the injury she sustained from your desk. You pray to God. Well, good, do something to gain God's assistance. Tell the truth, for once in your life. She didn't attack you. She never would do such a thing," Drake stated.

"No, she wouldn't," Jess added firmly.

"Don't tarnish her name here at the end, not when you have this last shred of hope for any redemption," Drake pressed.

The man sobbed on for a moment and then took one last calming breath before taking the plunge. "No, she didn't attack me. She told me what she had found. She demanded an explanation, and I didn't have any. I was scared and angry. I shouted at her and grabbed her. She scratched my face, and I threw her against the desk. I was so shocked at what I did that I didn't even stop her as she stormed out."

Drake nodded, walked to his desk, and picked up the phone he found there. He dialed the police, explained who he was and where he was, and then handed the phone to Robert McDonald, being certain he repeated the same story over the phone to the police.

Then they were leaving, with Jess shocked into silence.

They entered the car, and Drake gave directions she neither listened to nor understood.

"So, that's it?" She asked at last, partly in wonder but more in confusion.

"That is it," Drake confirmed.

"No murder, just a stupid, violent accident?"

"Yes, just stupid, thoughtless violence. She hit her head here, and the trauma caused swelling that killed her sometime later in the bathroom."

"But, it's all so ugly," Jess said.

"Sadly, my dear, that is pretty much the world. No heroes, no great villains, and the solution to most mysteries is mundane."

෴

The car jumped forward into the night and sprinted back into the streets of Boston. Jess was left alone once more in the darkness of her own confusion. Drake, though still there, seemed to have withdrawn his presence from the car. He sat there like a prehistoric marble figure hidden at the bottom of the sea.

The skyscrapers they passed now seemed more like bare bones than crystal towers. They were the carcasses of destroyed men, built upon the broken bones of the roadkill of time.

The car pulled up before the square in front of the Prudential Building, one of the tallest buildings in Boston, and parked. All was silent for a moment as the massive skyscraper raised its mighty head to heaven before Jess. Drake exited the car and opened the door for Jess. She stepped out into the night and saw that the clouds had completely fled, leaving the night sky to bend down and kiss the peak of the mighty tower before her.

Drake led her forward towards the center of the square, where a statue rested, some odd monument she had never taken notice of before. The statue was of a man, seemingly in flight, straining upward with one hand as if reaching for the height of the building of glass and light that rested just beyond him. The power of his gesture was such that it seemed almost as if the hand alone had caused the building to burst into being and climb to the heavens. The statue and the massive skyscraper were one in spirit. Drake nodded and spoke.

"You know, before a building such as this was built, it was considered an impossibility. The people who claimed they could do it, who dreamed of raising girders and glass to the heavens in challenge to God, were laughed at and called mad."

They strolled towards the building. Before they entered, Drake turned to Jess with unreadable eyes, "Where is your tower, Jess?" Then Drake turned and led the way into the building.

Jess was getting tired of following. She stopped him in the large, empty lobby of the building. This late at night, with no one working and the main lights turned down, it was a hall of echoes and shadows. "Stop," Jess said and waited as Drake turned from ahead of her to face her. "Who do you think you are? Leading me around. Preaching at me?" Jess's eyes flashed. He raised one eyebrow to her. "I'm not some helpless or unintelligent woman for you to save and educate. Is this how you treat everyone else?"

Jess's voice echoed back to her over and over, bouncing off the polished stone floors and marble walls of the empty business building. She was shocked at the tone she heard reflected back at herself, not because it sounded like someone else but because it sounded like her. She hadn't felt like herself for what seemed so long that to hear that old familiar casual sound of command in her voice, a sound that had been as comfortable to her as the New England farm where she had been raised, was chilling. For the first time, the possibility that she was still herself, beneath tragedy and resignation, dawned on her. She was angry, and it felt damned good. Her friend was dead, but she just might still be alive.

They stared at one another, with the echo of her voice hovering like a memory about them. Drake's face was bland, with the slightest smile playing on the edges of his lips.

"Of course. Jessica, I am deeply sorry." He bowed low to her, and for the first time that night, there wasn't the slightest irony in his actions. "I am often not good at interacting with people in a normal or comfortable fashion. So, yes, I fear I often do treat other people like this, and all the worse for me for doing so." Drake stared into space for a moment, realizing that he was learning as much or more about himself and the world as he had hoped she might. "I would like to invite you upstairs." He began again. "There is a surprise waiting for us that I think we may both enjoy. Please, will you grant me the honor of accompanying me?"

Drake gestured towards the elevator, intending for her to lead the way, and waited patiently. Jess frowned for a moment, not yet taking the lead. Then, with a slight look of suspicion, she walked to the open elevator door, and Drake followed.

The elevator swiftly carried them up floor after floor to the very top of the building. A restaurant sat slowly spinning atop the tower, as if it were a crown of luxury. The restaurant was empty except for one waiter who had been expecting Drake. It seemed the mystic had rented the entire restaurant this evening for some strange celebration of his own, a task of tremendous expense.

The servant led them to a table set with the finest foods and expensive wines. Two large silver candelabras lit the table that rested next to a wall of windows. The windows granted a constant view of the entire city as the restaurant slowly rotated beneath them. The sight was breathtaking. The sky was now flawless, strewn with stars and one perfect full moon preparing to set. The city far below them was cloaked in a light mist. It was as if the entire world, which seemed so small now, was a dream. Following the strange night, the entire situation felt surreal and dreamlike.

Drake pulled out a chair for Jess, and she noticed with a shock that the table was set for two and two only. He had anticipated taking her, or someone, here all along. He would have had to plan this all months ahead of time, if not years, in order to reserve the restaurant. The implications were staggering.

"What is all this? How?" Jess's voice trailed off in wonder at the view and the banquet, the beauty and impossibility of it all.

Drake smiled slowly. "What is all this, my dear? Hmmm, how to explain my little tradition? What is today's date?"

"It's April 30th." Jess answered, not seeing the importance. Drake laughed gently, his manner one of celebration now, and no longer judgment or challenge.

"No, it is not. It is well past midnight; in fact, we are here just in time for the sunrise." He pointed, and Jess realized the sky to the east was becoming a delicate pale blue; the sun was indeed preparing to rise. "It's the first of May. Beltane, a holiday older than writing itself, in celebration of life, light, and the achievements of the summer to come. It is also known as May Day. This is the day when, for the Catholics, Mary is crowned queen of spring by some pure maiden, the day when the Communists celebrate the freedom of the worker, and the day which originally was a celebration of the triumph of light over the darkness and the birth of a new season of growth."

Drake's eyes were distant for a moment as he lapsed into silence before he continued.

"May first, Beltane, has always been one of my favorite holidays, and I celebrate it every year. I usually celebrate it here, when possible, to witness the rebirth of the sun myself. Here, I can watch the blessings of light kiss the city and spread its loving arms of hope throughout the world." Drake gazed wistfully out the window, his expression making him look soft and even delicate and fragile.

"But I never celebrate alone," he continued, "it is a scene meant to be shared even as hope is meant to be shared; hope, like love and genius. It's the moment when, for a brief instant, the fire within the soul of every human is celebrated and blessed, purified and honored, by all the universe. It reminds us we, too, can advance against the chaos, the ugly and stupid, the horror of accident and chance."

As Drake spoke, the sky had begun to blaze in the east. Arms of color shot forth from the horizon, and shades of blue stretched across the sky to finally banish the darkness in favor of the light. Jess watched as Drake spoke, and then he was silent to watch as well.

Soon, the entire east was dancing with countless hues, like flowers of fire blooming then passing on so that another might take their place. The sky was music for the eyes, and it all was but a prelude, a triumphant announcement of the coming of the gods into the world. The colors grew more intense and reached further into the ether as the crown of the sun peaked from the sea in the distance. A burgundy gem slid into sight to drape the entire earth in borrowed glory.

A tear seeped from Jess's eye, a crystal gem born to add its beauty to the gold of the sky blazing in the east. So began the joyous march of the light through the spring and into a summer of triumph.

Jess turned to Drake, who now leaned back in his chair, sipping wine and smoking a cigarette. "Thank you for all this. But why did you do it all?" she asked softly.

He smiled for a moment and took a long inhale of smoke before answering.

"Many years ago, a dear friend of mine died. I have never gotten over the sense I could have helped, somehow." Drake sighed. "All things are possible for us, anything at all. I promised myself that I would prove this point to the world every Beltane. I promised that every first of May, I would do what I could to encourage a person to bring themselves back from death, in honor of my dear friend." His face grew morose for a moment, "Though I wish I could have done something more for your friend. But still, happy Beltane, Jessica. What are you going to do with your summer?"

For the first time that evening — and perhaps the first time in years — amidst the world's horror, fear, and loss, Jessica smiled a simple smile of joy. "I don't know," she said with some pleasure. And the sun, marching on its course, spared the time to throw one perfect ray upon the face of a newborn woman named Jessica, crowning her head and wreathing her face in a glorious blaze of gold. Drake raised his glass in salute and Jess tasted a drink she hadn't tasted in a very long time — the certainty of the divine in the human.

Witch Moon

In a patch of forest outside of Salem, Massachusetts, a fire was burning. It was June 21st, the summer Solstice, and the wind that wound through the woods was heavy with the whispers of spirits. In the air above the dancing flames, a sliver of moon shimmered.

In a circle around the bonfire, eight figures in green, red, silver, and black robes stood armed with swords, wands, staves, and bells. They raised their hands as they chanted, by turns alone and in unison. Outside their circle, several other figures sat in chairs in the shadows of the trees. Liberally placed candles about the clearing and up in the branches that interlaced above the heads of the celebrants added light to the night.

> *Hecate, Danu, Branwen! Goddess all!*
> *On this night of triumph, to you we call!*
> *Enwrap us in shadow!*
> *Embrace us in birth!*
> *Enlighten us with starlight!*
> *Come forth and join your hands with ours,*
> *In this place beyond place*
> *In this time outside of time!*

The red-robed figure ceased her chant, and the circle took up the chant "Hecate, Danu, Branwen!" as she drew forth from within the folds of her cloak a handful of herbs. As she cast these upon the fire, the clearing filled with a burst of sparks and thick clouds of smoke pungent with the scent of mistletoe and vervain. Next, a figure cloaked in deep green took up a new chant:

> *Pan and Hades, we call to you!*
> *When summer stands triumphant*
> *Over the winter pall,*
> *Come forth through the veil*
> *Heed at last our call!*

The gathering took up the chant "Io Pan! Io Pan! Pan, Io Pan Pan!" as the figure in green reached into his robe and withdrew a handful of herbs to cast upon the fire. Another burst of sparks and smoke wreathed the gathering, heavy with the scent of mandrake and musk.

Then the whole circle took up a new chant together:

> *Lords and ladies, stand with us!*
> *Let all spirits of the air and earth,*
> *Under the earth and beyond the stars,*
> *Beneath the seas and upon the fields,*
> *Be loyal and obedient unto us*
> *For we are the friends of the Lady and Lord*
> *The true servants of the highest!*

Four of the figures, equally placed about the circle, drew bottles from their robes and held them high. Together they joyfully sang out:

> *We celebrate the moon!*
> *We celebrate the sun!*
> *We drink to summer,*
> *And the verdant earth!*

Each figure drank deeply from the bottle and then passed the bottle to their left. The four then danced behind the others in the circle about the flame, singing all the while.

> *Thrice around the circles bound,*
> *Evil sinks into the ground!*
> *Thrice we rise and thrice we fall!*
> *Thrice we hear and thrice we call!*
> *Spirits rise and join us here!*

Spirits dance and laugh!
Goddess grant our fill of joy!
God grant the strength of pleasure!
Thrice about the wheel turns,
Winter to Summer,
Fall to Spring.
Year in,
Year out,
The God is Born!
The Maiden, Born!
Maiden, Mother, Crone
Child, Warrior, King
Mabon to Mathonweh!
Branwen to Hecate!
The wheel of time,
We dance and sing!

The remaining four figures joined the dance, clockwise about the fire. The bottles were passed liberally as herbs and fresh wood were cast wildly upon the fire. Those watching from the shadows joined. New bottles materialized, and the fire grew larger and larger. A series of calls and counter calls were taken up with one group chanting "Earth our body, water our blood, air our breath, fire our spirit!" While the other chanted, "Spirits dance and spirits sing, for living is a wondrous thing!" Someone produced a drum, another person a fiddle, and a final one a woodland flute. Music soon accompanied the dance.

Throughout it all, one figure cloaked in shadow remained seated. His motionless hand rested upon the head of a silver and black cane. Eventually, the wine was expended, and the energy had reached its peak. The robed figures stopped together and raised their hands to the sky; everyone went still and silent.

"All blessings to the summer!" they roared, and the congregation, with raised arms, roared back, "So let it be!"

The bonfire flared up one final time, and the breeze picked up into a full wind, whipping the robes and smoke about in wild spinning as if continuing the dance. Then flame and wind alike died, and all was silent for an instant. Far away, a raven called loudly, and the cloak of stillness was broken.

There was laughter and conversation as some sat by the fire, others retreated to chairs in the shadows. The musicians played once more, but there was no more dancing. Finally, the figure with the black and silver cane stood and stepped from the shadows towards the High Priestess and High Priest of the coven.

Drake, as was generally his want, was dressed in a perfectly fitted three-piece suit. Oddly, his attire seemed to match the robes of most of the other celebrants, and the cane that seemed an accessory to the outside world appeared as a magical implement to this one. He paused for a moment to light a cigarette and then completed his stroll to the spiritual leaders of the group.

"Drake, I can't express what an honor it is for you to have joined us," stated the High Priestess.

"Ah, Selene, it is my deepest pleasure to be here," Drake responded with a deep bow.

The High Priest had just lit a cigar and exhaled a large cloud of smoke before stating, "I still think you should have taken my place in the role of priest."

"I wouldn't dream of such a thing, Solinare. Besides, though related, our paths are different."

Solinare grunted, "Bah, all gods are one God."

Drake smiled mischievously, "I suspect we haven't been having tea with the same divinities, my friend."

Fresh chanting and dancing had started up behind them, less organized but just as wild, and scents of hashish and Salvia Divinorum were floating in the air. From the revels, one figure, a tall woman in a lovely summer dress with her hair woven with flowers rising in the breeze, detached itself and came towards them. It was Jess, Drake's recent friend, whom he had invited to her first witch's celebration for the sake of getting her out of the city. Her face was flushed and her eyes bright.

"Lady Selene, this is just amazing. I don't know that I have ever had such fun before in my life!" Jess said, laughing, "It's almost like something out of a novel."

"I'm glad you like it, Jessica. Please, come again. You are welcome amongst us at any time," The Lady Selene responded. Drake marveled to see her so happy.

"Come," Selene said, "I'll introduce you to a few you have yet to meet. And then we must have Robert cast the Rune Stones for you. He's the one playing the fiddle right now, but he will pass that on soon. Divination is traditional as the moon wanes."

The two ladies moved off, discussing the various traditions of Selene's eclectic coven.

"There are more things in heaven and earth," murmured Drake before making his excuses to Solinare and wandering off on his own. He had seen a bottle of mead somewhere, and this was the ideal setting for mead.

The revels continued straight through the night until the morning, with people stumbling off, alone or in groups, to wander the short distance throughout the forest to the farmhouse the coven owned for the sake of having a safe space and land in which to hold its rituals.

Finally, only Drake remained, reading the dying embers of the fire like tea leaves. He was standing there, mind lost in the ash and enchanted haze of the pre-dawn, when a scream shattered the still air.

Swiftly following the sound in the deceptive dawn light, Drake came upon a most unexpected scene. There was a young woman, one of the celebrants, still in her ritual robes, standing in shock and horror over the shirtless body of a man with his throat cut and a complex series of slashes across his chest.

"Are you alright, my dear?" Drake asked. The young lady looked ready to scream again, but chose to dive into Drake's arm instead, weeping wildly.

"My dear, you must tell me swiftly what has happened." As Drake was speaking, he disentangled the woman from his arms and knelt beside the body. Gently, he checked its pulse.

"I — I don't know," she stuttered. "I just stumbled over the body."

"And did you see anyone else?"

"N — no."

At that moment, Lady Selene and several other members of the coven arrived.

"My goddess," Selene gasped. "What has happened?"

"We must see," said Drake darkly. "But please, everyone, step back and stay still."

With surprising agility and delicacy, Drake approached the body once more. His depthless eyes missed not a detail. The man was of medium build, somewhere in his late twenties, with dirty blond hair. His face, locked in a death grimace, had an unfriendly cast to it as if its natural expression were unfriendly. Glancing around the body, it was clear that any footprints other than those of Drake and the girl who found the body had been brushed away.

Despite a terrible wound to his throat and many wounds to his chest, there was almost no blood. The man was shirtless, wearing only jeans and hiking boots, but Drake suspected that was not how he had arrived here.

"This man," Drake said, "was not at the ceremony."

Selene leaned closer and looked. There were several gasps from the others.

"By Hades," burst out Solinare, who had just arrived, is that —"

"Yes," Selene almost hissed. "It is Peter Crabtree."

"And he is?"

"Our worst enemy," the High Priests growled. "This is a

mess. We must search the grounds immediately."

"By all means," Drake said, "but it is unlikely to be helpful. This man has been here, and dead, for several hours."

Drake's eyes flickered around the space as the morning light revealed more of it. "Ah," he said with satisfaction and paced to a bush on the far side of the clearing. There, under a bush, he poked with his cane at a dark bundle. It was a shirt, cut up the front with what was most likely a knife. From within it, a flash of gold glimmered. Lifting his cane, Drake revealed a gold chain dangling from the end of it and, dangling from the end of that chain, a small gold cross. Drake held it high as the morning sun broke through the trees to blaze off it. With a raised eyebrow Drake looked to Selene.

"That would be his," she said. "He was the leader of Salem's Christian Coalition. They have been fighting for years to close the magic shops and make witchcraft illegal." She laughed harshly, "Honestly, in this day and age!"

"I think, my friends," Drake said solemnly as he dropped the cross back into the shirt, "that we'd better call the police."

"No," Selene said, "absolutely not. The press will destroy us! 'Christian activist found ritually murdered during witchcraft ceremony!' Just picture it. It would be national news. It would be the witch hunts all over again."

"What choice do we have?" Solinare asked. "Won't it be worse if we — what — cover it up?"

"We won't cover anything up," Selene responded. "We will solve this crime ourselves."

"I do not recommend this," Drake said softly.

"Drake, please," Selene pleaded. "Here you are in our moment of greatest need. You who have solved so many crimes. This is fate!"

Drake turned to Jess. "What do you think, my dear? Shall we extend our visit to clear up this rather murky situation?"

"Do you think we can?" she asked dubiously. "It might be best to include the police first."

"There is no doubt we can do it. The question," Drake ran his eyes over the still gathering crowd, "is whether we should."

"But why ever not?" Selene demanded.

"Because, my lady, I can offer no guarantee that the outcome of such an investigation will be to the good of the coven. I can offer you truth, but not necessarily assistance. You may be better served by a more mundane investigation."

"What?" Solinare burst out brusquely, "You can't imagine one of us did this!"

"And," added Selene, "if so, it is far better that we weed out the murderer and deliver them ourselves to the authorities with an explanation. That way, we conclusively cut off all rumor and speculation before it starts."

"Perhaps, perhaps," Drake said, staring down at the body. "There is one thing to note, before you decide. The wounds upon this man's chest."

Selene and Solinare stared down at the body for a moment, and then Solinare whistled softly. "Why, they are runes," he said, his voice troubled.

"Yes," Selene agreed, "but what of them?"

"Not just runes, but a complex pattern of them forming a hyper-sigil, a multileveled magical symbol intended for some specific effect," Drake added.

"But what is it for?" asked Solinare.

"I don't know," Drake said, and glanced at Selene, who also shook her head. "We shall have to have Robert, your rune expert, look at them. But one thing is troubling. If I don't know what the symbol means, and you don't, it was likely made by either an expert occultist or someone working very hard to appear like one."

Drake took out a cigarette and lit it pensively. "No matter," he said at last. "It shall be clarified in time. For now, I suggest we leave everything as it is and return to the farmhouse to gather everyone together and explain the situation. We won't want anyone leaving until our plans are settled."

"But," Jess objected, "aren't we risking losing evidence? DNA, fingerprints. Things like that?"

"That," Drake replied, "would only matter were we intending to rely on the police. As we aren't," he glanced at the others and noted their confirming nods, "there is nothing important to us we risk losing. Come, let us all return."

"Well," Solinare interrupted. "I, for one, would like to have a thorough look around the grounds."

"Of course," Drake agreed, "but be swift, disturb nothing, and come right back to the house for a meeting."

With that, they set off through the woods, the spectators in one direction and Solinare in the other. Drake and Jess lagged behind to talk as they trailed the others.

"Well, I must say this all brings Shakespeare rather to mind," Drake murmured.

"Really?" Jess asked. "You don't think a tragic love affair was involved, do you?"

"Perhaps," Drake said, "though it hardly seems likely, does it? I was thinking more of *A Midsummer Night's Dream*. It fits the day at least, and all this seems dreamlike enough. But who knows, perhaps we shall uncover a tale of mistaken identities, mismatched lovers, men changing into animals, and backfiring spells. Who can say?"

"But Drake!" Jess objected. "*A Midsummer Night's Dream* was a comedy."

"That it was," Drake agreed "but I am not certain it had to be."

There were, all told, about twenty-five people staying at the farmhouse, and it took some time for those who had seen the body to scatter and collect all those who had slept through the screams. Jess sat in the common room, with its large leather couches and chairs, rough log table, and cavernous fireplace, while Drake began brewing coffee.

Jess was thinking of the body, shocked more by how little

it had disturbed her than even by the events themselves. Perhaps it was just that after the long night and no sleep, things really did feel like a dream. She was lost in these thoughts when Robert, the Rune-Master of the coven, jogged in through the front door. He had retired early and seemed much better rested than most of the others.

"Hello Jess," he said with a cheerful grin. "What's going on? I was out for a jog and saw that everyone seems to be up and about." Robert was younger than Jess, in his mid-twenties, with dark hair and a dark Mediterranean complexion. He was very attractive, and Jess herself had noticed rather poignantly what a fine specimen his body offered to the eye the night before. Now, however, her every thought was laced with suspicion, and she dwelled instead on his story: going to bed early, waking early, and being up and about without hearing the screams.

Jess told him the story and, though he was surprised and horrified enough, his attention focused immediately on the symbol carved into the man's chest.

"Runes, you say?" he asked, and then a voice answered from behind him.

"Yes, just so. A hyper-sigil built of several interconnected runes, in fact." It was Drake returning with several pots of dark coffee.

"I should like to see that," Robert said, sounding worried.

"Of course. We shall return to the body when the meeting is over."

But then it was Drake's turn to be answered unexpectedly, because Solinare had just burst in through the back door.

"That's not gonna be possible," he fumed, "because the damn body's gone! I swung by on my way back for one last look, and it disappeared!"

There was a moment of shocked exclamations from Robert and Jess, but Drake merely looked thoughtful. "Mysterious appearing and disappearing bodies. Yes, a dream indeed," he said softly. Then the room was filling with people, both those rousted out of bed and those who had rousted them.

"Please, everyone, sit." Drake's voice effortlessly carried to the furthest points of the room, including both Robert and Solinare in his admonishment. "Have some coffee and we will discuss this all together." Drake set about distributing cups of coffee like a waiter, which Jess found to be the most incongruent thing she had ever seen. He was somehow both in command of the entire room and everyone's servant at the same time.

He paused, went down on one knee, and squeezed the shoulder of the girl who had found the body and spoke a few words of comfort to her. Jess had learned that her name was Karina. She was twenty years old and, while living in Salem, attended school for nursing in Boston. She was originally from the Midwest but had chosen to attend school in Boston to pursue her religious interests in Salem. She was, in fact, one of Selene's most promising protégés in the arts of witchcraft and holistic healing.

Then Drake was in the center of the room with the rest of the coven spread about him, most sitting and a few standing. Amongst those standing were Selene and Solinare, attempting to assert their authority in a reassuring way. Drake stood there, and the full morning sun blazed through the windows behind him. In his hand, he cradled a porcelain cup of coffee sitting on a saucer. He looked calmly at them all and sipped his coffee. Then, with everyone waiting in silence, he spoke.

"Well," he said, "we find ourselves, all of us, implicated in a rather precarious situation. A well-known public figure, rabidly prejudiced against us, has been found brutally murdered here during last night's revelries. Upon the body were carved symbols of an overtly occult character." Drake took another sip of his coffee. "So, not only are we all suspects, we are the main suspects." The atmosphere of the room grew far less comfortable at this point. "And now the body has disappeared, making matters worse."

"I'm not sure of that, all things considered," objected Solinare. "Where there's no body, there's no crime, I suppose."

Drake raised an eyebrow and sipped his coffee as Selene responded in shock, "Oh, Sol! That doesn't solve anything! Blood has been spilt viciously here on our sacred ground."

"It may solve some things," Drake disagreed, "in a legal sense at least. But I am unconcerned with crime or law. I am, however, very concerned with murder and, as Lady Selene points out, the violent spilling of relatively innocent blood."

"Well, I wouldn't say innocent," Robert broke in, "but this does make unraveling the mystery much harder. Damn, how I wish I could have seen those runes."

"I shouldn't worry too much," Drake drawled. "Murder is like a crack in the fundament of reality. No matter how much sediment you layer upon it, the instability remains. Fractures keep branching and spreading from the deep to the surface. The further the spread, the more apparent the original crack becomes. Every further development in this situation is a new sign pointing to the underlying cause. Murder, as they say, will out."

"So," Selene thought aloud, "the killer made a mistake in moving the body."

Drake held up one elegant, long-fingered hand. "Let us not move so swiftly. We have three questions, and we need not assume the answer to all three is the same. Who killed Peter Crabtree? Who carved the hyper-sigil in his flesh? And who moved the body? It is possible a separate person performed each action."

"There's a fourth question, and probably the most important one," Jess added. "Why was he here in the first place?"

Drake smiled and nodded. "Just so."

"So, what do we do?" Solinare asked gruffly.

"I assume," Drake responded, "that your search of the

grounds didn't turn up anything besides the fact of the miss-ing body."

"Yes," Solinare stated.

"Did you check all adjacent roads?"

"Briefly."

Drake frowned. "Then a fifth question presents itself. How did the victim get here? If he was driven out here by compan-ions, who and where are they? If he wasn't driven —" Drake frowned in silence. "No matter," he waved his hand dismis-sively, "first, Selene and Solinare, I would like you to inter-view everyone and get a clear timeline of where everyone was around the likely time of the murder."

"But when was he killed?" Selene asked.

"We found him at dawn, but he was cold, and rigor had set in. So, two or three hours before dawn, perhaps earlier. But how long did the act itself last? Was he killed swiftly or slowly? How was he killed?" Drake finished speaking and looked at them all.

Solinare cleared his throat, "Well, that seems easy. He died slowly, was tortured with the carvings into his flesh, and then had his throat cut, which killed him." His matter-of-fact tone and the content of his statements caused several of the mem-bers of the coven to look decidedly ill. The room was silent then, but Drake waited.

Finally, Jess broke the silence, "I'm sorry, but that doesn't make sense. The wounds on his chest hadn't bled or clotted. Nor had the gash to his neck. That means they were inflicted after death and were neither torture nor the cause of his death."

"Then what killed him?" Solinare demanded of Jess in ex-asperation, to which she responded with a slow shake of her head.

"I also do not know," Drake said, "leaving us another in a long list of questions. We have a crime which appears brutal, but probably wasn't. The cuts on his chest were not deep, and they were inflicted post-mortem, and the neck wound hadn't bled. Other than that, there was no other obvious trauma to the body. No signs of strangulation, blows to the head, stabbing, or shooting. The brutality was staged, which makes me wonder what else was staged and why. I would suggest, tentatively, that the murder itself was swift and may very well not have happened where we found the body. The symbol carving, however, did happen there."

"Why?" asked Selene.

"Because the shirt and cross were left in the clearing," Jess responded, her eyes bright as her mind ran through the problem.

Drake grinned, "Precisely. So, murder three to two hours before dawn, perhaps earlier. Body moving and symbol carving for an hour or so after that. We need to know everyone's movements from, say, four hours before dawn to one hour before. Perhaps even right up until the body was discovered."

Solinare and Selene gathered people to interview while Drake motioned Jess and Robert to him. "We three," he said, "have work to do." He led them upstairs to his own spacious room and motioned for them to sit.

"If we do not solve this by noon tomorrow, I suspect it shan't be solved at all, so we need to investigate those runes. It would be best to find the body, but there may not be time. Instead, we must recreate the carving. I suspect I can do so, but we need a second witness to test my memory against. You, Jess."

"But Drake, I don't remember them clearly," she objected.

"Consciously, you are right, but unconsciously, your mind caught them perfectly." He handed her a blank page and a pen while taking one for himself.

"Robert, sit to the side and keep your mind still. I don't want your thoughts interfering with ours. Jess, sit calmly and breathe deeply. Hold the pen loosely in your hand. I am going to guide you into a light trance to help you remember.

Then, when you are ready to start sketching, I will do the same."

Drake had Jess breathe and slowly let go of each of her thoughts and cares by dissolving them in a bright white light in her mind. Then he had her visualize the clearing, focusing on how the wind felt, the distant lingering smell of wood smoke, the rising predawn light, and the first morning bird song. He slowly narrowed in on the body but never mentioned the chest, carefully moving her mind's eye about the clearing instead. Then he had her simply stand in the clearing in her memory and breathe.

"Very good, Jess. I am going to go sketch. When you are ready, do the same."

In a flash, she saw the sigil as clearly as if it sat before her once more.

Moments later, Drake and Jess's sketches sat on the desk side by side. There was variation in style, Jess's bearing the telltale signs of her hand while Drake's looked as if even the imperfections caused by resistant skin had been captured in photographic perfection, but in all pertinent aspects, they were the same. Robert gazed upon them, amazed and frowning.

"It is definitely a legitimate hyper-sigil formed of many overlapping and interconnecting runes. This is not just an attempt to mimic occult symbolism. No one could craft one like this without hours, even days, of planning and research," Robert said grimly.

"Premeditation then," Jess said.

"Unless," Robert began to object and then paused. "Yes," he said at last, "it looks familiar. Wait, I'll be right back." He ran to his room and returned with a leather-bound book.

"Here we have it," Robert stated as he finished flipping through the text. "This is Edred Thorsson's book on hyper-runes, a type of hyper-sigil. They are incredibly difficult to create and equally hard to use."

"So, we are dealing with a rune master," Jess stated.

"No," Drake disagreed, "we are not. Go on, Robert."

"Drake is right. When I first learned of the hyper-rune, I was worried it was a rune master, but now that I see it again, I realize it wasn't. It was lifted directly from Thorsson's book! Here it is," Robert showed them a perfect reproduction of the sketches they had done in the pages of the book. "This was no master, but rather a plagiarist."

"So much the worse for us," Jess mused. "A rune master would have narrowed the search."

"Yes," Robert said sourly, "to a list of one. Me."

"You think you are being framed?" Jess asked.

"Well, what else?"

"Perhaps," Drake said, "but just a moment. We are missing the point. What does the rune mean?"

"Does it matter?" Robert asked.

"That depends," Drake said, "on who committed the murder or carved the runes. If it were an occultist, the runes matter very much. It may be plagiarized, but that doesn't mean it wasn't intended to be effective."

Robert read a bit in the book. "It's a hyper-rune to overthrow kings and topple the mighty," he said at last.

Drake nodded, but "So" was all he said, and then he muttered a line from Shakespeare, "How canst thou thus for shame, Titania?"

They frowned at him, uncomprehending, but Drake was moving on, "We should go check on how the interviews with the guests are going." They stood to move to the door, but Drake did not rise and instead interrupted their departure suddenly, "But first, I need to know why and where you hid the body, Robert."

"I don't know what —" Robert began to object.

"We don't have time." Drake cut him off, his voice cold and hard.

"Fine," he surrendered, unable to meet the mystic's eye. "I

came upon you all as I was out for my run, all of you focused on the body. I saw the hyper-rune immediately and thought the same thing then that I do now, that I was being framed. So, I got rid of the evidence after you all left."

Jess grimaced, "That was a terrible plan."

"I know!" he exploded, "but I was panicked and pressed for time."

Drake silenced them with a raised hand. "Where were you at the approximate time of the murder?"

"Asleep. You know I went to bed earlier than everyone else."

"Yes," Drake agreed. "Alone?"

"Yes." The two men stared at each other. Robert's eyes seemed caught, possessed, by Drake's. The silence was fragile and intense. Jess didn't breathe.

"Are you capable of murder, Robert?" Drake's voice was barely a whisper.

"Yes," Robert said at last. "Who isn't?"

"Why would you kill?" Drake pressed.

"To protect my loved ones."

"Did you kill this man?"

"No."

Drake stood suddenly. "Good. Here is what I need you to do."

❧

Ten minutes later, Robert was gone, and both Jess and Drake sat with Solinare and Selene to discuss the alibis of the guests.

Most had been in bed, or had retreated to hidden woodland clearings as couples or small groups. Of those who had gone to bed, most, like Robert, were without a confirmable alibi. Selene had been in a group with two others, who retreated to a clearing for a ceremony of their own. Solinare, rather surprisingly, had been with the girl Karina in another clearing right up until she left and stumbled upon the body.

He had been, he claimed, teaching her woodcraft. Selene and Solinare's stories were confirmed by their companions.

"This is a waste of time, I am afraid," Selene said. "We aren't learning enough, really, to narrow things down."

"Oh, I don't know," Drake said. "We have gone from twenty-five to about ten suspects."

"If it wasn't an outside job," Solinare objected.

"Just so," Drake agreed. "But still, we must press on as we are."

At just that moment, Robert burst into the room. "I've found the body!" he blurted out excitedly, "And, well, it's alive! He's alive!"

"Is he conscious?" Drake demanded.

"He was, but incoherent. I've carried him to the guest-house around back. No one is using it, and I thought it best not to move him further."

"Excellent, I will go see to him at once. Alone, I must insist. The rest of you, please inform everyone of the good news," Drake ordered succinctly and left them in various states of shock and confusion.

❧

The day passed with both a sense of relief and foreboding in the air. All seemed happy that murder was no longer the issue while wondering, at the same time, what the formerly dead man would say. What strange, horrific tale did he have to tell? The more thoughtful amongst them wondered whether a man with a slit throat could say anything, or how he could be alive. Yet Drake and Robert remained sequestered alone with him, allowing no one else to enter.

Throughout the day, Jess cycled through the group, getting to know people better and easing their anxiety as far as possible. Drake always said that you needed to know the nature of an action to find the perpetrator of that action.

Actions could be positive and creative, or they could be negative and destructive. Of course, all actions partook of both natures, but all actions also fit essentially into one or the other category. All crimes, by definition, were negative except a class of exceptional crimes that, Drake said, even he wasn't sure existed or were possible. So, this case dealt with a negative action, an action of destruction, which Drake claimed left a scar on reality. Such a bruise could be traced to its source.

More informative was the second distinction between actions. All actions were, in their essence, either active or reactive. When truly active, a deed originated entirely from the actor. These express fully a person's basic nature and insight. They were, Drake said, like light. When reactive, an action was a response to the deeds of others or various social and environmental pressures.

Where some actions were light, reactions were shadows cast by the light of others. They expressed weakness and ultimately disease. While crime was never, or almost never, positive, it could be either active or reactive. It was this question that told you the nature of the criminal. One need only figure out what the deed was in reaction to, and perhaps who was weakest or sickest of the suspects, or alternatively, who was most creative and active.

Drake had made it sound so simple when Jess pressed him on the nature of crime, but now that she was left to herself to work it out, it all seemed terribly vague and, truth be told, worthless. Drake, she had found, often spoke as a form of silence and was silent as a form of speech. His theory was as likely a smoke screen as anything else. But the message was that the nature of a crime was connected to the nature of its perpetrator. The only guide to unraveling that, Jess realized, would be her own intuition.

So, Jess spent that day exchanging small talk and comfort while attempting to gaze beyond the surface of people's faces and to listen for something hidden beneath their words.

Selene spent the day, much like Jess, trying to comfort her

people, but underneath, she was distracted. Jess got the image of a panther caged, pacing violently back and forth. The High Priestess felt like nothing so much as a warrior preparing for battle, restless and impatient for the kill. Solinare, on the other hand, was visibly distressed, whereas Selene was invisibly so.

Solinare paced, gnawing on the stump of a cigar and muttering to himself and others. Obviously, everyone was tense, but from Solinare, Jess also got the deeper sense of having been insulted. He was being kept out of the loop, and he knew it. He felt that his authority was being usurped.

Jess had no doubt that both Selene and Solinare were capable of this murder, given the right situation and motivation, but nothing about them seemed to point to guilt. Plus, something about the nature of the murder didn't seem to suit them. They seemed, both of them, people of direct action, and the murder was an oddly indirect and convoluted affair. It appeared violent, but wasn't; it involved staging and deception and, perhaps most importantly of all, it put the entire coven in danger. She couldn't imagine either of them willingly endangering the coven.

She had had the most time to observe Robert, and he seemed, if anything, without hidden depths in this matter. He was angry on the assumption that he was being framed and was primarily interested in catching whoever was responsible while clearing his good name. He, like Solinare and Selene, seemed an exceptionally direct personality. Even if he had committed this crime, the staging and misdirection seemed contrary to his nature.

Then there were the others, a hodge-podge of witches and healers. There was an older woman, Bernice, who had been a presence in Salem all the years of her life and was herself a descendant, so she said, of one of the victims of the original witch-hunts. She owned a shop in town and could hardly hide her jealousy of Selene. Regardless the topic of conversation, she turned every moment into a statement concerning how Selene was bumbling the entire situation and was clearly unfit for leadership.

Of Solinare, however, she had nothing but glowing things to say, and Jess got the distinct feeling that Solinare had been sleeping with her on and off for years in secret. In fact, Solinare seemed to get around rather liberally, which led Jess to think a bit more closely about the time he had spent "teaching woodcraft" to Karina on the night of the murder.

Karina herself was still a mess. It was obvious that she was a sensitive, even delicate, soul and that finding the body and the ensuing dramas had left her rather shaken. She was tearful, and yet prone to swing suddenly to worrying about what her family might think back in the Midwest if they heard she was involved in this whole thing. She was anxious for the entire situation to be resolved and wished the police had been called. On the other hand, she didn't want to have anything to do with the police or what would likely be a highly publicized investigation. She also seemed deeply sympathetic to the victim, Peter Crabtree, and Jess suspected she had no stomach for the suffering of any being, even a bigot.

However, she seemed even more horrified that he was still alive and repeatedly wondered about how much suffering he must be enduring, and whether they shouldn't call an ambulance. She seemed deeply drawn to Selene, who alone seemed to have the power to calm and comfort her, while distrustful of Solinare.

Jess suspected that what Solinare had in mind for their late-night forest lesson hadn't been what Karina intended. It seemed his advances may have been unwelcome. But then again, they had spent much of the night together.

The more Jess got to know the coven members, the clearer it became that there was a rather large amount of intrigue beneath the surface. There was clearly some sort of struggle for power between Solinare and Selene, and even Robert seemed to feature in the battle as one of Selene's strongest supporters. There was also talk of conflict with other covens within Salem itself. Several members of this coven were also members of some of the others, and it became clear that loyalties were divided and that the occult scene in the city of Salem was a vexed one. One person suggested to Jess that this whole thing might be a set-up by another coven in order to destroy this one, while another person suggested this would put an end to this coven, and that was "likely a good thing".

Finally, Jess found herself talking, for the first time, to a very old and reclusive member of the coven. His name was August McFarland, and he was an almost skeletal figure, gaunt to the point of being arresting and bald. His skin was tight but knotted with wrinkles, and he was by far the oldest person there, perhaps having passed his eightieth year. His eyes were sharp and contained perhaps a little too much fire to be entirely sane.

Jess had learned from Selene that he was an expert in necromancy, or the occult art of speaking with and controlling the spirits of the dead. He seemed little more than such a spirit himself, thought Jess. He made her uncomfortable in every way possible.

"So," he almost hissed, his voice a raspy whisper, "you have talked with them all, trying to bore your way into their souls, and now you are left with me. Well, don't waste your time, girl, I have no soul for you to read. Not anymore." He laughed harshly, and Jess smiled calmly.

"I haven't the foggiest idea what you mean," she said.

"Don't play with me," he shot back, "you are doing the mystic's bidding even now. It's exactly the damned man's way. Leave us all alone to stew in anticipation while his little servant scurries amongst us to weed out our secrets. And there are plenty of secrets, aren't there? Nothing but a basket of vipers, this lot, eh?"

"So, who do you think did it?"

"All of 'em, none of 'em. Who knows? The living are like that. Changeable and unpredictable. But the dead, the dead don't lie and never change. Give me a body and I can find out for you, get it to tell me itself. And that's just what Drake is doing now, isn't it, getting that body to talk."

"Perhaps, but it's a live body." August just grunted in response to that.

"That may be," he said, "but there is death here, nonetheless. I can smell murder and a corpse miles away. It's like lilac or jasmine at sunset, when the air cools suddenly and the rich buds release the perfume they have stored up throughout the day. You know, of all the seasonal holidays, Midsummer was often thought the most dangerous. All the creatures of the wild come out to revel, and demons walked freely upon the earth. Bonfires were lit to protect from the wandering devils. Well, there was a devil's revel last night, wasn't there?"

"I thought witches didn't believe in demons?" Jess asked politely.

"Bah, I'm no witch, pagan, or Christian. The dead are the dead just the same for each of them. And demons there are aplenty, no matter what myth you pick as your favorite."

The day had passed, and the sun was setting. As the last blood red blush of the sun glared through the common room's windows, Jess had a chill as she thought it was a terrible time to be talking to a necromancer.

"Listen to me, girl," the old man said with sudden fire, "the day is ended and the infernal mystic will be coming back any moment now to talk to us all about live bodies and dead bodies and murder. This isn't over, and this very night, another murder will occur before this is all over. You take care of yourself, you hear me?"

"What do you mean? What is it you know?" Jess demanded.

"I know only what the dead tell me, and they are restless

tonight," he muttered. "Ah, here comes the dragon now." And at that moment, Drake entered the room from outside.

"Peter Crabtree is not at all well," Drake said as everyone present pressed him with questions. "He was poisoned with digitalis, also known as fox, or witches', glove. Robert and I are nursing him back to health, and none of his other wounds are life-threatening despite their grisly appearance. He has told us what he can, but it hasn't been much. We hope, after a night of rest and care, that he will tell us more."

Several of the assembly pressed Drake to let them help, each having various talents in healing.

"No." Drake's voice cut through the noise. "My skills are adequate to do what must be done, and until we know more about this situation, it is safest to keep him in complete isolation. I do not mean to be rude, but you are all still suspects."

"You," Solinare's voice broke into Drake's speech, "I might point out, are as well. How do we know you won't kill him yourself and then claim he blamed one of the innocents here? You need witnesses if he is going to speak."

"I have a witness," Drake reminded them. "Robert."

"Who might himself be the killer, or in it with you," Solinare shot back.

"You all trusted me enough to place this matter in my hands," Drake said coldly. "You must trust me still or call the police immediately."

"But what makes you so sure you can trust the Rune Master?" someone shouted out.

"Based on the evidence, we can't, none of us, trust anyone," Drake responded. "But my judgment tells me I can trust Robert. And your judgment once told you that you could trust me. For now, that is all we have to go on. So please, enjoy some dinner and get some sleep tonight. Tomorrow morning, everything will be cleared up."

"I don't like this secrecy," Solinare insisted.

"And I don't like having my holiday turned into an inquisition, even if I get to play the inquisitor," Drake responded. "But for now, none of us is going to get what we want." With that, Drake turned and marched from the room and across the back lawn to the guesthouse where Robert and the ailing Peter Crabtree waited.

Everyone was tired, many having gotten little to no sleep the night before, so dinner was a silent, weary affair and most of the guests went to bed early. Eventually, only Selene, Solinare, Jess, and August remained sitting in the common room, sipping coffee or tea. August stared into the darkening sky, sipping peppermint tea. Selene read a volume containing the fragmentary writings of Hypatia while holding a steaming cup of coffee.

Solinare was restless and began building up a roaring fire. "It's a dark night," he muttered as he fanned the flames. Periodically, all of their eyes wandered across the lawn to the guesthouse where light could be seen leaking out from behind the closed shutters and pulled curtains.

August lit a cigarette, despite a disapproving look from Selene. "Grab some scotch, Sol," August said softly. "It will calm you and stop your damn pacing." Solinare glared at him, but went to the dry bar and poured himself a glass of scotch.

"So, do we all stay up all night and stare at that distant building until it unloads its fund of truth?" August asked softly.

"It wouldn't serve any purpose to do so," Selene said as she closed her book.

"No," Solinare agreed and threw back his glass of scotch in one gulp, "it is foolish to exhaust ourselves. I'm going to bed." He turned and marched up the stairs out of the room, despite having just lit the fire. He seemed, Jess noted, to become more and more cranky with each minute that the mystery continued.

Selene shook her head ruefully. "He doesn't do well with waiting," she said. "Patience is not one of his virtues. He has too much fire in his makeup, fire and the energy of Mars. A real warrior, but not a diplomat or judge." She shrugged and stood. "But we make do with what fate gives us, though, don't we? I'll be going to bed myself. August, Jess, have a good evening." Gracefully, the priestess followed Solinare up the stairs. Once more, Jess was left with the discomforting necromancer who continued to stare out into the night.

"Someone should keep watch," he said without shifting his gaze. "To protect the men laboring out there."

"What do you mean?" Jess asked.

"Well, think about it," August turned and pinned her with his flame-like gaze. "One of us is an attempted murderer, and our victim, the only person who can identify us, lies ill in that small cottage surrounded by the vast and hungry night. Two people watch him. Eliminate the three people in the building, and you eliminate the risk of discovery. At this moment, the would-be killer knows his or her capture is all but inevitable unless the occupants of that building are killed."

Of course, Jess thought. Robert and Drake had made themselves targets.

"So," he continued, "someone must stay up and keep watch. And, since you don't know that I am not the killer, it had better be you."

"But, you don't know that I am not the killer," she responded.

The ancient necromancer chuckled. "That is true," he agreed. "But unlike you, I don't particularly care about any of this or any of these people. So, I shan't bother myself." He stood, threw his cigarette into the now roaring fire, and wandered away to find his own bed, leaving Jess alone in the echoing room with the night. Sighing, she sat down in a large leather chair in the corner and prepared for a long night's watch. Inevitably, having stayed up for two days in a row now, she was lulled almost immediately to sleep by the soft warmth and crackling of the fire.

❧

She had no idea what time it was when she awoke. The fire had burned down to glowing embers. The lights within the house were all out, as were the lights in the guesthouse across the lawn. The embers, the stars, and the newly risen half moon cast the only light. Everything was still, except for a gentle, insistent breeze that seemed to sigh expectantly as it slid about the house. Jess wasn't sure what had woken her, but something had.

She stood and moved to the back door that let out onto the lawn leading to the guesthouse where Drake, Robert, and Peter Crabtree slept. The door was open, hanging slightly ajar. Someone had left and not closed the door so as not to make noise, Jess realized with a shock of horror.

Silently, she pushed open the door and stepped into the cool night air. The temperature had dropped, and it was much more chill outside than the fire-heated common room had led her to expect. The wind was louder, and the moon brighter.

The air felt thin and, if possible, extra transparent as if all the world were open to staring eyes hidden in the vast spaces above the earth. The night, Jess somehow knew, was waiting and watching. But who else was?

In a near panic, she cast her gaze about the darkened lawn, the distant tree line, the shadowed walls of the guest-house. Each movement of leaf or grass in the wind gave rise to visions of concealed attackers leaping from the shadows.

Someone was here, she was sure of it. She padded along the wall of the farmhouse, keeping her back to the building and her gaze sharp.

Suddenly, from the woods, a raven cawed and, at precisely that moment, she saw a human form detach itself from the surrounding darkness of the woods and slip silently to the side of the guesthouse.

The killer. It had to be. Jess faced her choices. She could call out to warn Drake, but risk allowing the killer to escape, or she could let things play out and perhaps even confront the killer herself.

It was foolish, she knew, but she needed to grasp this mystery directly. After spending the day trying to figure these people out, right here was the solution.

Having reached the side of the yard, caught in the deepest darkness, she slipped away from the guesthouse towards the far outline of the guesthouse. She was confident the murderous shadow would be too caught up in its own observing of the interior of the guesthouse and its search for a safe entrance to see Jess slipping up from behind.

She could see the outline of the one she hunted pressed beside one of the guesthouse windows. She set herself for a final sprint when an arm grabbed her from behind and a blow struck her head. She screamed once and then all went dark.

❧

"It's all right, my dear Jess. I never anticipated your initiative. I am so sorry." It was Drake's voice that roused her.

"What happened?" Jess asked, setting her head to a painful throbbing.

"Apparently, you were attacked by the murderer. I take it you were trying to confront the killer before he or she could sneak up on us. Did you see who it was?"

"No," Jess groaned. "And it wasn't the killer, or wasn't the person I thought was the killer. I was sneaking up on one of them as they tried to break into the guesthouse." Jess realized that she was lying in the guesthouse at that very moment. "But it was someone else who jumped me from behind and knocked me out."

"Yes, you suffered a bad blow to the head. You are rather concussed, I am afraid." She could hear Robert's voice outside the building, talking to several other people. She thought she heard Selene and Solinare.

"There were two of them," Jess said.

"I see," Drake said. Jess tried to rise, but Drake motioned for her to remain lying. "I had intended all along to flush the killer out, and was lying in wait for them. As I said, I never anticipated or intended for you to confront them first. I didn't, however, expect both of them to show up. To be honest, I hadn't been sure they were working together."

"They who?" Jess asked.

"That," Drake said, "has yet to be seen. But yes, I knew there were at least two people involved. One to commit the murder and the second to carve the symbols into his body and move it from where he was originally killed."

"Killed? I thought Peter was alive."

"Of course he isn't, and if our killer and accomplice were thinking clearly, they too would see that wasn't possible. The body didn't bleed when they cut into it, even when they slashed its throat. The poison did its fatal work successfully. But murderers are rarely self-assured enough to call one's bluff in cases like this."

"So, the people I saw, one was the killer and the other carved the symbols?" Jess asked.

"Precisely. And if I am right, one of them was panicking, and the other was coming to keep them from doing something stupid. You, however, got in the way, which I suspect saved one of their lives. It is likely that the more composed of the two would have killed the one who was panicking in order to keep their secret. Though it also risked yours." Drake cast her a slightly annoyed look following that last observation. "Still," he continued, "I suppose no one can fault your ingenuity. You've come closer to the killers than any of us."

"What do we do now?" Jess asked. "How do we figure out who the killers are, and who attacked me?"

"We are a long way towards that, now we just need to

look at the full picture. It makes sense two people were in-volved; the convoluted nature of the killing and staging at-test to that. A passive crime, poisoning, combined with active mutilation. Why make a premeditated and cold murder like poisoning appear brutal and passionate? Why make it appear like a ritual killing when, in fact, the poisoning at least was anything but? Moving the body might make sense, but the rest was odd to say the least. Now, we know we have two people of decidedly different temperaments and that both of them are still here, which was largely what this whole ploy was meant to determine.

"This murder is like a festering wound," Drake continued, "and I have been attempting to draw the poison to the sur-face. Now, quickly, tell me what you have gleaned from your day of observation, and then we can go solve the mystery for everyone who is, no doubt, waiting breathlessly at this mo-ment. It is now past midnight, and well past time this was all put to rest. When my friends start being attacked in the dark, you know things have gone too far."

Jess filled Drake in on the dubious intuitions she had gleaned from the day and, despite her own assessments, Drake seemed to find them useful. Then he aided her to rise and led her back out into the night. The moon was, if any-thing, brighter than it had been; something of the menace of the evening seemed to have dissipated.

As they entered the common room, everyone seemed to be present, roused from their beds by a late-night scream — this time Jess's. Drake ran his eyes around the crowd as every-thing went still, looking as if he were confirming everyone was present. At the far side of the room, near the stairs, stood Robert. Drake and Robert exchanged a brief nod, and Robert slipped, unseen, upstairs.

"Ladies and gentlemen," Drake said with aplomb and raised hands, "may I have your attention, please?"

The announcement was unnecessary, as the whole room

had already placed its rapt attention upon Drake.

"As you all no doubt know by now, my dear friend Jess was attacked this very evening, not moments ago, by the pair of criminals we are hunting. Yes, my friends, there are two of them, and they are in this room. Their identity is a secret no more; it is now well known to me. Peter Crabtree has been most forthcoming!"

"Rubbish," Solinare burst out. "I saw that body the same as these others, that man was dead as dirt when we found him, and he remains so!"

Drake smiled and bowed his head, "Most true, my dear Solinare. This has been, as it were, a bit of theater for the benefit of our killer. But I did not, of course, hope to deceive you. But, as our companion August will point out, even the dead can speak given the chance." August, who sat corpse-like in the corner furthest from the fire, chuckled dryly.

At that moment, there was a ragged gasp, and Karina grasped her chest, falling to the floor. Drake, swift as lightning, was on his knees at her side. "Her heart has stopped," he declared; immediately, Selene attempted CPR. Meanwhile, Drake had stood and taken Karina's spilled teacup in hand. He held it to his nose and lips, then shook his head sadly as Selene finally gave up trying to save Karina.

"It will be," Drake stated, "no use, my dear. Karina has been severely poisoned with digitalis, just like Peter Crabtree. At this point it is too late, though you should of course call the police and ambulance."

Selene was beside herself, both upset about this second murder and about inevitably being caught having withheld information about the first murder from the police.

"It is, indeed, very sad, my dear," Drake comforted her. "But do not fret too much, there is the balance of justice in this, and the murderers will be caught well before the police arrive."

Once things had settled once more, Drake resumed his

speech, though this time in an even more somber tone. "And so, we have a new murder and a new murderer."

"What do you mean, a new murderer?" Selene asked.

"This was not the work of the same person who murdered Peter Crabtree, because Karina herself killed Crabtree," Drake stated, to numerous gasps of disbelief.

"Then perhaps she killed herself to avoid capture," Solinare suggested.

"That would be possible, even likely, were there not a second person involved in all this who stood to lose should Karina speak." Drake gazed out at the gathered witches as tension built in the air.

"Karina poisoned Crabtree, right here in this house, after picking him up and bringing him here in her car. But she did not mutilate his body or carry him into the woods. And now she herself has died to cover up who did mutilate and stage the body." Jess looked from face to face as Drake talked, trying to ferret through the information herself and prepare for the coming revelation.

"That, my dear Solinare, would take a man of brutal, impetuous strength. A man who could restrain Jess and knock her out as she herself snuck up on the silhouette of Karina as she attempted to break into the building where Crabtree's body was kept."

Surely, thought Jess, August was too weak for that, and why would he have set her to watching the guesthouse if he intended to be part of a break-in, or worse?

"A man," Drake continued, "who could convince her to cover up the original murder, who would know enough of the occult to impeccably carve a hyper-rune into Crabtree's flesh, who would have an extensive enough occult library to contain a rather rare book on hyper-runes in his collection, who would wish to frame Robert, who might have a use for a hyper-rune to overthrow a leader."

Drake turned slightly to face the High Priestess of the

coven, "I am afraid you, Selene, were the target of that sigil's magic, as your right-hand man, Robert, was the target of the attempted framing." Selene looked disturbed and angry in the face of this revelation.

Drake took a deep breath and let it out softly as if in surrender, "Finally, there is only one option. Only one man provided Karina with an alibi and was, himself, provided with one by her."

"Of course," Jess said aloud, suddenly identifying the strong arm that had grabbed her and the smell of cigar which clung to it as Solinare's own. "It was you! I should have known immediately."

"This is garbage!" Solinare burst out. "Pure garbage, and you have no proof." He turned to talking to the group in general. "This is the real frame job, perpetrated by Selene and Drake alike to get me out of the way. Don't you see? They want sole control of the coven."

"Selene already has control," Jess shot at him, "and it has been you who has been working against her. Everyone knows that."

Drake held up a hand pale and firm as marble, "Please, we can settle this." Robert had just returned from upstairs, again unnoticed. "My good Robert, what have you found in our Karina's room?"

"A journal," he stated.

"Very good. And what does it say?"

Robert opened a leather-bound journal and began reading. "I can't take it anymore, that foul man's blackmail. For a year, he threatens to tell my family and demands more and more information on the coven from me. I shudder to think what dear Lady Selene will think of me, or what that brute Solinare will do if they find out. But I shudder as much to imagine my family's response to the discovery of my study of witchcraft."

"Very good," Drake interrupted. "So Peter was blackmailing Karina, providing motive enough for murder."

"There is more," Robert said.

"There must be. Why drive him here? Why last night, of all nights? What was his plan? And what pushed her to the final fatal act?"

Robert began reading again, "Now he has changed, the beast. Now he claims to love me, after all this time torturing me and making me into the worst sort of betrayer! Love! As if the monster knows the meaning of the word. He has demanded I meet him tomorrow, the night of the ceremony. He wants to tell me in person, he says, and what's more, he wants to join the coven. Join the coven! He doesn't just want to use me, he wants to own me, each and every part of me! I won't let him do it!"

Drake nodded, "So, she follows his plan. Leaves the ceremony and picks him up to bring him here. No doubt, he intended to speak with Selene and Solinare himself. But first they sit, he confesses his love, she makes him a deadly tea, and all is done."

"So, she killed herself. None of this implicates me!" Solinare barked.

"You forget the matter of the alibis." Drake reminded him chidingly, "and the attack on Jess."

"Fine. Yes. I lied, and she lied. She came to me, petrified, and told me what she had done. She said she had gotten Robert's help moving the body and carving the symbol, but she needed an alibi. I helped her and, yes, I knocked out Jess to keep her from catching Karina and to keep Karina from doing something stupid. I knew Peter was dead, and knew Karina was panicking and might do something stupid."

"All very plausible," Drake agreed, "except that Robert would never implicate himself in that manner."

"You overestimate his intelligence and pin this on me based on that," Solinare shot back.

"Bernice," Drake said, turning to the old descendant of Salem witches who was deeply loyal to Solinare, "Will you go with Selene to Solinare's room and search it?"

"I want nothing to do with this charade!" Bernice spat out.

"All the more reason you are to be trusted, my dear," Drake responded. With a little more pushing, she finally agreed. They returned a moment later, carrying a copy of Edred Thorsson's book and a bottle of digitalis. Bernice looked crestfallen. "So, the book and the bottle."

"What? That bottle isn't even mine!" Solinare burst out. "Look at the label, it's Karina's handwriting."

Drake looked to Selene, who nodded. "But Solinare, they are standing on the other side of the room from you. How did you know it was her bottle, with her handwriting? The bottle isn't yours, but you know it. Know it, perhaps, because you took it from her room. I am rather certain that if we ask around, we will find several people who saw you make her the cup of tea." Drake looked around inquiringly, and several people nodded.

"Solinare, how could you?" Selene asked, while Bernice marched up to him and slapped him. Solinare growled and raised his fist, but Jess was there already and grabbed his arm in an iron grip.

"I think you have hurt enough women tonight," Jess hissed into his ear.

"Get off me, bitch," He shouted and spun out of her grasp. He stood rigid, his fists clenched, before the fire; his eyes shot daggers at Selene. "And you, you have never been fit to lead this coven. It is mine by right, not yours and Robert's. I cut up a body, so what? It's nothing compared to what I will do to you."

"And Karina?" Selene asked, slowly stalking towards him like a cat.

"She was a traitor, and weak to boot. And finally, a murderer. There is no loss there."

"So, you killed her," Drake stated, waving Selene back.

"Yes, damn it! Yes, I killed her, like I'll kill you, Drake!" He was crouching forward now towards Drake, looking more like a wild-eyed animal than a man: shaking, red, breathing heavy. "I know you, Drake, I know all about you. I know your enemies, the enemies that are coming for you even now. Closing in around you."

"My enemies," Drake said with a smile, "are my own. And not the least concern to me, to be honest. Your time tearing this coven apart is at an end."

Sudden police sirens could be heard pulling up to the house. Solinare turned from Drake and sprinted towards the back door where August had silently positioned himself.

Although he was more animal than man in that moment, the cadaverous reaper of a necromancer pulled Solinare up short.

"Peter Crabtree says hello, Solinare," August said softly. "He says he felt it as you carved into his flesh, but not as much as he felt you hacking like an amateur into his neck. He watched you as you tore off his shirt and cast aside his cross." August took a step towards Solinare, and the man stumbled back. "And Karina, ah, Karina has so many games planned for you even now. She is waiting for you, Sol."

August's voice became an almost perfect impression of Karina's. "Sol, Sol, you were supposed to protect me. You said you would help me. Well, now I can help you, Sol. I can help you pay for what you have done."

"No!" Solinare screamed and collapsed on the floor as police and EMTs came storming into the room.

"Officers," Drake said, "please arrest that man for murder."

❧

It was late afternoon the following day, and Jess still hadn't really slept. Solinare was safely in police custody, and all the details had been worked out with the appropriate officials. The police were not pleased with the delay in reporting the crime, and even less pleased that the delay had led to a second murder. It was a price they placed at Drake's feet, but an extended conversation with various high-ranking officials in both local and Federal Government encouraged them to leave Drake and his companions alone. Finally, they had been allowed to leave; Drake had a private limousine take himself, Jess, Robert, and — oddly — August to a small country restaurant halfway between Salem and Boston.

"I am sorry our outing turned out to be rather more eventful than planned, my dear Jess," Drake said while sipping a cup of tea and eating a field green salad with sliced strawberries.

"But," Robert added, "you have certainly saved our coven and not just from the publicity surrounding the murder. Sol was a monster and would have destroyed everything Selene had built if he wasn't stopped."

"But Karina was not a monster," Drake added, "I fear the coven failed her rather terribly. They should have known something was wrong."

"Lay that at Brother Sol's feet as well," August commented. "It was only because of the distraction of infighting that the group missed Karina's obvious distress."

"But I don't understand Crabtree," Jess chimed in, "how did he go from rabid anti-witchcraft activist and blackmailer to lover and convert to the ways of witchcraft?"

"The ways of the heart," Robert said with a twinkle in his eye, "are always mysterious."

"Not as mysterious, I think, as all that," Drake disagreed. "Peter was clearly desperate. One day, he is a passionate Christian, the next a passionate lover, and so on. Too often, those who burn the brightest are also the ficklest, precisely because their passion is filling some emptiness. But nothing is ever right to fill the void, and so every opportunity that presents itself is leapt at with equal vigor."

"Of course," August said in his usual whispery voice, "he

had no substance, only fury. But none of this matters anymore; what matters is what Sol said about your enemies. He had some dangerous friends, and he likely knew what he was talking about."

Drake shrugged, suddenly bored. "Undoubtedly, he was right, but it isn't new information for me."

"Drake," August's eyes were as intense as Drake's, "something is building, and anyone with any talent at all can feel it. You and I, we are two old magicians, and we know rather a lot that others do not. We've both seen more than is good for us. But it doesn't make us invulnerable."

"August, my friend, you are right. Something is coming, but it is rather bigger than my enemies. And beside it, societies of black magicians engaged in international conspiracies are child's play."

August squinted at Drake for a moment, his eyes becoming slits, and gazed into the distance. Then he grunted. "I see what you mean. Well, then you can deal with Andrew and his circle. But, when this other something, this bigger something, this darker something comes knocking, I would appreciate a call. I've been through too much to miss that."

August cackled for a moment, a cackle that ended in a brief wheeze. "I'd like to see the threat that can concern the great Drake." August hefted himself to his feet and shuffled from the restaurant, but Jess had the clear sense they hadn't seen the last of him.

"If you are in danger," she said, "I want to help."

"I assure you, it is unnecessary. I don't need help — yet." Drake gazed into his tea for a moment in thought.

"Besides," he continued, "I did not bring you here in order for you to make this your life. You have a very successful and busy world of your own waiting for you. I only brought you to dance with the fairies, the demons, and the witches to show you that other lives are possible for us, always."

Drake sipped his tea and looked into Jess's face for an extended moment, "I can think of no more encouraging a fact than a person's ability to reinvent their existence through conscious effort. Yet, at some point, we build ourselves a garret and live out our lives in that dusty hideaway for fear of leaving." Drake sighed.

"Karina reinvented herself, but in the end lacked the courage for such an endeavor. Thus, this sad spectacle we have been a part of. But you, you have grappled with killers, faced down villains, and helped solve yet another mystery! Take that back to your world and remember, we are always more than even we can know."

Territorial Imperative

The Parisian night glimmered like the facets of a diamond. The air buzzed with passion and elegant vibrance as a soothing summer breeze caressed the lovers strolling through the city's wide streets.

Sentiment filled the air; sentiment and the thrilling undertone of deception. It was a deception that always grows out of any beauty that fails to exist for its own sake. A lie is that beauty's nature, which seems to express everything and in truth says nothing. To expect anything else is to fall for the lie. The sparkle and flash of hedonism is but an empty wonder. Each majestic building and lovely pose of the late-night wanderers presented perfection without purpose and magic without meaning. Each moment revealed itself like a taste that captivates the feaster for a time, but which, later, can never be remembered clearly.

To this shimmering city of style's slaves traveled Drake, the mystic and mage. A wanderlust born of sorrow had captured the dark lord of the esoteric multiverse.

The plastic mediocrity of America had worn on his emotions, following the sad death of Jacob Harris and the tragic murders at midsummer outside of Salem. In boredom and apathy, the mystic fled to the ancient passions of Europe, passions that birthed themselves anew every season. So, he left the dull gleam of America's manufactured falsity for the blinding spectrum of Paris' style-laden emptiness. Drake had always been one to pick his own poison, and the best poison is the one that complements the mood of the victim.

The ball was superb, as far as such gatherings go, and all the golden children of Parisian high society were there. Also gracing the scene were the obligatory traveling rich of Europe, comprising several examples of the spoiled British nobility and the elegant Viennese aristocracy.

The center of attention, however, was Drake. He flirted, he danced, he made the evening shine with his own glory. The sun around which the dull planets of Europe's finest orbited, and the candle to which the moths of the small-souled flew, was Drake.

The music unfurled about him as Drake lost himself in the flow and caress of a waltz. The personage with whom Drake danced was none other than the fair Lady Dunivan, the Goddess of Europe's opera houses. She, not unlike the rest of the eligible ladies of the fluttering female contingent, was absolutely charmed by Boston's famous mystic. The dark grace and old-world elegance Drake exuded brought all the false pretenses of the modern puffed-up dandies to their knees. His wit had grown into something of a legend amongst the gem-studded poodles and arrogance-draped pussycat lords of Europe's high society.

The music ended. Drake made his way, along with his lovely lady of the hour, to a group of waiting acquaintances. One did not have "friends" in a group like that; one had associates and acquaintances. Anyone who expected more loyalty than that allotted for a footstool or doorman was bound to be disappointed in the end, if not injured socially as well.

The group consisted of Lady Dunivan's female friends, Mistress Gates, a gossip column journalist for the rich and boring, and Prince Richter of Austria. Prince Richter, who was lost in clumsy attempts to woo the lovely Lady Dunivan, had decided that the swiftest way to raise his own intellectual standing was to engage in futile philosophical attacks upon Drake. Richter fancied himself quite the aristocrat's philosopher and, in this case, succeeded in little more than insulting the refined mental tastes of Drake.

"My dear Marquis," began Lady Dunivan, referring to Drake by his official title as Marquis de Montferrat, "how did you ever learn to dance so well? I swear your feet do not touch the ground! You glide like the wind!"

Prince Richter, though outwardly all smiles and attempted charm, boiled on the inside and began to see Drake as real competition.

"Why, my dear," responded Drake, "my dancing was but a poor attempt to imitate the purity and perfection of your voice. All music holds a hidden meaning, and the dance that accompanies the music is most beautiful when it translates that meaning into moving form. I but reflect the genius of the musician by flowing with the divinity concealed behind the sound."

Richter laughed. "Come now, old chap," he drawled, "I suppose, Drake, you're one of those who claim there is beauty and meaning in everything, eh?" He chuckled. "I, for one, try to avoid such sentimental slop, seeing how it is rarely found in the reality about us. Life is a mixture of spectacle and tragedy, all glorious and diverting but meaningless in the end. One can do little but appreciate the luxuries that come one's way and see them for the empty outcomes of a void deterministic universe."

Drake sighed. "There we disagree, my boy. Perhaps we do not always see the meaning, but I assure you it is there. Even in this jewel-encrusted fantasy world, there is meaning, though it is hard to find beneath the empty pomp and fashion."

"Is that so?" murmured the spoiled prince. "Allow me to present an example then. This current tragedy that has so shocked Paris, how do you explain the meaning of it?"

Drake shrugged. "I regret I have but recently arrived in Europe and have no idea what spectacles the news might hold. Please enlighten me, sir." Drake's voice was smooth and civilized, as was his manner. He was a wall of perfect marble that Richter's attacks found impervious to distress of any kind.

"Very well, then. Two days ago, Jon Garner, the brightest star of the Parisian stage, was murdered. The entire city is in mourning. He was the soul of perfection in the city's eyes; young, friendly, rich, talented, and kind."

"Don't forget handsome," Lady Dunivan noted, provoking a bit of a scowl from Richter. "So very handsome."

"Yes," Richter agreed grudgingly, "Quite handsome. No one could have found fault with him, and all who met him loved him to the core. The police are baffled, for there is no motive to be found. Surely, this is a meaningless and awful crime, proving the arbitrary nature of the world, for so wonderful a human specimen to be swept up by death's terrible claws for no cause. Most likely, the murderer had never met him and killed him in a psychotic frenzy. Find me meaning in that, Drake, and I will consider becoming a sentimentalist myself."

Drake smiled and snatched a glass of champagne from a passing servant. "I am not a sentimentalist, sir, I am a realist. As for this example of yours, I would have you know that no crime is without motive. Psychotic frenzy itself has cause and meaning in its heart. This case is no different. There is a motive and a meaning behind the entire affair."

"Well then, Drake, I challenge you to prove it. Show me some meaning in this pointless crime," Richter heatedly responded.

"I will do more than that. I will solve the crime itself. In solving it, I will demonstrate that there is no event without meaning in this world." The group was hushed; Drake's amazing abilities of detection were legendary. Indeed, a large part of his fame grew out of the claim that there was no challenge he could not win and no puzzle he could not, in some way, solve.

"To begin with, tell me about this Jon Garner and the circumstances surrounding his murder," Drake requested.

Richter frowned for a moment, worried that he had gotten himself in over his head. Yet he was sure the murder of the brilliant actor was unsolvable or, at the very least, chaotic and random. Finally, he responded.

"He is, or rather I should say he was, one of the most famous actors in Europe and by far the most loved. He was working on a production of Macbeth at the time, a very unlucky play, and was returning home from a rehearsal when he was murdered. The weather was rather warm, so he decided to walk, even though the hour was late. He never made it home. His body was found stabbed in a side alley. The neighborhood was not a bad one, and nothing was stolen, so it was not an attempted robbery. He is known to have no enemies; indeed, as I said, he is loved universally. That is the entire story."

Drake snorted in derision. "Entire story, indeed! There is more bubbling beneath the surface here than in a room full of philanthropists, lawyers, and politicians. Be that as it may, there are several obvious options. One, you say he had no enemies, yet he was a successful actor. That almost demands enemies. Every part he won was a part someone else did not win. What of his other actors? Surely there is jealousy."

Richter smiled before responding, "Not at all, my friend. In fact, he was particularly loved by his fellow actors, even those he beat out for a role. He was kind to everyone. He went to particular pains to see that there were never hard feelings between him and any other actor. He had given up more than one role when he saw it was likely to hurt his competitor. He had no enemies in the acting circle. You see, there are no leads."

"One moment, please. Was there a struggle? Signs of a fight? And do the police say he was murdered in the alley or elsewhere?" Drake moved inexorably onward like a steamroller.

"There appears to have been no struggle; he must have been caught by surprise and killed before he knew what was happening. And yes, he was killed in the alley itself," replied the smug princeling.

"Marvelous! That narrows the options down drastically. He sounds like a sensible boy, yes? Good. Well, no sensible person would ever wander into a dark alley late at night for no reason or for a stranger. So, he must have been called in or led there by a friend or family member, a lover even. It also explains why there was no struggle. He didn't expect it. Did he have a fiancée? A wife?"

"No," replied Richter, his face beginning to show doubt. "He was one of the most eligible bachelors in Europe–" Mistress Gates interrupted him with a discreet cough.

"I'm afraid that is not exactly true," she said. "He did have a lover. It was common knowledge in the journalist circles, but he had personally asked that we be discreet, and he was such a nice boy. We didn't want to complicate his personal or professional life, and he was always so accommodating to us reporters, so we kept it to ourselves. He also wanted to avoid stigma." Sighing, she sipped her champagne, "He was such a nice boy, it's very sad."

Richter lost patience, "What are you talking about?"

"Oh, dear me. Didn't I make it clear? He did have a lover, a Brit by the name of Benjamin." She smiled slightly, waiting for her news to sink in. Lady Dunivan seemed completely shocked and Richter choked on his drink.

"Benjamin!" the prince burst out. "Jon Garner had a male lover? He was gay!"

"Precisely, my dear prince," replied Mistress Gates. "Now you see why he was so discreet. As open-minded as Europe is these days, it is still not nearly as open-minded as it should be."

Drake chuckled to himself, "Ah, I thought that might be the case. So, now we have a prime suspect."

"Oh, dear me, no!" blurted out Mistress Gates. "Ben couldn't possibly have done it, he is positively the nicest boy

— besides Jon, of course. They absolutely adored each other. In fact, Ben worshipped Jon."

"Well, perhaps they had an argument and Jon threatened to leave."

"No, I'm sorry, my dear Marquis, but they were to be married in secret in only a few weeks. The police spoke to all his friends, and there was no argument. Ben himself is completely destroyed by his death," countered Mistress Gates.

"Well, I shall have to meet Benjamin and anyone else who was close to Jon, his fellow actors as well. Fear not, I shall be the very essence of discretion."

Mistress Gates nodded. "I can arrange all that. We will all be happy to see his murderer brought to justice."

Drake shook his head sadly. "My dear, I'm afraid very few people enjoy justice when they understand the full implications of it. To catch a criminal, I have to get to know him or her and understand what makes that person human. They are as human as the rest of us, if not more so, for their fatal flaws. Once you have done that several times, you realize that every criminal is a terrible tragedy. Often, they have suffered more than anyone deserves to, and that is what has brought them to crime. There is always a reason, though, always some meaning behind the crime."

Richter snorted. "That, my dear Marquis, has yet to be seen."

"Perhaps, my dear prince. Then tomorrow the hunt begins. By tomorrow night, I should have the killer for you all, and for you, Prince Richter, I shall have a meaning."

❧

The sun was kissing the pale morning sky as Drake sat in his penthouse atop one of the finest hotels in Paris. Before him, upon an engraved oak table, sat what remained of his breakfast. Smiling, he slid one more piece of escargot into his mouth and sipped his champagne. He was watching Mistress Gates, who sat across the table from him. She had been summoned to his far from humble quarters at what most of Paris would consider an insanely early hour. Drake's only explanation was that he would like to have the mess of solving the murder over and done with by lunch. He despised eating while he was in the middle of a puzzle.

"My dear Mistress Gates, or shall I call you Bethany? Yes, well, Bethany, you have not even touched your caviar. I understand it's early, but we must keep our strength up if we are to run the murderer to ground before we luncheon." Drake had already made reservations at one of the finest cafés in Paris.

Mistress Gates was unsettled. She was used to luxury, but Drake was taking the matter to an extreme she was anything but used to. He understood, of course, the source of her anxiety.

"Oh, you will forgive my moments of eccentricity, won't you? You see, I am a firm believer in the old 'when in Rome' theory. And I, never one to be beaten, come only to Paris when I think I can stomach such a level of luxury as to make even an ancient Roman Emperor ill. I find it best to always play the game that those I wish to converse with are playing, and it is best to beat them at it. So, our little Princeling shall sleep to noon and awake to his caviar and cream while we have already had ours, and better. By the time he crawls from the bed where he spends his empty hours, we will have given Paris the answer to its greatest current mystery." Smiling, he sipped one more time at his champagne and then lit a cigarette rolled in gold paper, smelling softly of red wine.

After a moment of discussing the police report, Drake discovered a short list of Jon's close acquaintances who could not provide a solid alibi for the time when the actor was murdered. Jon's director was to be the first one they would meet.

Drake and Mistress Gates took an upper-class taxi to the theater district, where the director, one Francis Russ, had his office. They arrived at about 9 o'clock and were immediately allowed in to see Mr. Russ. Drake's reputation had preceded him, and nearly all of Paris knew that he was on the hunt for Jon's killer.

Mr. Russ was a legend in his own right, having made his fame for years on the Shakespearean stage in England before moving to directing. All Paris was atwitter when he was called from London to direct this production of Macbeth.

He proved to be more than accommodating, offering Drake a seemingly endless monologue about Jon's personal relationships with the entire cast and the acting world in general. Following his speech, he offered Drake a cigar, which was refused, and asked if Drake had questions of his own. Mistress Gates looked on curiously. Drake's smile was like that of a beautiful and attentive predatory cat.

"Actually, my friend," he replied to Russ' inquiry, "I have only one question which is the basis of my entire method. Why was a boy like Jon killed?" Drake feigned a moment of boredom as if the hunt no longer amused him, but his eyes were orbs of all-seeing fire.

"Well, sir, to put it simply, Jon was just too good." The director coughed uncomfortably. "Well, ya see, it's like this. Our world isn't perfect, and Jon very nearly was. He was too kind, too trusting, too loving to live unharmed. This city is a lovely and dangerous place, and there are always those who just won't respect the type of purity Jon had. He was bound to get crushed in the rush of life; he was just too good for the world. It's a cold and cruel place, this globe, and people like Jon just don't stand a chance here, sad to say." Mr. Russ stopped expectantly, and Drake chuckled.

"Yes, it does seem like that sometimes, does it not, my friend? Eventually, however, the shadows part and we realize that the world has reason and events happen out of necessity. Good and Evil may seem irrelevant, but one thing is unavoidable — necessity. Justice is not good, it is not evil, it is necessary, and it can never be avoided, Mr. Russ. Everything which happens obeys the one unavoidable law of the essential." Drake stared into space for a moment, and it seemed the speech had been simply an oral contemplation. "Well, I believe that will be all, my good sir," he said finally. "Please, come to the Café de Sade tonight at seven to see justice achieved and Jon's murderer revealed."

The director showed obvious signs of surprise. "Do you really think you can solve this by tonight? Jesus, it can't be possible!"

Drake chuckled once more before responding, "Fear not, my friend, the murderer will be present and exposed tonight at the Café de Sade. That I can promise you."

With that, Drake and Mistress Gates left the office and proceeded out to their taxi to travel on to their next stop. This stop was at the apartment of David Regrades, a fellow actor and close competitor with Jon. Just like Mr. Russ, he had no alibi. He was also well known to be the most egotistical actor in all of Europe.

His apartment was as ostentatious as Drake's purposefully overdone abode. All was silk and gold, everything glimmered and glittered and exuded the feeling of a shrine to the apartment-owner's ego.

"Well, I certainly didn't kill him!" exploded David Regrades after Mistress Gates introduced Drake and explained the situation. "This entire thing is preposterous! I haven't been able to work since this entire thing began. I'm ruined! Ruined, do you hear me! I can't act, can't think, not with all those suspicious eyes staring at me." The divo paced and gesticulated wildly, giving the feeling that he was on stage and not standing in his own apartment before Drake and Mistress Gates. He continued to extol the suffering the situation had placed upon his weary shoulders as Drake smiled and watched calmly. Finally, he cut him off in mid-sentence.

"Well, that's fine and good, my dear sir," Drake said, his

voice slightly flavored by sarcasm, "But I've not come to accuse you, or to take up too much of your time. I'm sure this has all driven you to no end of suffering; it's so terrible when some other person's death must inconvenience the innocent, no? Yes, this is indeed a tragedy for you, for a personage such as you to have to suffer so. I sympathize deeply." The arrogance in Mr. Regrades' face seemed to increase even more as Drake spoke, though that would have seemed impossible a moment before. He obviously missed the sarcasm in Drake's tone. "All I would like to know, my dear sir, is who would have wanted to kill Jon, and why."

The actor smiled slightly, "Well, it's right you should come to me, of course. Who but I could know Jon well enough to help solve his murder? I, with whom he was always trying to compete; always attempting, and failing, I might add, to outdo. Indeed, if there were any leads, I would know it, but there aren't. No one killed dear old Jon for a reason; it was just a random act of violence." Mr. Regrades' voice had a false note of finality and authority that rang through the room like the clash of poorly made steel.

Drake nodded soberly and glanced at Mistress Gates.

"Indeed. A random act of violence," Drake sighed. "If only such things were possible, life would be much easier to bear. Well, that will quite be all. Allow me to invite you to the Café de Sade this evening, where all confusion will be cleared up. I assure you that, following tonight, your mind will be put to rest about this matter."

The actor seemed amazed and disturbed by this declaration on Drake's part.

"What, tonight? All done in one day, eh? I'll have to clear out my schedule — which, if I might add, will take quite a bit of doing. But I'll be there, I suppose. Whether this mystery is solved by then, which I fear I find rather doubtful, or simply to witness the first time in history your legendary personage is stumped. No offence, of course, but I think you've taken the wrong challenge. Not every question can be answered and—"

He would have run on with his dialogue had Drake not interrupted. "Yes, very good. You'll be there, then, for my imminent defeat." Drake smiled and swept from the room with Mistress Gates. Once they were back in their waiting car, Drake asked if he could borrow Mistress Gates' cell phone, which he used to call Prince Richter. It rang for a moment or two, and then Richter picked up. Gates listened attentively to Drake's words to him.

"Ah, yes, old boy. Quite good, and yourself?" Drake's voice sparkled with a tone of cheerful camaraderie she was sure he didn't feel towards the pompous prince. There was also a lazy undertone of disinterest so common to aristocratic ennui. "Oh, wonderful — what? No. No, no end to the monotony. Quite an uneventful day, all in all. Yes, indeed, I'm afraid your mystery has proven disappointing for me. Good heavens, no, I've not given up. That's the purpose of the call. A challenge once taken cannot be put down, no matter how much we may desire to do so. Yes, dinner. Tonight, at the Café de Sade. Oh, doesn't the location suit you? Well, I'm terribly sorry, I've already invited the others. What others? Why, the others, dear chap. Indeed. Tonight. You know where it is. Cheerio!" Drake hung up abruptly on the still talking prince.

He then smiled and turned to Mistress Gates. "Tell me, my dear, did our darling little princeling know Jon Garner?"

"Know him? Yes, to a limited degree. They had met several times, and Richter wanted very much to become close to Jon. It would have added much to his esteem in Europe's social circles. In point of fact, he wanted to sort of adopt Jon as his personal actor, give him a royal sponsor, so to speak. Something like a court entertainer in a modern way. Jon, of course, could not stand the prince's arrogant façade and found his insincerity appalling. He was polite as ever, of course, and very politely rejected Richter and avoided him from then on."

Drake nodded. "I knew there had to be a reason he brought up this crime in particular. Jon's refusal was an insult, and he thus takes some level of pleasure, unconsciously perhaps, in the poor boy's demise. That is why it has so been on his mind, why he leapt so swiftly to bring it up last night."

Drake frowned and muttered to himself in thought before continuing, "And you, my dear, obviously knew him as well. But how well? In short, what were your feelings towards him?"

Mistress Gates smiled sadly. "Ah, Drake, I loved him, as I've said, everyone did. But it goes, I blush to say, beyond that. I absolutely adored him." Her look was wistful. "The dear boy stole my heart. Why, he could have called me at any time to run away with him, and I would have dropped my entire life for the opportunity." She laughed slightly. "I sound like a teenager with a crush, I know, but it is how I felt. He glowed, like the sun itself. He transcended us all, both in his art and in his humanity. I hate to say it, but I painfully lamented his preferring the male half of the population. I assure you, I'm not alone either. Every woman who ever met him must have fallen immediately in love. He was a wonder, and a wonder lost to us. Such a shame."

Drake looked at her piercingly. "Such a shame? His being gay or his being dead, my dear?" His voice was, for a moment, flat and direct. Her eyes snapped to his in surprise, and then she looked away uncomfortably.

"Well, both, I'm sure. There are many forms of walls in life, and the boundary of his temperament was just as real for me, for us, as the harsh wall of his death." Her voice was defensive now, but Drake smiled and chuckled to put her at her ease.

"Many forms of death, then, my dear?" He chuckled again and then gazed out the window as their car eased through the city traffic.

"Drake, where are we going?" she asked.

"Didn't I say? Why, to lunch. I have worked up an appetite."

"But, you said you wanted to solve the puzzle before lunch, something about not eating while in the middle of a riddle, no?"

Drake smiled. "Of course, my dear, and I'm afraid I've quite solved it. The answer has been obvious for some time. There is only one possible person responsible. Now that I've concluded that, we can eat."

"But who? Oh, do tell me? And how can you be sure?"

"Whom? Come now, and ruin the surprise? No, no, my dear. You will have to wait, like all the others, until tonight. Now, to lunch."

❧

Lunch, which Mistress Gates had presumed would be an event to rival Drake's extravagant breakfast, was to be a very different affair. The place to which the driver took them, at Drake's behest, was a lesser-known, rather dim, and moderately seedy café in the more bohemian part of the city. The coffee was of the classic watered-down variety served in bars or diners, and the food was mediocre. It was the atmosphere, however, which Drake was hungry for. It presented a far more honest, eclectic, and interesting side of humanity.

Following the greasy lunch, Drake lounged back in the booth, gazing at Mistress Gates over the smoky light of a guttering candle while smoking a common cigarette such as one might buy in any convenience store. The contrast struck Mistress Gates hard as she struggled to understand this strange and confusing genius.

"Well, Mistress Gates, what has our little adventure today taught you of the paradoxical nature of man?" His voice was calm and content, but his eyes were acute.

"I'm not sure I understand what you mean, Drake."

Drake nodded. "Very well, allow me to elucidate for you.

Jon, the poor victim of some inexplicable tragedy, was by human measure perfect. Do you agree?"

She nodded.

"Universally loved, without any glaring flaw, undeserving of any animosity from any quarter?"

She nodded again.

"But what do we find? He has been killed violently. These facts point to an odd occurrence, a darker side to humanity."

Drake paused to tap his cigarette thoughtfully. "Observe the responses from those we have spoken with. Mr. Russ, his director, finds his perfection unnatural, a challenge to the fabric of reality, a thing lamentable. His purity becomes a weakness in Mr. Russ's eyes; it is a character flaw when placed within society, proper only for some recluse or hermit." Drake took a drag from his cigarette and exhaled a cloud into the air.

"Then we speak with David Regrades, who, jealousy aside, sees his death as a tragedy, if only because it places a burden upon his own shoulders. Jon's purity was a wall to Regrades; it was an insult to a man who works through deception and façade. It was an attack against Regrades' character. Thus, the simple act of 'being good' has become an assault."

Drake gave her a piercing look, "Hardly universally loved, my dear. Now, we get closer to home and look at dear Prince Richter, you, and me." Drake sipped his coffee and blanched slightly.

"To Prince Richter, Jon's amazing personality was also an insult because it refused to allow itself to be used for his own purposes. It was a tool that would not be of assistance, and thus an assault on his ego. For every perfection in Jon, Richter was made aware of an equally appalling lack within himself. Jon was everything Richter was not and could never be. He was real, and by being so, he revealed inadvertently that Richter was not. Jon reduced Richter to a shadow, and the prince was acutely aware of it on some level. Thus Richter revels in Jon's death, though he hardly admits this to himself."

Mistress Gates watched Drake closely, trying to discern the answer to the riddle Drake was weaving. From no suspects, he had suddenly made it seem as if everyone was a suspect.

"There is no virtue that goes unpunished," Drake continued. "Jon was all virtue and thus has been ultimately and completely destroyed by a world that cannot tolerate the insult of goodness. By being good, he made it obvious that goodness was possible; thus, everyone who is not good is blameworthy. He was the ultimate accusation against humanity. In point of fact, he was more hated than loved by many. Even in yourself, we find a gnawing bitterness and regret, seeing as how he was a perfection you could never have. Even in the nicest of individuals, his goodness bred disease of the soul."

Drake put out his cigarette and frowned, "Look at myself, who is even now using the glory of his virtue to my own ends. Where Richter failed to use him as a tool, I am succeeding. Thus, even within myself, his value breeds corruption and the drive to manipulation. He is the perfect playing piece in a game and a lesson, and I am using his disaster thus, with little in the way of a humane outlook on the matter. It is quite unforgivable." There was a long silence before either spoke.

Finally, Mistress Gates broke the uncomfortable silence. "But you're finding his murderer. Bringing the cold-blooded killer to justice! That, surely, makes up for any questionable motives on your part."

Drake smiled and shook his head. "Justice is a cosmic mechanism, my dear. Justice has been done, and I assure you the murderer suffers far more than I could bring about. I do not do justice; I reveal the workings of the universal imperatives. Justice takes care of itself, of necessity. And such justifications for my behavior you make are simply rhetorical; they in no way make up for the wrong. Now that we have finished lunch, we have one more visit to make and then we must prepare for the big dinner." Drake stood and offered his hand to assist Mistress Gates.

"But whom else do we have to visit?" she asked.

"Why, Benjamin, of course. Jon's bereaved lover may find closure in having his partner's attacker revealed. We go to invite the second half of the tragedy to the conclusive act. No loss is ever one-sided." With that, Drake sighed and led Mistress Gates to the door as if he were leading her to a funeral.

The address that Mistress Gates led Drake to was a rather expensive but nondescript townhouse in one of the nicer neighborhoods of Paris. The home had been shared by Jon and Benjamin, but now it was Benjamin's alone. They rang the bell and were met by a maid who told them directly that Benjamin was in no state to see anyone and would be indisposed all day. Mistress Gates pleaded, she cajoled, she maneuvered, all to no avail. The maid had obviously served her masters loyally for quite some time and was protective of the boy.

Drake murmured a word to Gates and took over the conversation. His method was direct. He looked the lady in the eye with an unbreakable and powerfully sincere gaze. "Madam, I appreciate and respect your concern, but please inform the master of the house that I have but a brief message and invitation for him, which promises to set his troubled mind at ease and place some closure upon this entire tragic business. He will not want to have me sent away, I assure you."

The maid scurried off to inform Benjamin about his visitors. They waited a moment or two in silence, and then the maid returned to show them in to see Benjamin.

They found him in the study. He was sitting, or rather hunching, on a couch and going through an album of newspaper clippings. He looked up as they entered. Benjamin was young, about twenty-eight years old, and had a slight build and dirty blond hair. His face was gentle, though now carrying the obvious signs of grief and prolonged weeping. His eyes were meek, and his voice, when he spoke, was soft and fragile. He seemed, at that moment, very much a small boy rather than a man of nearly thirty years.

He looked at them for a moment and then held up the book he was looking at. "My collection, every performance Jon—" His voice broke for a moment, and he looked away, and then continued in an even softer voice. "Every performance Jon had since the day I met him." There was another uncomfortable pause before he looked at them once more. "Hi. Of course, I've heard of you, Drake. How could one fail to? You are such an event in social circles." He then nodded to Mistress Gates, "Hello Bethany, it's been a while."

Bethany Gates smiled comfortingly and nodded back. "Yes, it has been a while."

The poor boy spoke again. It seemed difficult for him to talk, as if each word tore the terrible wound in his soul wider and deeper, "I'm sorry, I'm being such a terrible host. I never should have kept you waiting outside." He started to get up. "Can I get you two something? A drink?"

Drake quickly stepped forward. "No, not at all. We are alright, my boy. It is perfectly understandable." Drake's voice was warm and calming.

Benjamin sighed and sank back onto the couch. "Well, please, sit at least."

Drake shook his head in response. "No, we will not be staying long. We really do not want to disturb you. I would never have come at all had I not some form of comfort to bring to you."

The boy looked at Drake with a momentary hope, and then the hope died as if comfort were impossible.

"Having experienced all you have, this terrible tragedy. Having suffered and experienced so much, I am obliged to offer some form of release. Release from the terrible strain you must be under, and perhaps some closure to this awful situation. It is for that reason that I invite you to dine with me, and some other intimate friends of both ours and Jon's, tonight at the Café de Sade."

The boy flinched at Jon's name, as if feeling the loss all over again. Drake's voice became softer, smooth like silk, and Mistress Gates watched as the boy seemed to be enwrapped by it as by a comforting blanket. "This must be so hard on you. Losing Jon, such a brilliant blazing sun in an otherwise dreary sky. His spirit so potent, so vibrant."

Drake's voice had the tone of thoughtful reminiscence, as if he were thinking out loud. He didn't seem to notice as Benjamin stared at him and the let his shoulders shake with suppressed sobs of agony. After a moment of silence, Drake looked down at the boy.

He frowned in thought, then sighed. "It's ok, Benjamin, it's ok. Please, come to the café tonight, and everything will be alright. Let me give you at least some truth, by way of comfort. You will come, won't you?"

The boy looked up and nodded. Drake nodded back, "We should never have bothered you. I am sorry. I shall see you tonight. We can show ourselves out. Good day." Turning, the mystic led Mistress Gates solemnly from the grim and empty-feeling house.

❧

Night fell once more on Paris, bringing its lights like gems for sale under glass and its varied spectacles like accessories in a fashion show. The moon glimmered a bit too yellow, like thin layers of gold foil, and a bit too bright, like a cheap disco ball where once a chandelier had hung. The wind was soft and whispered; its words were suggestive but incomplete. Wine and spirits alone could add life to that brilliant hollow evening. Thus, people flocked to their parties, their galas, their bars and wineries to escape something that they couldn't see because it was an absence from which they ran.

The Café de Sade had all the dark, brooding, bohemian presence of a cheaper and less tasteful Parisian coffee house. But it also had the high prices and fancy clientele of the more extravagant section of Paris in which it was nestled. In brief, it was an attempt of the rich to capture the avant-garde, adventurous spirit of the middle classes and students. It was also a hangout for the incorrigible would-be philosophers and revolutionaries curled in the breast of Europe's rich.

Drake had specified, with the café's owner, that he was to have a large private party room in the back reserved for his six guests. One by one, they arrived to find the room furnished with fine wine, coffee, and quaint sputtering candles. Each appeared in turn: Prince Richter, Lady Dunivan, Mistress Gates, Mr. Russ, David Regrades, and finally Benjamin, who still seemed to be in rather poor shape and fled to the comforting presence of Mistress Gates. Their host alone appeared to be fashionably late.

There was little conversation, each person appearing to be rather surprised by the presence of the other guests. Many of them glanced at each other curiously, wondering who the murderer was that Drake was planning to unmask. When an appropriate time had passed for each guest to speculate long enough, for dramatic tension to build, and for enough coffee or wine to be consumed to calm the crowd once more, Drake strolled into the room.

"Late for your own party, Drake?" demanded Prince Richter. "That is hardly seemly. I do so hope you're not finding the challenge more difficult than you thought. There can be no backing out now." He stopped suddenly and glanced about, finally realizing that the whole game might be in rather poor taste. Everyone else was silent.

Drake smiled slightly, but seemed generally grim. "Not at all, old boy," he answered with a pointed condescension and familiarity that made the prince grind his teeth. "The puzzle is solved. In fact, it solves itself for any who would care to just look at it for a moment. But you'll forgive my pause, I'm simply parched." Smiling, he strolled to the table, sat, and poured himself some coffee. He sat back and sipped at it contentedly as everyone watched and waited expectantly. He seemed to lose himself in thought for a time. Finally, he came back and glanced around slowly, analyzing each person.

"Well, each of you is here at my behest, and each for a different reason. You, Prince Richter, are to learn that nothing is without apt reason, cause, and logic. You, Mistress Gates, are to be granted a top story for your paper. Lady Dunivan," he paused and smiled pleasantly at her, winking slightly, "are here to witness the prince's lesson and be sure he doesn't forget about it later on. As for the rest–"

The prince broke in brashly, "Oh, do get on with it, you puffed-up back-alley sorcerer!"

Drake frowned, his eyes sharpening. "Prince Richter, life isn't something that can be rushed through. Nor is it something which can be done with show and classy suits to hide lack of style and taste." Mistress Gates chuckled, and Lady Dunivan snorted in pleasure. The others seemed lost.

"Well, then," continued Drake, "onward. Each of you is here to receive a piece of truth, and more importantly, a piece of perspective. Life is all a matter of perspective, you see. Purity and torment, beauty and agony and fear, pleasure and pain, facts and deception, and lastly crime and justice; all are separated by little more than a twist of perspective. From one direction we see virtue; from another, we see the pain it can cause and the corruption it can spawn. Justice is one with crime. There can be no separation. The soul itself sews its own justice and reaps its own punishment."

There was a pause, and Drake sipped his coffee again. "Perspective. Now then, see Jon. The artist, the actor king, the talent. That boy, so beautiful, so full, so powerful. His virtue shone out into the world like a guiding star. That purity by which we can do nothing but measure ourselves as wanting, the mountain of humanity's perfection in whose shadow the rest of us can do nothing but toil on struggling, and from which we always fall short. Perfection, real or apparent, is a curse upon the denizens of an imperfect world. It makes every fault so much more vibrant in its ugliness. We have all stood in Jon's shadow, all bowed before his greater glory." Drake looked to Benjamin, "But none so much as you."

The man's eyes met and became locked on Drake's. "He must have been so strong, wasn't he, Ben? So kind, so good, so beautiful. And always with that driving will and blinding talent. He was perfect, wasn't he? He was everything and more to you, to the world, was he not?"

Ben tried to answer, but no sound came out.

"How did it feel, standing beside him as his partner and yet always feeling more that you stood behind him? Some are doomed to always overpower and always dominate their loved ones by accident. It is their nature. They are the sun from which we, simple moons, seek but to reflect their greatness back."

Drake's eyes remained locked on Ben's, "You were always a good man Ben, but never as good as Jon. You were always loving and loved, but not as much as Jon. Your talents were nothing beside his, your dreams as dust beside his actual achievements. How that must have made you feel." Drake sighed and shook his head. "He was your everything. It was deeper than that; he was more than your everything. He was you. He contained you, and you were but a part of him, while he was the incomprehensible whole. Not jealousy, but starvation. Not hate but love feeding off an emptying soul. Not anger but a sense of your own inadequacy."

Then Benjamin began to sob. "He — he — was too good — too good for me," the boy managed to say. "I — didn't deserve — no, he deserved so much — better."

Mistress Gates put her arm around the boy and tried to

comfort him. She threw Drake an enraged look. "Now see here, Drake, what is this all about?" she demanded.

Drake nodded. "I think," he replied, "that Benjamin is about to tell us himself." He looked at the boy who gazed weakly up at Drake. "Mysteries, while they add interest to life's monotony, are never healthy in the long run when left to fester within our souls. Come along, boy, it is over. Jon is gone. This won't ever end unless you speak, so speak now." Drake's voice was soft but firm.

Benjamin sobbed for a moment more and then sat up straighter and spoke, "I — I killed him." There were gasps from everyone at the table, except from Drake. "I met him after his rehearsal. I led him into that alley — and — and I stabbed him." The boy choked slightly and seemed to collapse on the table.

"But why, by god?" demanded Prince Richter, his face white with surprise.

Drake looked to him, his eyes spearing the man's soul. "Why, prince? Many men think themselves empty, lead empty lives and, more importantly, live meaningless lives. But they struggle through by denying all this to themselves. They can forget they are lacking any form of substance by losing themselves in jobs, in families, or perhaps in balls, parties, and high society. All these distractions from that terrible hole in themselves work to hide their own pain, their own sense of worthlessness. That is, until they meet someone who is not empty."

"In the presence of a person who is actually living his life the way it was meant to be lived — who has a sense of worth, purpose, and understanding — emptier people see the depravity of their lives. They have been hiding from themselves and thus have become nothing. Those who hide from their true nature and deny their own existence worship death by worshipping distraction."

"When they are taught by someone like Jon over a long

period of time what life can be, part of their mind turns animal. They can admit their own emptiness, their own lack of definition, meaning, and substance, which is close to a form of mental suicide, or they can escape or destroy the mirror that is revealing their true nature. Benjamin loved Jon. He could not leave him, could never flee him, as the earth cannot flee the sun. The only way for Ben to save his illusions and self-deceptions, which are the basis of what had been his entire life, was to destroy that which he could never bring himself to leave."

"It is one thing to stab swiftly with a knife, and quite another to escape the amazing gravity of a person like Jon, and stay away for the rest of one's life. The second option is just as much death as admitting all one's life has been a lie."

Drake glanced at the sobbing boy and sighed. "The curse of the strong is to live without a peer. The curse of the weak is to chance upon true strength in another."

matthew Macgregor sat in his study reading a copy of the *Aeneid*. Outside of his townhouse on Beacon Hill, a thunderstorm rattled the glass of his windows. The winds howled and clawed at Matthew's house as if they were seeking to tear the city of Boston to shreds. The thunder boomed like the voice of judgment, and the earth trembled before its terrible force. The gods seemed angry, working to dismantle the city stone by stone.

He mused that he understood why Zeus was god of thunder, and Thor, and all those most terrible and mighty of old gods. Thunder and lightning were the most fantastic forces that men hid from in terror, seeking desperately to make them reasonable and meaningful, until ultimately weaving their heavens and mightiest myths from them. His thoughts dwelt on myths of heroes, rising hope and crushing despair, fate and pride.

Fate and hubris were the topics Matthew kept returning to. The *Aeneid* was an epic poem about destiny, duty, and the individual who is always crushed on the way to destiny's fulfillment. Great things are accomplished at the cost of single lives, and countries are built on blood mixed with crushed bone. It was a powerful, if expensive, sealant.

The lives of the small, the innocent, the insignificant individual are always the ones sacrificed for the greater good. The hubris of greatness was to think that it is justified in demanding the sacrifice of the individual.

Matthew sighed as he realized all his reflections kept bringing him back to the same point. He was angry and felt more than a little betrayed. A confrontation was coming, one he had planned for the entire time his oldest friend had been away in Europe.

The time had come to teach Drake a lesson. He was, he had to admit, more than a little afraid — but he couldn't back out now that his mind was made up.

A particularly loud roar from the lords of cloud and sky shook Matthew out of his reverie even as a large gilded clock against the wall chimed the hour. Looking up, he cursed softly and stood to smooth his black three-piece suit. He would be late, and not just fashionably. He folded his maroon handkerchief to set off the black of the suit and neatly tucked it into his coat pocket, just peeping out enough to add some fire. He touched a button on his phone to page his chauffeur and strutted down the stairs to the door, grabbing a black umbrella with smooth ivory handle on the way out. He made a point not to open it until he was outside. Why take chances with luck? His Lincoln was waiting with its driver, and soon he was warmly ensconced in the back, smoking fine imported cigarettes smelling softly of rose.

He was at the Boston Museum of Fine Arts shortly after. He made a point of strolling into the reception hall where the gallery opening was being held as if time did not exist for him. To anyone watching who knew him, his nonchalance was obviously a front and defense for the poor social statement of being late. He tried not to appear ruffled and was soon sipping a glass of champagne and leaning against a pillar near the new acquisition for the museum. The entire contents of the gallery, mostly ancient Egyptian and Mesopotamian art, were new, but this specific piece was to remain after the rest of the show had moved on to New York and then Washington.

The piece in question was a religious statue, once central to a rather legendary and ancient religious cult in Egypt. The god, or rather goddess, depicted was the Egyptian goddess of Justice, Order, and Truth, Ma'at. The statue was black, and the figure was strong, stiff-backed, with a noble stance, and had a large ostrich feather projecting from the crown of her head. This was the feather against which the hearts of the dead were weighed to decide their eternal future in the afterlife.

Matt smiled and bowed his head, speaking his own silent prayer to the goddess, asking her to bless him. Justice, as so often pointed out by the illustrious Drake, was a terrible goddess who demanded almost perpetual sacrifice from her worshippers. Perhaps, this once, she would smile upon Matt and let her girlish whimsical side come out for a time.

Thinking of Drake, Matt glanced around slowly. He should have been back from his travels in Europe by now. In point of fact, Matt was supposed to meet him here. Matt was a little ambivalent about seeing Drake. Their last escapade, culminating in the death of Jacob Harris, had left Matt more than a little discomforted with his longtime friend. There was unsettled business, and part of Matt's prayer to Ma'at was inspired by the hope of bringing the brewing confrontation to a head sooner rather than later. It was, in fact, the reason he had been dwelling so extensively on the cruel treatment of humanity by the gods in epic poetry. Since the last time he had seen the mystic, the cruelty and inhumanity of fate and justice had become something of an obsession in his mind. It was unworthy of him, perhaps, but his thoughts often dwelt as well upon the topic of revenge.

Surely, Drake was not late as well. But no, there he stood in his impeccable suit, leaning on an elegant but ornate black cane with a fine silver handle carved into the form of an enraged dragon. He was in the corner with John Crisman, the inane king of Boston's offbeat social and artistic scene. The two stood before a stele depicting Osiris and his son Horus, and Drake seemed to be explaining the difference between the harsh authoritarianism of an Osirian worldview and the fiery and individualistic radicalism of a Horian philosophy.

Crisman seemed intrigued, but Matt was sure he understood not a single word. The man was friendly and distracting, but far from bright. Crisman had, however, been the leading political and financial force that arranged for both the arrival of this exhibit and the acclaimed acquisition of the statue of Ma'at. Crisman had mentioned to Matt that it was all done as some way to repay Drake for favors delivered. In other words, the statue of Ma'at was meant to be a monument dedicated, though secretly and personally, to Drake's almost divine sense of justice and amazing ability to establish it in all his dealings.

Matt chuckled to himself as he began to stroll over to the two. There in one corner stood human nature's extremes: the simple and happily ignorant, and the subtle, complex, aloof, and knowing.

"Greetings, gentlemen," exclaimed Matt cheerfully as he raised his glass to them. They turned, and Crisman smiled broadly, almost gushing.

"Ah, Mr. Macgregor, I had feared something had detained you, or that perhaps you could not make my humble show. I'm so glad you made it."

Matt nodded and smiled. "How could I miss such a spectacular display of antiquities, eh?" Matt turned and nodded to Drake, who stood watching, apparently deep in thought. "Greetings Drake, I trust your jaunt through Europe went well."

Drake smiled in response, a smile that was neither happy nor sad — a sort of reminiscent smile. "Europe has changed little over the years, and some things never change. My trip, however, was interesting enough. And you, Matthew, what have you been about?"

"Nothing much, just my usual distractions. I have been working on an essay for a journal of classical philosophy. It's a study of the concept of justice in the *Aeneid*. The book proposes a most interesting paradox and one, perhaps, which cannot be morally justified." Drake raised an eyebrow and then nodded.

Matt glanced about at the extensive and moderately bizarre collection of ancient relics and then looked pointedly at the stele depicting Osiris and Horus. "Well, it appears I interrupted you in the middle of a conversation concerning the progression of the equinoxes of the gods. Or am I very much mistaken?"

Drake smiled, and Crisman beamed. "Indeed, something to that effect, my dear Matthew," responded Drake.

Matt nodded. "Of course, I would expect such interesting conversation from you, my darling Drake," commented Matt, at which point Crisman broke in anxiously.

"But he had hardly even started to explain the idea. You must continue, I'm positively enraptured."

Drake nodded. "The idea is simple and can be developed into a surprisingly broad system. It was made public largely by the ceremonial magician and philosopher Aleister Crowley. Briefly, the world passes through certain periods of time during which given energies emerge as dominant for that moment of spiritual development. The idea uses the symbols of the Egyptian gods to explain a progression of Aeons. The first is the period of matriarchal societies, when the earth was worshipped under the guise of the mother goddess. The Aeon of Isis." Drake motioned with his cane to a large statue of the mother goddess Isis standing near the center of the room.

"Each Aeon lasts 2000 years or so, and following the age of Isis comes the time of her husband, the age of Osiris, the dying god. This is a time of authority, of patriarchal rule, and the key philosophical concept is that of a god who, like the sun, dies and rises again to bring a form of renewal or redemption to the world. Osiris is such a god, as are Mithras, Dionysus, and Christ. There are many such religions. The idea is that the similarities in religions, philosophies, cultural and political hierarchies, all grow out of a similar worldview expressing the predominant energies of that period.

"Within the last one hundred years, the beginning of a new Aeon was declared. Specifically, the Aeon of Horus, or the child god. We have had our time with the mother and the father. It is clear to us that the sun does not die and rise again. Rather, it is constant, so too are we learning that we do not need some external sacrifice to make us pure or redeem us. We alone can save ourselves. Likewise, one might hope we are realizing that external authoritarian governmental control is not necessary to rein men in, as if we were animals. Rather, we can learn to control ourselves and behave as civilized creatures rather than lowly beasts."

Drake twirled his cane in an off-handed manner while continuing, "This is all conjecture, of course, but the Aeon of the child is thought to be a time of stark individualism, massive creativity, and freedom in an absolute and stringent manner. The freedom to be precisely who and what one is, and nothing else. It's all a very interesting way to express the complex interplay of energy and historical movement."

"Perhaps you can assist me with a matter of slight confusion," Matt asked, smiling.

Drake nodded. "Perhaps."

"What of the Ma'atians? In the early 90s, a small group of Crowley's followers appeared with a book they claim was dictated by some inspiration from the goddess Ma'at, whose own Aeon, they said, was to follow that of Horus. Thing is, since Ma'at is the Goddess of truth and justice, she is an essential force in the makeup of the universe and does not seem to be constrained by the nice, neat time loop to which Isis, Osiris, and Horus correspond. Her Aeon is to be something much more like a state of mind, a dimension always present. Present even outside of time." Matt finished and awaited Drake's response.

Drake smiled slightly, enjoying the mellow challenge going on, "Yes, I've read *The Book of Ma'at*. What of it? It seems self-explanatory, not the book perhaps, but the idea."

"Well, it is, but the question is of the difference between Ma'at's 'justice' and the clear-cut authoritarian 'justice' of the Osirian age. What is the distinction?"

"Indeed, justice is a central issue of each age. Justice to the Osirians and Christians was based upon the concept of retribution, punishment, and revenge. An eye for an eye and all that. It was the justice of a king who swiftly smashed any resistance. Even the forgiveness supposedly ushered in by Jesus is bought through blood sacrifice. God the father, cruel and stringent, could only be placated by suffering. It just happened to be the blood and pain of his son and not all humanity. The base barbarism remains the same."

Drake's eyes grew distant as he continued, lost in the thread of his own ideas. "In the Aeon of Horus, justice is something which occurs naturally, or rather as a natural outcome of given actions. If a crime is committed, the criminals punish themselves or lead themselves to punishment. Justice becomes a fact of psychology, an extension of the laws of cause and effect. There is little moral right or wrong, but only a theory of balance, a dynamic balance that constantly adjusts itself. Every 'crime' is an act against the balance of the universe, but more so an act against one's own true self. If it is not, then it is not a crime. So, by committing a crime, I violate myself and am punished by my own will."

Drake frowned. "As for the Ma'atian justice, it's hard to differentiate it from any other. It's a complex theory with more than a little scent of fraud. I would imagine one would have to be part of the Ma'atian Aeon, which, as you said, is a state of mind or dimension, to understand its implications. I have made no such journey," Drake finished.

"It seems," Matt mused aloud, "that it will have everything to do with the heart and the feather. No stringent law of action and reaction, but rather a law of sympathy, passion, and the feather's touch of chance. A bit more chaos, a bit less cause and effect. Creation more than balance, and love over law."

At that moment, the curator of the museum appeared next to the statue of Ma'at to dedicate it and the rest of the collection. Crisman excused himself, having a part to play in the quaint little ceremony, leaving Drake and Matt together.

There was a moment of silence as the two stood together and waited for the speeches to begin. The silence was not to last, however, as the poet David Bore appeared and converged upon the two innocent gentlemen.

"My dearest Drake!" David gushed, "Oh, and the admirable Matthew Macgregor, so nice to see you both. How goes the life of the wise? Have you read my latest book? Rather daring, I know. Or so I've been told by hoards, and causing such a stir. I had no idea, I assure you. Who would expect such a humble piece to inspire such passion? I'm flattered, really. Who wouldn't be? So, I'm thinking of writing a mystery novel or some such next. I know. I know. It's not my style, but then neo-classical epics can get so old. You understand, I'm sure."

David appeared to be in one of his moods, which always tended towards the extreme, be they depression or exaltation. "Oh, and my next book, as I was saying. Yes, a mystery novel. Inspired, I might add, by your famous adventures, Drake. I do hope you won't mind. But—" Drake knew better than to even attempt to interrupt the flooding river of David's mind and speech, but finally he found cause to. With a word, he silenced the poet, though how none may ever know. It remains his greatest and most impossible accomplishment.

"Me?" Drake said softly. "I should think that a rather foolish idea, and would wholeheartedly advise against it. You will find nothing to write about but stolid pragmatism hardly worth anyone's notice. Plus, I am sure the public, with its usual acute and discerning mind, will swiftly smell any attempt at bettering its personal illusions, and thus tear the entire narrative to pieces through purposeful misunderstanding of the key passages."

Matt, finally finding room to speak, chose to add his own bit of humor, "Plus, I fear you'll find yourself enmired in the swamp of our brave hero's halo of mystery. Beware of sinking under the burden of the unknown. A reader can only take so many allusions to inscrutability and cryptic facial ticks."

Drake raised an eyebrow. "Come now, Matt, there is nothing mysterious about me. I simply keep to myself what there is no purpose in others knowing. I prefer not to air my every errant thought or the unimportant ornamentations of the past. People enjoy draping faded whispers of the past about them like pendants of honor or ermine cloaks of royal station, but they fail to see the dust and rot with which they become covered. We are what we are now, and that is what matters."

Matt nodded, "But of course. However, it is interesting to know the path that the vector has traveled to better understand the actions of the forces of the universe upon the object."

Drake smiled in return; the two seemed to be enjoying the sparring, but there was a tense current beneath the surface. David Bore watched, lost and stuck in a silence he despised.

"But my dear Matthew, the orbit of the star outlines the effect of all other bodies upon it. The presence of Pluto was clear long before it was discovered because of the force its gravity exerted upon the other heavenly bodies. So too with our lives. Our pasts can be read in the faces of the present, as the path of the future is writ in the current scene. These observations do not lie. But one can create any past one wishes while speaking of it to others. Call my silence honesty, perhaps, and the rest a practice in fiction."

"Oh, I say!" burst forth the poet. "What have stars or vectors to do with my book?"

At that point, the curator of the museum took the podium and asked for the audience's attention. It is this alone that kept matters between Drake and Matt from coming to a climax neither likely anticipated.

The curator looked like a model for the mummies it was his job to keep. Watching him, Matt was reminded of nothing so much as a weeping willow. He was tall and thin; in fact, every part of him was thin, from his narrow face to his string-like arms and legs. His skin was pale, almost like chalk, mirroring the white of the willow's bark. He was new to the museum, having taken on the post only that year after coming over from London.

His speech was academic and as bland as his looks, followed by a brief speech by Crisman that consisted of gushing. The audience found, a few minutes after the ceremony had ended, that they failed to remember a thing that either figure had said. Following the speeches, the evening rolled on with more champagne and conversations about the state of modern art, post-modernity, political debate, and similar themes. It ended with a universal invitation to an after-party at John Crisman's townhouse. The man was a glutton for parties, and a veritable whore for conversation of the avant-garde or artistic bent. Drake and Matt both bowed out for one reason or another, while the others enthusiastically continued the evening's entertainments.

๛

The next day found both Matt and Drake sitting in the Hasan Society, drinking tea and discussing the writing of James Joyce. Outside, the afternoon was a warm and sunny paradise whispering of the approaching autumn and the sun's imminent setting. The atmosphere of the club itself was relaxed and humble opulence, walking hand in hand with the dream of a society run by the intellectual elite.

On this given day, Matt chose to argue that Joyce's modern revolution in literature had, while brilliant, brought the art of writing to the very brink of the nonsensical. There could be no further development in that direction; rather, an entirely new approach must be found, or else all writing would tumble into the void of meaninglessness. Drake's response was mellow, and his entire form spoke of dedicated relaxation and ease. Within his own mind, he was on a hidden personal vacation.

"My dear Matthew, your view is too small, too precise. You miss the broad sweep of the history of artistic development. All new advances in the arts have walked the narrow ledge along the abyss of insensibility. Each new step is always breaking away from the old standards. To those who must think in the old standards, it always appears to be meaningless. By definition, anything outside of the ruling standard is meaningless. But the break from the old forms new standards that broaden the reign of meaning brings order to Chaos. Chaos remolds itself at our touch. Thus, we always find the insensible to have hidden meaning we never expected."

It was then that John Crisman charged through the club's doors in a panic. Crisman went directly to Drake, his face filled with anguish, while Drake raised one eyebrow calmly. "It's been stolen!" Crisman announced breathlessly.

"What has?" asked Matt with the air of one awaiting some new game.

"The new statue of Ma'at! Taken flawlessly from the museum of Fine Arts."

Drake sighed. "Calm yourself, my friend, have some tea. All shall be well, though I do fear you shall all make me nothing but a common detective."

In a short time, all were ensconced in comfortable leather chairs, sipping tea. "Now," Drake said once Crisman had calmed himself, "explain what has happened."

Meanwhile, Matt sat back and watched, interested in seeing what would come of this.

"Well, it's quite simple, really, my dear Drake. It's simply inconceivable."

"It is a rare man whose actions are inconceivable," countered Drake.

However, Matt spoke first, before Crisman could tell his tale. "How inconceivable must your own actions appear, Drake, when you chide us for turning to you as some petty detective, while you rush to the chase in the next moment. We simply turn to you as the disciple of that cold queen you would have for your goddess, namely Justice."

Drake watched Matt as he spoke, then frowned slightly and responded. "I do not act as some bloodhound, swift to track and slay my prey. Nor do I err in seeking to aid my friends. I seek and claim no queen, and I desire and need neither god nor goddess. Neither does Justice require me."

Matt smiled cheerfully in response. "How often have you expounded in flowing poetics upon the nature of Justice? It would seem you are indeed a thrall to love of this calculating maiden, Justice, the blind perpetual virgin. Perhaps the turns and mazes of man's destiny and soul are not so easily mapped as to be privy to the calculations of a mathematically minded blind hussy. There is a thin line, my darling Drake, between justice and cruelty."

Drake smiled slightly in return and sipped his tea before responding. "Fair enough, but there is a thinner line between sentimentality and the impotence of weakness. The minds of men are riddled with excuses and rationalizations. Each man makes his own destiny and answers to the dictates of that judgment which rests in the core of his being. We can but illuminate the workings of human nature."

Matt laughed, "Surely it is not necessary for one to be modest among friends. But the Wise must be wary since it is entirely unclear what is illumination and what is creation. But our friend is anxious," Matt said, glancing at Crisman, who appeared confused but still upset. "Please, tell us your story."

Crisman glanced at Drake, who nodded, and then he

spoke. "The facts are simple and completely mysterious. We had the dedication party, which we all attended, and then the party moved to my house, and the museum was closed. The guards made their rounds, and all was as it should be; the statue was still present. Then the cleaning crew showed up, at about midnight, and set to cleaning the remains of the party. They finished at about 2 a.m., the guard made another round, and nothing was amiss; the statue was still on display and did not appear to have been disturbed. The night passed calmly without any disturbance reported by the guard until the curator arrived the next morning. It was he who discovered the robbery and reported it immediately.

"It would seem the statue had been replaced by a new perfect replica, the only flaw was that the inscription on its base had been slightly misformed so that it no longer made sense. Now, the curator had spent time translating the inscription the night before because he was nervous about his speech and found that such exercises calmed his mind, and so he was certain that it had been correct the night before." Crisman finished and sipped his tea anxiously.

Drake frowned for a few moments and then spoke, "There is more to this than it would seem. The fake statue makes it unclear when the statue was stolen. The guard would not have known a real from a fake. Thus, the cleaners appear suspect, except for the fact that the statue has security precautions and alarms all about it. The guard would have been alerted to any robbery, and the guards were surely watching the cleaners on security cameras."

Drake spoke on while Matt sipped his tea and looked thoughtfully into the distance. "This would appear to leave one conclusion. The guard was in on it."

Crisman shook his head. "We were naturally suspicious of the guard who was on duty in the wing last night. We ran a background check, and he has worked for the museum for the last twenty years with a flawless record. Plus, the statue has almost no market value, aside from historical and academic considerations. The guard has no archaeological interests at all. He is a simple man with a wife and a son in college."

Drake nodded, "He would probably also lack the knowledge to create a fake statue. The museum is filled with works of much greater value; these are what should have been stolen if money were the motive. The guard is not the mastermind, but he could have been an accomplice. The key is that this crime was personal, and not about money." Drake stood up swiftly and began pulling on his long coat while reaching for his hat.

"Where are you going?" asked Crisman as he too jumped to his feet.

"To interview the guard. He may be the heart of this mystery. Meanwhile, you, Mr. Crisman, will contact your numerous friends in academic circles and get me a precise history of the curator's career."

Matt stood up as well, after taking his time to finish his tea. "I think I would like to propose a challenge and a bet. Call it something of a rematch of our ill-fated last wager."

Crisman nearly exploded upon this announcement from Matt. "How can you think of betting at a time like this?" he demanded.

"Oh, don't worry. The daring Drake is on the case. It is sure to be solved in no time. But just in case, I too will try to solve this mystery."

Drake raised an eyebrow as Matt continued. "I challenge Drake to a race. I bet my reputation as a master gambler that in two days' time, I will reveal who stole the statue of Ma'at. Drake, in return, will gamble with his reputation as a student of justice. If I lose, I am no longer a gambler. If Drake loses, he admits that his understanding of human nature is flawed and skewed to the side of calculation at the sacrifice of empathy."

The eyes of Drake and Matt met for a long moment, Matt's face frozen with a slight smile dancing on his lips.

Drake's eyes were as distant as those of Ma'at's statue. Finally, Drake answered, his voice puzzled.

"Very well, I accept. Though it would seem I have been flawed in some way already to not understand what has brought this on." There was another heavy silence. "In two days' time, we will meet at the museum, and one or the other of us shall disrobe this mystery."

Matt nodded, and the two shook hands, though Drake still looked perplexed. Neither Crisman nor Matt had ever seen Drake perplexed like this. It scared Crisman deeply, as if the foundation of the universe were shaking slightly. Matt, on the other hand, felt a thrill of pleasure coursing through himself. Drake and Matt left together to interview the guard while Crisman asked for a phone and more tea to be brought to his chair.

❧

A few moments later, Matt and Drake were speeding through the streets of Boston in the back of Matt's car. Drake spent several moments deep in thought and even confusion. Swiftly, however, this was replaced by his usual energy and hunger for the hunt. Drake longed to wrestle with the stubborn flowing chaos of reality and force the world to yield up its secrets to him.

They soon arrived at the guard's home, a simple apartment in the humbler parts of Boston. There, they found an abode rich in middle-class simplicity defined by cheap novels, football games, and the few feminine touches of style granted by a wife.

The guard, Francis Baker, was as innocent seeming as he had been described. He spoke with a heavy Boston accent, having lived in the city all his life and having never left the country. He was very distressed by the robbery and fearful that blame would be placed on his shoulders at the expense of his adored family's suffering.

"Please, do not worry," soothed Drake, "we are trying to

help everyone who has been touched by this crime. We were hoping that your recollections of the evening might help us in understanding this mystery."

Mr. Baker, though still nervous, calmed a bit and lost his defensive, frightened edge. "Well, it's as I've said, sir," he began, after his wife had offered everyone a drink, "I checked the displays after the party, and then again after the cleaning, and was monitoring the room on the cameras and watching the alarms at all other times throughout the evening."

Drake nodded while Matt just watched and listened. Drake took out his silver cigarette case and offered one to Mr. Baker, who refused. "Do you smoke, Mr. Baker?" asked Drake.

"Used to, close to twenty years back. But the wife wanted me to quit, for the family and all, so I haven't smoked since."

Drake nodded, "So you never left the guard booth to smoke? You don't have a set schedule of times when someone would know you wouldn't be in the security booth?"

"No, sir," said Mr. Baker.

"Please, call me Drake."

The man nodded.

"What is your relationship with the new curator?" asked Drake.

"My relationship? Well, there isn't much to it. Me being on the night watch and all, I've only met him a couple of times. We get along fine. Formally, I guess you could say as an employee to a boss. We've never had any problems."

Drake nodded again, his eyes sharp as an eagle's. "What do you think of him, his character?"

Mr. Baker thought for a moment. He seemed relieved that any implications of his own guilt seemed to have been dismissed.

"Well — hm — like I said, I don't know him well, just met him a few times. But he was reserved, like I said, formal — almost cold but more in a distant way than a mean or arrogant one."

"And you have never known him before? Never met him prior to his taking the job of curator?" queried Drake.

"No, sir, I mean, Drake. No, never met him before."

"And you saw no one unusual at the party last night? Anyone strange wandering around the museum? Anything else out of the ordinary?"

"Nothing of the sort. It was a perfectly normal evening. That's why I was so surprised by the robbery. There was absolutely nothing amiss all night. I would swear it, Drake."

Drake nodded. "Well, we thank you for your assistance. Please, don't be worried about all this. I am sure that it will not in any way reflect upon you. Please, excuse us, there is much still to do today."

Drake and Matt both stood and shook hands with Mr. Baker as his wife bustled into the room as well. Drake half bowed to her, and Matt went so far as to take her hand and gently kiss it as he bowed. They moved towards the door, but Drake paused along the way, as if having just thought of something, and turned back to Mr. Baker. "I am sure you are anxious to see all this settled, Mr. Baker. Please come to the museum tomorrow evening at nine, to the room where the statue had been housed. There, everything will be settled."

Then the two left the blushing Mrs. Baker and her husband.

In a few moments, both Matt and Drake were back at the Hasan Society, seated comfortably with John Crisman. Crisman, upon their arrival, asked them if they wanted lunch. He had already begun his own since he hadn't been sure when they might return. His lunch was a lovely platter of quail and mixed greens, admittedly a bit light for Crisman, but, in his own words, his "worried state made it hard to find the stomach to eat."

Matt smiled and requested escargot with puffed pastry, a

light salad, and the club's famous lobster bisque, along with a glass of imported Basque hard cider. Drake declined and asked for a cup of tea.

Crisman and Matt ate their lunches cheerfully while Drake sipped his tea and stared out the windows into the club's gardens. A violinist began to play in the entry hall, and Matt, having finished his lunch, sent for a glass of cognac and a cigar. Crisman joined him in this, and the two were soon cheerfully smoking away and discussing the state of British theater. Finally, Matt ended the discussion and asked what Crisman had found out. Drake's eyes seemed to come back to the present and focus on Crisman, who, for his part, seemed to have completely forgotten the crime and his earlier phone calls.

"Oh. Um, yes, but of course. Well, there isn't much to tell, really. I dare say our current curator is a frightful bore. Mr. Daniels is his name, Ferdinand Daniels in fact. He went to university at Cambridge and was quite a promising student of archeology. Went on several field studies in Yemen, Namibia, Cairo, and Brazil with several professors. He published a few papers while in university. Then he went to Trinity for his graduate work and got a doctorate in art history, French Impressionism to be precise. Around this time, his father died, leaving him quite a family fortune. He retired from academia and went into personal scholarship for most of his life. He has published several exquisite, if dry, papers on art theory and history. There has been talk of a book he has yet to complete. He then, apparently, got word of the opening for a curator in the Museum of Fine Arts here and decided to apply. Though his papers are few, they are greatly respected. He got the job easily and came to Boston.

"As for his personal life, there isn't all that much to say. He had a girl with whom he was supposedly quite in love during university, but she died rather suddenly shortly before he entered Trinity. He doesn't seem to have had any other lover since, and no one seems to know of any friends. He is a member of a riding club outside of London and has several acquaintances there. It seems he rode at least once a week and owns his own horse, which is still housed in England. He has no remaining family, and apparently very few personal attachments. He's a lonely and dedicated scholar. As for this crime, he has an impeccable history, completely free of any trouble, be it legal, academic, or social. I do say, Drake, I don't know what you were hoping to find out from that."

Drake nodded and took out a cigarette, lit it, and gazed once more into the distance. Matt took a sip of his cognac and puffed merrily away at his cigar. After a few moments, Drake came back to the present.

"John, do be a dear and contact the curator, Mr. Daniels, and have him meet us all at the museum tomorrow night around nine. Oh, call the foreman of the cleaning crew as well; he has a stake in this, also." Crisman nodded, and Drake turned to Matt, "Did you have anyone else you would like to attend the conclusion of our little game?" Matt shook his head cheerfully.

"Not at all," he said, then thought for a moment. "Though I don't see why we should trouble the foreman about it any, surely, he will hear about it when and if he is cleared of any blame. Let's leave him off the list, shall we?"

Drake nodded in agreement.

"So, this silly bet goes on, does it?" asked Crisman, glancing from Matt to Drake. "I hope you don't embarrass yourselves. Do either of you have any clue yet? It seems we have nothing to go on." Matt chuckled and puffed on his cigar some more.

"This is a wonderful flavor," commented Matt, glancing at his cigar. "I hazard to guess it's Cuban, quite adventurous, eh?" Matt chuckled again.

Drake looked to Crisman, who was looking confused.

Matt laughed softly. "Fear not, Crisman, darling," he said with a jovial tone, "both Drake and I are already certain about who is behind the replacement of the real statue with a fake. There really could only be one person behind it. Neither of us is likely to embarrass ourselves that much, at least not on that count."

Matt put out the stub of his cigar and finished the last sip of his cognac. "Well, gentlemen, if you will forgive me, I shall retire to my townhouse for the afternoon. I still have a touch of work to do on my *Aeneid* essay, and a few phone calls to make." He bowed and put on his coat with a flourish.

For Drake's part, the thought of the crime and who was responsible was hardly even present in his mind. Rather, his perplexity arose from Matt's behavior. He was mystified by the unexpected challenge and the apparent vehemence of Matt's hidden anger. Drake traced back the long history the two friends had shared, a history much longer and closer than those he shared with most. He finally found the core cause of Matt's feelings.

Months ago, during the painful strain of the vampire mystery, he had been too high-handed with his friend. He realized that he often forgot Matt's unique character in the flood of the far more common people around him.

Friends have a tendency to fade into the background, natural pillars of strength and warmth that one spends too little time considering. Drake, however, was rarely subject to such lapses of attention. He began to realize how distracted he had been for the last few years, haunted by a threat just beyond the horizon. The time had come for him to take greater care.

More so, he saw suddenly how his own character inevitably accosted those special parts of Matt that formed his impulsive charm. Drake saw how he could appear calculating to Matt, even though he had always been able to see beyond the arrogance that was often all others could see. Matt of all people, however, should know Drake well enough to realize that he was neither cold nor mathematical. It was, however, the air of understanding that Drake carried, which seemed to imply a certainty and determinism to all existence, that opposed and insulted Matt's impulsive and even romantic sensibilities.

Sighing, Drake looked across the room where the fine marble chess set sat before the fireplace. "Care for a game of chess, John?" he asked Crisman, who expectedly accepted. "Of course, it will just have to be a simple two-person game, I'm afraid, without a third player, we can't manage the more exciting four-player Enochian form."

Crisman nodded and finished his own cognac. "I suppose that can't be helped, Drake," he said, standing as Drake did. "What do you think of this whole challenge? Surely, you're not worried about Matt beating you?"

Drake smiled soberly in response. "To be someone's friend is to submit to defeat at their hands. In some ways, that is what love is, and why it is so dangerous. It's a knowing sacrifice of security and power. Matt had me beat from the start. But defeats obtained at such a high price are always more curative than injurious. Love can never really harm; it just seems that way sometimes. Shall we play?" The two strolled together over to the waiting board.

⁊

The next day dawned in the expected way, bright with a minimum of glory that was breathtaking nonetheless. At least so it seemed to Matt, who greeted the rising sun from the roof gardens of his townhouse. He sipped a cup of tea and looked far into the distance, imagining for a moment that his eyes took on that haunting visionary quality so many observed and feared in Drake himself.

Today was the day, he mused, as he sipped his lightly honeyed tea. He had gambled much, though few would realize it. Having taken Drake off guard was triumph enough, but he planned to play that slight advantage to its fullest. He had to if he was to make his point, and the situation lent itself to his goals perfectly. He had suspected it might, the bizarre lack of motive in the crime hinted at far too much, and a few phone calls of his own the night before had made it clear that he was right in his assumptions.

Today, the incomparable Drake would lose to his friend and learn a lesson that had been too long in coming. Somehow, however, Matt suspected that the lesson was not at all what he had first intended. The situation had metamorphosed, as the intended point seemed to shift. It seemed Matt, too, was to learn a lesson, and the day's dawning was heavy with the tint of fate. He felt driven like Aeneas, forced on by the destiny of the gods, but he reminded himself that he was instead a justified Dido, come again to defend the innocent from the strong arm of fate and cruel justice. Sighing, Matt turned and went inside to rest for a while. He would not see anyone until tonight.

❧

That night, the stars shone crisp and clear, distant and watchful with a hint of irony and expectation. Drake arrived a few moments early at the Museum, but the guard knew what was afoot and let him in as he had been instructed. He entered to find Matt already there, wandering about the room and looking at the statues of Isis and Osiris. "Hello Matthew, prepared for the evening?" said Drake.

Matt nodded cheerfully. "Indeed, I am, my friend," he answered, "but I wonder, are you?"

Drake smiled. "I suppose we shall have to wait and see, shall we not?"

The others began to arrive, and soon the whole group was present: the curator Dr. Daniels, the guard Mr. Baker, John Crisman, Matt, and Drake. Crisman seemed excited, anxious to see what would come as the climax of the evening. Dr. Daniels was more bemused than anything else, but in general, he remained formal and showed little emotion. Mr. Baker was worried and unused to being called to secret meetings.

Matt was the very essence of calm and even radiated a touch of joviality.

Drake knew this to be his poker face, one he used only during moments of stress while facing a major gamble. Drake remained Drake — calm, reserved, and apparently unruffled. The confusion that had so haunted him the day before might as well have been a dream. There was a moment of uncomfortable silence as Drake observed each individual, and as each person glanced about at the collection.

Finally, the curator spoke.

"Well, I for one would like to know what is going on here." He turned to Drake. "Mr. Drake, we met the evening of the robbery, at the party. I have since heard word of your special talents, which you have dedicated to the solving of our mystery. I assume you have some answers, sir?"

Drake nodded slightly. "Please, Dr. Daniels, the name is Drake and Drake alone. No 'sir' and no 'mister.' As for the mystery," Drake glanced to Matt, "both my friend Matthew Macgregor and I have dedicated ourselves to solving it. We have been in a sort of competition to discover the statue's thief. I assume that we have indeed solved the mystery." The curator nodded, obviously seeing himself as the authority figure in the group and thus the one in charge of the proceedings.

He was about to speak again when Matt interrupted him.

"We shall need your services, sir," Matt said to the curator. "You are to be the judge of our little gamble. At the end of the evening, you will decide which of us has discovered the person who is responsible for the statue's robbery." Matt then looked to Crisman, "John, you were present for the original bet, and so are to be a judge as well. You are also here to see that whoever loses lives up to his side of the gamble." Next, Matt looked to Mr. Baker. "Mr. Baker, you are here because you have a rather personal interest in the mystery and so should be present for its solution."

The curator looked confused by all this for a moment, then shrugged. "Well then, Mr. — umm, well then, Drake. And Mr. Macgregor, please enlighten us."

Drake glanced at Matt. They met eyes for a moment, and it was clear Drake was offering Matt the option of speaking first. Matt smiled at the kindness and waved for Drake to reveal his findings first. Drake nodded and ran his eyes over the entire room.

"The mystery of the robbery is a simple one, despite the fact that the perpetrator tried his best to cloud the entire issue in confusion and misconception. In point of fact, we were all led very smoothly to assume that the statue was stolen the evening of the party, but to an observant eye, it becomes clear that this need not be so. There is only one person who could have committed the crime due to knowledge and direct access to the statue. There is only one person who could say clearly that the statue was present before the party and missing the next day. Only one person could have had the knowledge to both create a replica statue and to replace the real with the fake. It is the same person who alone would notice and could show that the statue was a fake."

Drake turned to the curator, whose face was smooth as glass. "Dr. Daniels was the only man who could have noticed that the new statue was a fake; he is the one who identified it as such to clear his name of blame. For why would the perpetrator reveal his own crime, except that he realized it must eventually be revealed and that by revealing it himself, he would cloak his actions in the light of innocence. We have only Dr. Daniels' word that the statue disappeared the evening of its dedication; only he could know when it was real and when it was a fake. We were led to look to the cleaning crew, to the guard on duty, to any number of other seemingly impossible options when, in fact, the real statue had most likely never been present in the museum at all. We have only Mr. Daniels' word that it was ever present. Most likely, it was stolen the moment it was taken out of shipping, placed somewhere safe, and replaced with a replica from the start. All this was done by Dr. Daniels, the man who stole the statue."

Crisman gasped, and Mr. Baker whistled through his teeth. The curator's face was calm, accepting he was found out.

"Yes, I'm afraid that is quite true," the curator said softly in a sad voice.

"It would seem you win again, Drake," said Crisman in an awe-filled voice. Matt, however, stepped forward at that moment.

"I am afraid there is a bit more to it than that," stated Matt, glancing at Drake. "Are you finished, my friend?"

Drake nodded and replied. "Yes, there is something more, I am sure. I, however, am done, though I have yet to figure out the most important part. Namely, why Dr. Daniels stole the statue."

Matt nodded in response. "I can clear that up Drake," he said, just a touch smugly. "You see, you usually rely on me to do your side research during a case. My contacts tend to be more thorough, and I know the type of information you would usually be interested in. I knew, as I am sure you did, from very early on that the statue could be replaced by none other than Dr. Daniels. However, I was also confused about his motive."

Matt strolled to the empty display case where the statue had stood, then he turned back to face Drake. "You yourself said that the theft must be a personal one and not motivated by money. After hearing what information John had dug up on Mr. Daniels' past, I realized that the motive must rest there. That afternoon, I did my own research that, through only a little trouble, revealed the heart of the issue."

He turned to glance at Dr. Daniels. "John's contacts mentioned that when Dr. Daniels was in university, he studied archeology and spent a good portion of time abroad participating in actual digs. However, something occurred to turn him into a recluse and make him give up archeology for art history. John mentioned that he spent time at a dig in Cairo, and that is what sparked a thought in my mind. I looked up what dates he spent in Cairo and researched the history of the missing statue. Turns out he was present, working under Dr. Alfred Whaite, when the good doctor uncovered the statue itself."

Matt turned and paced to the large stele depicting Osiris and Horus. "In point of fact," Matt continued, "the statue's discovery won Dr. Alfred Whaite, who was already very influential both in scholastic circles and government circles for having served in the British secret service during the war, a vast amount of acclaim and fame in the academic world. This was interesting enough and hinted at several possible motives for the crime, but I needed more information.

"The next part was more difficult. I spent a good portion of time tracking other members of the dig and finally got in contact with several of them. They were at first unwilling to talk for fear of some form of repercussion, but eventually, I got the full story from one of them. This was due, I would imagine, to the fact that Dr. Alfred Whaite had just recently died and so was no longer a threat. It would seem that Dr. Whaite did not find the statue and the temple connected with it. Rather," once more, Matt rested his eyes on Dr. Daniels, "it was an undergraduate student who, through amazing insight and extensive personal research, pinpointed the temple's position and single-handedly uncovered the statue.

"It was an amazing find, but even more so for a promising young archeologist. It would have made his career, however, the already established and powerful Dr. Whaite wanted the find for himself.

"He could not stomach the thought of being outdone by a

student, practically an amateur. He used all his government power, academic strength, and reputation to take the find and the statue from the boy, claiming the discovery for his own. None of Dr. Whaite's colleagues would dare disagree with his claims, and the boy had no influence and so had no chance of achieving anything through complaining. I am sure the good doctor made it clear that he could, and would, ruin the boy's career forever if he spoke up."

Matt paused for a moment before continuing, "As should be obvious by now, the identity of the boy was none other than Dr. Daniels, who is the rightful discoverer of the statue." Matt paused again, and there was a weighty silence of amazement and shock. Drake nodded as he saw the pieces coming together and tears trembled in the cold Dr. Daniels' face.

"It was my find," the curator said finally, in a broken voice. "I worked so hard, I tried to share my research before the discovery, but the damn fool wouldn't listen to some silly student, so I went ahead on my own. I found that statue, I mapped its position, and I bloody well dug it up with my own damn hands. It was mine. It is mine. I raised it from the sands where it had rested, hidden for millennia, and only I had a right to it. It was my dream, my ambition, and he stole it all." Finally, the stern man sagged, tears running down his face, broken by the memory of his tragedy.

Matt nodded and spoke once more, "Indeed, you did find it, through the power of your own mind and your own perseverance. Against the odds of old fools and academic dogmatism, you uncovered the discovery of your career. Yours because your power retrieved it from the past." Matt's voice was soft and kind. Everyone else was silent.

"I couldn't stand it," the curator mumbled. "I would have, of course, given it to the world. I would have studied it and placed it in a museum where it belonged, having received my proper due. But all that was stolen. I hated it, hated that one man could take it away, my work and my dreams. I didn't want it on display for those who never knew its history, those who never aided me when it was taken from me, those who did not revive it from the grip of time and lost memory. I waited for years until I heard it was coming to Boston, and there was an opening for a curator. I leapt at the chance."

He looked to Mr. Baker, "I am sorry to have caused you so much worry, Mr. Baker, but you must understand that I was certain you would not be blamed. You had no motive and could not possibly have created a fake statue. If all went as planned, no one would be blamed. It would be an unsolved mystery, I would work here for a few years and then go back into retirement, with my statue — at last."

"And so," Matt concluded, "Dr. Daniels was only retrieving what he had earned." Matt turned to Drake. "I am afraid you did not reveal who stole the statue; you only revealed who the rightful discoverer of it was. The one who retrieved it. The thief was Alfred Whaite from the start, and the crime happened many years before the statue ever came to Boston."

"I concede," Drake said in a solemn voice. There was a moment of deep and timeless silence as the entire universe took notice of Drake's defeat. Then, as was his natural fashion, John Crisman broke the holy moment.

"But what are we to do about all this?" he demanded.

"It is really quite simple," responded Matt as he handed Dr. Daniels his handkerchief. "We do absolutely nothing. The police are at a complete standstill in this crime. They will never figure it out so long as none of us reveals it to them. Mr. Baker has already been cleared of guilt due to his past record and obvious innocence, and so no untoward effect will fall upon him. The statue was stolen goods, and so the museum and its insurance company are right to pay for the crime of trafficking in stolen goods. The point that the museum itself had no idea does not make things any better. It stands as a representative of the scholastic world and so should have done appropriate research into the matter. It remains responsible for what it displays. And, of course, the museum can keep the replica to display, now with an interesting backstory added to it. As for the statue itself, well, it is in the hands of the man who earned it. I would assume we can all agree upon that."

There was a moment of silence indicative of assent. "Well then, we all keep our mouths shut about this and continue as if nothing had occurred. Except, of course, for the matter of the bet," Matt looked to Drake, "the fulfillment of which we will have to discuss in private."

Then, the perplexing evening was over, those present dispersed and, with the bemused stares of the dumbstruck, went back to their homes. Most confused of all, perhaps, was Dr. Daniels, who, in one evening, found himself a convicted criminal and a vindicated victim.

⁊⦁

Later that evening, after both had retired to the Hasan Society for a drink to commemorate the end of the bet and the mystery, Drake and Matt strolled peacefully along the shore of the Charles River. There was a light breeze which set the water to lapping softly along stone and soil while the whisper of the overhanging trees played counterpoint to the solemn click of Drake's ebony cane.

Matt, in celebration, puffed on a cigar while Drake simply walked in contemplative silence, tasting the evening air like fine wine.

"Skewed to the side of calculation at the sacrifice of empathy, was it, Matt?" Drake said as they crossed a small bridge onto a long strip of island wreathed by water on both sides. The stars were reflected in the river's rippling surface as if the world swam with a sea of diamonds above and below.

"My darling Drake, I fear you have been mind and spirit so long that you forget what it is to be human, forget perhaps the heart or body," Matt replied. "But you have at long last received a lesson the likes of which you give others." A puff of smoke escaped his mouth to circle his head like a phantom crown.

"You are wrong, Matt. I learn lessons every day; only the monster stops growing. But I shall admit what you have won from me. I have at times fallen to the slavery of 'right' and 'wrong,' losing my perspective on the human heart. It is the risk one must take when creating or teaching. Men do not understand themselves, and so need objective illusions."

Matt chuckled, "So, your intimations towards justice are a lie?" he both stated and asked. They stopped walking and looked out into the river and into the night.

"A lie? Never that, Matt. All things are illusions when seen from even one level above them. Let us call it, rather, a generalization of nature. As I have said before, I do not accuse or punish. Nature does these things. I just seek to illuminate her ways to others."

"And develop quite an ego in the process, old boy. Very noble of you," stated Matt.

Drake shook his head slowly. "How long have we known each other, Matt? And you claim to not understand the difference between self-respect and some imaginary vice, the fear of which has been used to keep servants weak for millennia?"

"The difference is when self-respect harms others," Matt replied.

"You're right, I have learned a lesson. So many years spent together, and I never realized how I hurt you." There was a moment of weighted silence. "Well, I am sorry for that," Drake said, leaving it unclear if he meant the hurt or his failure to realize. "As for harming others," he said, "nature does not create equality, human fear does."

Matt puffed away at his cigar for a few moments thoughtfully. "Well, that is certainly true, but is not our destiny to rise above nature? Perfect its failures?"

Drake laughed in response. "Those thoughts don't even make sense, and you know it. If our destiny were to rise above nature, that would be completely natural. Reality has no failures, only complexities. We grow, we change, we learn, hopefully, all of which is the natural spiral."

There was a long moment of silence, and then Drake spoke again. "Fall is coming, I can feel the seasons turning. What are you to be about now, Matthew?"

Matt continued to stare out into the watery mirror of stars for a few moments, his eyes seeing distances that only he knew in that moment. "Hm, I don't really know. The wind calls me to fly, to put it poetically. I think that I shall away soon, to Europe perhaps." His words, though simple, seemed to hold a deeper meaning and carried a strange weight of import. Indeed, Matthew Macgregor was done in Boston for a time. He had spent too much time in the shadow of Drake, even if this shadow existed only in his own mind.

Drake nodded and knew that his friend would indeed be leaving soon, and that when they saw each other again, much would have changed.

"How about you?" Matt asked.

Drake smiled. "I, too, have the need to travel, only my path lies south for a time, and then west, I think. There are several old friends I need to check in on. It has been too long since I have seen much of the country. Though not, I think, just yet. Perhaps in a year's time, and then—" The wind picked up and the trees sighed a farewell to both of the parting friends. "Yes, the west calls me."

Archimedean Paradox

A city is not just a place of cold concrete and people lost in the rush of their own business. A city is more than cruel steel. It is built of the flesh of human fantasy and filled with the lifeblood of human passion. It is a monument to the indomitable force of humanity's arrogance and ambition. It is the ever-growing flood of the human lust for more. Every side of the complex creature Homo sapiens, every shadow of its multifaceted emotions, is entombed, embodied, and enshrined in the hodgepodge of the city's spider web of streets and alleys. Revelation lurks, it hides, and it dances in the dark throughways of the sprawling mind that is the city.

Thus, Derek found the city upon his move from a small town on the coast of New Jersey to the wild fluctuations of mass flesh that is metropolitan life.

"Derek! Boy, where is your mind?" asked the man he had just been conversing with before his eyes wandered to the window. He was one of a group of people standing in a finely furnished sitting room, sipping scotch and smoking rich cigars, except for Derek, who neither smoked nor drank often. The sitting room was part of the official building of an organization Derek had moved to Boston specifically to enter.

The *Order of the Golden Lamp and Ruby Flame* was an initiatory body dedicated to "bringing all the world to The Light."

Despite how it may sound, it was neither a Christian Missionary cult nor a den of rabid bigots; rather, it was an international organization of intellectuals participating in yoga, meditation, ceremonial magic, Qabalah, divination, and the basic disciplines of the Hermetic Western Mystery Tradition. It was more than a secret society of mystics, however. It was also rumored to be the political arm of a more mysterious group of "unseen superiors."

The small gathering was a party dedicated to Derek's initiation into the first degree of the order. Several of the order members were there to discuss politics, business, magic, or any other topic that might come up. Derek seemed to be of little importance to the group. Most were caught up in their own intrigues and lives. They ignored him or rambled small talk at him. All, except for one, seemed uninteresting, despite the fact that the group contained some prominent politicians, writers, and businesspeople.

The one who caught Derek's eye was a man in a three-piece evening suit leaning upon a black and silver cane and observing the gathering. He was tall, so tall that he hovered above the murmur of the other guests. There was something about this man that exuded power, a superiority that was real and not imagined, and yet a withdrawn, distant spirit and mind. He seemed to inconspicuously watch everything and everyone at once. Intimidating and yet reassuring, it was as if his presence meant nothing untoward could happen. Derek longed to talk to the man, but dared not even approach such an illustrious figure.

At just that moment, one of the older high-ranked fraters of the order walked over to interrupt the unknown man's vigil. Derek observed as the honored brother talked to the younger, elegant, and unidentified man. To Derek's surprise, the older frater was fawning and sniveling to the mysterious personage, who observed it all with a calm look of slight disgust. He waved his hand, seeming to shoo away the troublesome old man who was one of the most well-respected and feared men Derek knew. As the unknown man waved his hand, Derek observed that upon his finger was a most unusual ring. The ring seemed to have a lid that could flip back, possibly concealing a signet or seal of some kind. The lid was bent and dented, as if at one time it had been torn off. Upon it were several small pyramids made of the deep, rich blue stone known as lapis lazuli.

This stranger clearly had extreme power and universal respect to cause the older fraters to defer to him. Derek's curiosity was piqued but not to be satisfied. At just that moment, Brother Gregory Strob wandered over to Derek to discuss the importance of his vows of loyalty to the order and its members. Before being interrupted, Derek caught only a few words of the conversation he had been observing, but those tidbits revealed the mysterious man's name was Drake.

Frater Gregory was a teacher for Derek; he had been assigned as Derek's mentor, and it was Gregory who requested Derek's entrance into the order. Gregory was an older man of medium height and more than average girth. He had the look of an old librarian, wore lopsided bifocals, and was mostly bald. What hair remained to him was a distinguished grey. He was a kindly man who had been with the order many years and was widely respected for his vast historical and occult knowledge. In the politics of the order, however, he was a small figure, simply pleased to have the order's resources at his fingertips and never seeking political power beyond that which came with his age.

It was this man who swept Derek away from the mysterious Drake and into a boring conversation on inner order ethics and eternal fraternity.

The night rolled to a close, and Derek did not see the mysterious Drake again. He left the party, finally untangling himself from the long-winded lessons of Frater Gregory, and wandered to his apartment, which was situated on the campus of his university. The university was itself prestigious, and Derek was honored to attend with no strain on his already strained wallet. He had applied to the school with little hope of ever being able to attend, but somehow Frater Gregory and some other members of the order had pulled strings to get him a full scholarship. Derek was rather pleased with how his life was preceding precisely according to his dreams and plans, and slept that night with visions of greatness dancing through his mind.

The next morning, there was a voicemail from one of the University's deans. It seemed to be of a most serious nature. With a voice grim with worry, the Dean requested to meet Derek later that day to discuss a "grave matter that concerns you most intimately." Derek was troubled and called the Dean's office, where he was denied access to any information about the nature of the "grave situation."

Later that day, Derek sat in a self-important office as the Dean himself paced back and forth. Also sitting in the room were two serious gentlemen in official-looking suits. Derek smelled police, or something of the sort.

"My boy," said the Dean with a doom-laden tone, "I am sorry to have to involve one of my students in a situation of so serious a nature, but there seems little choice. These two gentlemen work for the Federal Bureau of Investigation. The school would like you to assist them in any way possible. Suffice it to say that your standing as both a scholarship holder and student here may well depend upon the matter." And with that, the Dean left the room, and Derek was left to the questionable mercy of the two officials.

The two mystery men left no time for Derek to wonder what was to come next. With crisp efficiency, they presented their credentials and badges and launched into the matter at hand. "Son, we are under the impression that you belong to a semi-secret organization that goes by the name of the *Order of the Golden Lamp and Ruby Flame*. Is this not true?"

Derek said that it was, in fact, true and waited for what was to come next. He knew enough never to volunteer any information not directly requested to any official of the Federal Government, especially when the information might bring him close to breaking the oaths he had sworn to his order. Derek was one of those rare humans with some shred of moral strength, one who actually considered holding to his word of honor once it was given.

"Boy," began the second man, "you may have inadvertently stumbled upon an international conspiracy and may be keeping company with a wanted criminal. Do you know a man who goes by the alias of Drake?" Both men's eyes bored into Derek.

Derek hesitated, so the other man continued. "This fellow, who goes by the name of Drake, is wanted by the FBI and the authorities in England in connection with a most serious charge of theft from the British Government and possible murder, as well as several conspiracy charges." The man who was not talking pulled out several pictures of Drake and then a picture of the odd ring Derek had seen Drake wearing.

"This is the item the suspect is accused of stealing. Perhaps you have seen it? It is likely that Drake would never go far without it, considering the trouble he has gone through to gain it. The ring was stolen from the private collection of a high English official who had it on loan from the British Museum.

"We have also received notification that this Drake is using the *Order of the Golden Lamp and Ruby Flame* as both a hideaway and a cover for several international crime rings. Now, you are a member of the order and privy to knowledge of Drake's movements. Have you seen him? Is he in possession of the ring? What do you know of his plans and movements?"

When Derek again hesitated to speak, the official raised his hand. "Please allow me to make your situation crystal clear to you, and I am terribly sorry that you have placed yourself in this position. As the Dean pointed out, the progression of your education here, and perhaps at any other reputable school, depends upon your participation in this investigation. Beyond that, should you fail to assist the Federal Government, it is not unlikely that you will be brought up on charges of obstruction and harboring an international criminal, to say nothing of conspiracy against the government. Think long and hard about your loyalties to your homeland, son."

Derek was not one to be threatened, nor was he prone to jumping conclusions without thinking a situation through. He smiled coldly and responded. "I am terribly sorry, gentlemen. This is a very shocking situation to find myself in. I am afraid it is so unexpected and shocking, in fact, that it has quite blurred my memory. If you could give me some time to think about it, perhaps I can assist you."

Both men grunted like predators who, moving in on their kill, are put off by a temporary obstacle. "Time, huh? Very well, boy. But don't take too long, we have been tracking this criminal for a while. We will be in touch, don't doubt that. Oh, and incidentally, this man Drake has killed before to obtain his goals. I would not doubt that he would do so again. Be careful, boy. Without the protection of the Federal Government, it is likely that you are in grave danger." With that, the interview was over. The gentlemen left without a word, and Derek walked numbly home, confused and angry at both the arrogance of the feds and the obscurity of his secret order.

A short time later, Derek sat dazed, confused, and alone in his small room, groping for some rescue from the illusions and lies lying all about him. His order was a circle of scoundrels and murderers, and their dark, sinful king was the man Drake. Were this true, then Derek's world was crumbling, and he had misplaced his trust. On the other hand, if it was not true, then he had been directly deceived by two federal agents and the Dean of his university. Derek was left with the choice of doubting the character of those he most respected or the columns of authority that upheld his society. He could afford to lose neither, or so he thought.

It was becoming more and more clear to Derek how fragile our sense of reality is, how dependent upon authority figures about which we never know much at all. An entire framework of realities is built around us by our own gullibility. Within these self-made prisons, we lie in a deep sleep, protected from any danger of awaking and seeing the real world which rises in all its glory before us. Yet, perhaps, even that world would prove to be as false as the bars with which we protect our imprisoned selves, were we to interrogate it. But one can't sleep forever and eventually stumbles, even if only for a moment, into the confusion of a world we never knew existed. It is the most dangerous moment in our lives.

His world swirling and tilting beneath him, Derek sought the only help he knew he could trust. He sought Frater Gregory. Derek's future was in jeopardy; it was a threat not easily ignored. However, Derek knew that his solemn oath to the order forbade him from assisting the federal agents in their investigation. He could not betray an order member or, if Drake was not a member, he could not betray a close friend of the order. The accusations cast by the investigators made it clear to Derek that it may, in fact, be dangerous to bring this up to the order heads. Frater Gregory alone could be trusted, removed as he was from any possible corruption by inner order politics.

Frater Gregory's face was stern and troubled as Derek told him the story of his meeting with the Dean and the government agents. Finally, the story was done, and Gregory sat and mused a moment in grim silence.

"Preposterous!" he said as if that settled everything. "You were right to come to me, and right to not betray your oaths to the order. That is beyond question, as you must see. As for these ridiculous accusations, there are many levels from which to view them. It is possible that they are true, on some level. Those high in the societies that run the world behind the scenes often act in ways misunderstood or mysterious to the common masses. To put it simply, they are above your reproach, and their business is in no way yours. You trust them, obey them, and leave it at that. There is also the possibility that all this is a plot or counterplot of some dark lodge that seeks Drake's demise. He has many enemies."

"Is he a very high member of our Order, sir?" Derek asked, wondering what made this mysterious man Drake so important.

"What? Our Order? Oh, he is not even a member, lad," answered Gregory. Derek sputtered in surprise.

"But— then what is the problem? Who is he?"

"Let me put it this way. Drake is not a member of our order, but he is a member of that greater, higher order which may well rule us all. To put it in perspective, if Drake decided he wanted to rule our order and be its Grand Master, he could but ask and be handed the entire bureaucracy on a silver platter. That, however, is not and has never been his way. He has more authority than even the head of our ancient and sacred order, and he is respected by countless other orders throughout the world."

"But who is he?" demanded Derek.

Gregory's answer only frustrated him more. "He is Drake. That is enough and more than any man can say. He is Drake." The old man saw the look of frustration on Derek's face and took pity upon him. "I am sorry they have put you in this position, child. Very sorry. But I cannot help you. The most I can say is that it is your future, and you alone must decide. It is my duty, however, to remind you of your sacred binding oaths. Break them if you feel you can and must, but understand that the penalty will fall upon your soul and your good name."

Derek wandered back into the streets more frustrated and confused than ever. When he arrived at his room, he found that there was a phone message from one of the two government men he had spoken to earlier that day. The voice spoke of the shortness of time, Derek's responsibility to the country, and the threat his silence placed upon his future. In agony, he sat in his room alone. He had to get out! He had to leave.

He wandered back into the now dark streets of Boston and caught the T to Cambridge, where a punk club he frequented was to be found. He dove into the masses of people and blaring wild sounds and sights as if to drown in the seas of humanity and no longer be Derek, no longer have to face these pressures. He allowed himself to be swept up in the chaotic music and soon was dancing and lost to all thought. Hours seemed to pass cheerfully away as he burrowed in his hole of induced trance.

Finally, he swept from the crowd, tired and relieved, still not thinking. The club was dark and set up in such a way that most of the place was open space for dancing. Only in one corner was there a dais-like section with a bar and several tables. He wandered over, bought a bottle of water, then set to finding a table or at least a chair for himself.

The only chair available sat at an already occupied table. At that table sat a man in a fine dinner suit smoking a cigarette. He should have stuck out like a spotlight in the dark, for the club was filled with sweaty, dirty, casually dressed college students, and this man most definitely did not fit a single one of the aforementioned categories. Yet, oddly, he blended into the dim lighting and dark. He simply sat back and watched everyone in the club, and seemed to be unnoticed by the crowd. It was only when he slowly raised a glass to his lips that Derek noticed the strange ring on his finger.

The man was Drake.

Derek was shocked forcefully from his escape, and everything he had been struggling with all day came crashing back into his mind. Here, in Derek's place of solace, was this man. Drake, who was the ultimate mystery, possibly an international criminal, dangerous, and yet the most respected man Derek had yet to meet.

Derek knew what he had to do; there was no other proper option. He had to bring the accusations he had been informed of before Drake and give the man a chance to defend himself. Shaking with nervousness, Derek walked as calmly as possible to the table and asked if he could sit. Drake's eyes met Derek's for a moment and seemed to bore through them into his soul. There was a second of complete stillness when the universe seemed to stop while Drake read every word of every sentence of every moment of Derek's life story. It all was open to him, or so it seemed to Derek. Then the strange mystic nodded, and Derek sat.

It was Drake who spoke first, "You are a member of the *Order of the Golden Lamp and Ruby Flame*, are you not, young man? Yes, I'm certain I saw you at the party last night."

Derek nodded, then found the nerve to speak. "You mean that you didn't follow me here?" This was all Derek could get out of his constricting throat. Drake scared him to death.

"Follow you? Why in the name of the gods should I follow you? Life is made of contrasts, as is all beauty. The aesthetics of the soul. I come here to appreciate that. Later, perhaps, I shall go to the opera and drive the point home." Drake's voice was calm and soft. His eyes had an unusual intensity, while his face showed some shadow of aristocratic boredom. He was scanning the hot, smoke-filled, rowdy room. He seemed to taste the atmosphere like rare wine, then he smiled languorously and turned to Derek again. "Well, speak. What is it that brings you over here? And why would I be following you? I'm Drake. Who are you?"

Derek stuttered out his name and began the story he had told Gregory. He had planned on being cautious, but that soon fled, and he found himself telling everything honestly and directly, including his own doubts about the honesty of Drake and the Order leaders and his fears for his future. When he was done, he fell into silence, and Drake watched him for a moment.

Then the man spoke, "And? What is your point, Derek? Why do you tell me all this?" That was the entirety of Drake's response.

"What?" Derek burst out. "Well, I wanted to let you know what was going on. I wanted to make you realize that I hold your life in my hands, and it's a responsibility I don't want. The authorities are hunting you, want me to help, and I can help to turn you in. Or I could keep silent and risk my future, but keep my oaths. Just defend yourself to me! Tell me it's not true. Tell me not to turn you in, or to turn you in."

Drake, to Derek's surprise, broke out into a laughter that seemed to ripple in the air and shake the entire structure of the place over the blaring music. "My life? You hold my life in your hands? I'm afraid you hold no one's life but your own in your hands, one way or another. And you incorrectly refer to the 'authorities.' Who are they? They hold no authority I recognize. I see that you have come to me so that I may make the choice for you. Well, that won't happen. This decision is your own. No one can or will make it for you."

Drake paused in thought for a moment before continuing, "Know this: if you do not help them, they will do everything they can to destroy your future and perhaps your life as well. These are not civilized or lawful men you are dealing with, even if they do work for the law. They may kill you as they threatened I would. You may indeed hold your life in the balance. You also hold your honor and your pride. You have sworn sacred oaths. Whether I am an angel or a devil doesn't matter. You are sworn to protect me, aren't you? The option is your future, and perhaps your life, or your honor and pride."

Derek stared at this man in agony, in wonder, in awe, and in fear. He spoke so calmly, so reasonably, as if he were only discussing the weather. "The question between life and pride is a contradiction. Ask yourself, rather, whether there is any life without pride. Can one exist without the other, or do you then exist only in shadow? I'm afraid all I can say besides that is that this ring is mine by right. It was promised to me a long time ago, and I have earned it. How I acquired it is my business, but it is my property. Those you have spoken with also seek it. I'm afraid it is currently the center point of a global game of chess. They will stop at nothing to acquire it, as, perhaps, did I. None of this concerns you, however. Your oath or your life. That is the entirety of your decision." Then there was silence, as if an iron door had slammed shut upon the conversation.

Drake sat, smoked, and watched the dancing kids while Derek stared in terror at the hopelessness of his position. He felt he had entered a game that there was no way he could play. He was a pawn. Everything the federal agents had told him was aimed at making him afraid, to manipulate him. Likewise, many things that Drake said could have an equal purpose. He was not sure who was manipulating who, and who was lying. Perhaps no one was, perhaps everyone was. The world had shifted from a concrete monument to certainty with given laws and truths, to a shadowy land of altering realities which were shredded and altered at the whim of any one of many powerful, mysterious figures. There was no reality, only an indistinct collection of claims backed by nothing but air.

Drake, the order, the government, the Dean, and his college might all as well not exist. Not a single one of them made the last bit of difference in the end. Each was, as far as Derek could know, inconsistent and illusory. Doubt had risen from its sleep to swallow Derek's universe and leave him with dust, ash, and images of memories and dreams. There was no certainty and no consistency; in the end, the boy had only himself.

Yet even one's moods and views waver and flow. In that dark club on that lonely night, Derek realized the world was shadow and his own self was twisting smoke. He could find nothing, no solid Archimedean point from which to build his reality. How changeable were his emotions? How alterable his being when a lack of food or sleep could set his reality swaying.

Derek had turned to Gregory and then to Drake for a solid point, and in each case, he had been given only a mirror. Upon looking into the mirror, he saw nothing solid, nothing certain, and no unbreakable or unbending law. Everything from the self outward grew meaningless in that moment. A seething black pit stretched beneath him, yawning for the shreds of his sanity, whispering for him to let himself go.

"Your oath or your life?" Drake had said. In a flash, Derek knew what he must do. He jumped to his feet, left Drake behind, and was soon outside in the crisp night air. Within moments, he was home.

When he arrived home, the federal agents were waiting for him. They had let themselves into his room, one sitting at his desk, the other standing over it, knowing that just a bit more of their scare tactics would crush the young student's resistance. Derek entered and saw them. Sighing, he sat on his bed across from them. They smiled a toothy smile, and one opened his mouth to begin an official-sounding speech consisting of veiled threats.

But Derek spoke first. "I'm afraid I cannot help you, gentlemen," was all he said in a calm, clear voice. They did not even bat an eye. They simply glanced at one another.

"Can't help or won't help, boy?" demanded the one. Derek shrugged.

"Is there a difference?" he asked.

"Boy, I don't think you understand the severity of this situation. If you are in any way withholding information, you are betraying your country," the second man said with intensity.

"Betraying my country? How do you two know how best I should serve my country?" Derek responded.

"You are aiding and abetting an international criminal.

You will not only be thrown out of school, you will be thrown in jail for so long your mother won't recognize you anymore when you get out!" The two men still didn't seem perturbed. It was usual for people to fight a bit at first, but the sense of calm about Derek troubled them. He should at least be nervous.

"You do not know whether or not I am aiding or abetting anyone," Derek answered.

The two men smiled grimly. "Yes, but we will know soon, and when we do—" The threat was left hanging. "Look, boy, we will get this man one way or another, with or without you. The only question is whether we will take you down with him."

Derek laughed. "That has yet to be seen, gentlemen. And I don't see any question at all. I'm doing nothing wrong according to my own morality, and that's the only morality which has any claim on me. You can threaten and bluster and follow through with your threats. But it will not change one single letter of my personal law. No other law exists. You can leave my room now. Good night!"

Both men seemed a little startled, but they were not about to give up. They could break this boy if they had to; all the paperwork had already been done to cover up any "unusual" methods.

"I'm afraid you will talk, boy," said the one man as he reached for his briefcase. "We have appropriate ways to create informants from accomplices."

Suddenly, the door opened wide to reveal Drake.

"Yes. You do have some interesting methods, don't you, Don? I always found them a little messy myself, though. I'm afraid you won't get the chance to use them here. This young man is not talking, that's his decision, and he will hold to it." Drake smiled and leaned against the doorway, spinning his black and silver cane idly in his one hand. He seemed cheerful, almost jolly, and completely at ease. "Well, Don, who is your lackey here? Why, Joey! How great to see you! I say, the government took you back? Even after that little incident in Taiwan with that hooker and the minister's strange death? How amazing! Andrew must have pulled a lot of strings to get you back to a position like this one."

Both men gaped at Drake in a surprise that melted into terror. They obviously knew each other. Suddenly, the man called Joey pulled a gun from his coat and pointed it at Drake.

The mystic in the doorway smiled before responding. "That always was your style, wasn't it? Force and muscle, but you lack fire, I'm afraid. Force is nothing without fire."

Drake continued to spin his cane and lean in the doorway. "So, Andrew must have sent you, no? Andrew wants the ring badly, doesn't he? Bet he thought he could have bought it from the thief in England who stole it from the rotting corpse. Now he is all upset I beat him to it, eh?"

Drake yawned slightly. "You all do get so tiresome," he mumbled and moved at last, strolling over to a chair while still ignoring the gun pointed at his chest. He sat and crossed his long legs.

The man called Don could take no more. "Shoot him!" he barked at Joey, who was obviously used to taking orders.

Drake swiftly raised a hand, the one on which the odd ring sparkled, and spoke. "Not yet, Don, not yet." Drake slowly and lazily raised both his hands, the cane still dangling in one of them. "I surrender. Andrew can have the ring, and me. Call him and let him know."

Don frowned, suspecting some sort of trick. "Keep your gun on him," he growled at last to Joey and pulled out a phone. He dialed a number and waited, and waited, longer than he expected.

"What the hell?" he mumbled.

"No answer?" Drake asked after Don had hung up. "Could he be busy?" Drake slowly smiled a predatory grin. "You see, things have changed a bit. Good old Andrew doesn't trust you very much. Not after you botched that assassination in Iran. Can't even kill one silly old sheik? Really, boys."

Drake put his hands down and resumed the slow spinning of his cane. "He has lost faith. Hired strong men are not good enough for him anymore. So, he resorted to his old tricks and decided the best way to get the ring from me would be to fight my fire with his. And you know what my fire is like."

Drake chuckled. "He has been spending the last three nights up in that silly tower of his in Scotland, chanting away over bowls of stolen blood and swirling about in the smoke of burning flesh. He was never any good at truly dark magic; he lacks the dramatic flair necessary for it. But I suppose he had done well enough for himself this time. He called up one rip-roaring hell of an infernal prince, horns and fire, howling servant demons, and all.

"Ironically enough, he was using the famous magus Crowley's copy of the grimoire *Lemegeton Clavivula Salomonis*. Allow me to mention an interesting historical gem, one of those quaint bits of odd knowledge that make such good cocktail conversation. On the front of every single copy of Crowley's edition of the *Lemegeton* is a magical seal to cause all magic done with that book to fail. During his life, Crowley used it as an assault on his one-time mentor, who helped him edit the book before the two became engaged in an occult war with one another. These days, it is just a jolly joke by the old Beast, Crowley; the seal has little power left."

Drake slowly raised his hand so that the strange ring with the pyramids of lapis lazuli sparkled and flashed. "But I have Crowley's ring, which he used as the focus of his authority. I knew what Andrew was up to and used the ring to recharge from afar the seal placed in the book.

"As I said, he got one hell of a nice demon prince to appear, along with a good hundred servant demons. That's when the seal interfered with his working. He lost his authority, and the demons went mad."

Drake smiled coldly. "They found his body today, at the bottom of his tower, broken into more pieces than you could imagine. The papers will call it an accident. But I think you and I know better."

Both men were now looking at each other in consternation. The hand holding the gun began to shake. "Well, boys? Don't believe me? Just check the papers tomorrow morning. Or call his second in command. You know he should have answered the phone or had someone answer it for him. Thing is, if I am telling the truth, then there won't be anyone with Andrew's authority and connections to protect you once you kill me and our fine Derek. Plus, neither of you has a use for the ring. You don't want to risk life in prison, boys. Or worse, maybe the chair?" Drake chuckled once more. "They hate federal agents in prison. Do you have any idea what they would do to you?"

Drake stood up swiftly. "That is what I thought," he said with a note of finality as his cane whipped forward and struck the gun out of Joey's hand. "Now leave here before I consider doing away with you glorified bumblers forever."

The two federal agents grabbed their things and all but ran from the room.

Drake chuckled deeply to himself one final time as he watched the fleeing feds. Derek stared at him in wonder and deep respect: he knew him now to be no man to trifle with.

"W—was everything you said true?" Derek forced out of his gaping mouth.

Drake turned to him suddenly as if he had forgotten the boy was present. "What? Oh yes — about Andrew? Of course," replied the smiling magician. "Andrew was a very old adversary. For many years, he was the head of the largest black lodge of magicians in Britain. It was located in the highlands of Scotland in an ancient castle he had renovated. As long as he stayed in Scotland, he was hardly worth noticing.

It was only after he began to go international that our interests started to clash.

"He wanted the world, you see, and using the funds from several corporate alliances, he began to purchase wide-ranging connections in most of the world's governments. He was looking to begin a full-fledged worldwide conspiracy, the silly old-fashioned fool. Well, we locked heads several times, and I never got around to dealing with him in any final way."

Suddenly, Drake's eyes became cold as ice and hard as steel. "He had a friend of mine killed in India a few years back and has been hiding from me, or trying to kill me from afar, ever since. I was waiting for him to show himself once more."

Derek still did not understand everything that had happened. "Is the ring really Aleister Crowley's? Did he really promise it to you?"

Drake gazed down at the ring for a moment. "Yes, it was Crowley's signet of office, and suffice it to say that those who gave him this ring promised it to me once he had completed his work. I was collecting what was mine. Andrew, however, had no claim on the ring but wanted to use it as the central spoke of a united occult front with which to achieve his own ends. That must never be and shan't be.

"You were a pawn for a time, not of me but of Andrew, and you proved yourself more than a worthy opponent. Fear not, however, Andrew is one necromancer who has botched his last rite. Crowley meant the seal he placed in the publication of his *Lemegeton* to be a joke, but it's a dangerous thing to overlook in the end."

Derek shivered, realizing that he had been given a glance into a strange world that lay behind the veils of everyday life. His entrance into the Order was also his departure from a simple life of ignorance. He was suddenly deathly afraid, for he realized he knew nothing of how the world really worked. Drake seemed to sense this and smiled.

"It takes most men who work their way through societies such as yours years to turn away from the illusions of child-hood 'realities' and enter a new one. Don't be deceived, though, the games always remain. The realities you see are just the edges of new lies that outline the form but not the matter of truth. Even old mystics must amuse themselves somehow, and one tends to develop eccentric amusements through the years."

Drake smiled a slow and casual smile that, for all its apparent ease, sent a shiver of anxiety to Derek's soul. He felt like a child who was being marched into battle before he could walk. He knew a world empty of security and was guided only by the constant star of his own will and integrity.

The crime was enigmatic, but more than that, it was frightening. An entire family was brutally slaughtered in the night: mother, father, daughter, and two sons, in Derek's hometown. He had a sneaking suspicion this was not an isolated incident and wrote to Drake in Boston.

The letter itself was simple, explaining how, having returned home for summer vacation, he experienced the collective horror and fear of his small coastal town at the sudden crime. Having spent enough time with Drake to absorb some of his unstoppable impetus, Derek had marched right to the scene and done some investigating of his own. All he had discovered was that the entire situation was a mess. The crime, while brutal, had been perpetrated with extreme precision, leaving only paradoxical clues. The police were at a loss, unable to find a motive of any sort. The victims, while a rich family, had no close relations beyond themselves. Thus, the inheritance was without an heir. Likewise, the father had long since retired young from business, leaving no business rival or vindictive partners. The mystery of the killer's motive was perplexing.

Derek closed the letter by stating that the FBI had been asked to consult on the case by the local police, but no one seemed to have the slightest hope of solving the riddle. For the families of the area, lest the massacre be repeated, Derek pleaded that Drake lend advice.

The day following the arrival of Derek's letter in Boston, Drake himself was driven into the small coastal New Jersey town Derek called home. As the young man watched the mystic's shining black Bentley pull up in front of his house, he felt he had witnessed the arrival of divine armies, angels come to harry Satan back to hell.

The form of the Boston sage, stepping from his car as his driver held the door, was salvation itself.

Derek met the man halfway down his modest front yard. "Drake," he said, amazed, "I never imagined you would come yourself."

"Derek, my friend," Drake said fondly, smiling. "How could I fail to come to the swift assistance of a comrade in distress? If I can, in any way, defend your noble family and silent town from harm, then may all the winds speed us on our course." Drake's overblown manner of speech revealed a certain joviality that nested in the hidden core of his mind, turning life into an opera or a farce.

Suddenly, the sparkle passed from the mage's eyes, as if they had been shrouded by storm clouds on distant horizons. "In truth," he said softly, "I come because I sense your instinct is correct, we face a very dangerous individual at work here. Brutal, smooth, and systematic. A machine, but one that can dream dark dreams. If he escapes us this once, he will never stop. We have this chance, this brief window while he is yet a young monster, inexperienced and more prone to mistake, in which to catch him. Mark my words, this demon is slick, terribly so, and his works will only become ghastlier and his trail ever more thoroughly covered. He is just beginning to learn his horrible art."

There was a pause filled by the sound of a lawnmower down the street, children laughing in a back yard, and a car passing, yet all of it seemed muted, strained with dread and expectation.

"Come," Drake murmured, "take me at once to the house where all came to pass."

And so together they entered the waiting car and proceeded the short distance across town to the grisly scene.

"What an interesting home," Drake said as they stepped from the car at the edge of the river that formed the southern border of the town. The house was designed with the river in mind, being positioned on a sprawling piece of land abutting the water. The front of the house faced the water rather than any road, and the gate that opened from the road led into a long, plain yard serving as a promenade along the water. Divided from this area by another smaller fence was a more private yard, complete with a deck and a pool.

"Why two yards?" Drake mused aloud.

Derek was swift to answer. "This first yard along the river was kept open to the public, to fishermen and sightseers, even though it was the family's private property. The other yard they kept more secluded."

Drake nodded. The house itself was ranch style, low and long, painted off-white with a red roof. An addition on its left side and of another story had left the once simple home looking haphazard and stacked, as if made of children's blocks. It was a testament to the swift rise from middle class to lower upper class that its inhabitants had experienced.

The scene itself seemed normal; the police had left no bright tape or warning signs to mar the character of the family's once-perfect utopia. Still, there was a lingering sense, an indelible mark, of what had occurred in this home. It was silence, a stillness that hung about the house as if the air itself were shocked into breathless horror.

Drake cocked his head to the side, as if listening to an unheard whispering. Suddenly, he spun around and stared out across the river, his eyes intently scanning the homes across the way and the fishermen scattered about. His face creased with a dark frown, and he turned slowly around to face Derek and the house.

"Let us go in," he said at last and set off, treading lightly, through the gate and up to the door. When they reached the door, which Derek was certain must be locked, Drake held the knob for an extended moment before trying it. When he did turn the knob, there was a resounding click, and the door swung silently open.

The foyer was empty of any sign of what had occurred, but Drake stood for a while, breathing the air like a bloodhound seeking a scent, before walking on unerringly towards the first-floor bedroom. The interior of the house itself was cool, and the air was heavy. If ever a place were haunted with restless spirits seeking release, it was this place, thought Derek as he followed Drake down the hallway.

"The killer came in through the front door, having forced the lock," Drake spoke absently. "He left marks there, slight ones as of a small crowbar. The family didn't use the deadbolt. He was certain, this killer, arrogant and sure of himself. He also must have been giddy, excited, for he could have been gentler on the door than he was."

They reached the door of the first-floor bedroom, which was slightly ajar, and the mystic nudged it open with his foot. Within, everything had been left as it was, with the bed slashed and covered in blood and the walls and floor splashed with gore.

"The parents' room," Drake said softly. His depthless eyes took in everything, though he touched nothing, and finally, he went over to a small marker that had been placed on the floor at the foot of the bed by the police. On the marker was a picture of the floor with a large, serrated knife soaked in blood lying in a small puddle. He frowned.

"He left his weapon here," he said. "I'm sure it was devoid of prints since it was left on purpose." Drake thought for a moment, then muttered, "No, surely not."

"What?" Derek asked.

"We shall see. Come, we must find the kitchen."

They left the room and wandered about until they found the kitchen. With delicacy, Drake opened the drawers and cabinets, using his handkerchief so as not to leave or disturb prints.

"I thought as much," he said at last.

"What?" Derek asked.

"Notice how clean and well-designed the kitchen is," Drake responded.

"Sure," Derek said with a hint of question in his voice.

"He left a kitchen knife in the bedroom. That makes it seem that he came in here first to grab the knife. He didn't, however. He wouldn't. It would be too dangerous to risk waking anyone. He had to get the parents out of the way right from the start, plus he was excited and wanted to go right to work. He entered and went to the parents' room, probably never even entering the kitchen. Therefore, he brought that knife in with him, and left it."

"But why?" asked Derek.

"Misdirection," answered Drake. "Our killer respects chaos. He knows that modern criminal investigation is a science, and nothing confuses science as much as random data and meaningless acts. He is giving the police leads to dead ends. Notice all the plates, silverware ,and knives in here are part of sets, all bought in groups. The first murder weapon doesn't fit a group; it doesn't belong here. The killer didn't know how neat and organized the kitchen was. He probably hoped that the knife would seem to have come from here.

"Despite his mistake, you can be certain the cops went over this kitchen in detail, finding numerous fingerprints of friends of the family, making them all possible suspects, while it's a dead end. This one is clever." Drake nodded and left the kitchen.

"You said nothing was stolen?" Drake asked.

Derek nodded.

"Hm — if my theory is right," Drake said as he led the way up the stairs to the second floor, "then we will find one room, perhaps a study, ransacked." And as they wandered through the empty house, they did find a small office that had been torn to shreds.

"What do you think, Derek?" Drake asked.

"I think we have come close to finding a motive. The killer

was searching for something. If we find out what is missing here, or what of value was held here, we can find the killer."

Drake nodded, "You are as good as any police inspector, and you may be certain that, even as we speak, the police and FBI are desperately in search of the mystery of this room."

Drake walked towards the children's rooms at the end of the hall. "However," he said, "if your theory is correct, then this room would have been the killer's main objective. Why the extreme slaughter? He could have broken in when everyone was out. Again, misdirection and confusion. That room was staged to distract investigators. His motive was killing and little else."

They reached the room shared by the two sons next and found it to be a classic kid's room, messy with toys, complete with bunk beds, but now stained on the floor and walls with blood. Drake didn't seem interested in this room, making only a few passing comments.

"Much the same carnage as the parents' room," he said in a precise scientific voice. "This, however, was done with a different weapon. Remember, the killer finished his work in the parents' room first, leaving that kitchen knife behind. He then came here and used a new weapon he had also brought along. One knife for the parents, one for the kids, as if the two were different crimes with one criminal. You see, he made a distinction, and that was purposeful."

Drake ambled out of the room, running his hand along the wall as if feeling the house's pulse. His face looked sad. Then they came to the daughter's room, and Derek felt his head grow light. The other rooms had been comparatively neat when faced with the atrocity within this last room. The walls, ceiling, and furniture were all splashed in vivid streaks with a little girl's sanguine life. Sheets, furniture, and even the wall showed marks of slashing, as if a wild animal had raged within.

Drake stood, silent and cold as a mountain staring at the endless procession of years and horrors of human history, while Derek grew lightheaded and felt himself slipping into darkness.

It was the hand of Drake, placed bracingly upon the boy's shoulder, that brought him back from the abyss.

"Hold, my friend," Drake's voice seemed to echo within the house-tomb, "this shall not go unanswered. This creature is dangerous beyond all account and, left un-caught, he shall do worse. But we, we are not allowed the luxury of horror or the retreat to oblivion. It has fallen on our shoulders to stop the beast that stalks these silent streets. Derek, for now, feel nothing, dismiss response, and let only your eyes see and your mind process.

"We must notice," Drake said in an analytic voice, "that the murder here far surpassed any of the others. Here, his savagery reached its peak. Why?"

Drake's eyes and question bore into Derek, who shuddered away from answering. "Is — was it a sexual thing?" Derek mumbled in disgust.

"A pertinent thought," Drake said, "and you can be certain the police have similar suspicions. This is false, however. Our society, our culture, is so thoroughly sexually repressed that we can never conceive of a sin or horror unconnected to sex. It is a fundamental self-deception, this clinging to the thought that our natural means of propagation is the heart of all life's horror; this deception is a hatred for the world and a fear of life.

"But this monster does not hate life, at least not his own. This is a great lover of pleasures, but not sexual ones. No, his taste is for the more visceral and primordial, the slaughter from the misty aeons when breeding was done in haste and rarely, but when violence and blood lust were constant."

Drake's eyes seemed to stare beyond the blank, bloodstained wall at which he gazed. "But let us not be mistaken," he continued, "this is no hunter we face, but a coward. He does not stalk police, the trained and the armed, but rather sleeping families, children — the weak." Derek noticed a tremble in Drake's arm, shivering down to his clasped fist, betraying his smooth face and empty eyes.

Suddenly, Drake was on the move, having spun around and begun a slow but purposeful walk around the room. "But there is sophistication in this evil. What of this enigma? Why the worst slaughter in this room, the youngest victim, the girl? Because — because this was the worst crime, the height of his evil. This monster has a conscience; he is no madman devoid of a sense of right and wrong. He knows the wrong of his actions, and this is what he enjoys, the forbidden pleasure he seeks. The hunger for sin, ever darker, but with complete consciousness and understanding of what he does. He knows good and evil, he just doesn't care. It pleases him to choose the evil in defiance, in crazed gluttony. The darker the act, the more the pleasure."

They left the house then, Drake leading with his mouth set in the grim determination of the hangman. "There is nothing more to see, for now," he said, but he was wrong.

As they made for the front door, Derek noticed something towards the back of the house, one more stroke in the tainted scene. To this, he drew Drake's attention. Upon investigation, they found a large stain, the remains of another puddle of blood, and a small stand holding a picture of the small dead dog that had occupied the puddle. "A parting joke, before he left the house," Drake said, his voice cold and hard as deep winter ice. He turned on his heel and stalked from the house.

When Derek caught up with him in the yard, it was to find him facing a police officer armed with a drawn gun. The cop was talking, demanding, covering fear with bombast. Drake seemed unconcerned.

"Well," the officer stated belligerently, his gun hand shaking, "they say the guilty always return to the scene of the crime."

Drake laughed lightly. "Only in cheap detective novels, my boy," he countered. "I am neither guilty nor a murderer. If you will investigate the note resting in my front right coat pocket, you will soon understand."

The cop seemed unsure, or at least unwilling to get too close to a person he suspected of being a serial killer. "How did you get inside there?" he demanded. "And what were you doing?"

"The door was open," Drake responded, "and I was investigating. Yet again, the letter will explain all. I would get it myself, but," he eyed the gun pointedly, "I wouldn't want there to be a misunderstanding."

Derek marveled. Drake was the only man alive who could look relaxed yet commanding while holding his hands in the air and facing a gun. So negligently were his arms raised with the hands opened to the heavens, as if in questioning, that one might believe he did not raise them by command but rather to illustrate a point.

Finally, the officer grew weary of the standoff. He cautiously edged over to Drake and drew a neatly folded collection of letters from his coat. He perused them, looking rather silly trying to read, hold his gun, and watch Drake all at the same time.

The letters were from the chief of Police in Boston and several high officials in the FBI, all commending Drake's crime-solving abilities to the officials in New Jersey.

"I could have letters sent from Scotland Yard as well, if you like," Drake offered.

The cop missed the joke. "My chief will have to look into this," was all he said.

"By all means," Drake agreed. "How nice to be offered a ride to headquarters. Coming, Derek?" It was only then that the cop noticed the young man, swinging the gun towards him.

"Oh, put that away before you hurt yourself," Drake said in exasperation, "and take us downtown or whatever a half-mile square town might call its cop shop."

The officer conceded defeat, and in moments, they were on their way towards "headquarters" with Drake's driver following behind in the Bentley.

They were brought to a small conference room within the police station, while the officer who had escorted them brought Drake's papers to his superiors. The police station was an old-fashioned affair, a one-story brick building located on what the town considered its main street. In the front was a small reception room with one person occupying a front desk. Beyond this point was a small, shared office, with one other private office for the chief in the back, and the conference room. Beyond that could be seen a jail space with two cells. That appeared to be the entirety of the town's police headquarters.

Drake was unconcerned; in fact, he seemed downright amused, while Derek felt profoundly uncomfortable.

"Don't worry, Derek," Drake said as they waited, "It is important that we meet with the officials involved in this case to gain access to them later when we may need them. This is quite convenient for us."

Within moments, the door opened to admit two men. One was the town's chief of police, predictably stout and ill-tempered, and the other was dressed in a common business suit that identified him as the FBI's man on the case. Drake's smile broadened while the agent's scowl darkened.

"Drake," the agent said with distaste.

Drake stood in feigned cheerful excitement, "Why, Agent Burroughs! How delightful that you're on the case," the mage gushed.

The agent grunted, "Yes, well, we don't need your help.

What are you doing out of Boston?" It was clear that the Fed knew Drake, and just as clear, he didn't care for him.

"Don't need my help?" Drake asked. "Delightful! Case closed, then? Mystery solved and killer captured. How wonderful! Capitol, truly capitol. I'll be on my way back north then, since everything is cleared up and there won't be any more murders cropping up." Drake grabbed his coat. "After all, my only concern is for the safety of this distressed town. I am sure you both agree that this case is too serious to allow matters of ego to interfere. But if peace and safety are restored—" He put on his coat. "Well, Derek, glad my help wasn't needed! So, gentlemen, who was the villain?"

There was an uncomfortable silence as Drake stood watching them in his long overcoat. "Well," the chief of police spoke at last, receiving a glare from agent Burroughs that made it clear who was in charge and who should be silent. The chief cleared his throat and began again anyway. "Well, we haven't apprehended the suspect just yet. But, well, we're doing just fine."

"Uh-huh," Drake said, his face betraying disappointment. "Perhaps, then, I can be of minor assistance in clinching the matter." Drake took his coat back off and sat down again as if the matter were settled.

"For Christ's sake, what are you doing here?" Burroughs demanded, causing Drake to flinch.

"Please," Drake said, "there is no need to use such language. I am here because my help was requested."

"Requested? By whom?" Demanded Burroughs, eyeing the chief suspiciously.

"Why, by this fine lad here," Drake stated, motioning to Derek. "Chief, Agent Burroughs, please sit. Make yourselves comfortable." Drake motioned to the chairs as if they were sitting in his own study back in Boston, and the two grudgingly sat at Drake's behest like servants in an audience with the king.

"Now," Drake cut off the agent as he was about to speak and looked at the chief of police. "You do not know me, and so are rightfully suspicious — what was your name again?"

"Uh, Benjamin, Howard Benjamin," responded the startled chief.

"Ah, of course, well, Howard, you are undoubtedly curious as to my credentials. By way of introduction, and to prove my aptitude as a — shall we say a consultant — I can reveal to you an element of the case which you already know, but I would be unable to know, unless I was as good as Agent Burroughs has no doubt said I am." This elicited a grunt from Burroughs, which made it clear he had said no such thing. "What's more," Drake continued, "I will reveal more details about this singular element than either of you has discovered."

The chief waited skeptically, the agent scowled even more, and Drake winked at Derek.

"You have by now had the bodies examined, and this examination has turned up a strange fact. You have found foreign, non-human, animal blood within the wounds of each of the victims."

The chief gasped, and the agent growled.

"But how could you know?" burst out the cop. "We have just gotten the results today."

"It's quite simple," stated Drake. "What's more, since the results are so recent, you don't yet know that the blood is that of fish. The labs will take more time to decide that. There is fish blood in your victims because the murder weapon, the one the killer brought with him and didn't leave behind, is a fillet knife used for cutting fish."

"Dear god," the chief gasped.

"Pointless speculation," the agent grunted.

Drake stood and put his coat on again. "Now, I must be off to arrange somewhere to stay for the duration of the case." Drake motioned the sputtering federal agent to silence,

"Don't worry, Agent Burroughs, it shouldn't take long."

Drake nodded for Derek to follow and swept from the room. "I will be in touch," he said as he left the two perplexed and still seated law enforcers in an empty room.

❦

Firmly ensconced in Drake's car on their way to Derek's home, the lad turned to Drake in surprise, "How did you know about the blood and the knife and everything?"

Drake smiled, "You mustn't be mystified by a bit of drama, my friend. The observations were really very simple; you yourself could have put it together just as well had you expended the effort. I am just more practiced, that is all."

"But," he insisted, "I still don't see it."

"Well," Drake responded, "let me elucidate for you. Look at what we know already. The killer was clever, seeding the scene with false leads. He spent a lot of time thinking about the crime before doing it, and he must have been familiar with the house. Now, we also know he used two weapons: the butcher knife he left behind to obfuscate, and another weapon he took with him. So, he has his own special weapon." Drake paused to tell his driver to drive along the beach to provide time for the two to talk.

"But now, to the heart of the matter, the killer's character. I mentioned that he is brutal, his psychology ultimately savage and sub-human. He loves slaughter, and he is also a coward because he doesn't seek armed game but rather the sleeping and children. Having no taste for the danger of the powerful prey, a formidable opponent, or even the dark woods, he is no hunter per se. This is further evidenced by the choice of murder weapon: a knife as opposed to a gun. In daily life, such a person will surround himself with blood and the chance to kill, but without extreme personal danger.

"So, he spends time taking part in the intimate, hands-on killing of smaller, weaker creatures. He must be a fisherman. This would give him time to watch the house and hatch his horrific scheme. And it fits his cowardly but brutal hunger. A rather common monster, this one, who revels in the blood that soaks his fillet knife and cutting board as he cleans his day's kill. The knife is central to his consciousness, so he uses it in his human slaughter as something of a joke — though it is rather more to him. As another joke, he doesn't clean his knife well, further joining his little victims from the briny deep with his larger, human ones."

Drake paused and stared out at the empty evening beaches and the endless expanse of the sea. "The sea is depthless, as is its memory. It may wait a lifetime to extract its price for misuse, but the account is always balanced in the end. The sea will have its repayment."

Drake seemed to realize his reverie had wandered and looked back at the young man. "You must always remember, Derek, that those hungers and drives which scream for murder are always the most bestial parts of the human mind. As such, they are the simplest as well. Murder may seem inexplicable, and killers somehow enigmatic and demonic, but most often they are as transparent and predictable as the common dog when you see through the smoke of your own horror. It is the complex and intriguing man who can suppress or redirect violence within himself. It is always the weak person who lashes out."

The car pulled in front of Derek's house. "Here we are. Go get some sleep," Drake commanded.

"Oh, Drake, you must stay here with my family," Derek insisted.

The mystic laughed and shook his head.

"Nonsense, I would never impose. Plus, my hotel suite will be far more comfortable than any guest room. Now, you must sleep well, for I will pick you up at dawn. Tomorrow, we go fishing."

Strangely, that night, Derek did sleep well despite the horror that inhabited a now-empty house only half a mile away.

If Derek thought that Drake had spoken metaphorically of fishing the night before, his mistake was swiftly corrected when Drake arrived with two fishing poles precisely at sunrise. Drake's driver took them back to the crime scene, and Drake informed him that he could leave the car and stroll along the boardwalk or visit whatever entertainments the small town might offer. They would have no need for his services until dinner.

Then the two strolled to the river, and Drake positioned them a little past the house. The day was spent fishing, though Drake never caught a thing and only half-heartedly held the rod. Most of his attention was focused on the other fishermen, whom he analyzed in an inconspicuous manner. He even wandered over and talked to a few of them about fishing, the area, and the identities of the most dedicated fishermen who frequented the river. Twice, Drake and Derek walked the short way to the beach and crossed the bridge to the other side of the river to analyze the people there.

By the time dinner approached, Drake seemed unsatisfied and even a little frustrated, while Derek had a nice catch of young bluefish for dinner.

"I'm certain I haven't overlooked anything," Drake muttered to himself as he packed up his things, then the air was pierced by the deep-throated roar of a boat horn. The two drawbridges that crossed the river, both upstream and down from where they stood, had opened wide, and along the river came a line of large fishing boats, some extending up to a hundred feet in length, all with strange names. The decks of the boats were crammed with what seemed to be individual fishermen, fisherwomen, and families. Drake's eyes lit up, the boats had passed several times that day, early in the morning and at lunch, but he had not taken notice.

"What are those boats for?" Drake asked Derek.

"They are called party boats."

"Ah, they take people fishing who pay to get on?" Drake asked, and Derek nodded. "How often do they pass this spot in a day?"

"Most of them pass four times," he answered. "They offer two trips a day, so they pass twice going out and twice coming in. Some of them offer a day trip and a night trip."

Drake nodded and smiled. He waved to the passing boats and then turned to head back towards the car. The driver had returned by then and helped to carry the poles and tackle, though he conspicuously showed no interest in helping carry the fish.

Then, with Drake in the lead as they approached the car, it exploded with a deafening roar into a solid ball of flame, showering debris everywhere. Derek screamed and threw himself to the ground, and noticed the driver had done the same. Drake, however, stood perfectly still — silhouetted by the inferno of his car as flaming ash settled on his shoulders.

Derek had never seen the enigmatic Drake angry, even when he was threatened by men with guns. He had never thought of anything that would make the mystic angry; it was too much like imagining angering a mountain or an ancient oak tree. But in that moment, Derek was sure he would witness the unimaginable.

The lad was suddenly very afraid, not of car bombs or killers, but of an anger that would resemble nothing so much as an act of God. Surely lightning would fall in terrible rain as an expression of rage at this insult. Surely the sea would turn wild with gales, and the Earth itself would rise at the mage's command to decimate his enemies.

All was still as if the sky held its breath and nature herself waited for the command to unleash her righteous justice. And then, Drake laughed.

With his head thrown back and his body shaking with the hearty depth of the sound, Drake laughed, and the tones soared to echo off the vaults of heaven.

"Come!" he said merrily, "It seems we must walk home. Lucky, the weather is so clear."

He set off at an energetic pace across the town for Derek's home with the two men running to catch up.

"You know, it isn't just clear, it is an absolutely fine evening. Just lovely," Drake said as they reached him. Then he laughed again.

"Are you all right?" Derek asked as Drake dusted char from his shoulder.

"Never healthier," Drake said lightly.

"Guess he just wants to scare you awake," Derek said, and received an odd look from the mystic. "Well, he set the bomb off before you got to the car and all."

Drake laughed again, though softer this time, and laid a comforting hand on Derek's shoulder.

"He didn't set the bomb off, Derek; it was undoubtedly connected to the vehicle's engine. But, you see, the car was equipped with a remote control starting device. My noble chauffeur had just pressed the clever device in his pocket used to start the car when the bomb went off. I'm afraid our killer very much wanted to kill us all. Worse luck for him."

A chill shot through Derek's body, and they walked in silence as he worked through the implications of Drake's words. Shortly, they arrived at Derek's home.

"I think we shall spend the night here after all," Drake said at last, "this man is more impetuous than I thought, and thus more dangerous. I could not stomach the thought of having anything happen to you or your family." Drake sniffed prudishly, "Plus, I can't stand taxis, and tomorrow we have another early morning fishing trip planned. Tomorrow our nets will bring in the big catch!"

❧

Drake didn't sleep that night. After protesting extensively, Alexander, his driver, gave in to the direct order to occupy the home's guest bedroom. Meanwhile, Drake spent the evening in a lonely vigil on the house's front porch.

There he sat, wide-eyed and almost motionless, sipping tea and periodically enjoying a cigarette scented lightly with sage as the still evening unfurled before him. He had mistaken the swift ferocity of his prey once, and it would not happen again. The man was a coward, but a dangerous and aggressive one. He would allow no harm to come to Alexander, Derek, or his family.

When Derek crawled from bed at sunrise, it was to find Drake fresh and energized, sitting in the family's kitchen, sipping dark coffee and having made a full breakfast. The thought of Drake cooking was ridiculous, yet the presence of bountiful bacon, scrambled eggs, pancakes, and even homemade biscuits was a testament to the man's cooking skills.

"Come eat!" Drake commanded. "And for the gods' sake, drink some coffee. We have a big day ahead of us, and it wouldn't do to allow the shadows of sleep to blur your mind."

Derek did as directed and launched into the delicious breakfast with abandon. When they had broken their fast, Drake threw on his heavy overcoat ("appropriate for a day at sea," he said) and set off on foot at a brisk pace for the boat basin in the neighboring town, where the large party boats committed to fishing were docked.

It was still rather early in the morning, but already the basin was a flurry of activity with the captains and crews of the ten party boats hawking and yelling in attempts to get the milling costumers on their boats.

The boats were many and varied, including several charter boats which took out only singular prearranged groups. There was the *Sea Queen*, a massive metal beast that fished for the rather brutal adult bluefish far out at the edge of the continental shelf, and which boasted a boisterous and rugged crowd. Beside her sat the smaller fiberglass *Captain Jerry*, a boat fishing for a variety of more delicate fish requiring a higher degree of skill, such as sea bass and fluke. That boat seemed to have a regular clientele made up of rather serious, older anglers. Then there was the *Soaring American*, a boat looking perpetually on the verge of sinking or complete deterioration, and the *Colonel*, which was so impeccably kept that it shone in the early morning sun.

Drake observed everything that occurred along the fragrant docks and discerned quickly the nature of the business rivalries and alliances. It had taken Derek two summers of working in the basin during high school to begin noticing these dynamics, and he filled in details Drake may or may not have needed. Some of these businesses went back generations and harbored generations of alliances, competition, and grudges. Others were new and desperate to destroy the older, more established businesses. Some boats were run by the former employees of others, and many of those breaks had not happened pleasantly. Crews were loyal to their captains, and while the captains themselves might try to stand above bickering, the crews sometimes engaged in savage acts of sabotage and manipulation. It was a lively, messy, and potentially dangerous place.

After lengthy observation, Drake began wandering the docks and talking to people about casual matters. His wandering had a focus, however, and he soon ended up at the far end of the docks, where he struck up a lively conversation with the captain of a dive boat dedicated to taking divers out to wrecks and reefs, who was not preparing to leave that morning.

The captain was an older gentleman who had spent most of his life running his boat. He was animated and talkative, a natural gossip.

As all the party boats filled with people, Drake discussed varied subjects involving the strange society of fisher people with the captain. Finally, he slid the topic to military veterans and his observation that they seemed to love the sea.

This was the trigger the captain needed to launch into an endless discussion of all the military veterans common to the basin, be they customers, captains, or crew. He listed their names and natures, one after another. All this Drake noted with particular interest.

About thirty minutes before the morning boats were to leave, the two companions returned to strolling along the docks with Drake observing each captain and crew member of each boat while remaining inconspicuous.

"Why the interest in veterans?" Derek asked at one point.

Drake shrugged. "It's a long shot, but any information may be useful," he responded. "After all, the making of a successful car bomb is no easy thing. We need someone with knowledge of demolitions and explosives. It could just as easily be someone who has worked in construction, a former mafia member, or a veteran. But an experienced hit-man doesn't match our man's profile."

"Neither, however, does a soldier who has seen action and shown bravery," Derek countered.

Drake nodded. "You are right, of course. Our man is a worm, not a hero, but not all military men have seen action or acquitted themselves well in the situation."

There was a sudden roar of many engines followed by the deafening notes of boat horns as the morning fleet pulled out.

"We shall wait to embark with the afternoon fleet. If we have no luck, then we shall look to the night boats," Drake said.

They spent the morning in the basin's small diner, where Derek read the newspaper as Drake stared abstractly into space, lost in thought. They had until noon before the boats that would return and depart once more for the afternoon would be back. Drake passed the time by talking with the elderly Greek lady who ran the diner and her charming daughter about the quality of the different boats and which would be the best one to secure a place with.

There were only two boats that had trips in both the morning and the afternoon. They both fished for the same prey, had an extreme level of competition with one another, and an accompanying violent mutual hatred.

As the two boats pulled in at noon, Drake and Derek stood in the parking lot and observed from afar as an odd bit of showmanship played out. The crew of each boat talked loudly with passengers about the size and bountiful nature of their catch. Fish were weighed against each other on large metal scales, held dramatically in the air for everyone to see, to determine who won the competition for the heaviest catch. People posed for pictures. The entire scene was designed for each boat to display its superiority over its neighbor to the waiting afternoon fishing crowd.

There could hardly have been a greater difference between the two boats themselves. One, *The Iron Hawk*, was a large metal vessel made up of flat planes and sharp corners. The other, *The Merry Princess*, was smaller and made of fiberglass, constituted entirely of graceful curves and with a prow that seemed to reach over the water in arching pride.

"Here is a pretty riddle, and a simple one," Drake murmured to Derek. "Take note of the people leaving each boat. Notice the differences in the crowds and ask yourself why some people gravitate towards one boat or another."

So, Derek observed, scrutinizing each custumer as he or she disembarked. At first, he didn't notice what Drake was getting at. The patrons leaving *The Merry Princess* seemed normal enough — classic fishermen, old retirees, and families with overexcited children. Derek began to see what Drake was suggesting when they turned to look at *The Iron Hawk*.

At first glance, this crowd seemed to be rougher, wearing ragged clothing and carrying decrepit equipment. But that observation didn't hold up for long. There were wealthy patrons there as well, driving away in their Cadillacs and Town Cars. There were families, too. The crowd wasn't more rugged, it just felt that way.

It was as Derek noticed the boat's captain that his subconscious observations clicked into place. The captain was tall and lean with dark hair peppered with gray. He had hard, cold blue eyes. As he bid his patrons goodbye, he failed to hide a sneer of contempt for them, and each of them held a similar smirk somewhere in their faces. Each smirk was different, but all shared the common gluttonous satisfaction of having gotten away with something.

Here was true camaraderie amongst thieves, the guilt of cheats worn as badges of honor. Here was the shrewd businessman, the bargain hunter, the wheeler and dealer — all stood as brothers and sisters bound in the filial bond of having cheated someone. They each felt they had cheated the world; they had gotten something by paying half its value, the captain had sold them something of no value, and they were warm and safe in each other's contempt. In reality, they had cheated only themselves. They had caught fewer fish than those on the other boat, but it wasn't about fish. They had received far less service and had far less fun, but it wasn't about service or fun.

Derek shuddered to think what it was about. Perhaps a subconscious hatred of all things honest and clean, and a life-long oath never to show enough respect for themselves or anyone else to match a thing's value with an equal value of their own. These weren't traders; they were thieves one and all, paying a few dollars less but robbing themselves of the entire point of their every purchase. Their sneers said that none of that mattered, only having somehow defrauded on payment. There were more of them than the simpler patrons of *The Merry Princess,* and that frightened Derek in some radically metaphysical way.

"That," Drake said, "is the host of our afternoon fishing excursion." Derek thought his choice left much to be desired.

At Drake's insistence, Derek maintained his careful observations as the two of them boarded *The Iron Hawk*. There were two "mates," or deckhands, and the captain. One of the mates was a middle-aged man, short and overweight, with the scarred and hardened features indicative of rough living. Derek noticed with a shock that he was missing a finger, and the mate took time to explain, "My father was a longshoreman out of Montauk, and he always insisted on one thing: never get on a boat without a knife."

The man pulled a long hunting knife from his belt and showed its wicked edge to Derek. Drake stood at the railing watching as the boat slid through the river's water and past the haunted house where a full family was slaughtered.

"I never much liked my old dad. He was a violent bastard away for months at a time at sea and drunk as hell when he was home. So, I get a job on a sport fishing boat that only does one thing — shark fishing. Figured I'd one-up the old man by going after real game. Didn't have the money for a knife, didn't think I needed one. After all, nothing else the old bastard ever said did me any good. So, we head out from Montauk with some rich guy from Colorado who wants to bag himself a big, nasty beast of a shark. We take him to the Canyon — don't know what that is, do you? About a hundred miles out to sea from here, the water from the Hudson River has dug out a huge canyon in the ocean floor.

"The ocean drops from two hundred feet deep to six hundred, and then gets steadily deeper from there. Nine hundred, eleven hundred, three thousand, till at the end it hits six thousand feet and breaks off into the endless dark beyond the continent's shelf. It's a damn Grand Canyon none of us will ever see. Depending on the speed of your boat, it can take up to eight hours to get out to the start of it, and then you are as far from the world as you can get. No land in sight, and often no other boats either, just the endless rolling sea and the sky and the beasts that live beneath it all. Ain't nothing like Canyon fishing, out beyond any real hope of rescue and some of the ocean's nastiest creatures swimming beneath you."

"You see, the warm water of the Hudson River flows along that canyon, and it makes it perfect for fish. You can find anything there: swordfish, tuna, marlin, bluefish, and shark. All there, hungry and hidden in the deep, and our job is to dredge it all up by giving it food. Depending on what you're fishing for, you do different things. For shark or something like bluefish, you can either run around the canyon with lines trailing in the water like swift prey fish, or find a spot and anchor if you can. Then you cover the area you are in with chum. It's chopped-up fish you throw in the water to attract sharks, with all that blood and flesh. You chum and wait, chum and wait, knowing the flavor of all that death is just seeping out into the sea like a supper bell calling everything that is big, hungry, and mean. When they come, they all come together.

"Nasty, stupid bluefish and big swift sharks, all getting wild in a feeding frenzy around your boat. You fall in that water when they are in that slick of blood feeding like mad, and you don't last too long at all." The hardened fisherman smiled a lopsided smile, showing off his many missing teeth, waiting for something.

"Um, so, did you fall in?" Derek asked at last. The man answered with a wheezing laugh and lit a cigarette.

"Hell, no. What'd I just tell you? Fall in and you're done. No. So, we are chumming up the beasts, and bluefish are hitting us all over. They hit fast, as do sharks, and are strong. They hit and run, out of nowhere, your line goes tight and starts shooting away from you. Then the fight starts. Bluefish big as you, cruising away from you at the speed of a car. But that ain't nothing like the hit of a shark. When they hit, it's more like a jet plane just took your bait.

"So, these rich tourists are fishing. Don't know shit about what they are doing. One of 'em lets their fishing line get all tangled when a bluefish hits quick, so I am helping him untangle the line. Luckily, the bluefish must have just taken a chunk of the bait, then run, because the line didn't snap as it usually would. There I am, with my hands full of tangled line, when the shark hits the bait the bluefish just played with. The line goes taut like a noose, and there is my finger caught in the tangle. The shark is pulling the line, the line's wrapped around my finger, and all of me is being pulled out over the water.

"If I had a knife, I could have cut the line; instead, all I could do was hold myself in the boat as best I could. Didn't take long, really. A few seconds fighting to stay aboard, and the shark won. The line pulled straight, and my finger wasn't there anymore. I swear I saw a bastard bluefish swim by and gobble it up." The man held up his hand, considering his missing finger melancholically.

"That was years ago, so long, I've lived without the finger longer than I did with it, but I still miss the damned thing. So, now, I carry a knife, always. You know, they made me keep working. Wrapped the hand in a dirty cloth, tied it tight, and fished for the next five hours. Caught a huge mako shark that day, and I like to think it was the bastard that took my finger off. Then we went home, taking about five hours, and I went to the hospital."

The other mate came over from the stern of the boat and cursed at the nine-fingered mate for talking rather than working. He also gave Derek a dark, angry glare before stamping away. This mate was a different thing from the other. He was younger, somewhere in his twenties, and had a hard, cruel expression on his face. Derek noticed track marks on his arm and frequently saw him drinking from a flask while chopping bait at the stern of the boat. Derek didn't feel up to trying to engage the man in conversation. He seemed angry and dangerous, the exact type of person you would avoid in a bar or on the streets.

They left the inlet of the river and hit the sea, the boat suddenly riding up and down the long swells of the waves in a pleasant motion. The wind blew off the land, warm and humid, carrying the smell of suntan lotion and barbecues from the people on the beaches as the boat began its chug north. For a time, Drake stared at the shore, his eyes distant and thoughtful as the wind whipped around him, looking as remote as the ocean horizon. Then, slowly, he turned to Derek.

"So, what do you think?" he asked softly.

"I'm not sure," Derek responded.

"Of course, it is too soon for certainty, but what do you feel?"

"Well, I don't think it is the mate I was talking with. He is rough, sure enough, but he didn't seem cruel or — wicked." Drake nodded and waited.

Derek went on, "It could be the other mate. He does seem cruel and dangerous. I suspect he likes causing pain."

"Indeed, he does," Drake agreed. "Cruel, taking pleasure in the pain of others, lacking in sympathy, ruled by uncontrolled hungers. He is a type of monster, surely enough." Drake paused once more, looking at Derek questioningly.

"But," Derek started, then paused. "I don't think it was him either."

"Why?"

"Well, if he can't make it through a day without drinking since morning, and he seems to be addicted to heroin too, I don't see how he would have the self-control necessary to make and rig the car bomb. Break into a house and slaughter a family, maybe, but not the bomb."

Drake smiled. "Very good," he said. "Notice how it is the

bomb that keeps aiding us in our assessment, how the killer gives himself away with it. I'm not sure that poor fellow would fit the house killing either, he seems more likely to bash the door in than to use a crowbar, even if it was a bit of an overly enthusiastic job. Nevertheless, the bomb clearly rules him out — I agree. So, we wait. We wait and see."

The boat stopped several miles up the coast off the beaches of the wealthy town of Deal. Mansions dotted the shoreline on high cliffs with winding stairways down to private beaches. Luxurious backyards with waterfalls, pools, and tall palm trees. The boat set up a drift, stopping broadside to the wind, allowing the wind to slowly push the boat over a hidden underwater hill where fluke like to hide in the mud.

Derek watched Drake for a moment while the people around them prepared their fishing poles for use. "Do we fish?"

"I don't approve of causing pain for sport," Drake said softly, his face looking troubled for a moment, "but you, of course, may do as you see best."

"It would be less conspicuous to fish," Derek said.

"It would, but inconspicuous bait catches no fish," Drake responded. The people were beginning to fish, and the crew was positioning long nets around the boat. "It doesn't seem as if our fearless captain is planning on joining us on deck. You should fish, and I will do the same."

Derek prepared his pole, but Drake did not; instead, the enigmatic mage wandered to the bow of the boat to the unoccupied prow in clear sight of the captain's wheelhouse on the top deck of the boat. In the prow, Drake gazed for a moment out into the distance, long enough to catch the attention of the captain seated above and behind him, and then, he slowly turned and stared unblinking into the wheelhouse. Derek watched from the side of the boat, his pole held forgotten in his hand. Drake stood with his long black coat flapping in the wind — a garb distinctly unsuited to the weather and out of place amidst the other costumers — and stared unflinchingly into the wheelhouse like a specter of death. Derek could feel a tension building, uncertain if any form gazed back just as unflinchingly from the captain's seat on the top deck.

Ten minutes passed, and slowly the wind died, and then came about to blow from the east. Suddenly, the boat's horn blew, the signal for everyone to draw in their lines because the boat was going to move. Then, before everyone had gotten their line fully up, the engines roared to life and the boat turned sharply to point out to sea. As if in anger, the boat shot east.

Drake stood for a moment or two more and then, despite the pitch and bounce of the boat as it strained into the wind over the choppy waves, walked unfailingly back to Derek.

"Now," Drake said grimly, "we have a shark on the line."

The two mates walked back, trying to gather up the nets that were liable to bend or break in the force of the boat's forward motion and the oncoming wind.

"What the hell is he doing?" asked the man missing a finger. "We didn't even give the other side the drift, and the fish were biting!"

"Who the hell knows," growled the other mate, "he's been like an angry dog for days."

They passed on, and Drake glanced meaningfully at Derek.

"So, it's the captain?" Derek asked.

"I wasn't certain, but it fit. Let me tell you what I found out. The captain was in the military and, more specifically, in demolitions as well. He was dishonorably discharged years ago, supposedly due to the use of excessive violence. Specifically, killing civilians. Of course, those weren't the official charges; such things would require jail or worse, but whatever official charges were stated, they were a cover for murder.

"Then we have this, the filthiest boat catering to the most despicable clientele in the entire basin. A boat and a captain who would hire someone like that second mate, drug addicted, drunk, and angry."

The boat was going fast and hit a wave broadside, throwing everyone to the starboard side. Drake added, "So, I baited him, and he took the bait."

"Folks," the voice of the captain boomed over the boat's sound system, "we are gonna try some deeper water for some bigger fish." It was the voice of an energetic man, and an angry one. It carried the undertone of a growl, and a disconcerting hint of pleasure, almost like a purr. Then there was silence, aside from the whistle of the rising wind and the crash of the waves on the boat's bow.

"Look," Drake said grimly, pointing out to the chop where small birds looked like they were dancing along the white foam, "storm petrels. To sailors, they are harbingers of dangerous weather. There is rough water ahead." The boat launched over one of the remaining swells, sending Derek falling to the deck, but he could hear Drake murmur, "I fear I have underestimated how dangerous this man is."

The passengers were gathered in the cabin, and the spray from the bow repeatedly soaked the length of the boat. In the rising mist, any sight of the land was lost behind them. Drake stood for a time at the railing, grim and brooding, unfazed by the crowd of people going inside and ignoring the ocean spray against which his coat now seemed appropriate. Derek stood beside him, clutching the railing desperately and being thankful he wasn't prone to sea sickness. Then Drake slapped his hand down upon the railing, having made a decision, and walked smoothly once more to the prow to retake his post against the railing with his back to the howling wind, gazing up at the wheelhouse. The engines growled louder, deeper, and the ship sped up. Derek glanced to the back of the boat and saw the younger mate staring up towards the wheelhouse, looking scared. But it was clear the boat could not outrun the specter of judgment that stood in its prow and, as suddenly as the wind had changed, the engines cut out and the vessel wallowed to a stop, tossing back and forth in the rough water.

"I need my crew. Now," the captain's disembodied voice barked over the speakers. The two mates scurried to the front and up the stairs, and Derek followed to stand beside Drake, who hadn't moved.

"What is going on?" Derek asked him. "What are we doing?"

"Calling a very dangerous man's bluff." There was sudden shouting from the wheelhouse. "And I am worried it wasn't a bluff at all."

"What do you mean?" Derek asked, chilled by more than the crisp ocean wind. Drake did not respond.

The two mates scrambled down from the wheelhouse. "We need you both to join us in the cabin," they yelled to Drake and Derek before shooing the few people who had wandered from the cabin back inside.

"Derek, my friend, I am sorry I brought you along," Drake said at last, "but you and I shall see this out. Now, listen closely. I don't know for sure what is going to happen next, but I have some ideas. I need you to head away from the bow. Pay attention to what is going on up here, though. If you get a chance to climb to the top deck without the captain seeing you, once he has come down here, do so and radio for help. It doesn't matter who you radio, just do what you can. Say we need immediate assistance." Derek nodded. "Now, go towards the back. Stay out of the captain's sight."

Then, as if mentioning him summoned forth the man's voice, the captain once more used the ship's speaker system. "Ladies and gentlemen, I am sorry to inform you that this boat is sinking. Its engines are damaged, and I am worried there might be a risk of fire. We are evacuating immediately." One mate ran from the cabin and climbed the stairs back to the top deck, where he began unstrapping several lifeboats. Then, one by one, he handed them down to the other waiting mate. Together, they carried the two boats to the back of the boat that was closest to the water and opened a gate. They glanced questioningly at Drake, who hadn't moved, tried shooing him a few times, but he was as immobile as a mountain.

The passengers, garbed now in life jackets, lined up to board the lifeboats. In the urgency to assist the passengers, the crew never noticed Derek hanging back and watching the prow of the ship. Once everyone was aboard, the crew yelled up to the captain, but the man stalked from his wheelhouse back to them and growled, "Go. Both of you, all of you, just go!"

"But—" the man missing a finger objected.

The captain pulled a gun from his coat, "I said go!" he yelled and fired into the water beside the lifeboats. The crew, seeing their captain had lost his mind, jumped into the lifeboats and pushed off, the wind and chop carrying the frightened passengers away. All the while, Derek hid inside the cabin. There was a moment of silence as the boats bobbed away, and Derek imagined the captain staring grimly after them.

And then, the slow, firm footsteps of the man paced along the upper deck towards the prow where Drake still waited. Derek ducked from the cabin and crouched down with a clear view of Drake.

"Come now, captain, you aren't going to ruin your prized possession. There is nothing wrong with this boat," Drake yelled to the man who must be standing at the head of the stairs, "But we are alone at last. Are you ready to face someone who isn't a sleeping child?"

Loud stomps marked the man descending to the deck,

and then Derek could see his back and the gun held before him, pointing directly at Drake. "Who the hell are you?" he demanded.

"Just a man," Drake responded, "a man who can't stand cowards who take pleasure in the pain and fear of those weaker than them. Why did you kill them?"

"Why?" The captain was shouting in a tone that made clear he wasn't accustomed to being questioned by anyone. "Because I wanted to! Because I could! I could just walk in, cut them, watch them bleed, and no one could stop me."

"Well, I can stop you now," Drake said calmly.

"Can you?" The man asked and pulled the trigger of his gun just as a large wave hit the side of the boat and threw him off balance. The gunshot was deafening. Derek flinched, but Drake did not. The bullet went wide.

"Oh, come now, captain," Drake said just loudly enough to be heard, "that isn't how you want to do this. Look at me, an older and less fit man. Probably less trained than a former soldier as well. You didn't kill them with bullets, from a distance. Isn't that a little boring? But then again, you are a coward. Wouldn't it be better to kill me yourself, with your own hands, with—"

The captain let loose a roar and drew a long fillet knife from his belt.

"Yes," Drake said almost lovingly, "with that."

The captain's hand whipped out, and the gun went whistling through the air into the hungry sea. Derek realized he had to move, and now. He jumped up onto the bench and pulled himself up to the railing of the top deck. He swung over it easily and, crouching low, he moved into the wheelhouse. The wind had picked up significantly, and the boat was buffeted in circles by wave and wind. Clouds were rolling in from the sea, and bursts of rain hit the front windows of the wheelhouse. It was a summer thunderstorm; wicked lightning flashed in the distance. The two men in the prow of the boat faced each other in the rising storm, unmoving. Drake now stood straight, no longer leaning back against the rail, and the captain crouched slightly a few feet from him. The lightning flashed off the wicked blade of his knife.

Derek, feeling more than a little panicked, glanced around the small room and saw two radar screens, a "fish finder" sonar machine, a large compass covered in a glass dome, a GPS device, and a radio that had been torn from its casing and thrown on the ground. Leaning down, Derek saw that it had also been smashed with the heel of a boot. The radio was dead. Looking back up, Derek saw the confrontation at the prow of the ship reach a climax.

Drake looked as if he could have been standing on any street corner. His hands hung limp at his waist, his face was relaxed, but his eyes held those of his opponent. Then his opponent launched at him, the knife drawing back and then striking forward towards Drake's stomach. Drake did not seem to intend to move at all, but, at the last moment, he flowed to the side, and the captain's knife hand was firmly held in Drake's. The captain was pressed against the front railing, leaning far over the water, Drake's steel grip around the wrist with the knife, extended up in the air, and the other around the back of the man's neck.

The killer kicked back, and Drake flowed away from him. With a spin, their original positions were reversed, with the knife-wielding captain crouched in the prow and Drake standing with his back to Derek a few feet away. The killer's face contorted in rage and hunger, his lips drawn back from his teeth and spittle hovering in the corners of his mouth. He launched at Drake once more, and Drake shifted beneath the jump, flipping the man over and behind him. Drake spun, and the two came together once more, grappling in the boat's bow — the knife shivering and inching back and forth between them like a serpent.

Derek had to do something. He yelled, but couldn't be heard through the wind. He looked for a weapon, but worried he would just get hurt himself or lead to Drake being hurt. He knew he had to do something. Then he saw them — the two keys that controlled the boat's engines. Spontaneously, he reached out and turned them. The engines burst to life.

It was a gamble, likely to throw them both off balance, but Derek bet on his faith that nothing could shake Drake's balance. He grabbed what he assumed were the dual throttles and leaned them forward, and the boat shot into motion.

The killer captain let out a howl louder than the wind and motor's roar as he felt the only thing he loved taken from him. Guided by Drake's smoothly bending body, he was flipped up and over the railing of the bow and into the sea. The knife seemed to hover in the air for a moment, knocked from his hand, before Drake snatched it. Then there was a dull thump as the boat hit its captain as it sprinted over his body.

Swiftly, Drake sprinted up the stairs to the wheelhouse, where Derek was trying to get the boat's controls in order. Both Drake and Derek were relieved to find the other unharmed. "That was rather a brilliant move, my boy," Drake stated as the two of them figured out the details of how to navigate the vessel.

Together, they were able to relocate the drifting lifeboats and assist the crew and passengers back on board. They explained the minimum necessary, dismissing most questions and instead determining which of the crew was fit to captain the boat back home in the storm. Once the coast was back in sight and the cellphones regained reception, passengers called the police and the coast guard.

Drake did all the talking, explaining the situation in detail to the cops, all the while sheltering the murder weapon used at the house inside his coat as evidence of the story. Soon, a coastguard cruiser was there to guide them safely back to their dock, the waiting police, and Agent Burroughs of the FBI.

"What the bloody hell is going on here, Drake?" was Burroughs' enraged first words.

"Yes," Drake said, "hell has been going on."

"Why do you have the coastguard sweeping the seas for the body of this boat's captain — a man you confess you threw overboard? And what is this about him being the killer?"

"You seem to have the full story, Agent," Drake stated.

"The hell I do. You've done it this time, Drake. You and your unjustified speculations have led you straight off the deep end. Killing, murdering a man at sea! You are through now, and I will see you in prison where you belong. That or a mad house, which is more likely. Though, honestly, the chair would be the best choice if they ask me."

"Good lord, you are dramatic," Drake said as he felt the other officers' gaze upon them, pulled the knife from his coat, and handed it to Agent Burroughs. "Have this blade analyzed, and you will find it matches the wounds at the house, and that there is dried blood from the family upon its blade. Talk to the crew of this boat, and you will find that this was the knife of the captain, a knife with which he never parted, and you will also find that he has been acting oddly. Dig deeper and, undoubtedly, other horrors will rise to the surface. There will be confirming evidence at his home. In fact, you will find that Derek and I have risked our lives and defeated a monstrous killer — one you had yet to identify. Now, if you will forgive us, we are tired and must be going."

The police were, predictably, unhappy about the dramatics that had occurred at sea, and the coastguard was unable to recover the captain, alive or dead. Soon enough, Drake and Derek were allowed to return home, with the incriminating fillet knife safely in the hands of the authorities.

They didn't speak much. Drake seemed troubled, and

Derek thought it best not to inform his parents of the full extent of the dangers that had occurred while the two had been at sea. Drake agreed to spend the night before heading back to Boston the next day.

The next morning, Drake and Derek were up early, Drake having once more made breakfast. In front of Derek's home sat the new Lincoln Towncar that Drake's driver had rented to get him back to his home city. Before leaving, however, Drake asked if Derek would like to go for a walk with him along the beach. The day was cloudy, windy, and cold for the summer, so the beaches were mostly empty. The two walked along the angry sea in silence until Derek had to break this brooding mood.

"Thank you for coming, Drake," he said.

"I only wish I could have been more successful."

"But we found the killer and stopped him," Derek objected.

"Perhaps I judge success more harshly," Drake responded. "I put you in terrible danger, not once but twice. And I killed a man."

"You killed a monster," Derek corrected, "and I willingly placed myself in danger."

"All men are monsters, my friend, only sometimes we are not. That doesn't change the horror of killing. I would have liked this entire affair to have gone differently."

"And I would have liked for it never to have been necessary, but then I wouldn't be the same me I am now. So, I am satisfied, because I think I became more than I was before."

Drake looked to Derek suddenly, his face showing surprise, "Well done. There are few who can successfully scold me. You are right, and so I shall rest content with the way things have gone. Nay, I shall even be pleased for this chance to benefit from more time with you."

"With the mysteries all solved, do you return to Boston?" Derek asked.

Drake stared at the stormy sea for a moment, "I do return to Boston, for a time at least. I'll see you in the fall, and then we shall talk some more."

&

"Are you well, sir?" his driver asked him later as they made their way back to Boston. Drake had sat in a brooding silence for most of the drive, and his face was troubled.

"I've asked you a million times to call me Drake, Alexander," he said with a pained voice.

"And I have told you just as often that it would be inappropriate. I think we have worked together long enough to get used to this. Now stop changing the subject. What is bothering you?"

"Despite what I allowed Derek to believe," Drake said slowly, "not all the mysteries of this case are solved. The confrontation with the murderous captain made me realize a few things. First, the killer didn't recognize me. He had never seen me before. Second, he was truly obsessed with a hands-on mode of killing. And finally, he didn't gloat over the act of blowing up my car, which would have been a natural taunt for him."

"Ah!" Alexander said, his eyes widening with surprise. "So, he didn't plant the bomb."

"Precisely," Drake agreed. "The bomb, the very thing that directed me to the correct killer, wasn't planted by the killer at all."

"What does that mean?" Alexander said in a perplexed, near whisper as if to himself.

"I don't know, Alexander. But it is beginning to seem that someone — someone very clever and very dangerous — is playing games with me."

Homunculean Condition

Every year, the Hasan Society — Boston's premiere private club for the eccentric, rich, intellectual, or insane — held a banquet in memory of Jacques de Molay, the heretic Grand Master of the Knights Templar who was burned at the stake in France in 1314.

At the event, one member was chosen, either for the sake of merit or (more often) demerit, to give a speech on the "Human Condition." When one considers that members of the club are repulsed by speeches, it becomes clear what a perilous honor being chosen was.

On one such occasion, Drake was selected to speak at the banquet of Molay as punishment for having brought about the untimely suicide, but more terribly, the enlightenment, of one of the club's honored members — Jacob Harris.

Within the grand hall of the Hasan Society, wreathed in cigar and pipe smoke, Drake stood to face those with whom he had just shared a delightful feast of pheasant. Glasses of champagne and port wine were raised in salute as the chandelier lights were lowered.

"The Human Condition," Drake's voice filled the hall like thunder but sounded no louder than a whisper, as if he confided in each of the club's thirty-three members. "The Human Condition can be characterized in one of two phrases: either as a perpetual process of death or of birth. The sides of every war ever fought have been determined by their adherence to one of these two principles. Yet, all warriors have inadvertently served the first principle. A shame it was lost upon the Bishops, Kings, and politicians that the terms are synonymous.

"I have been brought before this inquisition under the charge that I have uncorrupted the aged. It is claimed that I have been the cause of death, and so I shall speak of birth.

"Stephanos Pryderi was a member of this distinguished club many years ago. He had been driven out of Salt Lake City for the crime of cavorting with the devil in his search for the secret of turning base metals into gold, and so had settled in Boston in 1920.

"Stephanos was something of a fop for an alchemist, with long white gloves and a jaunty bowler hat. He was also a good citizen, donating to all the right charities and attending several different churches, all for the sake of keeping his neighbors happy, benign, and out of his business.

"His only crime was being raised in France, where he learned to drink absinthe like Van Gogh and think like Huysmans. Following his graduation from university, his taste for the morbid brought him to the American Midwest. His interest in the eccentric life and alchemy didn't well please his more humble neighbors, and, having had his fill of the western style of the American dream and beginning to fear fire and the stake, he found himself here. He took rooms in the old haunted Italian north end of town and set about his search for the secrets of the Philosopher's Stone with abandon.

"One thing stood in his way: Stephanos Pryderi was a very poor chemist. Following several cases of mercury poisoning and repeated explosions that disturbed his neighbors, he decided he needed to go about things in a different way. Having failed in the working of metal, he turned his thoughts to the nature of organic life and so started to create a homunculus.

"The creation of a homunculus is an ancient alchemical art in which the alchemist attempts to repeat the action of God when he created man. One artificially creates new life within an alchemically sealed glass container. One then draws into the new life form, through occult intervention, the soul of an entity from a higher place, leaving one with an angel in a bottle, as it were. Such experiments were accomplished by Paracelsus and were written about by Aleister Crowley. Paracelsus was reported to have a large crystal bottle in which two miniature people, a robed king and queen, would dance with knowing glances and nods to onlookers.

"Stephanos was inspired by the story of one visitor to the abode of Paracelsus who gazed in wonder upon a massive, clear orb in which the master alchemist had created an entire world, complete with miniature mountains of gold, flowing rivers of quicksilver, and swaying crystal trees.

"This was Staphanos' path, the way of the alchemist as artist, and not as scientist! But how to go about it?

"He filled his old leaning lodgings with books on the subject, poring over the personal records of Cornelius Agrippa, Paracelsus, and Hermes Thrice Great. He spent days lost in the Harvard archives and, having become a member of the Hasan Society based upon the shining recommendation revealed in the extreme rage in which he had left the people of Salt Lake City, ransacked our own extensive private collections.

"Soon, his mind was aflood with stories of vitalized cow fetuses left to quicken in horse manure for eight months, and serpent's eggs blessed in the soils of fresh graves.

"It was clear he had to use the matter of life as a basis for life, but the thought of decaying remains repulsed him. In a frenzy, he wrote to the arch-magus Aleister Crowley himself for advice. The terse reply was that the knowledge needed was reserved for high-ranking members of Crowley's own secret society, the Ordo Templi Orientis. However, with a hefty monetary donation, membership could be acquired. Stephanos decided to rely, instead, upon himself.

"Rather than use animal matter, he turned to the stuff of plants and launched into an involved study of herbalism. In this study, he discovered a bright perfumed garden of possibilities, a forest flowering with a thousand sweet poisons and brilliant promises. And so, he could be found in his self-made laboratory decocting obscure herbs, capturing the breath of mandrake root born under the hangman's gallows, and dissolving deadly dream-inducing wormwood in macerations of mistletoe."

Drake's audience was captured in the hypnotic rise and fall of his voice, and a small smile played on the magus' lips as he spoke.

"See him now, bent in concentration over an ivory bowl grinding to powder the rare resin known as Dragon's Blood while the light of a simmering beaker reflects off his golden hair, curled in perfect ringlets. Some had speculated that his alchemical quest was born of a desire to recreate the amber glories of his own brilliant hair. While he worked by antiquated candlelight, he sang softly to the muses:

> *Roll back the Sea,*
> *Get with child the evening star.*
> *Set all mankind free,*
> *Laugh at the crossing of the bar.*
> *Sing the song homunculus,*
> *Sweet sovereign birth, homunculus!*
>
> *Speak to me your secrets*
> *Speak them now with velvet voice.*
> *Set me free of weakness,*
> *Guide the way through maze of choice.*
> *And sing the song homunculus*
> *Sing it now my waiting child!*
> *Wise born, waiting, homunculus!*
> *Wily, lovely, lofty, wild!*

"And the muses were questionably kind to Stephanos."

Drake paused to take a slow sip of his champagne and a puff on a cigar, which he then allowed to smolder beneath him on a china plate as he continued speaking.

"The homunculus must be born and live suspended in a stasis of liquid, but what basis to use was a dilemma for

Stephanos. Something like quicksilver, while traditional, was too opaque and hostile to organic life, while water was not buoyant enough, and was also far too aesthetically mundane.

"Finally, to fit his theme of making life out of the stuff of life, rather than the more classically chemical approach of alchemists, Stephanos decided to create his child in a universe of thick, fresh honey.

"With the preliminaries of his experiment clear, our noble Oscar Wilde of the alchemical world set to work in earnest. He measured and balanced herbs to represent each of the many faculties of life; chamomile for the fresh living breath, myrrh for muscle and bone, mandrake for animal impulse and mental instinct, and so forth.

"Several such herbs he burned within the confines of a magically consecrated chamber while calling out invocations to the potent primordial gods from whom the foundational mysteries of life issue. Hulda and Dagda, Ishtar and Ouranos, Gaia and Prometheus — he called them all, pleading that their breath might enliven his work. The flames danced and left him with his herbs reduced to a perfect carbon ash.

"Other components he dissolved into oil, stirring in an elixir of sulfur, salt, and mercury he had prepared earlier. For over a week, Stephanos never left his home. The neighbors noticed strange lights flickering at night from his windows and heard otherworldly chants rising from his cellar, accompanied by bizarre smells.

"Finally, all his materials were prepared and set before him: five cups, one vat, and the large Mason jar in which he would place them all. One cup held fine ash, another a thick black liquid, another white powder, another a reddish oil, and the last a collection of fresh herbs and several seeds on the verge of sprouting.

"In the vat, he slowly heated a large portion of honey and then stirred each of the duly blessed ingredients into it. He allowed the honey to reach a good rolling boil in order to dissolve all the ingredients within. With the honey popping and sputtering, Stephanos screamed for the fires of Purgatory to purify his work, as he stirred it all with a large ritual sword.

"When he had exhausted his call to heavenly fire, he poured the concoction into the jar and sealed it tight. Traditionally, the sealed home of a homunculus was buried in horse or cow manure for eight months so that the warmth of the waste's decay might replace the warmth of a mother's womb. Stephanos had been unwilling to depart from tradition entirely, and so he had purchased a healthy mound of manure.

"Stephanos' experiment, however, was as much occult as it was alchemical, and so he had single-handedly moved all the manure into his cellar where he had piled it within the confines of a large magic circle drawn on the floor in salt, chalk, and sulfur. This circle would guard the homunculus, forming a barrier that only the highest spiritual entity might cross to inhabit the new body of the waiting child.

"And so, he buried the jar in the manure, calling upon the seventy-two powerful names of God to bless the womb and child within. With solemnity, Stephanos called to the armies of angels to descend and lay their hands upon his pile of excrement and thus bless his work and the entire world.

"Now, it only remained for the alchemist to wait and call upon the heavenly hosts at the rising and setting of the sun each day.

"It was during this eight-month reprieve that the members of the Hasan society first began to get to know Stephanos Pryderi. He spent his days within the society's house in downtown Boston, sipping tea and playing chess while discussing the miraculous birth that was to come.

"The members of the Society found him a delightful companion. He would regale them for hours with his stories about Parisian whorehouses and absinthe bars. Likewise, they adored his tales of Salt Lake City, each of which had the ring of farce. They never, however, visited his home on account of its ghastly stench, which had become something of a legend.

"Finally, the eight months were up, and Stephanos, with many a spasm of excitement, clawed his way through the hardened pile of manure to extract his ambrosial jar of putrescence. In the cool midnight air, bathed in the silvery light of the full moon, he cleansed the surfaces of the jar with purest warm spring water.

"Surely, he thought as layer upon layer of grime was washed off the smooth glass, surely there was a sparkle of life within. Was that a tiny form in the darkened ooze? An eye, a hand? Had he felt some motion? Heard a tiny voice or heartbeat? Did it have lungs? Rich flowing hair? This was its moment of birth. How would it see the world? What stories would it tell of the worlds beyond this one?

"With shaking hands, he carried the jar back inside and placed it upon his dining room table amongst the soft light of candles. The once golden liquid within was now dark and opaque, but cloudy forms moved within the sludge of honey and ash.

"With silk, he draped the sealed jar, not wanting to hurt his child's tender eyes, as he studied his homunculus. For a father, it was a rather unimpressive birth with little to be seen within except tantalizing hints of what might be hidden there.

"The child was newborn, Stephanos reminded himself. It needed time to awake from its embryonic sleep. The liquid would settle and clear, and his child would smile and speak. In Dionysian exhaustion, Stephanos crawled into bed and dreamt of the voices of angels. He would name his child Andrea.

"The next day, a layer of fine sediment had settled like the soil of the Earth at the jar's bottom. The color of the liquid had changed from pitch black to a dark brown with a more solid, darker form floating in the center. 'My precious Andrea,' sighed Stephanos as he stroked the jar. The glass was warm, surely, and he knew he felt a fluttering beat or breath within.

"It was several weeks of gentle care with little change before Stephanos heard Andrea's voice for the first time.

"That is not to say he heard it, actually, but then again, it is hard to speak with a mouth full of honey. Rather, his child, who admittedly was a potent spirit from a higher plane come to inhabit honey and ash, spoke to him in a dream.

"One night, he dreamt that he got up from bed and went down into his dining room at the behest of a silent summons. There on the table sat his jar, only now it blazed with a blinding light, and within it stood an angel fanning its wings of ruby and silver while holding aloft a sword of flames.

"'Andrea!' Stephanos exclaimed, and the angel nodded.

"'My father, who art in Boston,' it responded in a voice like song, 'hallowed be thy name! What would you with me?'

"For an instant, Stephanos was frozen. What did he want from his glorious child? Then, in a crash, his lifelong search returned to his mind, the quest for the secret of making gold. In his excitement over the creation of his homunculus, he had forgotten. He babbled a reply, begging for the secret of gold.

"The angel Andrea nodded solemnly and responded, 'Unwittingly, you seek the elixir of knowledge. Follow my instructions and drink of the sacred medicine I shall teach you to make, and you will have the power to turn all you can see into gold.' What followed was a complex lesson on the secret method of distilling the living essence of mercury through the use of a catalyst derived from small amounts of molten lead and silver, a lost process once known by the ancient priests of Egypt.

"When Stephanos awoke, he remembered in detail every

step of the process and swiftly wrote out several pages of notes. It was so simple and beautiful — well actually, no, it wasn't simple exactly, rather it was a vast web of simple steps. But it was indeed beautiful.

"With a cry of joyful exaltation, he clothed his nakedness in a red silk kimono and sprinted down the stairs to surround his homunculus, which still looked deceptively like a jar of dark brown piss and mud, with candles and fresh flowers in gratitude. He then set to work melting lead and silver to a glowing sheen while collecting the precipitate from several ounces of swiftly heated and cooled quicksilver. It took all day, but finally, come midnight, he had a gold chalice full of an elixir derived from the sweat of certain metals mixed with balanced portions of lead and silver nitrate.

"He placed fresh flowers and candles around his precious child, Andrea. And, toasting the sealed jar with a delightful clink, he raised the holy elixir."

Drake paused and dramatically held up his own crystal glass of champagne, admiring the shimmer of it in the candlelight. "Then, in a rush, Stephanos drank down the secret potion of knowledge." Drake downed his own champagne and paused, as if awaiting an effect.

"Stephanos stalwartly ignored the searing pain that the cool drink caused on the way down and awaited the climax of the medicine's work.

"He did not have long to wait. Stephanos Pryderi was dead within moments, having passed into oblivion where there is no force of sight, but, were there one, it could surely grant the power to turn all to gold. Or perhaps, having ascended to a higher plane, Stephanos' very desire for gold perpetually births celestial riches."

❧

The grand dining hall of the Hasan Society was silent as Drake paused to pour himself another glass of champagne. The chandelier sparkled as did the mystic's eyes as he sipped the drink and studied the faces of his confused companions.

"I know, my fellows," he said at last, raising his hands to reinstate a silence that had never been broken. "Your minds worry over the same problem contemplated by my own. Fear not. Upon its father's death, the brave homunculus Andrea was freed from its jar prison and adopted as a full member of the Hasan society. Stephanos Pryderi was declared one of our society's honored, and thankfully few, martyrs for having died in pursuit of truth. Andrea gave him a truly moving eulogy fit for the great Paracelsus himself, who also died at a blissfully early age. In the end, Andrea was one of the most fulfilling conversationalists our humble halls have known these many long years, proving that the apple does not fall far from the tree even when the apple is somewhat artificial.

"Following a delightful life of scholastic insight and the publication of several books on the faults of modern correctional facilities, Andrea retired to a house in the country where she became an avid beekeeper.

"Thus, my friends, the story ends well for all, and I have paid my dues by the time-honored method of Odysseus, who knew better than all men that it is wiser to tell a story than argue a point. As for the human condition, rare is a truer illustration. Our illusions outlive us and, in the end, are more real than we are. And so, let my crime and my story stand as a testament to my innocence. He who can well understand one will see to the depths of the other just as clearly."

The applause that followed was thunderous but perplexed as Drake sat back down to enjoy a rich dessert of crème brûlée.

Bill Koch

Bill Koch has had a lifetime love of mystery and detective stories and has been haunted by Drake since they first "met" when he lived in Boston. During the day he is a college professor teaching philosophy and by night he is a practicing occultist and pagan. Under the pen name of Kadmus he has published the book *True to the Earth: Pagan Political Theology* with Sul Books and has a new book *Learning from Legendary Practitioners: A Necromantic Journey into History, Myth, and the Practice of Magic* with Hadean Press. With future volumes of the Drake Chronicles already in progress, he has many more mysteries to share.

Sphinx and Sul Books

Sphinx is the fiction imprint of Sul Books.

Born from a collaboration of two long-time independent esoteric publishers, and named to honor the Suleviae — the sisterhood of goddesses revered at springs throughout Europe — Sul Books is dedicated to publishing works that manifest aspects of the sacred sight that heals what humans have harmed.

As with the thrice-fold kinship of the Suleviae goddesses, Sul Books combines the publishing strength of three resilient imprints: Sphinx Books, RITONA, and Gods&Radicals Press. Arising from these continuing legacies comes a fourth imprint, Sul Books, committed to stand-out works of powerful transformation.

Each of our imprints is guided by a commitment to pluralism, dissent, and the autonomy of humans, with a core focus on the importance of indigenous, animist, and non-industrial ways of being in the world.

Find out more at SULBOOKS.COM

www.ingramcontent.com/pod-product-compliance
Lightning Source LLC
Chambersburg PA
CBHW071234190726
48292CB00007B/2280